US, NOW AND THEN

LORIE SMITH SCHAEFER

US, NOW AND THEN

A Novel by Lorie Smith Schaefer

ISBN: 9780463056776

Cover art by Judy Bullard at

customebookcovers.com

Copyright ©2020 by Lorie Smith Schaefer

To Don, with love and gratitude
for quietly toiling away in the engine room so that
I may live life out loud up on the promenade.

And to old dogs everywhere proving
that they can indeed learn new tricks.

"It's never too late to become
who you might have been."
~George Eliot

CHAPTER ONE

Now: So Far Away

Sweat trickled down Claire Jordan's neck in her makeshift office at the sticky Haitian internet café. A plastic tumbler of iced coffee sweat along with her as a sweet roll remained mostly untouched except by a persistent fly. She checked her email, skimming past all the work-related stuff when she saw a message from Jack.

"Libby's biopsy came back. Breast cancer. Oncologist appointment next week. Thought you should know."

Claire looked up from the screen. She touched her left breast, her heart. Her connection to Libby had been formed in the primordial mud pie of early childhood. Pressing their thumbs together and solemnly reciting Robert Frost, they'd become blood sisters at twelve. *Promises to keep.* Over the years Claire had tested that bond, mostly by her absence. Libby had stayed in their hometown to marry Jack, have children, teach school, and take care of her parents. Everything Claire had chosen not to do. And like her mother had always said, "Life is living with your choices."

The belief that she'd failed Libby tore at her heart, which she imagined must look like a cartoon wall that Wile E. Coyote had just run through. Only hers had more holes. The father-shaped hole was the oldest. Then there was the big space for Sam. And a baby-sized one for... Sometimes she forgot about those holes. But other times, like today, despite the heat, a chill leaked in. She shivered.

Usually, Claire was happy that nothing bound her to a place or person. Nothing except her mother and Libby, that is. The only people she trusted completely. The only people who had never, would never disappoint her. And with the internet, the world felt as though she and Libby were once again passing notes in junior high. Even her mother had mastered email. Neither Libby nor her mother had mentioned cancer.

But, no. She couldn't. Flying home now was impossible. Claire hadn't even gone home for Libby's fiftieth birthday last month. She couldn't take the time.

Claire's team coordinated funding for several global relief organizations, prioritizing and matching needs with donors. After decades in the field, she was finally making a real difference. The deadline loomed for the next round of grants and micro-loans. Much depended on that money. Desperately poor women whose small cooperative awaited grants to buy sewing machines and fabric. Money to turn that old bread truck into a mobile health clinic. Renewed contracts for two primary school teachers. Not to mention the three young women applying for scholarships to midwifery school. Those projects would save lives and lift entire communities. Women counted on her. They trusted her. And that funding deadline was what, two weeks away? So no, not now.

Years ago, she'd chosen to stay away. Going home hurt too much. Still...

Her young co-worker, Enrique, tapped intently on his own keyboard, the rickety wooden table at which they sat wobbling with every keystroke.

Just how sick was Libby? Could this trip wait until spring?

2

Could Libby die? Frustrated, Claire scrubbed her fingers through her short, sweaty hair. Honestly, what could she do for Libby?

The answer came quickly. Be there, as Libby had been for her. Damn. Besides, how long could it take to show her support? A few days, a week at most?

"Do you think you could handle things for a while?" Claire asked. Enrique had only been on the job for a few months. But he was a college grad with a big smile and a bigger heart. And he spoke three languages, for God's sake.

"What's wrong?"

"Something's come up at home. A friend is sick."

"Sorry. In New York?"

"No. Nevada. Where I was raised." Enrique's brows raised in surprise. He wouldn't know this about her. She didn't talk about her past. "There are only two interviews left. And you can help the ladies finish their paperwork. You can still text or email or…" Claire said, offering him training wheels.

"You trust me?" His shiny brown forehead wrinkled. She was known for being hands-on, guiding her applicants personally through each step, from the development of their project through funding and implementation.

"Yes, I trust you." Although saying it didn't make it true. Enrique looked as uncertain as she felt.

Ignoring the rest of her inbox, Claire went directly to the airline website. She swatted at the fly and sucked noisily at the straw of her drink as she waited for the site to load. Even the internet seemed slow in this climate. Finally, she typed in her destination: Reno, Nevada. Not too many choices if she wanted to leave today. All routes involved several stops along the way. She opted to stay well south of winter. Fort Lauderdale, Dallas, Vegas, Reno. The trip would take nearly a full day, with several plane changes and layovers.

The cursor hovered over the "book now" button as she once more weighed her obligations. Shit. Click.

"Done. The flight leaves at eight tonight." Claire looked at her watch. Plenty of time to pack and check out. Transportation to the airport would mean a bumpy two-hour ride to Port-au-Prince. She'd be in Carson City tomorrow afternoon. "You sure you're ok?"

"No sweat." Enrique smiled at his little joke as he dabbed at his face with a paper napkin. Everything here involved sweat. He flashed a dimpled grin. Ooooh, Why was she always a sucker for dimples? She shook that thought from her head and emailed her mother with her plans. After finishing the rest of her tasks, she gathered up her laptop, said good-bye, and strode back to the small guest house where they'd been staying. She had promises to keep.

───────

THIRTY YEARS of life on the road had taught her three things. One: Never check your bag. Two: But if you do, be sure it's so outrageously ugly that no one would claim it accidentally. Her battered orange duffel certainly fit the bill. Three: Bring only essentials, but be prepared for emergencies—a second pair of shoes, a small water filter, antibiotics, wet wipes, and Band-Aids. But last week, when she left her tiny apartment in New York City, she'd packed for the tropics, not February in Carson City where altitude and proximity to the Sierra Nevada Mountains meant freezing temps and ever-present chances of snow. She groaned just thinking about the layers of clothing she'd need. The best she could find was one wrinkled pair of khakis and a thin cardigan sweater. She stuffed them into her backpack for a quick change when she got north. If she needed more clothes, she knew she could borrow something from her mother's amply stocked closets. At a spry and savvy seventy, Sylvia

Jordan still ran her real estate business and maintained her reputation as something of a style maven, at least by Northern Nevada standards.

Her mother liked to say that Claire had inherited the travel gene from her traveling salesman father. Some of her earliest memories were of the roadmap tacked on her bedroom wall with his route traced in red crayon. Every Monday morning he'd drive off to sell medical supplies in communities all over the west. The names became a mantra of sorts—Las Vegas, Needles, Pahrump, Eureka, Ely, Elko, Moab, Winnemucca, Pocatello. She also recalled how the knowledge that he'd soon be gone again clouded each happy Friday homecoming.

And yet she'd followed the same path, first as a guide with a travel company after college, though that had been a second choice after her dreams of the Peace Corps fell through. Fell through due to her own actions, but still.

Claire took a long shower in tepid water to cool off. Thinking about Libby, she soaped her breasts and checked for lumps. Afterward, she wrapped a towel around her body and fluffed her closely cropped hair with a quick glance in the mirror. "Pretty butch," she'd told Libby when she'd first cut it. It was simply more practical for her life in the third world, where amenities like hot water and electricity were often nonexistent. What had once been golden blonde, had dulled and darkened with age, but lately, she'd spotted troubling strands of white. Slathering heavy-duty sunscreen on her face, she noted the fine web of lines around her eyes, the creases beside her mouth. Fifty years of damage done.

As she reached for her underwear, the towel slipped and she caught a glimpse of not only the pale scar that ran low across her belly but her naked backside in the full-length mirror. What was this with her skin? Dimpling? Sagging? Running had kept her weight in check, her long legs lean and muscular, but jeez!

How long had this been going on? She quickly pulled on cargo shorts. Note to self: No more skinny dipping.

Once packed, she pulled out her laptop to edit a few documents and tried to focus. However, her mind pulled her to the past, to another flight, and that desperate call to Libby.

And as always, Libby had complied. Which was why Claire was heading home now. And why doing so was complicated. Claire was indebted to Libby and yet had stayed away. Sure, they emailed one another, spoke on the phone, but in the last fifteen years, they'd seen each other only twice. Claire blamed her work but knew there was something more to it. Something deeper she rarely admitted even to herself. Envy. Some part of her wished for the one thing Libby had she would never, could never have.

CHAPTER TWO

Now: You Can't Always Get What You Want

$\mathcal{L}$ ibby Cooper waved good-bye to the last yellow bus as it pulled out of the school's driveway. An icy wind off the snow-capped Sierra caused her to pull the hood of her coat over her head and stuff her mittened hands deep into the pockets as she walked back inside. After-school bus duty was the worst. The kids were hungry and tired. The teachers were hungry and tired. And from time to time, like today, the bus ran late. Twenty-five minutes late. On a Friday.

And her day wasn't finished yet.

Kimberly Landon's mother had booked an after-school conference with the principal. And now Libby was late. She could have asked someone to trade duties with her but hated to impose on anyone on a Friday. Besides, the mother had just scheduled the conference this morning. Libby learned about it at lunch when she found a note in her mailbox. She hurried to the office where the principal stood in the doorway and gestured her in.

"Mrs. Cooper!" He wore a sweater and tie beneath a tweed sport-coat. His glasses perched on top of his balding head.

"Mrs. Landon has already arrived. Will you step into my office, please?"

"Of course, Mr. Bridges." She removed her coat and mittens and sat in the unoccupied chair opposite his desk. A thirty-ish woman dressed in a forest green smock indicating a job at a local supermarket occupied the other. Her blonde hair, pulled into a tightly braided pony-tail held in place by a scrunchy and several barrettes, showed dark roots, suggesting she was long overdue for a touch-up. Her nametag read, "Summer." The principal closed the door.

"Hello, Mrs. Landon. I apologize. The bus was late. I had to wait with the kids." Libby offered her hand. The mother turned away and made a point of looking at her watch before looking back at Libby.

"I'm here about the homework you keep assigning. Every day. Those of us with real jobs don't have time to do your job. Aren't *you* supposed to be teaching her to read? I can't do your job and mine too. I don't get off work at three o'clock every day."

Libby took a deep breath and pasted on a tight smile, resisting the urge to check her watch.

"Homework? Do you mean the twenty minutes a day of reading?" Libby didn't believe in burdening six-year-olds with homework. They needed to be kids. Those twenty minutes were meant to establish a habit and some closeness between parent and child.

"Yes. I barely have time to … I can't…I can't…" Something cracked in Mrs. Landon's expression. Her shoulders sagged and her chin quivered. This conference wasn't about homework. Something else was going on. "Kimberly's father left us. Right before Christmas. We may have to to move. I–I–I can't afford the rent. Even working extra shifts."

Libby handed her a box of tissues. "I had no idea. I'm so sorry." Guilt niggled at her. Had she missed something with

Kimberly? Libby always thought of Claire when she heard of fathers leaving. And in over twenty-five years of teaching, she'd heard it more times than she could count. Children imagined all kinds of horrible things, even believing divorces were somehow their fault. She reminded herself to give Kimberly some extra TLC.

"I'm sure Kimberly misses her father. Those few minutes could be very comforting and reassuring to her."

Mrs. Landon quietly wept as Libby and the principal went into problem-solving mode, reminding her that parents and teachers were allies, not adversaries. First, they signed Kimberly up for free breakfast and lunch. Then they agreed to assign a fifth-grade reading buddy and to get her into a group with the school counselor. Small things, Libby knew. Mrs. Landon wiped her eyes and thanked them both before leaving.

With Mrs. Landon gone, Libby collected her things and stood to go.

"One more thing." Libby felt her eyes narrow. What now? She sat again and looked at her watch. Mickey's hands indicated 4:07. "Thank you for your work on the school improvement committee. Especially with the literacy stuff. I learned a lot from you." *Stuff* made Libby smile. Bridges' last job had been as a middle school science teacher. At least he was smart enough to realize he didn't know everything about running an elementary school.

"You're welcome." All she'd done was share the research on early intervention she'd compiled for her Master's.

"It couldn't have been easy to carve out time for the committee and to go to school while teaching and raising a family." Libby smelled a buttering up job and braced herself.

"Jack was very supportive. Insistent, you might say. He picked up all the slack. And our girls are pretty much grown now." Libby liked to give credit where credit was due. "But...?"

"The district is assembling a team to develop new literacy

standards." He leaned forward, his hands flat on the desk. "They need someone to chair the committee."

In her mind, that added about seventeen more side dishes to her already overloaded plate. No one at school knew about her cancer. The principal noticed her hesitation.

"They'll pay you a stipend for running it," he offered, as if money could buy time.

"It's not that. It's. . ." What? It was rare when the administration offered teachers extra pay for extra work. Or for input on important decisions. "Shouldn't one of the younger people do it?"

He shook his head. "We need someone with a Master's to chair. And frankly, you have the experience, the organizational skills, and..." Now he looked directly at her and smiled. "People respect and like you, Libby. Somehow, you can be assertive without alienating them."

She returned his smile and sighed. "When does it start? How long?" Did he hear the resignation in her voice?

"The process will continue through next spring. A year's commitment."

"May I think about it? I have several other things going on." Breast cancer, for one. And a father who'd forgotten who she is. A mother who can't leave him alone. And the girls, even in their twenties, they still needed her, don't they? And Jack? Why was he always last on the list? "I won't take on anything without running it by Jack."

"Fine, but get back to me soon. Right now, there is no second choice. It might end up being someone from the high school."

"Gee, thanks. No pressure." Libby managed a weak smile. What does a high school English teacher understand about teaching little kids to read and write? The idea was as scary as it was laughable.

"Enjoy your weekend, Mrs. Cooper."

"Thanks. You too." Libby looked at her watch. 4:25. She walked back to her classroom and went through her mental checklist. Today there were five items. Five fingers, five things to do after school.

One: Stop at the supply closet for poster paint (white, green, orange) and glitter. *Done.*

Two: Check cupboard for supply of empty butter and yogurt tubs for Monday's art lesson. *Done.*

Three: Find last year's note to parents in the St. Patrick's Day file. *Done.*

And what's this? An open bag of leftover conversation hearts? She popped a handful of them into her mouth.

Four: Collect plan book and teachers' manuals. She brought the candy with her and nibbled as she assembled a book-bag full of what would be at least part of her weekend's entertainment. Lesson plans for the next couple of weeks would need to be more detailed, in case there were extra doctor appointments. No one understood that planning for a sub took more effort than teaching. Teachers never knew what they'd come back to or what needed to be re-taught. Or un-taught. By the time Libby finished packing up, the bag of candy was empty.

That's four things done. But what was five? She wiggled her pinky finger. Pinky—p-p-p—pills. That's right! She'd promised to pick up her dad's prescription at the pharmacy. Quick stop. Unless there's a line. Then she'd need to drop it at her parents' house. Probably not a quick stop. Her mom liked to tell her everything that had gone on between Libby's daily visits. At least Jack said he'd bring home supper tonight.

At nearly five o'clock, a sliver of sun remained above the Sierra as Libby drove toward the pharmacy, dreading what she'd hear in her mother's voice, what she'd see in her father's eyes. Robert Frost often came to mind on days like this. She had miles to go before she'd sleep.

CHAPTER THREE

Now: Somewhere Out There

Claire's eyes shot open. That dream. Again. A crying baby she could never find. And it always ended with Claire awakening to her own desperate, tearful apologies. She looked around the plane. Had anyone noticed? She swiped at her tears with the back of her hand as they landed in Reno. Stifling a yawn, she called Jack as the plane taxied to the gate.

"Office of the Attorney General. How may I direct your call?" the cheery receptionist answered.

"Jack Cooper, please. Claire Jordan calling."

Moments later Jack was on the line. "Claire! What a surprise! Where are you?!" His husky voice sounded the same.

"Reno. Just landed."

"Libby should be home from school around five. Unless she has errands to do."

"She's working?" Claire muscled her duffel from the overhead, shouldered her backpack.

"You know her. She knows she'll have to take time off at some point. Says she will. Want me to call her?"

"I'd rather surprise her." Claire didn't want Libby worrying about preparing anything. And Libby would worry.

"You'll stay for dinner, right? I told Libby I'd pick up a pizza, but maybe I'll make it Adele's instead. There are a couple of cases of good wine in the dining room. We went over to Napa for her birthday a few weeks ago."

"Dinner sounds good. See you soon."

THE HOUR DRIVE south from Reno to Carson City, through Washoe Valley was one of Claire's favorites: the jagged, snow-capped Sierra Nevada to the west, Washoe Lake, and the Virginia Range to the east, and the ribbon of US395 running straight down the middle. Whatever the surrounding weather was, it was always worse here. The wind blew harder, the snow fell heavier, but still, it was beautiful. And today, even with the wind buffeting her small rental car and threatening to force her into the lake, this place caused her heart to ache with joy and sadness, comfort and pain. She had stayed away too long.

She remembered the last Christmas she was home, when she'd taken Libby's then little girls to see "An American Tail." No one would ever think of that as a disaster movie, but it was. A story about love and separation. Claire had sat in the dark, sobbing, as the sad little mice sang that killer lullaby, "Somewhere Out There."

"Don't cry, Aunt Éclair," six-year-old Annie had whispered and reached for her hand. Claire still smiled at "Aunt Éclair," the sweet, conflated name for her. "It's just a movie. It's not real."

But it was real. Too real. Two people looking at the same sky, wishing on the same star, even though they were apart. She had too many people somewhere out there. And the guilt over what she'd done meant that seeing Libby's little girls grow up was simply too much to bear. No one could protect her from that. She had to protect herself. So, she stopped coming home.

Instead, she poured herself into her work, more than once using it as an excuse for her absence. As Libby's girls grew, Claire kept her distance, sharing letters, her best wishes, gifts —but not her presence. Of course, that only added to the guilt. Would Libby even want to see her after all this time? Or would it just remind her of how Claire had failed her?

Claire parked in front of Libby's house near the snow-dusted foothills on the west side of town. She saw no lights on, although it was close to five-thirty. She'd finally changed out of her shorts at the Reno airport, but the khakis and sweater provided little protection from the icy wind. She shivered and jogged in place as she rang the doorbell and waited. No answer except a dog barking in the backyard. Claire ran back to the car and restarted the engine and the heater. She called her mother on her cell phone.

"Hi, Mom. Nobody's home at Libby's yet. God, it's cold!" While it had been years since she'd been home, regular emails, phone calls, and vacations with her mother made for easy conversations between them. Somewhere along the line, she and her mother had become friends. They shared everything. Or nearly everything, Claire reminded herself.

"Glad you made it. There's another storm due tonight. I'll make up the sofa bed in the office for you. Use your key if it's late." Claire laughed at their shared joke. How many keys had she lost as a child? The key would be under the mat.

Headlights shone in Claire's face. The garage door opened. "Oooh, Libby's here. Bye." Libby pulled in, got out of her car, and stared at the strange car parked on the street. Claire turned off the engine, opened the door, and got out.

"Hey, Libby! It's me." Claire shouted and waved, walking into the pool of light from the garage.

"Claire? Why? How?" Claire wrapped her arms around Libby and felt a small sob rise in her friend. "I'm gonna kill Jack."

"Don't you dare! You've got the one good man in the entire Western Hemisphere. And believe me, I know what I'm talking about." That earned a smile from Libby. Claire's romantic exploits were a source of great amusement for her monogamous friend.

"I didn't want him to tell anyone yet."

Arm in arm they walked into the open garage. Libby hoisted an overloaded book bag from the car and let in an excited border collie before closing the garage door and entering the kitchen.

"Let me feed Maggie, then we can chat."

"Fine, I need to pee anyway." Claire stepped down the hall past a photo gallery that documented the lives of Libby's daughters. Claire's honorary nieces, her fairy goddaughters. One brunette, one blonde. Two chubby babies grew into toddlers, then through a blur of school years. Braids, bangs, and braces appeared and disappeared. Her throat tightened. Somewhere in another hallway, in another house, photos of another child attested to a life she knew nothing about. She looked away, swallowed, and continued to the bathroom.

"You. Sit," Claire ordered when she returned to find Libby straightening the living room. She pointed to an overstuffed chair. Libby looked paler and puffier than Claire had ever seen her. Libby had always struggled with her weight and often joked about what birthdays, babies, and bread machines did to one's waistline, but she'd always been so rosy, so lively, she'd carried it well. No longer.

Libby collapsed in a chair. She put her feet up on the ottoman and kicked off her shoes, revealing Dr. Seuss socks, then lifted a remote control, igniting the gas fireplace.

Claire called out from the dining room. "Jack said there's some wine with our names on it. Here it is. Merlot or Cab?"

"There's also a case of Pinot Grigio in the garage, but I like reds in the winter. How about Cab tonight?" Claire wasn't picky. She'd drink almost any wine that hadn't turned to vinegar. Another side-effect of time spent in the third world.

Claire opened a bottle and carried it with two big glasses into the living room. She poured ample portions and handed one to Libby, setting the bottle on the coffee table.

"Salud!" Claire clinked her glass with Libby's before settling onto the couch. "So, how…?"

Libby fluttered her hand nonchalantly as if she wanted to brush the issue away. "I found it myself. In the shower. Still don't know anything about treatment or prognosis. That's why I don't want to tell the girls."

"How will they feel if you don't tell them?"

Libby shrugged. "They wouldn't be much help." Claire sat back. She'd argue that point another time. Libby seemed ready to drop the subject altogether, so Claire resolved not to mention the cancer again unless Libby brought it up. How could she avoid that elephant in the room? Libby's girls seemed a good place to start.

"Annie still wants to teach?" In Claire's mind, Libby's younger daughter was still toothless and wearing lopsided pigtails. Annie was now in college.

"You bet. It's the only thing she's ever wanted to do."

"And Norah?" Growing up had not been a smooth path for Libby's strong-willed older daughter. Nor a straight one. An eating disorder and some drugs in her teens had scared Libby and Jack and reminded Claire of her own trouble-filled adolescence.

"Tending bar at a brewpub downtown. With a college degree. I'm so proud." Libby shook her head. Was she embarrassed or merely exasperated? Carson City was still a small town. Everyone would be aware of Norah's failings, just as they had been of Claire's.

"Don't forget what I did after I graduated—cocktailing at the Ormsby House. And that ridiculous costume I had to wear?" Claire empathized with Norah, recalling that horrible winter.

"It took me a while to find my niche. I was thirty, remember? And then it was only by accident." Claire felt a smile curve her lips as she remembered that chance meeting in a Puerto Rican hotel bar while on vacation with her mother. That trip had been memorable for several reasons. Dave, then an undersecretary of something or other with UNICEF, had been coordinating relief efforts in the Caribbean after Hurricane Allen. During a long walk on the beach after dinner, the waves had glowed with bioluminescence, which reminded her of Sam. Still, Claire couldn't ask enough questions about Dave's work. Within six months she'd left the tour company and taken an entry-level job doing grunt work setting up health clinics. She'd also gained a sometime boyfriend/bed-buddy who valued his independence as much as she valued hers. Certainly, meeting Dave had changed Claire's life, but not in the usual way that a man does. Probably better in her case.

As the wine took effect, the reason for her visit faded into the background. Claire recounted the events of her latest trip to Haiti and the charms of her coworker, Enrique.

"He's so smart. So kind. Sadly, a little young to even flirt with. But I'm sure Norah or Annie would like him," Claire said. An idea began to form in Claire's head. She'd talk it over with Norah. Later.

"You're matching my daughters up with your rejects now?" Libby teased.

"He's not a reject, but I'm old enough to be his mother. I do have some standards." She laughed.

"Good to know. But there isn't much chance of a romance if he's in Haiti."

"Maybe that's the secret to lasting relationships."

"Absence?"

"Proximity never worked in my favor."

"Is Dave still in the picture?"

"No." Claire shrugged. He'd called at Christmas to tell her he was getting married. Even the original lone wolf was heading for home.

"I don't think you've ever given a relationship a chance, but I think there's still hope for you. You would need to plant yourself somewhere though." Claire shrugged. Her last serious relationship—perhaps her only one—was Sam. And she'd burned that bridge long ago.

The back door opened and Jack walked in, carrying three fragrant bags and the mail. He bent to kiss Libby tenderly. He is one of the good ones, Claire thought, even if he has lost a little hair and put on a little weight. Claire stood to hug him.

"Thanks for coming," he whispered in her ear, then nodded toward the nearly empty bottle. "I see you found the wine"

"Medicinal," Claire asserted with a wink. "Apply as needed for whatever ails you." She followed Jack into the dining room and opened a second bottle, pouring fresh rounds for the three of them.

Jack set the table as Claire opened take-out containers, placing a spoon in each one. These must be Libby's favorites. Three appetizers—baked brie, smoked salmon, an antipasti plate. Three entrees. Pasta carbonara, something with rice— curry maybe? —and a Caesar salad with large shrimp. Three desserts. The conversation stalled as they savored their first few bites.

Libby spoke through a mouthful of gooey brie. "How long can you stay?"

"Not long. A few days. A week, maybe. I have reports due, but I can do some work from here." Claire imagined her inbox overflowing, forced herself not to check her phone messages, and took another bite of curry. "How's your dad?" she asked, switching subjects. Mike McCormack had taught fifth grade for forty years, teaching nearly everyone in town, including them.

Mr. Mac was known for his crew cuts, bow-ties, and love of poetry, making his students memorize a poem every month. At least ten lines. Claire adored him. He was one of the few adults Claire never sassed. Not out of fear, but out of pure respect and love for a father who stayed. His loss felt like losing her own father all over again.

Libby shook her head slowly. "Alzheimer's has taken away everything we knew and loved about Dad and left this stranger. Mom can't leave him alone. I try to help, but I'm working. Then, of course, I feel guilty for not being more help."

"Your mother understands what a teacher's life is like."

Libby pursed her lips and sighed. "Yes, but you know her. There is always something martyred in her voice. 'Fine, fine, don't worry about me.' Catholics invented guilt, didn't they?" Libby stabbed a shrimp with her fork and popped it into her mouth.

"Well, if they didn't invent it, they certainly turned it into an art form," Jack added. Libby laughed and nodded in agreement. And in Fran McCormack's hands, guilt was a weapon.

"You aren't an only child. There are five of you, after all," Claire said.

"Only theoretically," Jack said. "John's been a real ass about this."

Claire loved how Jack defended Libby, especially when she wouldn't stand up for herself. Three of her four brothers had left the situation entirely in Libby's lap. John, the oldest, was a former Navy commander, stationed in D.C. Pat ranched in Montana. Mitch was here, but drank too much and was always between jobs. Keith, the youngest, was a therapist in Sacramento and the only one in Libby's corner.

"Tell her about the latest with Mitch," Jack chuckled as he stood up from the table, cleared empty containers, and started a pot of coffee.

"Mitch moved back into his old room. Says he can help

Mom." Libby rolled her eyes. "He has an opinion on everything. Especially if he's been drinking, which is most of the time. Plus, he's come out of each of his three marriages angrier and more bitter. Each of his brides was more gullible and codependent than the last."

"Three marriages? I haven't even had one!" Claire said. "What's that say about me, if stupid Mitch can find three people to marry and I can't find one?"

"As you said, you have standards. And taste," Libby responded.

Jack reentered the dining room, carrying a large brown envelope that he set in front of Libby. "From Aunt Ellie. You knew Uncle Matt had died last year, Claire?" Claire nodded. Libby's Uncle Matt—Dr. Matt McCormack—had changed her life too, and in an extraordinary way. He and Ellie held a special place in her heart.

Libby picked up the envelope, unsealed the flap, and pulled out the contents. It was another envelope, which she tore open. A snapshot of a young woman slipped out.

"Oh, my God, Claire. Look!"

CHAPTER FOUR

Now: My Girl

*C*laire couldn't speak, but stared at the photo—a close-up of a young woman, whose wide grin and freckled cheeks nearly hid her dark eyes. Claire felt a shiver of recognition at that tumble of auburn curls. She knew who that hair belonged to. Sam. This was their child. The child she began calling little Sam soon after she'd felt the first flutters of life.

Libby read aloud from the handwritten letter, stopping to wipe her eyes and sniff between sentences. Claire gulped for air that was suddenly in short supply.

Dear Dr. and Mrs. McCormack,

My name is Grace Bassett. I am the granddaughter of Louise and Bob Thorsen. They lived in Bridgeport, California in the sixties and seventies, but now live in Bishop. My parents, Tom and Gail Bassett adopted me in Bridgeport in 1972. From what I have learned, my birth mother stayed with you while she was pregnant. I would like to learn more about her. Do you know how I might reach her? I would appreciate any information you can provide.

I have enclosed a photograph of myself.

Thank you for your help.

Sincerely,
Grace

LIBBY HANDED Claire the single sheet of cream-colored stationery. The handwriting was a tidy, rounded hybrid of print and cursive with little slant. Claire reread it while Jack served dessert and coffee. Still, no words came. She'd never told a soul about this child. Only Libby and Jack knew.

Libby's uncle, Dr. Matt McCormack had found the adoptive parents in the small California town of Bridgeport, a few hours south of Carson City. The Universe had provided a perfect solution at the perfect time. Each person fulfilling a role they seemed destined to play. At the time, Claire believed she could have another child later. When she was ready.

While Claire had promised herself she would never be the one to make the first contact, she'd asked Jack—then a law student—to insert something in the adoption agreement saying that she was willing to be found. Someday. Claire had hoped, but never dared expect this would happen. Now little Sam—Grace—wanted to meet her.

The guilt, the regret, the—what was it, exactly? —had weighed on her heart for twenty-eight years. She tried to wall off thoughts of the circumstances of her child's birth, but they remained just below the surface of her consciousness and troubled her dreams. She knew her relief work was an attempt to atone for this one choice. However, it had the opposite effect. Time and time again, Claire saw other women—in far more dire circumstances—keep their children and care for them. No matter what. It only reinforced her belief that she didn't have it in her to sacrifice herself for her child. For anyone. She simply couldn't be trusted.

Libby tapped the shell of the crème brûlée and asked, "What

do you want to do?" Jack busied himself tidying up in the kitchen.

"I don't know." Untrue. Claire did know. She wanted to run to her daughter, right this minute. "But what if she asks about Sam? About why I gave her up?" She doubted she'd ever be ready for that conversation.

"Don't you wonder about your father?" Libby spooned the custard into her mouth.

"Uhm-hum." Claire remembered searching for her father in every hotel phonebook. She crunched her spoon into her crème brûlée and let the sweet, silky center melt on her tongue. "So, I should write to her?"

"That's a good start." Libby lowered her chin and looked at Claire. "And think about telling your mother. Sylvia ought to know she has a granddaughter."

That revelation could destroy the trust they'd established. Claire wasn't willing to risk that. "But then I'd have to..."

"You'd have to tell the truth."

"The truth. . ." The word caught in her throat. Halfway through her custard, Claire put down her spoon, unable to swallow another bite.

This was why she didn't come home. Too many secrets. Too many ghosts.

CLAIRE'S MOTHER now lived in an apartment occupying the entire second floor of a charming old commercial building, but tonight the rental car steered itself toward the little house where Claire had grown up. She parked across the street in the dark and recalled that summer morning—her sixth birthday—when the first seed of suspicion had planted itself in her consciousness. Her first lesson in mistrusting not only her feelings but also what she saw. That day, Claire learned that appearances could lie.

With one last glance at Grace's letter and photograph, she tucked them both deep into her backpack on the passenger seat and drove the few blocks to her mother's apartment.

CHAPTER FIVE

Then: Que Sera Sera

*L*ittle Claire stood barefoot on the back step hugging her Tiny Tears doll and breathing in the new plastic smell. The smell of birthdays and Christmases. The smell of happiness. The summer sun filtered through the tall cottonwoods in dancing, sparkly patches.

"Where's Papa?"

Claire's mama looked up, bit her lip, and smoothed back the strands of blonde hair escaping her ponytail. "He left early, honey. Didn't want to wake you." She continued to stuff dew-dampened crepe paper, sagging balloons, and a pin the tail on the donkey poster into a trashcan.

Something felt wrong. Mondays were for leaving. Fridays were for coming home. At four Claire had even learned to tell time and read a calendar, just so she'd always know how long it was until Papa came home. Today was Sunday.

"It's Sunday! Papa never leaves on Sunday." Never. Sundays meant bringing Papa his coffee, pancakes for breakfast—maybe even Dutch babies—and reading the funnies on the living room floor. Little Lulu. Alley Oop. Dick Tracy. Sundays belonged to them.

"Help me finish cleaning up the party stuff and then we'll make breakfast."

"But where is he? He never leaves without kissing me good-bye." Papa's job as a salesman kept him away from home five days a week. He never left on Sundays. Never.

"He's just…not here."

Claire couldn't decide if Mama was angry or sad.

"And he left me to clean up this mess." Ok, angry. Still suspicious and holding Tiny in one hand, Claire stepped into the backyard and half-heartedly helped to fill the trashcan. What had happened since her birthday party? Had she done something wrong?

Yesterday at her sixth birthday, she'd opened one present after another—Yahtzee, Silly Putty, and a game of Sorry. When the time had come to blow out the candles on the cake, she'd squeezed her eyes shut and made her secret wish, that her Papa would never leave again. Then after everyone had left, Mama and Papa had given her their gift. She'd torn at the wrapping from a Tiny Tears doll in a pink cardboard trunk, complete with a pink layette. Exactly like the one she'd seen on TV commercials. Mama sat on the couch, smoking while Papa helped her to dress and feed the curly-headed baby doll. When he'd shown her how to make Tiny cry real tears, Mama left the room.

Later, Papa had tucked her in with Tiny, kissed them both, and shut off the light. "Sweet dreams, Claire Bear."

"Sweet dreams, Papa Bear."

"Always dreaming about you, honey, so I know they'll be sweet."

He wouldn't leave without saying good-bye. He just wouldn't.

Claire helped her mother drag the now full trash can back to its place beside the house, and climbed the steps to the backdoor.

Mama turned her back to Claire. lit a cigarette, and gazed

out the window over the kitchen sink, "Damn that man," she whispered, shaking her head, and exhaling two ribbons of smoke through her nose. Like a dragon.

Damn what man? Papa? "Why did he leave early?"

Mama turned to face her, bit her lip, and closed her eyes. "Let's make breakfast. Then we'll talk."

She stomped her foot. "Where's Papa?"

"He's gone." Mama blinked hard, turned away again, and took another puff on her cigarette.

"Where?" Claire dropped Tiny, whose head clunked on the linoleum floor. She struggled to understand. "You sent him away, didn't you?" Sudden anger prompted her to pound her fists into her mother's back.

Mama turned, grabbed Claire's shoulders, and gave her little shake. "Stop it, Claire! Stop it now!" Mama never raised her voice. Something must have happened. Something bad. Claire tried to free herself and refused to look at her mother.

Mama sank to her knees on the kitchen floor and held Claire's face in her hands, trying to look Claire in the eye.

"I told him how much we missed him, how much we loved him." Her voice was softer now. "I told him we wanted him home more. But he said he couldn't be home more and keep his job."

Claire heard the emotion in her mother's voice. "You had a fight?" she whispered, shocked because she'd never heard her parents fight. Ever.

Claire's mother only nodded.

"Then say you're sorry. That's what you'd make me do."

"It's not that simple, Claire."

Claire trembled. She didn't understand. But her mother stopped trying to explain. She stood and took eggs and milk from the refrigerator. Like nothing had happened. "How about Dutch Babies? You did a good job cracking the eggs last time."

"No, I want Papa!" Claire swept the egg carton onto the

floor. Eggs splattered the linoleum where Tiny Tears rested in her pink nightie. The yellow yolk would leave a stain.

Claire grabbed Tiny, ran down the hall, and slammed the door. She fell to the floor and shuddering sobs wracked her chest as she rocked her baby. "It's okay. I won't—I won't leave you. We'll find Papa and—and bring him home."

THREE YEARS LATER, there had been no word from her beloved Papa. He had simply disappeared from her life. No more father-daughter lunches at the Pine Cone Cafe, no more bedtime stories. Not even a birthday card. Claire had seen one letter from him, addressed to her mother. The return address—Ruby Drive, Placentia, California—made her think of Dorothy's magical ruby slippers. There's no place like home, Papa. There's no place like home.

But there had been no magic, only dreams filled with the search for him, opening door after door in a huge house with a maze of dark, endless hallways, and waking up crying.

Once or twice she was sure she'd caught a glimpse him standing outside the school playground, watching her from behind a tree. But when she looked closer, whoever it was had disappeared. Like a ghost.

Claire didn't mention these incidents to her mother. Talking about Papa always seemed to make her mother sad. Certainly, Claire's fierce anger was big enough for both her parents for doing this to her. Nonetheless, she couldn't ignore the fact that her mother was the one who stayed, the one who tried.

Claire tried too, believing that if she were a really good girl her father would return. Good grades, good conduct, Girl Scouts, school choir—all to prove her worthiness, to bring her Papa home. But as years passed without contact—without him —a ten-year-old Claire gave up. Why bother? Maybe by not being good, she'd show her mother how this whole dad being gone thing was going. Not good. Not good at all.

Today, Claire was alone in the house while her mom was at her office—again—straightening out some paperwork. After working as a receptionist, her mother had gotten her real estate license, which meant she was gone even more. But on this Saturday morning, inspired by her recent obsession with Nancy Drew, she planned a little detective work. There must be some clue that would lead her to her father. Something that might even lead him home.

She began in her mother's room. The top dresser drawer revealed lacy bras and underwear, a garter belt, and stockings in various shades of tan and beige. Not helpful.

The second drawer held more lingerie: nightgowns, pajamas, and slips in black and soft pastels. Claire touched the silky fabric before slipping a lavender nightgown over her head, enveloping herself in her mother's Estee Lauder scent. The nightie overwhelmed her thin body. Six shiny, bullet-shaped tubes stood on the dresser tray like little soldiers. She twisted each shade up and set it back down for inspection. Now each soldier wore a tall, rosy hat. Choosing the bright pink, she carefully outlined her lips and pressed them together as she'd seen her mother do. Oops. Smeared. Rubbing it with her finger only made it worse. Oh well, she shrugged and continued her search.

Bottom drawer. Socks. Sweaters. No clues.

Still wearing the nightgown, she moved on to the den closet where winter coats hung on the tightly packed rod. She carefully touched each garment. There. Crammed between a brown coat with a fur collar and the wall. Her father's raincoat. Is that a clue? Maybe it doesn't rain where he is. Her fingers found their way into the pocket. A handkerchief. Ticket stubs from the last movie he'd taken her to —Danny Kaye in "The Court Jester." A hard stick of Juicy

Fruit. She unwrapped it, bit down hard, and started to chew.

With both hands, Claire pressed her nose into the dark blue fabric. The faint smell of aftershave brought him into the small space. Papa. She pulled the coat from its hanger and slipped her arms into the too-big garment. Hugging herself felt as if Mama's and Papa's arms were wrapping around her again. They were everywhere. And nowhere.

The kitchen door opened and closed. Footsteps in the kitchen, down the hall.

"Claire, I'm home." Claire froze and couldn't answer. The sweetness of the gum mixed with her salty tears. She looked up and saw her mother slowly shaking her head as she knelt to hold her. "Awww, honey. What are we going to do with you?"

A BRISK NOVEMBER wind whipped the cottonwood leaves as Claire and Libby walked the few blocks to the McCormack's big white house on Westview after school. As fourth graders, they were expected to see that Libby's little brother Keith got home safe before they could play. They climbed the steps to the back-door and a sweet and spicy smell surrounded them as they entered the kitchen. Mrs. Mac, a flowered scarf covering her curlers, had just taken a pan of ginger cookies out of the oven. Dozens more lay cooling on the counter. Libby's mom always made huge batches of everything.

"Can I go to Claire's?" Libby asked. "Miss Mabel is there." Claire frowned at the thought of Miss Mabel, the latest in a string of babysitters. Each one more hated than the last.

"*May* I...and yes, you may. Change out of your school clothes first. Don't forget to hang up that skirt. I don't have time to iron things twice. Do you have homework?"

"Only reading," Libby said as they went to her room. Libby

changed into her brothers' hand-me-down jeans, a sweatshirt, and faded red sneakers.

Mrs. Mac shook her head as they re-entered the kitchen. "That's the best you could find to wear?" Sometimes there was no pleasing Libby's mom. Libby only shrugged as they sat down at the kitchen table, each with a paper napkin, two warm cookies, and a glass of cold milk.

Afterward, the girls walked the few blocks to Claire's house. Miss Mabel was ironing in the living room and watching an old-timey movie. Some skinny guy was twirling a woman in a swirly dress. Miss Mabel "Moocow" Snooks, was about a hundred and fifty years old. She came over from next door to do a little housework and watch Claire. She wore awful print dresses over her enormous bosom and gigantic butt. Her doughy, purple-veined ankles spilled over the tops of her fat-heeled black shoes. Sometimes she would start dinner if Claire's mom was extra late. But mostly, she just watched TV and ironed.

"Hi, Miss Mabel," Libby called as they entered.

"Hello, Libby dear. Claire. Did you have a good day?" Claire grunted a response as she eyed the day's mail on the dining room table with a practiced disinterest. She couldn't say why she still looked for something from her father, but she did. And as years went by disappointment replaced her anger—at her father for leaving and herself for still caring. Just the Sears Christmas catalog in its brown wrapper and the new National Geographic. She grabbed both and indicated Libby should follow her down the hall.

"We're going to my room," Claire yelled over her shoulder.

"Your mother will be home after her hair appointment. I'm supposed to start dinner and you're to set the table and make the salad."

"Moo," she whispered to Libby. They giggled and ducked into Claire's room.

Claire took off her school clothes and left them on the floor while she dug around in the bottom drawer for her jeans. She found a freshly ironed blue plaid shirt hanging in the closet.

The girls flopped onto the bed with the Sears catalog and played "dibs," pointing to the thing they wanted most on each page. New Barbies—a blonde for Libby, a brunette for Claire—and new wardrobes for both. Claire's heart jumped a little when she saw a new Tiny Tears, but she didn't let on. Her Tiny Tears lay sleeping under her bed, tucked away in her pink and white suitcase. Claire only played with Tiny when she was alone now. No one needed to know that playing with Tiny made her cry tears of her own.

They giggled their way through men's and ladies' underwear, ending up at luggage.

"Oh, let's get matching suitcases and go to Hawaii when we grow up," Libby said.

"We'll go everywhere!" Claire asserted. Claire set aside the catalog and picked up the *National Geographic*. The photo of a pretty lady with a powdered face and a fancy hair-do promised a story about Japan. "How about Japan?"

They giggled and stood up to practice bowing to each other.

At 5:30, Miss Mabel appeared at Claire's bedroom door to remind her to make the salad. Claire ignored her and continued looking at the magazine.

"I'll help," said Libby, who led the way into the kitchen.

Claire groaned. Libby was always so helpful. Still, she followed and together they tore iceberg lettuce into a green Pyrex bowl. They peeled and grated the carrots, chopped the celery and green onions. Claire carefully measured the oil and vinegar into the Good Seasons bottle. She sprinkled in the seasoning packet and put the lid on. They took turns shaking it while singing and dancing "The Twist."

They had just finished setting the table when Claire's mother walked in smelling of Aqua Net, her blonde hair done up in something she called a "French twist." Little curls danced in front of her ears.

"Guess what I bought today?!" Claire looked for shopping bags.

"Um, shoes?"

Her mother smiled and shook her head. "Bigger."

"A color TV?"

"Bigger!"

"A new car?"

"Bigger!"

"What's bigger than a car?"

"A building!" Her mother seemed thrilled about this. Claire thought a color TV would be much more exciting.

As much as Mrs. Mac might complain and scold Claire and Libby, for making a mess or getting into some mischief, it was their mothers' fault that they became best friends. After Claire's mother got her real estate license and bought that stupid building, Mrs. Mac started watching Claire after school. While Claire still didn't believe she needed a babysitter—and bristled at Mrs. Mac's endless nagging—she enjoyed being part of Libby's large, normal family.

Libby's dad taught fifth grade at their school and would often walk home with them. Or they'd stay late, helping Mr. Mac by doing little jobs like stapling packets of purple mimeographed worksheets or cleaning chalkboards.

And summers meant whole days of adventure. One week, a gang of kids played "jail" in the Kings Canyon storm drain, putting prisoners—mostly their younger brothers and sisters—behind the grate. Or that time they'd roller-skated through the Capitol building. By the time they got back to Libby's though, someone had called Mrs. Mac to tell her and they'd been in trouble. Again. Claire couldn't count the times they'd been scolded and then given some hateful task as punishment for their crimes. Pulling weeds. Doing dishes. Or the worst, picking up dog poop.

One good thing about each of those escapades was that afterward they'd stop at Austin's Market and charge Juicy Fruit gum, Cokes, and their favorite Abba-Zabas. They especially liked them pulled from the back pocket of their jeans where they'd grown soft and warm. In Claire's mind, those treats made up for getting Libby into trouble.

One morning Claire entered the McCormack's kitchen through the backdoor. Libby sat reading Nancy Drew at the kitchen table.

"What do you girls have planned today?" her mother asked over her shoulder as she defrosted the freezer with a steaming bowl of hot water and a spatula.

"Maybe a trip to the library?" Claire suggested.

"I'm almost done with my book. Let me finish," Libby said.

They spent the morning sprawled on the floor of the McCormack's den. Claire occupied herself with a set of second-hand encyclopedias as Libby finished her Nancy Drew. Mr. Mac came in just as Claire was looking at Africa on the globe and measuring how far away it was with her fingers.

"Planning a trip, Claire?"

"Someday."

He nodded and gave Claire a puzzled look. "So anxious to go away?"

Claire shrugged. Away was always on her mind. She wanted to find her father and he might be anywhere. Anywhere but here, that is. Her complicated emotions swung wildly when she thought about him. Anger. Longing. Hate. Love. And jealousy that Libby's dad was never more than a few blocks away.

"I understand the urge to travel. But remember, the earth is round." Mr. Mac spun the globe. "You can only go so far in one direction before you start coming home again."

Was that true? Did all roads lead home? Even for her father?

An hour later the girls were outside on their bikes.

"We're really going to the library?" Libby asked as they rode toward downtown. She seemed a little disappointed. "I thought the library was just an excuse to get out of the house." True. Claire was known for exploits, not errands.

"The library keeps phonebooks from all over the country." They parked their bikes and climbed the stone steps.

"Who are we looking for?" Libby whispered as she placed her book in the return slot.

"My dad."

CHAPTER SIX

Now: Rescue Me

*W*ell, that happened, Libby scolded herself as she prepared for bed. The carbonara—not to mention the brie and brûlée. And all that wine. None of it had done her weight or cholesterol any favors. Her efforts to keep track of all that had gone out the window tonight. But she had cancer, for God's sake. Nobody expected her to fight every battle at once, right?

And Claire's arrival had been a complete surprise. While they had kept in touch, the fact that Claire flew halfway across the world on some sort of rescue mission was unexpected, to say the least. Ridiculous. Rescuer was Libby's role, her forte. Always had been.

Sure, it had caused its share of conflict, like after that awful thing on vacation in Hawaii with the surfing instructor. Libby had called Claire's mom with her worries. And early the next morning they'd both flown down to Orange County where Claire was in college. Claire had lashed out, accusing her of tattling. It wasn't tattling if someone was hurt or in danger. Claire had been hurt. She had been in danger.

They hadn't spoken for nearly a year after that, during

which time Libby met Jack and Claire met Sam. They all seemed headed for happily-ever-afters until Claire broke up with Sam. Which led to yet another rescue. No, Libby's part was rescuer, not rescuee. Still, her heart went out to Claire whose life hadn't exactly gone as planned. Maybe Claire was hoping to balance their friendship account by coming home.

Libby stood in the bathroom doorway, smoothing lotion onto her face and hands.

"Isn't it strange the letter from Grace arrived the same day as Claire came home?"

Jack sat up in bed with his laptop, his reading glasses resting on the tip of his nose Jack didn't look up. "Uh-huh."

Plumping her pillows and settling herself between the sheets, she wiggled her toes over to Jack's warmth.

"I think it happened for a reason."

Jack turned now and looked directly at her. "What would that reason be, oh Oracle of Ormsby County?" He liked to tease her about her search for patterns and connections, but she was rarely wrong.

She shrugged. "I think we all have lessons to learn. If we don't learn them right away, God—or the Universe, or whatever —gives us a second chance. A third."

"The Universe? That doesn't sound very Catholic. Where'd that come from?"

"Maybe the church doesn't have all the answers. It can't tell me why I got cancer, why my dad has Alzheimer's, why Mitch is. . . Mitch." Her jobless, addicted brother and her ailing father living in the same house? Hard to find a purpose in that.

"Some things remain a mystery, Lib. We can't see the big picture and some things just happen."

"And don't you think little Sam—er, Grace—will want to know about her father? Maybe Claire should tell him, too." Keeping that secret had been another point of conflict between Libby and Claire.

Jack closed the lid of the laptop, removed his glasses, and turned out his light. "Libby, think about what that disclosure could do to Sam. You have no idea..."

"I guess," Libby agreed, sort of. Still... she thought of the letters he'd sent in the months after that break-up, pleading for Claire's whereabouts. The letters Claire had never wanted to see.

"By the way, while we're on the subject of full disclosure, I invited the girls to dinner on Sunday. I told them Claire was here. They need to know about your cancer."

A hot, angry flush rose from her chest to her ears. Her fists clenched. "I can't believe you did that without asking me."

"Honey, they need to know." His voice was tender but firm.

"But it's my business." Tears stung her cheeks.

"It's our business. It affects all of us." Jack reached for her hand. Libby pulled it away.

"No. It affects me. I'm the one who might die. I might never see my girls get married. Never have grandchildren." Thoughts of a future in which she was not present overwhelmed her. She felt as if she were falling. Nothing solid beneath. Nothing to grasp. No hope of slowing her descent. "Don't you realize how out of control I feel? I should at least be able to limit who knows and when. You shouldn't even have told Claire. Did you invite my parents too? Send out a press release?"

"Libby. . ."

"Well? Did you?" She was shaking now. And yelling. Even as she argued, she saw the futility of trying to keep this a secret. She knew everyone in town. Everyone knew her. Receptionists, nurses, pharmacists... Someone—anyone—could let the cancer cat out of the bag. By staying in Carson City she lost any chance of anonymity, of privacy.

Jack responded by lowering his voice. He always did this—with the girls, with clients. Tonight, it pissed her off.

"I did not. Just Claire and the girls. I'll cook. A big pot of pozole, okay? You won't have to do a thing."

"The soup cure isn't going to fix this. No, I still have to tell my daughters I have breast cancer." Libby pulled a tissue from the box on her bedside table and blew her nose.

"Our daughters." Jack was nearly whispering now. He wrapped his arm around her, kissed her forehead. She sniffed again. How could he have done this? "You're frightened, honey. You're imagining the worst."

"Of course, I am imagining the worst. I have cancer. I could die." A horrible, painful, wasting death. And then who would...?

"Let's let the girls share in this part. That way when the doctor gives you good news, they can share in that too." When, not if. Bless his heart.

The fire had gone out of her argument. Jack was being sensible. As always. She'd pressed Claire to tell her secrets. Libby hated secrets, hated lies.

"Libby?"

"What now?"

"I love you."

"Love you, too. Mostly." She kissed him goodnight, turned off her bedside light, and settled herself onto her pillows. She pulled up the down comforter. Sleep didn't come quickly. It rarely did. Not until the flurry of worries about the people she loved stopped stirring her thoughts. Often, on the brink of sleep, in the blurry terrain of semi-sleep, a concern would resurface. Her anxiety would return. Her cancer. Her weight. Her blood pressure. Her little students. Her father. And she'd start over, reciting her childlike prayers. God bless Jack. God bless Norah and Annie. God bless Mom and Dad. God bless Claire and Grace. God bless Sam. And herself always tagged on at the last.

THE FOLLOWING WEEK, when Libby awoke after surgery, her first thought was for her left breast. She felt a bandage, but, yes, it was there. She hadn't realized how much she wanted to keep her breast intact. In the past, she'd even joked that her goal was to be a very old lady. And if she lost a body part or two along the way it was not a big deal. Still, relief swept over her like a wave and she was crying when Vicki, the recovery nurse, and a friend from her days in PTA, came in. Vicki, who had survived her own cancer scare, handed her a tissue, checked her temperature, her pulse.

Jack arrived with Norah, Annie, and Claire. Dinner together had been a good idea after all, despite all the tears. Norah promised to move home when Libby started therapy. She'd help with meals and such to allow Libby to focus on getting well. Annie would drive down from UNR to spend weekends at home. Even Claire would stick around a bit longer. Libby was proud of her girls and grateful to Claire. The gang was happily chatting when the surgeon stopped by with his good news. The lump was indeed small with clear margins. About one and a half centimeters. He was pretty sure he got it all.

A WEEK later at the oncologist, Jack held Libby's hand as she sat on an exam table. They listened to the treatment plan laid out by Dr. Guo, whose unlined face and tight ponytail made her look much too young to be giving medical advice. A month of daily radiation treatments would start the following week. They'd give her weekends off. Then more tests. Then several months of chemo, followed by more tests. Libby sighed and asked about continuing to work.

"That's up to you. Be prepared. You may not feel great.

Some patients only feel fatigued, others are laid pretty low," Dr. Guo said.

"But. . ." Libby had been off work for over a week already and she still couldn't move her left arm over her head.

Jack interrupted. "We'll see how it goes. And we'll do whatever it takes, Doctor." He squeezed Libby's hand.

Afterward, they had lunch at City Cafe.

"Turkey on that sour wheat walnut bread and iced tea," she told Jack as she found a table by the window. Only a few people here. And no one she recognized. Being out on the town on a school day—even if she could justify it—looked bad. Was it Catholic guilt or being a teacher that made her feel like she was playing hooky?

"See? Nobody here. You're safe," Jack said as he set down the tray of lunch. He handed Libby the basket that held her sandwich and sat in front of his bread bowl of steaming clam chowder. She removed the ruffled toothpick from her sandwich and took the first bite. Jack stirred his chowder before lifting the spoon to his lips.

Libby weighed her situation. "I guess doing radiation after school won't be too bad."

"How many sick days do you have?" Jack looked up from his soup. Behind his glasses, she saw the lawyer, the negotiator. She also saw his concern, his love. And something else. Was he afraid?

"Over two hundred," she answered with her mouth full. More than an entire year of school days.

"You have cancer. I think that's what they're for."

"But. . ."

"No 'but.' Your first priority—my first priority—is you. I want you well." His voice was firm now. Jack was arguing a case. Libby's heart swelled with love for this man who, throughout their marriage had sacrificed repeatedly for her happiness. He'd been offered better paying, more prestigious jobs in Las Vegas and San Francisco, but had turned them down. For her. For their family.

"We'll see," was all she'd give him. Who was she without work? Teaching defined her place in the world. It both consumed her and fueled her. Libby wouldn't give it up without a fight.

CHAPTER SEVEN

Then: We Gotta Get Out of This Place

*L*ibby lay in bed reading late on a chilly autumn Saturday night, her bedside lamp making an amber pool of light in her otherwise dark room. The house was silent. No radios, no voices, no footsteps intruded as she turned another page of the tragically romantic scene near the end of Jane Eyre, an assignment for her sophomore English class. The torment. The fire. The love.

Tapping at the window jolted her from the dark manor house at Ferndean and back to her room. She looked toward the window. Probably the wind, she reasoned, but her heartbeat quickened anyway. She tried to reenter the book. Now sirens. Pretty close. Smoke pricked her nose. But it was November. Smoke from fireplaces was normal.

Tap. Tap. Tap. Scratch.

A twig on the screen?

Tap. Scratch. Tap. Scratch.

She stood and lifted a corner of the shade. Peering through the opening, a shaft of orange light shone dimly on a shadowed face outside. Her heart thudded into her throat. The face moved into the light. Claire. Crap. What has she done now?

Libby pointed toward the kitchen door and rushed to meet Claire there. The sirens wailed and then stopped. Not more than a street or two away.

"What happened?" Libby smelled smoke on Claire. Woodsmoke. And alcohol. She didn't want to connect the dots but smoke and sirens left little doubt.

"Can I come in?" Claire whispered.

"What happened?"

Claire's finger went to her lips. "Anyone up?"

Libby shook her head and led the way to the little bathroom off the hall and clicked on the light. Claire's face and hands and clothes were smudged, her blonde hair flecked with ashes. She dropped her pea coat, pulled her sweater over her head, and stood there in her bra. Libby found a few old, dark towels her father and brothers used after working on cars and handed them to Claire. She stood in the doorway as Claire washed her hands and face. When her face was clean, Libby handed her a sweatshirt.

"What did you do?" Libby asked in an emphatic whisper. Excitement danced in Claire's eyes while worry twisted Libby's gut.

"I—we—me and Tony—broke into one of my mom's vacant houses. He had a bottle of rum. We thought it was the perfect place to...you know." Libby didn't like to think about Claire's sex life, which was miles further along the road than her own.

Tony was the latest of Claire's boyfriends. All had been the same dark and dangerous type. To Libby, Claire's exploits seemed to be all for show. She didn't love any of these boys. What she loved was the danger, the thrill. Sex was just part of it. Libby also believed that deep down Claire didn't think she was good enough for anything serious. And Libby's attempts at setting up double dates with nice boys always caused an argument.

Once Claire had set up a double date and it had been a

disaster. They'd parked near the waterfall up King's Canyon. Claire and her date had taken off into the hills for some privacy. That left Libby with her date, a former football star who'd graduated a year before, in the backseat. A flask appeared from somewhere. When she refused, he'd taken a long swig, retightened the lid, and leaned into her with a long, sloppy, rum-soaked kiss. Libby pulled back and opened the car door to get out. He grabbed her arm to pull her back, but she escaped by bending his middle finger back until he released his grip. Being raised in a house full of boys had taught her a few things. He'd followed her out of the car and tried again to pin her, but her knee knew just where to go. He dropped in pain, cursing. Libby walked three miles home that night.

But these adventures were no longer fun or cute. Breaking and entering? Booze? Sex? A fire? She could land in juvey for this kind of stuff. Or worse.

"I've done it before. A couple of times last summer." Claire shrugged and looked at the ceiling for a moment. "Anyway, it got cold. We built a fire."

"But that doesn't explain…"

"The smoke. It didn't go up the chimney."

"You didn't open the flue?"

"The what?"

"The flue. The damper." Libby swirled her finger in the air. "To let the smoke go up the chimney."

"I don't know anything about that, but we couldn't breathe. We took off. Somebody must've seen the smoke, cuz we heard sirens."

"But the house isn't on fire?"

"I don't think so. But I couldn't go home. At least not smelling of smoke. And the Fire Marshal's car was already in front of my house." Was Libby aiding and abetting a crime? Was she hiding a fugitive? When did helping her friend become breaking the law?

Libby opened the medicine cabinet and took out a pink and blue can of baby powder. "Here, sprinkle some in your hair and brush it out. I read about it in Seventeen. It's sort of dry shampoo."

A white cloud billowed around Claire's head as she worked the powder through her hair. Libby helped her brush out the residue and nodded at the result.

Libby sniffed. "Better, but not gone." She held out a bottle of Jean Nate'. "Good thing it comes in such a big bottle."

A squeak on the stairs caused them both to freeze. Claire's brown eyes shone big and bright with panic. She rarely saw fear on Claire's face. Perhaps she sensed what discovery would mean for Libby. She knew Claire's anxiety wasn't for herself but Libby.

"Libby? You okay?" Her mom said in a loud whisper from the top of the stairs.

Libby's hands went up and waved wildly at the air between them. "Yes, Mom. Just getting a drink of water."

"Back to bed now. It's late."

"Gonna finish a chapter. 'Night!" Libby trilled.

They listened for the click of the bedroom door, the creak of the bed before breathing again.

CLAIRE HURRIED home along the dark streets in the November chill and ducked behind a tree as the Fire Marshal's car rolled past. The porch light was on, and most of the house lights. Had they been looking for her? Shit. She knew from experience that the sneakier she acted the more suspicious her mother became. Better to be bold. She strode up the front steps and opened the door.

"Hey, Mom. Still up?"

"I was getting ready for bed when I heard sirens. Then the

Fire Marshal rang the doorbell and told me there'd been a fire at one of my vacant houses. Over on Hillcrest."

Claire nodded and kept her face as blank as possible, but her mother's stare would not leave her. Finally, she looked away. "Yeah. I heard the sirens too."

"Well, there doesn't seem to be much damage. Some fool broke in and lit a fire in the fireplace. Kids or a homeless person, probably. They didn't open the flue and the house filled with smoke. The police are investigating the break-in though. Looks like they used a window at the back."

Claire nodded, relieved there was no damage.

"Anyway. Is that a new shirt?"

Claire looked down at the too-big sweatshirt Libby had loaned her. "Um. No. Not really. I spilled a Coke on my other one. This is Tony's."

"And your jacket? Pretty cold to be outside without a jacket."

Claire shrugged and walked down the hall to her room. Had she left her jacket at Libby's? Or at the house when they ran out? Shit.

The next morning Claire's mother woke her early. Too early for a weekend. Especially after last night's little incident.

"What?" Claire growled.

"Fran McCormack just dropped this off." She held up Claire's jacket at her bedroom door. Even from across the room, she smelled the smoke. "Somehow it was in Libby's room this morning. You lied to me."

Claire imagined Mrs. Mac feigning concern for Claire's well-being. She'd be thrilled with the I-told-you-so retellings. Not to mention the consequences.

Claire nodded, her brain suddenly wide-awake. "Sorry, but…"

"And the fire last night?" Her mother shook her head slowly, disappointment oozing from every pore.

"We broke in. Lit the fire."

"You and Libby? That doesn't sound like…" Of course not. But Libby was involved now.

"No, me and Tony. We didn't mean to …" To what? They didn't mean to get caught.

"That's breaking and entering, Claire. That's a crime, not a prank." Her mother's voice was low and controlled, which was much scarier than if she'd yelled.

"But nothing was damaged, right? No harm, no foul?"

"No Claire, this is one step too far. I've looked the other way, tried to be understanding. But you must accept responsibility for this. Get dressed."

"What? Why?"

"We're going to the Sheriff's office. Today."

Claire tried not to implicate Tony, but her mother told the Sheriff they'd been together. As if appearing before the judge hadn't been awkward enough, she and Tony had to serve interminable community service hours together picking up trash along the river. Tony and the rest of the crowd shunned her as a rat. Mrs. Mac banned all contact with Libby indefinitely. Claire couldn't remember ever feeling so alone. She sulked and stewed for the rest of that year, barely passing her classes. God, she hated this town, these people, and being sixteen. But saw no way out for now.

MRS. MAC'S RESTRICTION—AND Claire's mood—only lifted the following summer when Claire and Libby both got jobs at the A&W and Mitch started causing more trouble. Maybe Mrs. Mac realized that some things and people were simply beyond her control.

While they hung out with very different crowds at school, the girls' friendship remained strong. Libby was a natural choice for student council, cheerleader, and honor society. Claire unsurprisingly still chose the outsiders, who loitered under the bleachers, smoking, and perfecting their eyerolls. And yet Libby and she passed notes in the hallway at school and talked on the phone almost every night.

She knew how people here judged her, what they said: Poor, wild Claire. Such a disappointment. Such a shame. Sylvia— bless her heart—did her best, but she had to work. No wonder Claire got into so much trouble. But, when your story starts with your father leaving, what do you expect?

So, in the wake of the fire, Claire did what could only be described as soul-searching. Somewhat surprisingly, she'd learned a few things from her misdeeds. First, she never wanted to taste or smell root beer again. But more importantly, she believed that if she stayed in town after high school, her life choices would be limited by the low expectations of those around her. Claire longed for a bigger, more important life. One that mattered.

She had to leave town, to shake off her past. Nevertheless, Claire was also smart enough to know that merely running away wouldn't solve anything. No, she must run toward something. Her father, maybe? No, his last known address was that Southern California town and there was no guarantee he was still there.

It was only then that Claire decided she had to go to college. A respectable alternative. College would give her four years to find a path, a way to that larger life in the larger world.

Early in her junior year, Claire began camping out in her school counselor's office. After some understandable skepticism, given Claire's history, he had agreed to help. What finally convinced him of her commitment though was earning solid Bs in French, Algebra, and History. He compiled a list of ten schools in Arizona, California, and Oregon. Claire studied it alongside a large map, eventually settling on Cal State Fullerton for two reasons: its proximity to the beach and the return address on that long-ago letter from her father. Placentia was next to Fullerton.

Claire's mother agreed to pay her rent and school expenses. She'd even given her a Sears charge card to buy a few pieces of furniture for her apartment. Nonetheless, Claire would need a part-time job for food, entertainment, and incidentals. On principle, her mother said. Claire accepted the arrangement without complaint, knowing her mother had learned self-reliance the hard way.

One August evening as the sun was setting, they began packing items into her graduation gift—a baby blue VW convertible. A breeze rifled through the cottonwoods overhead, making that incongruous sound of ocean waves and making Claire feel the tiniest bit wistful. Her mother looked a little sad as she set a box of kitchen things in the bug's little trunk.

"Not going to lie, Claire. I'm going to miss you."

"Even with all the trouble I caused?" Claire set a portable typewriter on the floor of the back seat and stood back to see what else might fit. Fitting her belongings into the little car was like solving a Chinese puzzle.

"Even with. I know I made mistakes. But I did the best I could. Isn't that what all moms say?" her mother said with a chuckle.

"I didn't make it easy for you. Sorry." And she was.

"But we survived. And I'm honestly proud of how you turned things around the last couple of years. You could have chosen a very different path. But you showed yourself just who you are, how smart and capable you are. You can do anything you want. College will show you that, I'm sure. The world is waiting for you, Claire."

"Gee, thanks. No pressure." A lump rose in her throat, unaccustomed as she was to someone having faith in her. Claire wanted freedom from expectations as much as she wanted to matter, to make a difference in the world. But now she realized she also didn't want to disappoint her mother. Walking that line would be a challenge. At least away at college, she could make any future mistakes without an audience.

"And while I wish you were going to stay here, I know you have to go." Her mother sighed and shook her head. "There is something so much like your father in you. Always needing to see what's on the other side of the mountain." Claire detected no judgment in her mother's words, just a statement of fact.

ON HER FINAL day in Nevada, Claire and Libby hiked up to the waterfall at Kings Canyon. In August it was a mere trickle, but it was still cooler here than down in town. While they had hoped they could go away to school together, Mrs. Mac had refused to even consider the possibility. It seemed Libby too yearned to escape Carson City's restrictions and expectations. Maybe after college.

They took off their shoes and waded in the pool below the falls. Claire picked up pebbles absentmindedly, tossing them into the water and watching the ripples. Libby pulled a warm Abba-Zaba from her pocket. She unwrapped it and tore it in half, offering Claire a hunk of the warm, gooey sweet.

"As soon as I get settled, I'm going to campus health," Claire said while chewing. She knew enough to know that her early sexual exploits had put her at risk. But she wouldn't or couldn't go to a doctor here, where everyone knew her. "Birth control pills, finally."

Libby seemed incredulous. "Not sure I'm comfortable with the notion of purely recreational sex. Don't you want love? Or commitment?"

"Those are pretty high standards. Not sure I've ever been in love." She enjoyed sex, period.

"What about the future? Don't you want to find 'the one?' You know, get married, have kids?" Libby skipped a flat stone across the still water. Three perfect little hops.

Claire shrugged. Those ties, responsibilities, and obligations sounded like some awful version of hell to Claire. She chafed just thinking about it.

Libby said, "I guess I worry about what I'll think of myself in thirty years. I don't want to look back and think of myself as. . ."

"A slut?" Claire smiled and completed the thought. "And I don't want to look back and regret any roads not taken. I'll only be young once. I'll be old for a long time."

Libby hesitated, drying her feet with her socks. Perhaps she was considering her words before speaking. "We can't predict what we'll regret. Only that time will pass and one day we'll be old. Someone's wife. Someone's mother or grandmother. Someone's role model."

Claire replied with a chuckle, "Or someone's horrible warning. That sounds more my style."

CHAPTER EIGHT

Then: Mele Kalikimaka

*C*laire's cheek stung as she looked around the hotel bar for her mother, her breath coming in small gasps, her bare sandy feet sticking, and grinding on the cool stone floor. Her torn dress hung from one thin shoulder strap. A tacky Hawaiian arrangement of "White Christmas" played in the background.

She spotted her mother's perfect blonde French twist first. She sat alone, perched on a barstool, wearing the short, flowered dress they'd bought at Hilo Hattie's that afternoon. She drank something with an umbrella, smoking and chatting with the bartender.

Thinking she might faint, Claire trembled as she crossed the room and reached out to touch her mother's shoulder.

"M-m—Mama?"

"Claire, you're back early." Her mom turned, smiling. Her expression altered immediately. She dropped her cigarette into a shell ashtray and stood to take Claire into her arms. That's when Claire's tears came.

"Claire, what happened?"

"He, he, we...he wouldn't...stop. I tried to leave. I tried to, but he...." Each word fought its way through her sobs.

"Claire, who? The surfing instructor?" Holding her at arm's length now, her mother looked at her more closely. Pain filled her eyes.

Claire nodded. "B-B-Billy. He, he hurt me."

"H-h-hurt? You mean he—raped you?"

A sob caught in Claire's chest. She shook her head.

"Sh, sh...It's all right, baby." Her mother held her close again. "Let's get out of here."

Claire stumbled as her mother guided her to the elevator, grit scouring her thighs. The desire to sink into a deep, dark hole and let the earth swallow her muted her surroundings. Entering their dim room, her mother pulled back the covers on one of the beds. Claire crawled into the cocoon of clean, crisp hotel linens which made her feel even dirtier. Sobs rose again and her mother lay down next to her, wrapping her arms around her. Claire snuggled against her mother's neck, breathing in her familiar scent—Estee Lauder with a hint of tobacco. Eventually, Claire's breath grew more regular. The tears subsided. Her mother said nothing. What was there to say? Claire's inner voice more than filled the space with blame as her past rose to accuse her.

Her mother whispered. "You know, Claire, good men don't act that way."

"But I ..." She hadn't wanted to but... "I wasn't r-raped."

"Yes, honey, you were. If you told him no." Claire turned to see flashes of rage beneath her mother's usually composed features. "That monster hurt my baby." Her mother kissed her hair, paused a moment, sighed, and added, "I know you've been having sex for a while."

"You knew?" How much more did she know?

"Yes. We live in a small town. And Fran loves to gossip.

Always says she's trying to help." Mrs. Mac, professional busybody.

"God. I'm sorry." Her mother had known about her escapades all along and loved her anyway. She'd been disappointed, probably embarrassed by Claire's behavior. Claire felt a new emotion now. Shame.

"Of course, as your mother, my first instinct is revenge. Castration. With a machete." Her mother pushed herself up on one elbow and hacked at the air with her other hand. "Like the one Hawaiians use to open coconuts."

Claire almost laughed at the image of her sophisticated mother wielding the massive blade.

"But we need to get you to a doctor first. And the police. And say something to the hotel. He is their employee, after all."

Claire's breathing grew ragged again. "No," was all she could get out as her mother held her again. No. All she wanted was a shower. A long, hot shower. Filth clung to her legs and—well—everywhere.

The phone rang as Claire stood and started to undress. "Hello...Yes, this is she...Yes. They were on a date." Her mother's answer was cautious, her demeanor controlled. "He took things a bit...um...too far..."

Claire shook her head, silently pleading with her mother not to tell. Please. No. Don't say anything more.

"Why in the world didn't you fire the son-of-a-bitch then?" Her mother's composure cracked. Her jaw tightened. "Yes, it would certainly seem so...I see, well...all right."

Once again, Claire watched her mother regain control. "That was the hotel manager. The bartender overheard you mention Billy and reported it. This isn't the first complaint they've had about him. Should have fired him before. The manager seems truly sorry. He's sent security to have Billy pack up and leave tonight. And he's sending up the hotel doctor."

Claire started to argue, but her mother insisted saying, "He can see if—well—see if you're okay."

"I'm okay." Claire protested, knowing it wasn't true.

"At any rate, he might give you a sedative. The manager also asked if we wanted him to contact the authorities."

Claire shook her head. No. No one needs to know.

"I told him I'd talk to you."

"No." The idea of facing Billy again or the police was unthinkable.

"But Claire, he shouldn't get away with this. If someone had reported him before, maybe it wouldn't have happened to you."

Claire shook her head. Her past had led to this. She knew who was to blame.

"No. I want to go home and forget this ever happened. I don't want to tell and retell this story." She took a breath. "No. No police."

"I don't agree, Claire. He should pay for this."

"He will." Someone else will accuse him. Someone more blameless.

Pulling the rubber-band from her hair, she shook her pony-tail loose and ran her fingers through the tangles and moved toward the bathroom. "I need a shower."

"You can't just…"

A knock at the door stopped her mother's argument. A sixtyish, spectacled man wearing a Hawaiian shirt and sandals stood at the door. He carried a small black bag.

"I'm Dr. Hiramatsu. I'm here to see your daughter." He stepped into the room. Her mother opened the sliding door to the balcony, in a weak attempt to release some of the tension from the room. The sound of the waves and a slight breeze whisked in. That sound might never have a calming effect again.

"Let's get your vitals first, Miss Jordan. Have a seat, please." She sat on the edge of the bed as he checked her pulse, her temperature, and her blood pressure. "Is this your first trip to Hawaii?"

The thermometer lodged in her mouth, Claire only nodded. She looked down to avoid his kind, hooded eyes. The hem of her short dress didn't quite cover her thighs, which were still sticky with sand and… God, she wanted a shower.

"The bruises on your legs are beginning to color now. He gently turned her face to look at her left cheek, which now burned with humiliation. "He did this too?"

"Uh-huh." The doctor looked sad.

"Some ice would help the swelling."

Her mother turned then and sniffed. Had she been crying? "Sorry. I should have thought of that. I'll run down the hall." She grabbed the plastic ice bucket and left.

With her mother out of the room, the doctor asked, "Any chance you might become pregnant, Miss Jordan?"

"Not much. I'm on the pill."

He nodded. "The pill doesn't protect you from everything. You still need to see your regular doctor when you get home, Miss Jordan."

"But…"

The doctor put up his hand. "The fact is you were assaulted. And I feel compelled to advise you to not only see your doctor but also to press charges. If you were my daughter…"

Her mother reentered the room then, carrying the filled ice bucket.

"That's what I told her. Besides, don't you have to report this?" No, Mama. Please, no.

The doctor shook his head. "You'd think so, but no. Rape is not a medical diagnosis. It's a legal term. The decision to report it is up to the victim. And make no mistake Miss Jordan, you are a victim here."

Claire shook her head.

"I understand, but if you change your mind or need

anything, don't hesitate to call. Anytime. Ring the desk. They'll find me." He pressed his lips together and frowned a bit, gave her mother a tiny envelope with several Valium, and left.

Claire lay back down and curled up, closing her eyes and trying to disappear. Her hair fell across her face. The smell of Billy's cologne, sweat, and sex enveloped her, nauseated her. She uncoiled herself and got out of bed.

"I smell of him," she gasped. "He's still on me."

"A bath. We'll wash him away. I'll run the water." That might be a good first step, but Claire doubted it would be enough.

Her mother turned on the taps and added some plumeria bubble bath they'd bought earlier. As the hot water thundered into the tub, the sweet fragrance filled the air. Claire undressed and tossed her torn dress and bloody panties into the trash. Her mom steadied her as she stepped into the tub. Relief seemed to seep into her as she lay back and closed her eyes. If only she could stay here and not have to face the world. She knew she'd brought this on by her recklessness, confirming everyone's beliefs about her. With a deep moan, she slipped under the water. When she came up for air, her mother was kneeling beside the tub with a soapy washcloth.

"Shall I or do you want to do it yourself?" When Claire didn't answer, her mother started with her face and back. She allowed herself to be soaped, shampooed, and rinsed as though she were a child.

When the water started to cool, she looked up and nodded. As Claire stood, her mother patted her dry and wrapped her hair in a towel, then pulled a soft cotton nightie over her head. She sat Claire down in a chair facing the mirror and tenderly combed out her hair. Claire closed her eyes against the site of the bruise purpling on her cheek and the sadness in her mother's eyes. Claire obediently took the Valium her mother offered.

They curled up together in the bed and Claire drifted off to sleep.

———

THREE DAYS LATER, her body leaden, Claire lay on the couch in her dark apartment, where she'd collapsed last night after her shift at the restaurant. She had lain here all day. Now the winter sun had set again. While she'd managed five hours at work—barely—she hadn't been able to face her classes today. Her mouth was dry and tasted of stale rum—a bottle left unattended and slipped into her bag at work. She'd hoped drinking would help her sleep, but the effect hadn't lasted long. Besides, it had muddled her dreams. Or maybe she shouldn't have combined it with the Sominex. Visions of dark beaches and sinking quicksand grasped at her from the edges of half-sleep.

The phone stirred her from her stupor. She'd ignored it throughout the day, but whoever it was wouldn't give up. Maybe if she answered they'd stop.

"Hello?" Her tongue felt slow and stupid.

"Claire! I finally caught you!"

Libby. Shit. "Oh, yeah. Sorry...um..." Claire should have called her, told her something. But she'd wanted to keep Libby in the dark about this. Had her mother said something? No, probably not.

"I got your postcard. And your date with the surfing instructor? How cool was that?" Libby sounded too sunny, too perky, too normal. The ordinariness jangled Claire's nerves.

"Um, not really."

"Why? What happened?"

"I don't want to talk about it."

"What do you mean?" Claire would have to say something.

"It's just. . ." What? Naming what had happened would make it happen all over again. And explaining would make

Libby part of the story. Claire's throat tightened with more impending tears. "I don't want you to be—oh, I don't know. Disappointed in me?"

"Never," Libby asserted, but Claire wondered if that were true. She remembered her glib remark about wanting to be a horrible warning. Be careful what you wish for.

"He kinda messed me up." Claire wiped at her face with the sleeve of the now wrinkled and soiled white uniform shirt she'd hadn't changed out of, catching a whiff of her own stale body odor.

"You mean he beat you up? Are you hurt?"

"I was r—raped." Sobs welling in her chest now escaped.

"Raped? Oh my God. Your mom knows, right?"

"Yeah." Claire wished that she'd been able to shield her mother from this bit of knowledge. That regret added to her shame, her guilt. Nevertheless, there'd been no "I told you so" in her mother's reaction. None. Her mother had simply taken care of her.

"Did the police arrest him?"

"No, I didn't report it." How could she explain to law-abiding Libby that she hadn't reported a crime?

"Didn't your mom want you to?" Questions and more questions. Couldn't Libby just shut up?

"Yeah. But I couldn't. The hotel knows though. They fired him."

"That's all?" Claire heard Libby's Irish temper rising. "So now he's free to do it again?" Claire felt her anger growing along with her guilt. It would be her fault if it happened to someone else.

"Damn it, Libby! I can't accept responsibility for that. Gimme a break! Jeez. I couldn't face him again. Besides, maybe I did or said something that made him think I wanted to…"

Libby would never have let it happen to her.

"Sorry, it's just..." Libby's tone softened as she tried to apologize. "This was not your fault."

"That's what Mom said, but I can't talk to her about it anymore. She just sounds sad and sorry and . . ." Claire gasped and gulped.

"I can't even imagine. Did you get checked at least, by a doctor, I mean?"

"Yeah and I've been to the school clinic." The cold fluorescent light, the faint smell of bleach as the kind nurse examined her. The blood test, just in case.

"God. I'm so sorry. I don't know what to say. I'm probably saying all the wrong things." This was why Claire didn't want to tell Libby. Or anyone. No one would know what to say, and then she'd find herself in the position of comforting them. Shit.

"I'll be fine. But I can't sleep. I can't get it out of my head." Claire sniffed again and reached for a box of tissues as more tears escaped. "I only want to stay in bed, but every time I close my eyes, I see Billy's face. Last night at work, a guy at one of my tables was wearing that horrible English Leather aftershave. That's what Billy wore. I started sweating. My heart raced. I couldn't breathe. I had to trade tables with one of the other girls."

"God, English Leather is pretty hard to avoid."

It wasn't simply aftershave that could set her off. It was men. Any men.

And in some weird way, it felt like it was still happening. "After work last night, I had to have someone walk me to my car. I was too freaked out to walk through the stupid parking lot. Maybe I should go back to the clinic. Not sure they can do anything, though."

"I wish I was there with you."

LATE THE NEXT MORNING, Claire awoke to knocking on her door. Someone called her name. She stumbled to the door, unlocked it, and squinted into the daylight to see her mother and Libby standing outside looking worried. They'd flown down to check on her. Instead of gratitude though, Claire felt betrayed and angry. She directed her rage at Libby.

"How could you? I thought I could trust you. Never again." If this is how Libby treats a confidence, Claire couldn't, wouldn't trust her.

Libby stood, mouth agape, unable to respond. Tears filled her eyes.

Her mother tried to intervene. "Claire, Libby was trying to help you. She was worried about you. I'm worried about you too."

"No. I told her I'd be fine. But Miss Goody Two-Shoes tattled. Period." Claire refused to look at Libby the rest of the day while her mother got Libby an earlier flight back to Reno.

After a night of rage and tears, they'd dropped Libby at the airport this morning. Now, a sulky Claire had nothing left to fight with as she and her mother stood on the porch of a small Spanish style house on one of Fullerton's tree-lined streets. Her mother rang the doorbell. Supposedly this was a doctor—a shrink—but this wasn't an office. Maybe a home for wayward girls?

"She's expecting us. Let's go in and at least meet her." Her mother's voice was gentle, but Claire detected an edge.

"Why?" Claire heard futility and frustration in that one word.

"Let's not start that again. You know why. We need you to feel better. To get better."

"There's nothing wrong with me," Claire tried to argue, but she knew that was a lie. What she wanted was to be left alone. Why wouldn't everyone leave her be?

"Someone hurt you, Claire. Scared you. And you seem to be

stuck there. Maybe the doctor can help you get—I don't know —unstuck." Claire looked at her mother who was biting at her lip, scraping off a wide swath of coral lipstick with her teeth. A nervous habit.

The door opened a moment later and Claire felt a smirk twitch her lip. Standing in the doorway was the oldest hippy Claire had ever seen—at least sixty! —complete with a long gray braid wound around her head and tiny glasses balanced on the end of her nose. Large, pendulous breasts appeared to be unconstrained under her baggy sweater. This ought to be good.

"Hello, I'm Louella Kozel. Please, come in." She opened the wooden screen door and led them into the small living room furnished with a hodge-podge of slightly shabby furniture. Quilts and afghans draped the sofa and chairs. A fire crackled in the tiled fireplace. The effect was nest-like. Nothing like a doctor's office.

"How do you do, Dr. Kozel. I'm Sylvia Jordan. This is my daughter, Claire. Thank you for seeing us so quickly. And at your home. I'm sorry if we…"

"I find it more convenient, more comfortable to work from my home. For clients and myself. And please, it's Lou. Just Lou."

"I explained a little about my concerns…"

The doctor put up her hand to halt her mother's explanation.

"Yes, but I want to know what concerns Claire. Perhaps you'd leave us now. Come back in an hour or so and we'll chat more then." Confusion swept across her mother's face, but she left when Lou showed her to the door.

Lou padded toward the kitchen, calling back as she walked. "Would you like some tea, my dear? Something herbal, perhaps? I have a special blend here that I find calming. The water's hot and I'm having some, so it's no bother." Claire only nodded as she watched Lou press loose tea into a tea ball, set it in a cobalt blue pot, and pour boiling water from a copper kettle that had been rattling on the stove. She set the pot on a brass tray with two cups, a spoon, and a jar of honey.

"Please, follow me, Claire." Carrying the tray, Lou led the way down a dark hallway. The older woman's long print skirt swayed over her ample bottom as she walked, revealing thick socks that looked hand knit. The room at the back of the house held no desk, no chair, no couch. Richly colored fabrics swathed the walls, cushions and pillows covered the dark wood floor. Claire smelled incense.

Setting the tray on a low table in the center of the room, Lou sank onto a large cushion, with surprising ease considering her age and bulk. She gestured to Claire to join her. Claire obeyed.

"While we're waiting for the tea to steep, why don't you tell me a bit about yourself."

Claire shrugged. "Not much to tell. I'm a student at Cal-State. I'm nineteen. I work at The Velvet Turtle."

Lou nodded and smiled and waited.

What else was she supposed to say? Claire picked at her nails. "I'm not sure what else there is."

"What are you studying?"

"Haven't settled on a major. I like French though."

"I sensed that your mother is worried, that she cares for you. How does that make you feel?"

Claire shrugged. "A little angry. Like she's butting in. Like I've disappointed her or something."

"Has she said she's disappointed?"

"No. But I've screwed up so many times. And now this…"

"That's the thing with mothers, the good ones anyway. They keep loving you no matter what."

Claire said nothing. When she thought about mothers, it seemed that most of them had little time to spend, time to spare. Libby's mom was ever-present, ever-critical, harried, worried, and domineering. Mrs. Mac gave orders. Pick up. Clean up. Don't do that. Eat this. Don't eat that. Calling, "Be home by six," over her shoulder as she swept the kitchen or folded laundry.

On the other hand, Claire's mother was rarely at home. She spent much of her time at her office, showing properties, or at some business meeting. And yet, when she was home, she floated above her surroundings, amused, somewhat indulgent, serene, and a little sad. Nothing ever seemed hurried. She was efficient, calm, affectionate, and encouraging. Her mother left notes reading, "Have fun and come home safely. XO."

"Who else cares about you?"

Claire shrugged.

"Your father? Brothers and sisters? Friends?"

"My father left when I was six. So not him. And I'm an only child. My best friend is Libby. Or she was 'til she called my mom about this—um—little problem."

"This problem?"

"Yeah, you know." Did she have to spell it out again?

"What do you think the problem is?"

"You mean besides being scared to leave my apartment? Wanting to sleep all the time. And then being afraid to sleep because of the nightmares? And the crying that won't stop? That problem?" Rage roiled up. Again. Tears came. Again.

Lou poured the tea, stirred honey into each cup and handed one to Claire. Claire inhaled the minty aroma and took a sip. The tea was warm and sweet.

"Tell me about Libby."

"My best friend from home." Anger and betrayal still burned deep inside her. "We grew up together. She flew home this morning." Claire's fury hadn't even allowed her to say goodbye as a tearful Libby tried to justify her actions.

"I see. Do you have friends here?"

"A few people at work, but no one close." She wouldn't

count the dozen or so boys she'd dated in the last year. "No. No one."

Lou nodded. "Are you okay with that?"

"I think so. Or I was."

"Something's changed?"

"I—I—I seem to be—scared all the time."

"And all this started…?"

Lou was going to make her say it. Shit.

"It started after Hawaii. In Hawaii, I guess."

"Hawaii?" The old woman tipped her head up to look at Claire through her little glasses.

"That's where it happened."

"It?"

Shit. "The attack."

"Attack?"

"Yes, well, the rape. But it was a date."

"This was different?"

"Uh-huh." The terror rose in her chest and overtook her. She was back at that beach. "He—he—he hurt me. Slapped me. Held me—held me down." In spite of herself, she cried. Again. Lou waited in silence and handed her a box of tissues.

"So, you felt…?"

"Scared. Angry. I couldn't do anything to make him stop. Powerless, I guess." That was it. She wasn't in control. "And I think it was my fault."

CHAPTER NINE

Now: Stay Just a Little Bit Longer

Claire was on the steady downhill grade after a run up Kings Canyon in the brisk early spring air. The cottonwoods lining the streets held the merest promise of green. She had gradually acclimated to Carson City's altitude, which had left her gasping when she first arrived. Yes, she'd stayed longer than she'd intended. Much longer, although she'd been in daily —sometimes hourly— contact with Enrique and her headquarters in New York City. Her work and her life were waiting for her elsewhere.

Libby, halfway through her radiation treatments was only fatigued. Only. How anyone not at physical peak could spend her days surrounded by whiney, demanding six-year-olds, Claire couldn't understand. And Libby's nagging about contacting Grace was getting on her nerves. Why wouldn't she give it a rest?

Nevertheless, Libby's friends demonstrated the benefits of the ties Claire had always thought of as burdensome. Jack, their daughters, neighbors, and co-workers rallied to Libby's aid, calling themselves her "rack pack." They brought meals, ran errands, did housework. Perhaps, Claire's efforts to be free of those ties had been too successful. If she were ill, who would care for her?

Still, Claire was beginning to feel like a fifth wheel.

This morning's email from Enrique said aid requests were once again piling up, needing her attention. She felt pulled in too many directions. Surprisingly, a part of her saddened at the thought of leaving. But no, she had a job, a life, an apartment in New York City. She couldn't live in her mother's den forever. It was time to go. She'd make her travel arrangements today. Relief replaced anxiety as the historic Sweeney building came into view.

The first property her mother had bought currently housed an antique store on the ground level. Or perhaps "Time After Time" was more of a second-hand store, with its street-facing windows crammed with charming, somewhat dusty displays of miscellaneous household items. Stoneware dishes. A potato masher with a green wooden handle. An enamelware colander. Vintage advertising. All things Claire remembered from her childhood. Could these things really be antiques?

As Claire reached under the mat for the key, a battered, marmalade Tom cat wound around her feet. Mom told her that the old stray had appeared some years back and she'd taken pity, setting out food and water for him.

"Good morning, Buster." They had no idea what his name was, but Buster suited him. Claire bent and scratched behind the remnant of one ear. Poor old guy.

Claire unlocked one of the double doors that led into the stairwell and up the long flight of stairs. She turned the knob, but the door only budged an inch or so. Something blocked it. She peered in through the etched glass. Her mother lay crumpled on the hardwood floor of the entry. She wasn't moving.

"Mom! Oh, my god, Mom!"

Panicked, Claire reached her fingers up through the sliver of an opening between the two doors and found the latch that released the fixed side. She knelt beside her mother, took her hand, and tried to rouse her.

"Mom! Wake up. It's Claire. Please, wake up." When she didn't respond, Claire pulled her cell phone from her jacket pocket and called 911. Moments later, she heard the sirens.

CHAPTER TEN

Then: Just One Look

*C*laire's mother arranged twice-weekly appointments with Lou. And on their advice, Claire dropped a couple of classes and took some time off from the restaurant. Lou recommended a yoga class and taught her some breathing techniques to help her relax. Claire took a self-defense course at the Y. And she began running.

A few months later and despite her initial scoffing, she felt less afraid and more in control. Nonetheless, guilt still gnawed at her for lashing out at Libby. Could Libby ever forgive her? Claire refused to consider the permanent loss of Libby's friendship and made two promises to herself. She would redeem herself—in her own eyes as well as her mother's. And she'd find a way to apologize to Libby.

At today's appointment with Dr. Weaver, her shaggy-haired advisor, they mapped out the next two years. With his help, Claire settled on a major—French, with a minor in Geography. Both subjects she liked and did well in. "Well" being a relative term in her case. After dropping those classes, she'd need to make up a few credits this summer and then dive in with a full load in the fall if she wanted to graduate on schedule.

"And after graduation?" Dr. Weaver looked into her eyes through his smudged wire-rimmed glasses.

Claire couldn't see herself settling into a traditional life after college. "I'm applying to the Peace Corps." Perhaps she could atone for her youth.

Dr. Weaver nodded and smiled. "I like that idea. But you still need three credits of life science." Looking up from the class schedule, he continued. "Botany would fit. Monday and Wednesday nights at seven. Is that going to be a problem with your job?"

"Shouldn't be. My boss is pretty good about arranging shifts around school." He'd been very understanding when she'd quit in January. "Can I at least take it pass/fail?" she pleaded, knowing she'd nearly failed every science course she had ever taken.

Dr. Weaver studied her rather shaky transcript. "Yes," he sighed, "but don't fail."

THAT FALL every seat in the Cal-State Botany class was full when Claire arrived a few minutes late. Looking around she noticed one vacant seat in the middle of the tiered lecture hall. She'd have to step over half a dozen people and their books. Mouthing silent apologies as she made her way to the seat, she took out her notebook and dug into her bag for a pencil. Where was it?

"Shit," she muttered.

"Here." Someone seated to her right offered one.

"Thanks," she whispered without looking at her rescuer.

The professor, Dr. Stearns, was a balding little man who appeared to be in his 60s. He frowned and gave her a quick shake of his head as he continued passing out the syllabus and going over the grading system. Claire tried to reassure herself, after all, she only needed to pass. Points. Good. Extra credit. Good. Okay. She could do this. Maybe.

When the class was over, Claire looked up to see who had loaned her the pencil.

"Thanks," she said, handing it back.

"Don't mention it."

Who was this guy? His neatly trimmed red hair, his clean, new-looking Levi 501s, and that blue button-down shirt were out of place. And that briefcase, for God's sake. Like someone's dad. Or one of Libby's clean-cut, business major boyfriends.

Thoughts of Libby pricked at her conscience. She still hadn't apologized, though she knew she had to. Was that what caused her pulse to race? Or maybe that mess in Hawaii had heightened her senses. This was going to be a long semester if every harmless-looking male caused her to panic. Something else to talk over with Lou tomorrow.

"Can't figure out what happened to mine." Did she sound normal? She couldn't tell. "I'm Claire, um, Claire Jordan."

"Sam Wylder. And like I said, don't mention it."

His name is Wylder? Jeez. Could he be any tamer?

LIBBY RUSHED through the crowded UNR cafeteria, balancing not only her books but also a tray loaded with a tuna sandwich, a bag of potato chips, two cookies, and a large fountain Coke. Suddenly her right foot slipped out from under her. Down she went as her lunch flew up.

A long-haired stranger jumped up as the Coke and ice hit him.

"Uh, what the f...?" He looked around but when he saw Libby sprawled out on the linoleum floor, he stopped in mid-curse, shook his head, and smiled. The crowd streamed around them.

"Oh God. I'm so sorry." Mortified, Libby looked around and saw the item responsible for the slip—a mimeographed flier announcing an upcoming Derek & the Dominos concert on campus. Whoever they were.

"Are you hurt?" he asked as he offered his hand. Libby took it and stood.

"Just my pride. And my lunch." She'd been looking forward to that sandwich. The stranger helped her collect her books and salvage the remnants of her meal. At least the chips and cookies seemed safe. She dashed off to grab handfuls of napkins. He stood flapping his striped t-shirt away from his body. When Libby returned, she dabbed awkwardly at the young man's clothing, carelessly discarding clump after clump of sodden paper on the table. When she noticed a stray clump of tuna salad in his long hair, she couldn't help herself. She laughed before removing it with her fingers and depositing it on the pile of wet napkins. Libby wiped her hand and held it out earnestly.

"Libby McCormack, resident klutz, at your service. I'm so terribly sorry. What can I do to make it up to you? Laundry maybe?"

"Jack Cooper. And that's not necessary." Why did that name sound familiar?

"Well, if you're sure. I'd still like to make it up to you."

"Like I said, not necessary," he replied then added, "How's your typing?"

"My typing? Pretty good. I have a portable back in my room. You need something typed?" It was then that she noticed where all the Coke-soaked napkins had landed—on top of what had been a neatly typed essay. "Crap. I'm so sorry. When's it due?"

"Three this afternoon, but it's only five pages."

"Tell you what. You go change clothes and I'll start typing. I'll meet you back here in an hour."

Back in her room, Libby sat down and inserted paper,

grateful for that summer school typing class and her nearly error-free 60 wpm. Claire had taken the same class even though she'd stubbornly refused to become proficient, saying she had no intention of being anyone's secretary. The sticky copy was titled "Abbie Hoffman: Hero or Villain?" Seriously? What would her Dad say about that?

In less than an hour, she was stapling the pages. She checked her hair and headed downstairs. Jack waited for her in the cafeteria dressed in dry clothes, his freshly shampooed hair tucked behind his ears and dampening his t-shirt.

"So, Abbie Hoffman, huh? Pretty radical."

Jack shrugged. "Not really. I'm pre-law. I might need to defend someone like that someday. Angela Davis, the SDS, Black Panthers..." His gaze narrowed as if he were trying to decide something about her. "You aren't for the war, are you?" Then she remembered. He'd been one of the organizers of the big protest last spring. The one after those students at Kent State were killed. That Jack Cooper.

"Well, no. But..." She did have two brothers in the service. John was even a naval officer. Jack smiled then and a glint of mischief shone in his hazel eyes.

"Do you like Derek and the Dominos?"

"Um, sure," she said, not admitting her ignorance.

"Would you like to go to that concert? It's the first week of November."

"Okay." That would give her nearly a month to learn who they were. They agreed to meet back at the cafeteria for supper.

It was only after Jack left that Libby remembered that she still hadn't eaten lunch. But for some reason, she wasn't hungry. That was a first.

CHAPTER ELEVEN

Now: Stand By Me

"Where? What?" Claire's mother whispered, opening her eyes only briefly, looking confused, lost.

"You're at the hospital. You fell."

Sylvia tried to respond. "Fell...stairs," was all she seemed able to say.

"You broke your hip, a couple of ribs, and your wrist. Banged your head too." With a nod, she closed her eyes again.

"Mrs. Jordan?" Claire looked up. It was Nick, a bearded, burly nurse. "The orthopedic surgeon will be here soon. We need your permission to replace your hip."

"Permission?" Claire argued. "She can barely keep her eyes open. Her right arm is in a cast."

"Unless you have medical power of attorney, ma'am, yes."

Claire quickly read through the release. Standard stuff, she supposed. "Mom, you need to sign." Her eyes opened again, but squinting, trying to focus. Her glasses had broken in the fall. "I've read everything and it's all okay." Nick placed a pen in her mother's good hand and held a clipboard, pointing to where she should sign.

"Initials are ok," Nick said. Her mother scrawled an approximation of her SJ, dropped the pen, and closed her eyes.

Claire patted her hand. "I love you, Mama."

"You too," she murmured as the gurney rolled down the hall, leaving Claire alone.

Claire found the waiting room, the soda, and snack machines. After purchasing a bottle of water and some trail mix, she settled into one of the chairs and called Libby. It went to voice mail. Claire checked the time. 10:45 A.M. Of course. She's at school. Scanning the available reading material, she knew politics and celebrity news wouldn't hold her interest today.

She selected a travel magazine with a turquoise seaside on the cover. She recalled that first trip to Hawaii with her mother.

Her mother had always put Claire first, stood by her. Through everything. Through that Hawaii mess and its aftermath, her mother's support never wavered. Not once. Residual shame and regret arose. Small and ancient, but still there.

HOURS LATER, Libby and Jack walked in as Claire finished washing the smeared make-up from her mother's face and smoothing on lotion.

"What did the doctor say? What kind of recovery?" Claire heard the concern in Libby's question.

"Weeks, months," Claire answered without looking away from her mother's face. A heavy sigh escaped her chest. "She'll need help. And there aren't many good choices." Claire flashed back to other conversations about choices—with Sam, with Libby. With her mother, who always said, "Life is living with your choices." What choice could Claire live with?

Libby patted her shoulder. "Whatever we can do to help, let us know." Claire shook her head. Libby's face was practically gray with fatigue. She couldn't, wouldn't put any more onto Libby. Not now. Not ever. Claire sent them home.

How could she justify leaving her mother now? Or putting her in a rehab hospital? A nursing home? Just so Claire could fly off to Timbuktu, again? What kind of daughter was she? She knew the answer. The kind she'd always been, more concerned with her own needs and those of strangers—than with her mother's. The kind who left. Like her father.

"Claire?" Her mother stirred. Her voice was thick, her words muddled by medication. She reached for Claire's hand.

"Right here. Need anything?"

She shook her head slightly and closed her eyes again. It seemed to take more effort than she could muster to keep them open. "When are you leaving?"

That was always the question, wasn't it? It tore at Claire's heart. "I'm not."

Her mother opened her eyes. The space between her pale brows wrinkled. "Your job?"

"Don't worry about that, Mama." Claire smiled. "The work will go on. With or without me." There. She'd said it. No more running away from responsibility, from commitment. Claire stroked her mother's hand and watched the worry lines disappear as her eyes closed.

CHAPTER TWELVE

Then: Can't Hurry Love

*W*ith midterms looming, what worried Claire most was passing that stupid Botany class. The scientific names left her baffled, desperate, and wishing she'd taken Latin instead of French in high school. That mild-looking guy from class—what was his name? Sam? —seemed to know a lot about this stuff. Maybe she'd ask him to help. But they hadn't shared much more than a hello and a nod. It wasn't like Claire to be frightened, but her defenses were always up now. She'd simply ask him for help. That's all. Besides, he wasn't her type. Dimples or no dimples.

When the professor announced a Saturday morning field trip to the Botanical Gardens in Claremont, she decided this was her chance. She loitered in the hall after class and summoned her courage.

"Um, Sam?? I—um—I still don't—um— know my way around the freeways here. Could I hitch a ride on Saturday?" Playing the dumb female was not her usual approach. Would she ever get over this?

"Sure, glad to have you along. By the way, Ron and I are going for coffee." He pointed to a lumpy-looking fellow coming out of the door. "Wanna join us?" he asked, nodding in the direction of his unkempt sidekick.

Claire smiled politely in Lumpy's direction. "I guess," she managed as nonchalantly as she could. Two men. She took a breath, trying to calm herself. On the way to the parking lot, Ron suddenly begged off. Claire and Sam agreed to meet at the Denny's near campus. A well-lit, public place. Okay.

With its bright orange and pink interior, Denny's was accustomed to college students spending half the night for the price of one cup of coffee and maybe a piece of pie. As a waitress herself, Claire made sure to over-tip when she overstayed. Seated in a big corner booth, Sam and Claire talked about the class. His openness, his boyish confidence—without a hint of arrogance—put Claire at ease. When she admitted she was struggling with the class, he volunteered to help her study.

"Piece of cake," he said, disarming her with those deep dimples that made him look ridiculously like Howdy Doody.

"How do you know this stuff?"

Sam's blue eyes brightened as he told Claire of his parents' large nursery in Yorba Linda, a few miles from campus. He'd worked there since he was a kid and planned to run it one day. He was majoring in Business, minoring in Biology. His younger sisters, Joanie and Kate, already did odd jobs after school and on weekends.

Claire mouthed a thank-you as the waitress refilled their cups.

"Where did you grow up?" Sam asked.

"Carson City, Nevada." Most people had no idea where it was and assumed it was near Las Vegas. She was always prepared with a little geography lesson. It's the state capital, she'd tell them. Or it's near Lake Tahoe.

"I've been there on a trip to the Eastern Sierra with my family. It has a great view of the mountains." Sam leaned back in his seat. "What does your family do?"

"My mom's in real estate."

"And your dad?"

"He left when I was six." On her birthday. Without a word.

"Where is he now?"

Claire stared into her coffee cup. "He may live around here somewhere, but he's not in the phonebook."

Sam leaned forward and cocked his head. A series of freckled Vs formed on his forehead. "You checked the phonebook?"

"Yeah. I always check. Everywhere I go." Sam continued to stare at her. "When I was a kid, I spent hours at the library looking for his name in all the phonebooks they kept."

"Your mom doesn't know where he is?"

"If she ever knew, she never said. All she'd say is, 'He's not coming back. We'll be fine.'"

"And were you fine?"

Claire shrugged. Heartbroken, but fine. Broken hearts weren't fatal, right?

"I can't imagine not having my dad in my life." Sam shook his head.

"I guess it taught me not to count on anyone." Claire remembered proudly making her own breakfasts and packing her own lunches in second grade. As she grew older, she was surprised that her friends' mothers still made their breakfasts and lunches. She found it quaint, as if she were viewing some primitive culture in the National Geographic magazines she went to bed with every night. Independence had become a habit. But the knowledge she didn't even have Libby to turn to sat in the pit of her stomach like a stone.

WEEK BY WEEK, Libby and Jack spent more time together. She liked him. A lot. But he was different from anyone she'd ever dated. She worried about her parents' reaction to his long hair and tattered jeans, not to mention his politics. What if they jumped to judgment before getting to know him? He looked like one of Claire's scruffy beaus. Although she had no idea who Claire was dating now. They hadn't spoken since January.

She stirred her coffee and looked across the cafeteria table at Jack. "Want to come to Carson for the Nevada Day parade this Saturday? My little brother Mitch is marching in the band." That Derek and the Dominos concert wasn't until the following weekend. Her brother, Keith had told her the lead guitarist was Eric Clapton. But who was Derek?

"Mitch isn't exactly little," Jack responded. Her baby brother was close to six feet tall and was the wildest of the McCormack clan. Mitch had started smoking, drinking, and ditching school in sixth grade. He practically lived in detention now. But for some reason, he liked the band.

"Yeah, but he's only fifteen. And he's still the baby. Anyway, my folks have an open house after the parade. Mom makes chili. Dad buys a keg. The whole neighborhood drops by."

"You Carson people like to go all out for Nevada Day, don't you?" Jack was from Las Vegas and seemed to think the rest of the state was a bit old-fashioned and backward. Libby's defenses went up.

"I know, it seems corny, but it's fun to dress up in Western clothes. And there's the parade, the rock drilling, the Indian tacos…"

He laughed and nodded. "I'd love to go with you."

Libby was relieved when Jack picked her up early Saturday morning wearing a plaid Western shirt and denim jacket. His long hair was pulled into a ponytail under a frayed straw cowboy hat. They headed south on US395. The weatherman had predicted a chilly but sunny day in the upper 40s. A perfect day for the parade.

When Jack parked in front of the McCormack's house, Libby's younger brother, Keith, was opening the garage, her dad was stomping toward her and shaking his head.

"Hello." He held out his hand to greet Jack, then turned to Libby. He planted a kiss on her forehead. "Go in and see your mother, Little Bit. I have to get Mitch out of jail."

"Jail? What happened?"

"He and a few of his buddies played a little game of Halloween trick-or-drink last night. They got their hands on a bunch of liquor then drank and drove all over town until they ran the car into a tree in front of the Governor's Mansion."

Halloween and Nevada's admission to the Union shared October 31, so trick-or-treating was usually accomplished the night before the parade to keep the little goblins safe from the drunks. That was the intention anyway.

"Is Mitch all right?"

"Yeah, he's fine. Or he will be until I get him home."

She and Jack walked through the open garage door and into the kitchen where her mother, still in her house slippers, was chopping onions for the chili. Tears streamed down her cheeks.

"That boy will be the death of us." Libby's mom continued chopping and crying. "You know what it's like at the mansion on Halloween. Little kids everywhere." Libby's mom looked up from the onions. "What was he thinking?"

"Sounds like he wasn't thinking. Mom, this is Jack Cooper."

Her mother gave a helpless gesture with the big knife. "I'm sorry you have to see this bit of family drama, Jack. It doesn't make a very good first impression."

"That's all right, Mrs. McCormack. Stuff happens in every family." Libby wasn't sure that was true, but it was nice of him to say.

"Call me Mrs. Mac, please. Everyone does. And Libby, would you pick up the newspapers from the living room?"

"I'll take care of it," Jack offered as he stepped out of the kitchen. Was he trying to escape or simply being helpful? "Would you like them stacked or put in the trash?"

"Trash, please. Beside the garage. And thank you."

"The party's still on?" Libby asked as she assessed what might need doing.

"Sure," her mom said as she scraped the onions into the huge pot that already contained several pounds of ground beef then turned on the heat and rinsed her hands. "Your dad and I talked about it last night after we got the call from the Sheriff. We're not letting Mitch spoil everyone else's Nevada Day."

"You found out last night? But. . ." Libby stopped. They'd let her brother spend the night in jail?

"We could have picked him up earlier, but we thought waking up in the pokey might be good for him. Logical consequences. Of course, neither of us slept a wink. It was the hardest thing I've ever done."

"But, Mom. Jail?" Libby couldn't believe what she was hearing.

"We've tried to keep it quiet. But this is still a small town. Everyone knows everybody's business." But usually, it was Libby's mother spreading the news. What goes around...

They continued to work in silence, having rehearsed this bit of kitchen choreography often enough. Her mother dumped the soaking pinto beans into the colander. After opening cans of tomatoes, Libby handed her mother the chili powder.

Sometime later, as they finished wiping the counters, yelling and slamming of car doors signaled that the boys were home. Keith was the first one through the door, rolling his eyes and shaking his head when he saw Libby.

"You left me in jail?! What kind of parents are you?" Mitch's stringy, dark blonde hair was matted. His clothes reeked of stale liquor and a hint of hemp, thought Libby. His eyes were puffy, his face blotchy.

"Jesus! You could've killed someone," her father answered. This conversation had begun earlier.

"It wasn't my fault."

"You were drunk." Libby's dad waved an official-looking paper at Mitch. "This Sheriff's report says that Michael McCormack, Jr. was 'drunk and disorderly' and 'resisting arrest.' What part wasn't your fault?"

"God, I hate this town!" Mitch spat out. "There's nothing to do and when you try to have a little fun, the cops show up."

Libby's mom stepped in and put her index finger firmly on Mitch's chest. "Upstairs now, young man. Strip and shower. You're under house arrest until further notice."

"House arrest? It's Nevada Day. I'm in the fucking band!"

"Not today, you're not. You're not going anywhere, except to your room."

"Oh, yeah? Who's going to make me?" Her mother looked up and didn't flinch. Mitch towered over their mother's five-foot-two frame. And simultaneously, Libby's dad, Keith, and Libby all stepped up. Mitch's shoulders slumped in defeat. He turned and stomped upstairs, hurling curses down at them with every step.

———

AFTER THE PARADE, the family took turns standing watch in Mitch's room. Jack sat with her during her turn on guard duty. Mitch's only words were to call them traitors and toadies, or worse. That night, when the last of the guests were gone, Jack and Libby rode back to Reno.

"I'm sorry about today," Libby said, thinking this might be her last date with Jack. Now that he knew her family was crazy.

"For what?"

"All I wanted was to take you to the parade. Stupid Mitch."

"Yes, but when it comes to family stuff, you do what you

have to do. There will always be another Nevada Day." Jack gently patted her thigh. She leaned her head against his shoulder. Mitch's misdeeds had certainly taken the pressure off the whole "meet the parents" thing. Jack's kindness and heart had shone through. Ponytail or no ponytail.

Libby ached to tell Claire about Jack, but they still hadn't spoken since Claire turned on her. Libby's mother had been none too sympathetic. Of course, her mother didn't know the half of it.

———

THE DECEMBER SUN glinted through the crystals hung in Dr. Kozel's windows, casting little rainbows around the walls.

"How's Botany going? Did that young man help?" Lou asked. The semester was almost over. Claire would pass Botany.

"Yes. Sam helped."

Lou gave her a knowing look and nodded. Claire now recognized that as her cue to "go on." Lou would wait—and wait—for a response.

"At least he doesn't make me crazy like other guys." Surprisingly, Claire found herself relaxing with Sam.

"Why do you think that is?"

"He feels, you know, safe. Not my type." Not one bit. Did she even have a type anymore? Her radar had been off since Hawaii. She could be misreading signals. "Besides, I'm focused on school right now. I plan to leave the country after graduation. Peace Corps. I don't want to start anything—you know—serious. And I certainly don't want anything unserious either." No. She'd had enough of that for a lifetime.

"Hmmm. Graduation is still a year and a half away. That's a long time." Lou sipped her tea—fragrant cinnamon today—and waited.

Claire only nodded. Right now, the thought of a boyfriend, of sex, caused her skin to itch, her throat to constrict.

"What about the rift with your friend? Have you figured out how to mend that?"

"No." She hung her head, raked her fingers through her hair, scratching at her scalp and finally burying her head in her hands. The knowledge that she was in the wrong had lain in the pit of her stomach for most of a year now. Nothing made it go away. She'd lost count of the times she'd dialed Libby's number—or most of it—before her shame kept her from dialing the last digit. Once, she'd finished dialing and Libby had answered. Words had thickened and stalled in her throat. After several awkward moments, she'd hung up cursing her spinelessness. Nonetheless, Libby's absence put her off balance. A piece of her was missing and it ached, like an amputee sensing pain in a phantom limb.

"What could I say?"

"'I'm sorry' is a good place to start," Lou said firmly. "Perhaps a letter?"

"Maybe. But she might tear it up without reading."

"Would you?"

"No, not from Libby."

"Don't you think she feels the same? And if you never ask, the answer will always be 'no.'"

The results of that session filled a wastebasket with empty words of regret.

I behaved badly.

You are a good friend, maybe my only friend.

I was wrong to turn on you.

I'm so sorry.

Now, Christmas vacation was here and Claire still hadn't apologized. When her mother picked her up at the Reno airport, she asked the only real question.

"Will you see Libby?"

Claire shrugged. "I hope to. I need to. But I can't..."

"Hmmm. I ran into Fran at the market yesterday. She wasn't very friendly. You know how she can be. I asked about Libby. She said something about a pretty serious boyfriend. Did you know about that?"

Claire shook her head slowly. Libby in love? What else had she missed?

"Anyway, Fran said Libby was home for vacation. Maybe..."

"Yeah. No way through, but through."

Her mother pursed her lips and nodded.

The next morning broke clear and cold with only a few patches of snow left on the north sides of houses and parked cars. Claire put on her running shoes, bundled up in her old hooded Carson High sweatshirt, and started a run. Running had become a meditation for her. She'd learned that all meditation starts with a single thought and hoped it would prepare her for what she had to do. She repeated I'm sorry—I'm sorry— I'm sorry as her feet found their rhythm on the street. She intended to run up Kings Canyon, but halfway to the top, she turned back downhill, toward Libby's. Now or never.

When she reached the McCormack's house, she jogged in place on the front porch, cajoling herself to press the doorbell finally and firmly. Then, her feet planted firmly, her muscles taut, she clenched and unclenched her fists, repeating I'm sorry — I'm sorry—I'm... The apology would be the first words out of her mouth, no matter who answered the door.

The door opened and there stood Mrs. Mac. Shit.

"I—um—I'm sorry"

"Well, I should think so," Mrs. Mac sniffed. Somehow that five-foot-two woman managed to look down her nose at five-foot-nine Claire.

"Is Libby home?"

"I'm not sure she wants to…"

"Mom! I'm right here!" Libby stepped in from the kitchen, still in her robe, her expression unreadable. Claire felt a fluttering in her chest.

"I'm sorry. I'm sorry. I'm sorry." Her mantra ran on automatic-pilot now, as her throat filled with tears. "You were right. I was wrong. I'm so sorry. Can you ever forgive me?"

Libby's mouth remained a straight, tight line, but her chin began to tremble.

Claire held her breath.

"Of course, I forgive you," Libby choked out, wrapping Claire in a warm terrycloth hug that smelled faintly of maple syrup.

"I've missed you so," they both uttered at once.

Mrs. Mac left them there in the doorway, shaking her head and calling back over her shoulder, "In or out, girls. Make up your minds. And shut the door, Elizabeth!"

CHAPTER THIRTEEN

Now: Stayin' Alive

*A*lthough it was nearly nine o'clock on a May morning, Libby had neither eaten breakfast nor dressed. She lay in bed, as still as she could, her eyes closed. Earlier, Jack had brought her a cup of chamomile tea which now sat on the bedside table, untouched. She tried to work up the courage to raise her head, perhaps even to sit up, but with every attempt at movement, her stomach pitched. Chemo.

The good news was that the treatments were only once a week—two weeks on, two weeks off. The bad news was that after two rounds of this so-called lifesaving therapy she was so sick, so exhausted, she considered death a viable and perhaps a more desirable alternative. The toxic stuff they pumped into her for an hour and a half on Thursday was supposed to poison the cancer without killing her. And there was no telling how long the treatments would continue. After eight weeks, they'd do tests to see if she needed to go another eight weeks. She hoped—she prayed—for the strength to survive the cure. A sob heaved her chest with the knowledge that she needed to surrender to the treatment.

This realization was hard to accept. Cancer was now taking

away the strong, caring, capable person Libby believed herself to be. She'd excelled at every job she'd ever taken on. Teacher, wife, mother, daughter, friend. She gave 100%. More. She prided herself in putting others first. Her students—she knew —often came before her family. Herself last of all. Who was she without her work? Who was she if she could no longer be a dutiful wife, mother, and daughter?

Libby now doubted she'd be able to finish the last few weeks of school. Heck, she questioned she'd make it through the day. Knowing what she needed to do didn't make it any easier. A tear escaped and ran down her cheek as she thought of calling her principal, of not seeing her precious students again. Of giving up control.

Jack—freshly showered and shaven—leaned over and patted her shoulder. "I'm calling the oncologist, Lib." He picked up the bedside phone. "There has to be something she can do. You can't go on like this."

Libby opened her eyes and lifted her head from the pillow. "I've heard marijuana helps. I'm sure Mitch could. . ." and she put her head down again before bolting upright and stumbling to the bathroom. Jack set the phone down and followed her.

After vomiting, she sat on the floor beside the toilet, a bitter taste in her mouth. The chill from the icy tile floor rose through her hips and spine as a cold sweat soaked her cotton pajamas. She shivered. Vomiting made her feel better, though certainly weaker, and emptier. Spent.

Jack helped her stand, closed the toilet lid, and sat her down on it. He dampened a washcloth with warm water and wiped her face. "You want me to stick around this morning?"

"No—well, maybe 'til I'm out of the shower." She knew he had a full morning. And he didn't need to hang out to watch her sleep. Or puke. "Is Norah up yet?"

"Not yet. She worked until two this morning. I thought I'd let her sleep."

"Can you give me five minutes to shower?"

Jack looked at his watch and nodded. "Sure, take ten. Maybe I can get through to the doctor."

Libby stripped, letting her pajamas puddle on the floor. As the water warmed up, she stepped on the scale. An old habit. She and the scale had always had a rocky relationship. Hmm, down twelve pounds. She smiled in spite of herself.

Standing still, allowing the pounding water to soothe her, Libby enjoyed the brief respite and escape a hot shower could provide. She reached for her orange-scented shampoo and closed her eyes, reveling in the fragrance, massaging her scalp with the rich lather. Moments later, she screamed.

A breathless Jack arrived and opened the shower door.

"Libby, what happened?" He reached in to turn off the water.

"My hair. . ." she wailed. "My hair." Clumps of dark hair littered the shower floor. She sank to the floor as the water cascaded around her. Masses of her brown locks hung between her fingers like limp seaweed. Jack reached for a towel and helped her up from the shower floor. He swaddled and held her shaking body, rubbing her back to dry and warm her.

"I'm so sorry," he murmured. "Tell me what you want me to do."

He couldn't make it stop. He couldn't take away the cancer or the chemo or. . . "Just hold me a minute. Then help me get dressed." Jack rocked her gently. Her sobs subsided and Jack helped her to the bedroom and found fresh pajamas. He steadied her as she stepped into the bottoms. He helped her with the buttons. Libby caught a glimpse of the pale gray stranger in the mirror above the dresser and gasped. She looked like a dog with mange. Jack wrapped his arms around her and kissed her forehead. Libby smiled weakly to herself. His forehead had increased in acreage as well.

"You knew that was one of the side-effects, Lib." Jack's tone was gentle, but matter of fact.

"I know. But it's such a shock. And there was a chance that it wouldn't happen."

"It's hair, honey. Remember Norah's purple hair? It grows back."

"I look so. . . ugly. I used to be cute, right?"

"Libby, I love you. To me, you're always beautiful—inside and out." She knew he meant well, but really, how could anyone love someone who looked like this? Someone who was sick. He ran his hand over his own balding head. "You still love me, right?"

"Yes. Mostly."

"Well, then don't you deserve equal rights? What good is feminism if you don't have the right to be loved?"

Bless his little lawyer's heart. This man made her fall in love with him again and again. She smiled at a memory. Norah had been a colicky newborn, Libby, an exhausted new mother. She'd awoken in the middle of the night, alone in bed. A light down the hall drew her forward where she discovered Jack dancing in the kitchen, cradling Norah, and softly singing "Be my baby..."

"And Jack? I think you should call the school." The words she needed to say caught in her throat. "I can't—I can't finish the year. Let them make—make whatever arrangements they need to."

Jack nodded and gave her a small, tight-lipped smile. "I'm glad you reached a decision, honey."

"Not like I have much choice. Even that shower kicked my butt."

"And it's such a nice butt." Jack patted her bum, kissed her cheek, and left for work.

AN HOUR later Maggie lay sleeping beside the bed. Libby sat up reading the paper and sipping tepid chamomile tea. It was staying down, at least for now. She heard the garage door open. No doubt it would be Claire. They'd given her the code and done away with the formality of knocks and doorbells.

Sure enough, Claire strode in brandishing newly purchased electric hair clippers. Libby's dad had used similar ones on her brothers, lining them up for identical buzz-cuts in his backyard barbershop.

"Oh, God. What are you thinking?!" Libby had resisted the idea of shaving her head. "Can't I wear a hat? Or a wig? I still want to look like a girl."

"No doubt about your gender. Those ta-tas of yours are a dead giveaway." Only Claire could get away with death and boob jokes. Only Claire would risk them.

"But. . ."

"But nothing. You're doing battle. You should look like a warrior." Claire looked her in the eye. "Fierce instead of fragile."

"But shaving my head?" Easy for Claire to say. She'd cropped hers years ago.

"What are you afraid of?"

"You mean besides dying?" She couldn't look any worse than she did now.

Claire's eyes lit up, flashing the mischief that reminded Libby of their childhood adventures, like jumping out from the state museum's mine cars to yell, "Boo!" at the tourists. "I've got an idea. Follow me." Claire marched into Libby's bathroom with clippers held high. Libby trailed timidly behind. A wary Maggie watched from a distance.

It was only then that a sleepy-eyed Norah emerged from her room, her long dark hair a bird's nest of tangles. "What's going on?"

"Ask your Auntie Claire." Libby cocked her head toward the bathroom.

Mother and daughter stood at the bathroom door, uncertain —and skeptical—of what Claire was about to do. They watched as Claire plugged in the clippers and pressed the on button. She held the buzzing weapon to her temple.

"No, Claire! Don't!" Libby shrieked in horror.

"Too late!" Claire said with a slightly mad gleam in her eyes.

Norah stood back, open-mouthed, shaking her head. Claire's dark blonde hair fell into the sink.

Once again, Claire took the bold, dangerous first step. Once again, she dared Libby to follow. Like jumping off the high-dive when they were eight. Or secretly shaving their legs in Claire's closet at eleven. Not much of a secret with all the bloody bits of TP on their legs. Claire held the clippers out to Libby.

"Oh, crap." Libby knew what the next step would be. Still, she hesitated.

Claire shrugged and went back to the mirror. "I'd better even it up." She buzzed the other side of her head, leaving what looked like the start of a lopsided Mohawk. "Well?"

"Crap. Okay. Hand 'em over." Libby held the clippers to her forehead. Her hand shook. "I—I can't."

"*Can't* you don't want to or *can't* you want help?" Claire asked.

"Help. Please."

Norah retrieved a chair from the bedroom. Libby sat as Claire wrapped a dark green towel around her shoulders. Norah grasped her mother's hand. Libby chewed her lip. The three of them held their breath as Claire ran the clippers along Libby's scalp, removing the first strands of brown hair. All three were crying by the time the last wisps fell. Only a bit of fuzz covered Libby's pale round head. She shivered. The effect was not what she'd expected.

"I don't look like a warrior." Her chin quivered. "I look like my brothers."

Norah opened a drawer and pulled out a tube of bright red lipstick and some blush. She carefully applied the make-up as Libby watched in the mirror. "Some light artillery, Mom. Don't leave home without it."

"Better," Libby admitted. She looked at Claire and giggled. Even though Claire wore her hair short, those two swaths of shorn scalp looked pretty funny. "Your turn, Claire."

Libby stood and Claire took a seat. They were both laughing when Libby finished. Empowered now, Libby pointed the shears at Norah with a sly grin.

"Next?" Norah retreated to the safety of her room.

LIBBY PULLED up the hood of her sweatshirt against the chill then settled on the couch with an afghan and the remote.

"Hungry?" Claire asked.

"I think so. Maybe some milky tea and toast?"

"Cinnamon toast?" Claire offered.

"Not too much trouble?"

"No trouble at all."

Libby heard Norah in the shower. The phone rang and she started to jump up from the couch. Claire stopped her.

"Sit. Stay. I'll get it." Claire said as she picked up the cordless from the kitchen counter. "Coopers, Claire speaking." She smiled and nodded, handing the phone to Libby.

"Are you any better?" It was Jack.

"A little, I think. Amazing what a little treatment from the bathroom beauticians can do."

"I don't understand."

"Never mind. You'll see. Claire's making me some toast."

"That's a good sign. The oncologist finally called me back.

She's calling in some anti-nausea meds. That's why you've been so sick."

"Shouldn't they have done that before now?"

"Yeah. You'd think. . . Anyway, the pharmacy will deliver the prescription within the hour. Also, I talked with the principal. Now you can focus on getting well."

A lump rose in Libby's throat.

"It's all set. Jan will stay for the rest of the year. That should make you feel better." Yes, indeed it did. She loved and trusted Jan, as did her students. Claire brought her the tea and toast, setting the cup and plate on the table beside Libby.

"Thank you, Jack. I don't think I could have made the call." She hung up handed the phone to Claire. It rang again.

"Coopers. Claire speaking." Claire frowned and shook her head. "Not sure she's awake, Fran. She had a pretty rough night. Let me check." Claire held the phone against her chest and whispered to Libby, "Are you sure?"

Libby sighed, nodded, and reached for the phone. Claire shook her head.

"Hi, Mom. What do you need?"

CHAPTER FOURTEEN

Then: To Make You Feel My Love

*B*ack in her Fullerton apartment on a morning in February, Claire's bed shook. Books and candles tumbled from their precarious perches on shelves. The spider plant swung wildly in its macramé nest. Somewhere in her not-quite-awake fog, it registered: earthquake. What was it she was supposed to do? Stay away from. . . what? Stand... where? She remained in bed gripping the sheets, her gut rumbling in concert with the earth's tremors. Then it stopped. Everything was quiet. She waited for the shaking to resume or the roof to collapse. When it didn't, she took deep, measured breaths—that technique she learned from Lou—and willed her pulse to slow. Breathe in-two-three-four, out-two-three-four. In time, it obeyed.

Stepping down the hall and into the living room, her steps were tentative. She opened the curtain and peeked out, fearing what she might see. The freeway, carports, the eucalyptus, and palm trees stood unchanged. Out of habit she started a pot of coffee and turned on the TV. How bad was it? Was anyone hurt? The morning news guy might say something. The perco-lator gurgled and sighed as the announcer regained enough of his composure to say what everyone already knew. Yes, there had been an earthquake. No, they didn't know how bad it was. Stay tuned.

The phone rang, startling her and returning her pulse to racing speed.

"H—hello."

"Hey, Claire. You okay?" Sam. His voice instantly calmed her.

Claire stretched the long phone cord to turn down the TV's volume. "Yeah. No real damage here. But it woke me up." She poured a cup of coffee, sat at her table, and stared across the room at the TV.

"Me too. I'll bet folks with waterbeds got sloshed out of bed this morning."

Claire chuckled at the image, blotting out more troubling scenes for the moment. "How—how bad do you think it is?"

"Dunno. Not 'til they hear from the seismologists. But as big as it was here, it would be way worse nearer the epicenter. Houses, freeways...could be bad. Anyway, I wanted to make sure you were okay. Still up for dinner?"

"Sure." Dinner with Sam's family again tonight. They had become her surrogate family. "Thanks for calling. For checking up on me."

THROUGHOUT THE SPRING, she and Sam shared quick meals on campus, or coffee between classes. They ran together several times a week. And she started doing stuff with his little sisters, Joanie and Kate. Movies, shopping, Joanie's French homework. She and Sam had shown each other their emotional scars. His girlfriend of five years had been cheating on him for three. Claire revealed a bit about Hawaii, explaining her wariness of men. They accepted each other's trust issues and brokenness and remained content and comfortable behind their respective walls.

Late one summer night, Sam knocked at Claire's apartment door. It was nearly ten o'clock. "Come with me," he said. "I want to show you something."

Without questioning, Claire slipped into her sandals and followed him down the stairs. A recent rain had freshened the air and washed the sky of its usual haze, but the night was warm enough for the Jeep to go topless. They got on the freeway and headed toward the beach. She trusted Sam, but the beach still triggered anxiety. Once again, she breathed slowly to calm herself as she corralled her wind-whipped hair into a rubber band.

Gravel crunched as Sam parked at a turnout along Pacific Coast Highway. He turned off the headlights. Claire's uneasiness resurfaced as she followed him to the barrier at the edge of the cliff.

"Look!" He stood behind her, one hand pointing out to sea, the other resting on her shoulder. As always, his voice steadied her.

"What?" What was she supposed to see?

"The waves."

"Yes, Sam. I see waves. It's the ocean." Duh.

"No, look! They're glowing."

Then she saw it. The white foam of each dark wave glowed, luminous and radiant.

"My God. I've never. . ."

"Bioluminescence," Sam explained in her ear, his breath sending a pleasant shiver down her spine.

"Bio-what?" She turned her head slightly and leaned into him but kept her eyes on the water.

"Bioluminescent phytoplankton. The fireflies of the sea."

"Bioluminescence," she repeated. "What makes it do that?" she asked, unable to look away.

"It's a chemical reaction. Hundreds of little single-cell algae called dinoflagellates. Sailors see it in the bow wake of their ships."

"How did you know about this?"

"I was here earlier tonight."

Claire turned to look at him. "You were here already?"

"Uh-huh," he said with a nod.

"Wait. You were here, left, and drove all the way back to get me?"

He shrugged. "I thought you'd like to see it."

Now a chemical reaction sparked a glow within her. It warmed her from someplace deep inside. She felt something she hadn't felt since she was very young. Not merely safe, but cherished. Worthy. She turned, reached up, and fingered the fresh-haircut bristle on his neck, breathing in his smell. Coffee and Juicy Fruit gum. Kissing him softly and slowly on the mouth, she felt something inside her open, like a flower turning toward the sun.

Sam pulled away from the kiss and looked down at her through narrowed eyelids.

"What?" she asked.

He grinned his stupid Howdy Doody grin. "It's about time." He kissed her deeply.

For a long moment, Claire lost herself in that kiss. But when Sam's hand brushed her breast, she panicked and pulled away. A struggle churned inside her. Her brain—or the rational part anyway—argued that Sam was good and kind and true. But the ancient reptilian, reactionary instinct for survival made her recoil as if she'd been burned.

"I—I can't..." Her breaths came quick and shallow. She felt light-headed and bent over with her hands on her knees.

"Can't?"

"I like you so much. It's just..." What? Can't stand to be touched?

"That guy messed you up pretty bad, didn't he?"

Her words stuck in her throat with tears of shame and rage that she'd believed she was done with. "I'm sorry."

"You've done nothing to be sorry for."

"But…" Shivering, she straightened slowly. She couldn't meet his eyes.

"No 'but,'" he said, touching her chin and gently turning her face toward his. Claire leaned into him as she rested her head against his chest, feeling the sturdy bulk of him and the steady beat of his heart. He held her and kissed the top of her head. Her breathing calmed. Again. Her heartbeat slowed. Again. "We'll wait," he whispered. "We'll wait 'til you're ready."

And they did wait. And wait.

A LONG FRUSTRATING summer passed and school started again. One night that fall they sat at Claire's kitchen table finishing off the last bit of pizza, Sam said, "I've been thinking."

"About what?" As if she couldn't guess. It's all she'd thought about for weeks now. Since that night at the beach.

"Maybe we need to go away. To the mountains, maybe?"

"Together? Alone?" She felt apprehension creep into her words.

"Yes. Together. Alone." He smiled that sweet dimpled smile. "My folks have a cabin at Lake Arrowhead."

"Why would that be different?"

"You've never been there. No triggers. No sand. No beach."

"Maybe, but what if that doesn't work?" What if nothing worked? What if she couldn't be fixed? Maybe it's a good thing she was leaving after graduation. Sam could find a normal girlfriend. One who didn't have a stroke every time he touched her.

"Then we'll try something else." She exhaled slowly, licking her lips in cautious hope.

They picked a date on the calendar, less than two weeks away, before the holidays when things got hectic at the nursery. Sam drew a little heart in the calendar square.

"This seems weird. The opposite of spontaneous." Claire said.

"Spontaneous hasn't worked for us."

CLAIRE HAD LOST count of the time and tissues she'd spent in Lou's office over the past year and a half. Naturally, she'd resisted at first and scoffed at the incense and cushions, the sitar music and herbal tea. But it had worked. Or so she thought until Sam kissed her. Lou looked at her over her glasses.

"I feel like a born-again virgin. Or like I'm back in high school," Claire admitted.

"Has he made you feel uncomfortable?"

"No. He's been so good. So patient. The worst part is that I want this as much as he does. I simply can't get over this panic I feel whenever we get—you know—close." She'd started birth control pills again. Just in case.

"How far have you gotten before the panic sets in?"

"Kissing is good." So very good. Thinking about kissing gave her a pleasant little shiver. "But when he touches my breasts or—you know—I—I—I can't go any further."

"When he touches you. What about when you touch him?"

Claire loved the feel of his neck, his chest, his back, his... "That's ok. That's good." More than good.

"It could have something to do with being in control. You said the rape made you feel powerless."

"But sex is about losing control, isn't it?"

"In a way, yes. But it's also about feeling safe to let go. Trusting the person you're with."

"I trust Sam. Or I think I do."

"Um-hmmm." Lou stirred her tea. "What if you took the lead? What if you initiated and set the pace?"

"You mean tell him what to do?"

"Even more. Show him. Put his hands where you want, when you want..."

CLAIRE'S HANDS fidgeted as she packed a small suitcase Friday morning, her stomach tense, troubled. Would she be able to follow through on Lou's suggestion? Or would it end in one more humiliating disappointment? Underwear, jeans, sweater, extra socks. PJs? No, a nightie. No. Nothing remotely sexy. Not this time. She tossed in an oversized Wylder Nursery t-shirt to sleep in.

She and Sam rode most of the way up to the cabin in silence. Claire tried to relax, but the knot in her belly refused to loosen as Sam maneuvered along the twisty mountain road. They arrived at the redwood-sided cabin as the sun was setting. The pine-scented air reminded her of home and summers at Lake Tahoe. Maybe Sam was right.

Sam opened a bottle of wine which they drank while making a simple meal of spaghetti with jarred sauce. They settled on the floor in front of a blaze in the stone fireplace with their plates and more wine. Claire felt pleasantly buzzed as the edges of the world grew fuzzy.

"You've got a little sauce on your lip."

She licked. "Still?"

"Let me get it." He kissed her. "You taste good."

"Mmmm, you too."

They lingered in the kiss, savoring it. This part they did well. Very well. Sam held her head tenderly in his big hands, kissing her eyes, her earlobes, the hollow of her neck. She moaned and lay back against the sofa. This place, this feeling was at once familiar and new. Claire lost herself in the sensation of warmth and pleasure. Sam's hands caressed her neck, her belly, sending divine tremors to her core. Yes. Please. More. Her body urged her forward although her pulse quickened in what she recognized as pre-panic. She sat up and then, trembling, breathless, took Sam's hands in hers and held them at his sides. A question washed across his features.

"Everything okay?"

"I—I think so." She stared into his eyes. "But, let me do this," her words muffled as she pulled her sweater over her head. Slowly, she unhooked her bra and let it slip off. Her nipples stiffened in the chill, but the prickles of panic seemed to be holding back, watching, waiting. Deep, slow breaths came without thinking as she unbuttoned Sam's flannel shirt, revealing his freckled shoulders. His coppery chest hair danced with electricity beneath her fingers. Unzipping and removing her jeans brought a slow smile to his lips.

Claire—her heartbeat roaring in her ears—now reached for Sam's belt, the buttons on his jeans. He let her tug at his clothes and straddle him. In the firelight, she could see a longing flame in his eyes. Her fingers, her lips explored and aroused him until at last, she let him enter her. They rode their yearning to its peak until they had both achieved what they had been longing for.

Breathless, she collapsed against his chest, her cheeks damp with tears.

HER FINAL FALL semester nearly done. Claire sat at her kitchen table, feet propped up on a chair, talking with her mother on the phone.

"I got my Peace Corps application into the mail today. Now all I can do is wait and hope."

"So, what happens if you're not accepted? Do you have a Plan B? Stay in California with Sam, maybe?"

"No. I want to go away for a while. Travel. Work. Do something different."

"What about Sam?"

"I don't know."

Falling for Sam had happened slowly, like a car heater on a cold morning, warming up until at some point you realized you were no longer shivering. And it was only weeks old. She wouldn't change her plans because of it.

In addition to her job at the restaurant, Claire had been pressed into service at Wylder Nursery a few times, cashiering mostly. And now with holiday preparations, Sam's mom, Inez had asked her to help Sam's sisters make evergreen garlands and wreaths for the holidays. Her hands bore the scratches where the branches and wires had nicked her inexpert fingers. The more her life became entangled in Sam's, the harder it would be to leave. It muddied her escape route. Still, her mind was made up.

"So, you're not thinking long-term with Sam?" her mother asked.

"Like getting married? Jeez, no! I'm not thinking about that right now."

"So, you'll be like Scarlett O'Hara?"

"Hmm?" She wasn't at all like Scarlett.

"You'll think about it tomorrow?" A little chuckle erupted from her mother.

"Ha-ha, very funny." Sam wouldn't want to get married

after graduation, would he? And she didn't want to marry anyone. No, she was leaving.

"Have you thought about coming home for Thanksgiving? You could show me how to make a wreath while you're here."

"Actually, the Wylders invited us for Thanksgiving."

"Oh, my! With his whole family?"

"Yes." Claire couldn't remember ever wanting her mother to meet her boyfriends. Partly because she'd relished the secrets, the deceptions. But another part was that none of them had been important enough. Sam was different. He was important. Just how important, Claire refused to admit.

THANKSGIVING DAY WAS warm and fair as Claire balanced two shopping bags in her arms and rang the Wylder's doorbell at their house on a quiet cul-de-sac in Yorba Linda. She could hear voices and the bright sounds of Herb Alpert and the Tijuana Brass.

"My goodness, what all did you bring?" Inez said as she opened the door wearing a butcher's apron appliqued with a cornucopia, her salt and pepper hair cut in its functional pixie cut. She brought with her the smells of roasting turkey.

"Well, it started with a few hors d'oeuvres and wine. I guess we got carried away." Claire shrugged and introduced her mother.

"Inez Wylder, this is my mother, Sylvia Jordan."

"It's so good to finally meet you. You've become such a big part of Claire's life," her mother said.

"Well, she's become a big part of ours," Inez smiled and wrapped an arm around Claire's waist. Sam's father wiped his hands on a tea towel as Joanie and Kate crowded into the entry hall.

"Come in! Come in! I'm Lee." He offered his hand. "Can I offer you something to drink? Wine?"

"Wine would be lovely, thank you. We brought some," her mother said gesturing toward the bags that were disappearing into the kitchen with Joanie and Kate. "I wasn't sure what you preferred, so there's an assortment. One red, one white, and one sparkling."

"I prefer whatever's open!" Sam called as he descended the large staircase into the entry hall, smiling and looking freshly showered and shaved. When he bent to kiss Claire on the cheek, she inhaled deeply and fought the urge to nibble his ear. He greeted her mother, "How do you do, Mrs. Jordan."

As they shook hands, Claire recognized the appraising look in her mother's eye, the way she looked for good value in people as well as in property. Foundation, structure, quality of materials. And potential. Always potential. While Claire worried when that look was directed at her, she doubted her mother would find anything lacking in Sam.

"Please, call me Sylvia."

"Yes, ma'am." No, Claire had nothing to worry about.

Joanie and Kate emptied the bags onto the counter, oohing and aahing over the exotic cheeses, imported crackers, and assorted olives. All of it had been her mother's doing, of course. Lee poured generous helpings of wine into stemmed glasses for the adults before opening the oven to baste the turkey.

"What can we do to help?" Claire asked.

Inez answered, enumerating the list on her fingers. "Peel and dice potatoes. Set the table." She paused before holding a large, unfamiliar vegetable aloft. "And this butternut squash needs attention."

"I can do potatoes," Claire asserted. Peeling and chopping were within her skill set.

"Kate and I can set the table," dark-haired Joanie added.

"I'll do the squash," Sam offered. "You old folks can take it easy."

She and Sam worked side-by-side, paring and chopping. Sam wielded a huge knife, muscling it through what looked like the shell of the squash, revealing bright orange flesh.

"What's that going to be?" Claire gestured with the potato peeler.

"Mom bakes it with apples. It's one of my favorites, so I don't mind doing prep for it."

Yes, Sam's value kept growing. What she couldn't understand was why he loved her. Why he protected her. No one had ever treated her that way before. Not since her father, anyway. Even her mother had encouraged Claire's independence, given her grown-up responsibilities early on. Sam seemed to sense some need in her that no one else had. A need she'd never let anyone else see. Not Mom, not Libby. He allowed her to be soft. And for the long months during which she was recovering and they were becoming friends, she'd shown him little to contradict that perception.

But now she felt her old self returning. And it wasn't all good. She worried that Sam would have trouble accepting and loving the free and fierce Claire who she felt re-emerging. The stronger she grew, the less she needed Sam. Wanted, yes, wanted very much. But not need.

CHAPTER FIFTEEN

Now: Only Love Can Break a Heart

*A*n evening out with her friends and playing bridge was exactly what Fran McCormack needed. Maybe Libby was right. If Mitch were going to stay, he'd better start helping with Mike. Staying with his father while she went out was the least he could do. The very least.

If she were honest, lapses in Mike's memory had been happening for years. Asking the same question over and over again. Forgetting neighbors' names. Repeating stories. The final straw came to be known as "The Chicken Incident." Mike had roasted a chicken countless times. A little oil rubbed over the skin, some seasoning, and into the oven for an hour and a half. Easy. Except this time, Mike got out a bunch of random ingredients and got lost somewhere. He forgot what to do next. Fran had patiently walked him through the process and watched as he put the chicken in the oven, set the timer, and sat down to watch CNN in the den. Fifteen minutes later, he was back in the kitchen taking the chicken out of the oven and saying dinner was ready and that she'd better make a salad. Of course, the chicken was raw. Mike accused her of messing with the oven.

Fran hated to argue with him. Poor guy, he simply didn't remember.

When she finally told Libby about her concerns, she'd felt as if she were being disloyal by sharing secrets. Mike would be embarrassed. It simply broke her heart.

"I'm going out, Mike," Fran said. He looked up at her from his recliner in front of the TV, but otherwise didn't respond. She leaned over and kissed his cheek. "I'll stop at Libby's before dinner and see how she's doing." Chemotherapy had weakened her daughter, but at least the nausea was under control now. The sight of her daughter's shaved head was an unwelcome reminder of the unseen cancer threatening her child. She knew that had been Claire's doing. Libby never could resist her influence, but shaving her head? Good grief.

"Libby's a good girl. Has she finished her homework?" Mike asked.

Fran took a deep breath. "Libby's a teacher now, Mike. She gives homework; she doesn't do it."

"Libby doesn't do her homework?"

This could go on indefinitely and Mike would never remember. "I'll tell her to finish her homework."

"She'd better. Or no dessert."

Fran turned to her youngest child stretched out on the couch. "And Mitch? Keep an eye on your father. Make sure he doesn't leave the house alone. I've left a number by the phone."

"Sure," Mitch replied, barely looking away from the TV.

"I mean it." Her two men, both damaged in some irreparable way, sat before flickering images on the television oblivious to the world around them and their place in it.

IT WAS NEARLY TEN O'CLOCK. Later than Fran had

expected, but she'd so enjoyed the evening of dinner and bridge.

"Hey, boys, I'm home!" Fran called as she entered through the garage and dark laundry room. She flipped on the light and shook the rain off her umbrella, leaving it open to dry on top of the washer. "I brought you dessert!" Thunder clapped and lightning snapped directly overhead. "Quite a storm out there."

The house was quiet except for CNN droning from the den.

"Mike? Mitch? I'm back." Worry flashed through her mind. She dropped her coat and began searching the downstairs room by room, her heart beating more desperately at every door. Thunder echoed what was happening in her chest.

The den? No.

The living room? No.

Maybe there had been an emergency? Certainly, they would leave a note, a message. The kitchen, next to the phone? No. Nothing.

Finally, she walked upstairs to Mitch's room. That's where she found him, face down on his bed. An empty fifth of store-brand vodka rested on the floor next to him, his arm draped over the edge of the bed. She tried to wake him. He stirred a bit but was incoherent.

"Mitch! How could you?! Where is your father?! You were supposed to be watching him."

"Hey, Mom—wha'zzup?" Mitch lifted his head to look at her, then seemingly exhausted by the effort let it drop again. "Le' me ssshleeep. . ."

Fran dialed Libby from the kitchen. Jack answered.

"I can't find Mike," Fran sobbed. "He's—he's gone."

"We'll be there in two minutes. Call the sheriff."

One of the benefits of living in a small town for a long time is that everyone knows everyone else. The 911 dispatcher was a former student of Mike's. So was the Sheriff.

"What's he wearing, Mrs. Mac?" the dispatcher asked.

"Blue jeans and a plaid flannel shirt. White sneakers. And most likely a blue Wolfpack baseball cap." For years, she'd tried to update Mike's wardrobe to add a little variety. Now she was glad she could accurately describe him.

"We'll find him, Mrs. Mac. We'll bring him home."

Another clap of thunder shook the house as Libby and Jack arrived breathless and frantic, raincoats over their pajamas. Libby wore slippers and a knitted cap. Jack wore sneakers without socks. They looked awful. Libby was so thin and pale. Fran felt guilty for involving them, but who else could she call?

Jack took charge. "Libby, you stay here by the phone while I take your mom and drive around the neighborhood."

"But. . ." Libby started to argue, but both Fran and Jack put up their hands.

"No, we can't have you getting any sicker, honey. I have my cell. We'll call if there is any news. You do the same."

The house went dark.

"Power's out." Fran felt her way to the bottom drawer in the laundry room and pulled out two flashlights. She handed one to Libby then retrieved her still dripping umbrella.

Jack held the door. "Come on, Fran. Let's go find Mike."

Jack turned right from Westview onto Fifth Street before creeping north on Thompson.

"The way he walked to Bordewich School," Fran nodded. "Every day for thirty-five years. A good place to start."

"Just a hunch. After that, we'll try the church. Then we'll see what happens."

With the street lights out, the scene outside was deserted and dark except for the frequent electric flashes. Fran jumped at each boom and crackle. Jack parked in front of the school and helped Fran out of the car. He grabbed his flashlight from the glove box.

Another boom.

They walked around to the north side of the building, where

Mike's class had been. Their flashlights' beams revealed the new entrance to the school. A mural had been added.

"Mike? Dad?" Jack called.

"Mike? You here? Come on, it's late. Time to go home."

They rounded the corner and looked out at the playground behind the school. It had changed since Mike taught here. Fran didn't recognize it. Mike wouldn't either. If he were here, he'd be confused, scared. Lost. Her heart sank.

"Mike? It's Jack! Where are you?"

"Mike, honey?"

Jack tried another tack. "Mr. Mac? Come on, the bell rang! School's over. It's time to go home!"

Their two beams of light continued to sweep the empty darkness. Then they saw him. Sitting on the steps at the back of the building. Hidden from the street. He was crying.

"I—I—I don't know how to get home."

Fran shook her head sadly. "Oh, Michael Patrick McCormack. For goodness sake. It's okay. We're here now. Let's go home."

Jack was already calling Libby.

———

WATCHING her father slip away while his body remained healthy, was the hardest thing Libby had ever done. It sapped what little energy chemotherapy left her. He could no longer read nor carry on a conversation. When she looked at old photographs, she tried to see when exactly her father had gone away. Three years ago? Five? More? Something changed around his eyes. They became vacant, like looking into a house after everyone you knew had moved away.

The first time he didn't know utterly shattered her.

"But Daddy, it's me. It's Libby."

"Glad to meet you, Libby. Take a seat by the window."

He might recognize her the next time, but she couldn't count on it. It was a gift if he did. Or at least that's how she tried to think of it. Libby talked to friends, checked out books from the library, and searched the Internet. There was advice, but little hope.

And caring for her father had become more and more difficult for Libby's mom. During that spring and early summer, the frantic, middle of the night phone calls from her mother increased. It was time for her brothers to accept that there was a problem. Libby had notes in front of her, with the specific times and situations where Dad was having difficulties. Something needed to be done. Soon. She dreaded the conversation with her oldest brother, John, so saved it for last.

"I can't believe we're even talking about this." John dismissed her. Libby felt her heart rate increase, her blood pressure rise. She hated confrontation—especially with John—although she had learned to stand her ground when she had to. "You want to put our father in a home? Can't you help Mom? Can't you just...?"

"Just what? I already stop by every day. I call at lunch. Are you saying I should move home?" John didn't get it.

"Well, no, but. . ."

"But nothing. I have cancer, John, remember? I'm still getting chemo and will be for at least another eight weeks. I can barely take care of myself." She ran her hand up and under the soft, knit cap Aunt Ellie had sent to cover her bald head.

"Well, then hire someone to come in and help out."

"He needs more than help, John. He leaves the house and gets lost in the neighborhood. I told you what happened that night of the storm."

"Then lock the damn doors. God. It's so simple. You have a duty." The retired Navy commander was big on duty.

"But nothing. No one lifts a finger to help. It's Jack and me. That's it."

"But I don't even live there. I can't help."

"Precisely." Did he even hear himself?

"If Mitch would only. . ."

"We can't count on Mitch." Their youngest brother was in rehab again. A residential place in California. Maybe that stormy night had done some good.

"What about Keith?"

"He's here every other weekend. I can't ask him to do any more. Of course, if you think you can do better, I can put Daddy on the next flight to DC and you could deal with him." She was bluffing, but still. . .

"He's your father. How could you. . ."

"Ditto, John. Ditto." She banged the phone down with such force that it bounced out of its cradle. It took her two hours and a long walk to calm down enough to call him back.

"I'm not asking for your permission," Libby stated matter-of-factly. Using Jack's technique, her voice was soft and steady, belying her anger. "I'm merely informing you of a decision that Mom and I have made."

"So, you decided without any input from anyone?"

"Decisions get made by those who show up, John. Keith was here. He agrees. And Mitch."

"Mitch—as if. He'd sell his vote for a beer."

"Of course, if you want to take him to live with you. . ."

"This is ridiculous. I don't have a place for him. Besides, I work, you know. You at least. . ."

". . . At least what, John? Dad needs twenty-four-seven care. I can't do that. Neither can Mom. Unless you can, he must go somewhere. There's a memory care facility here in Carson. We can visit him every day." Libby took a breath and took out the final item in her arsenal. "I'm most worried about Mom."

"Why? What's wrong with Mom?" His tone softened a bit. John hadn't seen their mother in over a year. He didn't see how thin, how weary she was.

"She doesn't eat, can't sleep. She looks awful. The doctor said her blood pressure was through the roof. At this rate, Dad could outlive her. Then what, John? Then what?"

SETTLING her father into his room at Carson Pines took most of the morning. The room resembled a nondescript hotel room, so the staff encouraged families to bring photos and personal items to help residents feel more at home. Libby and her mother also wanted to remind his caregivers of who he used to be. Libby hung her dad's "Teacher of the Year" plaque next to the small bulletin board where her mom had already pinned a few photos, including their wedding picture and a school photo from the 70s. In both, he wore his trademark crew-cut and bow tie. Libby shook her head remembering that a bow tie had been his secret code to expect a pop quiz. He'd collected dozens of them over the decades. Several even lit up.

Libby busied herself putting away his clothes, trying not to think about the next step—leaving. She was glad that her father couldn't comprehend what was happening.

A few minutes before lunch, the social director came to escort her dad to the dining room. They both kissed him goodbye and stepped into the hall where big band music played on the PA.

"I'll be back tomorrow, Mike. I love you," her mother called after him. They watched him shuffle down the hall, away from them. He barely registered their presence, let alone their departure. Her mother shouldered her handbag and marched toward the exit. Libby had to run to catch up.

"Get me out of here," her mom said under her breath.

"But Mom, you know. . ." The automatic doors slid open and they walked into the late June heat.

"I know everything," her mother gasped. "That is—or was

—the man I fell in love with. The man I married and promised to stick by for better or worse." Then her voice cracked. She turned back to look at the low, neatly landscaped building. "My God, what have I done?!"

"You didn't abandon Daddy. You gave him what he needs."

"Then why does it feel like I've broken a promise?" Her mother reached into her bag for a handkerchief. Her hand trembled. "I was supposed to take care of him. In sickness and health."

Libby had no answer other than her presence. She held her mother, whose grief shook them both. When sobs slowed to sniffles, they got into the car and drove to Libby's. Not wanting her mother to be alone, she'd made up the guest room.

Her mother quieted along the way. Try as she might, Libby couldn't imagine the pain of watching your sweetheart, the love of your life, disappear into someone who didn't recognize you. Then realizing you simply couldn't take care of him anymore? Libby wondered if it were possible to die of a broken heart.

They ate lunch without speaking, except to remark about the chicken salad—an old family favorite with celery, grapes, and cashews. Afterward, Libby suggested her mother lie down. She fought her a bit before realizing that yes, she was a little tired.

"Maybe I'll stretch out and rest my eyes for a while. Don't let me sleep too long though."

"Sure. And when you get up, we'll have tea."

NEARLY TWO HOURS LATER, Libby looked at her watch. She hated to wake her mother, but she put down her book and tiptoed down the hall. The guestroom door was ajar. Her mother looked more peaceful than she had in months. Years maybe.

"Mom?" Libby tapped her mother's wrist. "Time to wake up."

Something wasn't right. Her mother wasn't breathing. "Mom? Mom! Oh. . . Mom."

Libby sank to the floor. Sobs shook her shoulders as she held her mother's cold hand.

THE DAY BEFORE THE FUNERAL, Libby stood looking at herself in the dresser mirror. Crap. Her one good black dress sagged. Over thirty pounds gone now. Everything in her closet was simply too big. She resisted buying anything new at this weight. It always came back. Always. She picked up the phone and dialed Claire, who within an hour, arrived with several outfits for Libby to choose from. One hers, two of Sylvia's, complete with scarves and handbags.

They settled on a deep violet pantsuit of Sylvia's. She'd need to hem the pants.

"But it isn't black. What will people think?"

"They'll think you look lovely. Besides, my mom wouldn't steer you wrong, fashion and etiquette-wise, right?"

"True." Sylvia dressed impeccably.

"And I'll tie that scarf around your head Haitian-style."

"Haitian?"

"Trust me." And Libby did.

NOW LIBBY STARED at herself in the mirror, head wrapped in vibrant silk, a pouf of fabric at the nape of her neck and smiled. "Fancy."

"Told ya."

Jack had tried to convince Libby to use the church basement

for the reception afterward, but she'd refused. It had to be in their home. Weak as she was, some things had to be done right. This was what was called for. No matter what. Only to herself did she admit her standards were perhaps unrealistic.

Fortunately, Fran's friends organized everything, including the food. They borrowed tables and chairs from the church and rented linens. Fran's garden club arranged mountains of flowers in every available vase, urn, and jar. Norah and Annie had cleaned.

All four of Libby's brothers and their families arrived earlier in the week. They were staying at their parents' house and had started sifting through fifty years of belongings in preparation for putting it on the market. Sylvia's office would handle the sale. Libby was determined to stay out of it. There was nothing worth fighting over. And frankly, she didn't have the energy for the divvying up, the inevitable squabbles. However, she had retrieved their mother's jewelry box. There wasn't much of value. A strand of pearls, a gold locket on a chain, a charm bracelet, a few rings. Each of her mother's granddaughters could have something. She'd let them choose.

ORGAN MUSIC FILLED THE COOL, dark sanctuary at St. Teresa's, while quiet conversations buzzed in the background. A potpourri of fragrance wafted through the space. Honeysuckle. Asiatic lilies. Furniture polish. Libby tugged at the floral scarf covering her itchy head.

Libby's father sat between her and Keith in the front pew. Keith had volunteered to stick by him throughout the day. Dad's behavior had become more and more unpredictable. Jack sat on the other side of Libby and took her hand. Her father looked at his old Timex watch, then turned to look up the aisle.

"Where's your mother? Church is about to start." His pale blue eyes darted nervously around the church.

Libby took a deep breath before answering. Again.

"Dad, remember? Mom died. This is her funeral."

"Your mother's dead? Why didn't you tell me!?" His lower lip trembled. A tear escaped. He whispered, "My Franny's dead?"

"Yes, Daddy. I'm so sorry." Libby and Keith exchanged worried glances.

"I don't remember. . ." How many times had she told him? And each time was like hearing the news for the first time. As if she were ripping off a scab, renewing his grief and shock. The loss, the heartache never had a chance to fade.

Keith wrapped his arm around their father's shoulders. "We're here to say good-bye, Dad." His voice was soothing. Libby silently vowed to never tell her father again. She'd lie to him and allow him to believe his wife was merely asleep or out somewhere.

Libby found a hankie in her father's jacket pocket and dabbed at his face. He took the hankie from her and blew his nose. "My Franny's dead."

BACK AT THE HOUSE, her brother John immediately started to berate Libby.

"What do you mean you're not going to tell him that Mom's dead? He needs to know."

"I have told him. Many times." She sighed in exasperation. "He can't hold on to new information. Every time is like the first time."

"He deserves to know, Libby. It's cruel to lie to him." John raised his voice.

"And it's crueler to tell him that his wife is dead over and

over again." Watching him hear the new:
time. That was the worst part. Not the tel

"He has to accept that she's dead." H
her now. Libby swatted it away. John step]

"Why? What purpose does it serve?"

"He needs to know," John asserted.

"Fine. You tell him. Every day. You l
break his heart. Every day." From acr
watched as one guest after another stoppe
her father, pat his bony shoulder or kiss
looked away and walked to the buffet ta
plate for him. Handing it to him, she s
beside him.

"This is a nice party. Where's your mo
room. "She should eat something."

Libby pressed her lips together befor
kitchen." Her father nodded and took a bi

CHAPTER SIXTEEN

Then: Baby I'm Amazed

Claire awoke trying to remember where she was. The wind was blowing. There was a flapping sound. She was in a tent. Camping with Sam. She smiled involuntarily. Flipping onto her stomach, she inched to the tent door and peered out. The sun was coming up over the desert. A few pink clouds spackled the sky. The sage and other scrub brush trembled in the warm Santa Ana winds. Behind them, rocks towered but provided little shelter from the eddying sand.

"Hey, sleepyhead," he said. "How're you feeling?"

"Pretty good. Hardly coughed at all last night." A case of bronchitis a week ago had meant a trip to the health center and a course of antibiotics.

"Coffee's ready. Want some?" He stood at the makeshift kitchen—the Jeep's tailgate—gray sweatshirt over green flannel shirt and jeans, copper hair sticking up.

"Sure."

Claire wriggled into her jeans and sweatshirt. She shook out her socks and boots—cautious about bugs and snakes—and crawled out of the tent before racing to find a boulder to pee behind.

The wind was fierce, but somehow Sam had managed a substantial enough windbreak to get the Coleman stove going for coffee. She wrapped her arms around him from behind, using him as an anchor as he poured her a mug of coffee from an ancient blue enamelware pot.

"Cowboy style," Sam said.

"Cowboy?"

"You throw the grounds directly into the water and boil it."

"Boiled coffee?" She was skeptical but sipped anyway. "Hmmm. No grounds."

"You sound surprised."

"I am, a little." Not really though. Sam was kind of magic.

"The secret is to pour cold water on top when you're done boiling. It settles the grounds to the bottom."

"You gonna try to cook?" she asked before taking another swallow of coffee. "I threw some Sugar Pops into the bag. There's milk in the ice chest."

"I've got it all planned. It's too nasty to eat out here unless you're partial to grit. Why don't you go back inside the tent? I'll bring it to you." What could he have planned? She hadn't seen anything special when they stopped at the market on the way out of town last night. Sam wedged a roll of paper towels under her arm and handed her two paper cups. "Take these." Claire obeyed.

A moment later, Sam crawled into the tent, carrying a bottle of champagne and a package of cinnamon rolls. "This is Christmas breakfast at my house."

"I remember. But it's not Christmas."

"Yeah, but I feel like celebrating," he said. He popped the cork outside the door of the tent and filled the cups. They talked and ate and drank and kissed and laughed and kissed some more until the champagne and the cinnamon rolls were gone and the bubbles and sweetness were inside of them.

Without fanfare, Sam simply said, "I want to do this for the rest of my life. With you."

"Do what? Camp in the wind?" Claire slowly realized what he was saying.

"Camp in the wind. Drink champagne from paper cups. Bring you coffee. See your little face all smooshed and wrinkled in the morning. All of it. With you. Always."

Without thinking, Claire answered, "Be careful what you wish for." Which wasn't an answer. As much as she loved Sam, "always" wasn't a word she used.

Confusion and hurt clouded Sam's blue eyes. He sat up and pulled away from her. Her belly constricted, knowing she'd caused that wounded look. She hated herself for it. How could she make him understand? Her whole life, she'd held back, not given in to loving, to needing anyone. People thought it was because she didn't value commitments when really, it was just the opposite. She valued them too much to take them lightly. They petrified and paralyzed her. To break a promise, to disappoint someone you loved as her father had done? No. She didn't want anyone loving her like that, needing her that way.

"I like what we have now, Sam. I'm just not sure…"

"I love you. You love me, right?"

"Yes, of course." She looked away. "But I'm not sure that's enough."

"Of course, it's enough."

"Says the man whose parents have been married forever."

"So that's it. You're afraid?"

"Yes, I'm afraid. I know what happens when people fall out of love. I know about collateral damage."

"I'd never hurt you, Claire." He turned her to face him. "Don't you trust me?"

"I trust you. I don't trust me."

"That's silly. Because of your parents." He shook his head.

"It's not silly." She looked into his bewildered face. "I know you'd never hurt me, but I might hurt you. And I couldn't bear that." She felt tears brimming as she leaned forward to kiss him gently. "I'm not saying 'no,' just 'not yet.'"

The wind never did die down. Instead of spending another night camping, they drove back home to Claire's apartment with the eight-track playing The Mamas and the Papas. She sang along. Sam didn't. They stopped to pick up Claire's mail from the kiosk of mailboxes in front of the apartment complex. She unlocked her box, gathered the contents, and slid back into her seat next to Sam.

"What's that?" Sam asked pointing to the large envelope with the Peace Corps logo.

"I applied last fall...remember? Hadn't heard anything back from them." He had to know her plans. "I told you I wanted to go after graduation."

Sam said nothing as he released the brake and put the Jeep in gear. His jaw set, he drove the short distance to her apartment, parked, and turned to look at her.

"What?" Claire asked.

"After graduation? What about us?"

"I don't know."

Again, Sam said nothing. He got out of the car and grabbed her duffle bag from the back. They trudged up the stairs. Claire unlocked the door.

"Maybe they don't want me," Claire said as she tore open the envelope. She hesitated before pulling the letter out. Peace Corps had been her plan, her chance at redemption, to make up for all the trouble she'd caused. But Sam was another kind of chance, one she hadn't planned on. If they accepted her, she'd go. If not, would she marry Sam?

Slowly, she withdrew the letter as if it were a splinter, not wanting it to hurt more than necessary. Skimming for the pertinent information, she found what she needed. Accepted. Africa. July. Details to follow.

"They want me," she whispered.

Sam's jaw tightened. "So do I."

———

FOR WEEKS THAT SPRING, the push, and pull of wants and needs, plans and expectations were unbearable. Claire had a constant stomach ache from the stress. Finally, she convinced Sam to submit his own application. His knowledge of botany and business would be valuable in any developing country. If things worked out—and she honestly hoped they would—they could be posted together. His application was in the mail. The decision rested in someone else's hands now. Their life went back to normal. Claire couldn't help but think of it as a reprieve.

Looking at her calendar, Claire counted down the days and weeks. Eight weeks till graduation. Twelve weeks till Peace Corps training began in Puerto Rico. Then finally off to Kenya for two years, possibly with Sam. She'd teach health to young women and help at a village clinic. School was number one, but she needed to update her passport, her inoculations. Paperwork. Packing. Moving. She'd scarcely started a to-do list when the phone rang.

"Hello?"

"It's me." She heard a shudder in Sam's voice. "I need to talk with you. I need to see you. It's my dad."

"What's wrong?"

"He's sick." Something in Sam's voice told her he wasn't talking about a cold or the flu.

"Sick?" she repeated.

Claire waited, not wanting to hear what would almost certainly be something bad. "Cancer," he choked out before his sobs started.

"I'll be right there."

Claire grabbed her purse and keys, slipped into her sandals. Outside her living room window, the sun was setting over the freeway. She ran down the stairs to her car in the carport. When she put her VW in reverse she heard a honk and slammed on her brakes, and barely missed rear-ending a van behind her. "Sorry!" she yelled and started again. Her car knew the way to Sam's apartment.

She knocked on the door. Sam opened it. His eyes were puffy, his face, blotched. Claire wrapped her arms around his waist, leaned against his chest and held on, whispering over and over, "I'm sorry. I'm so sorry."

"I keep thinking about my mom and the girls." His voice broke.

"What do the doctors say? Surgery or chemo or radiation? Something?" she asked, leading him to the couch and settling herself beside him.

"Nothing." Sam looked away, blinking back tears.

"What do you mean, nothing? Of course, it's not nothing. He's what? Fifty? He can fight this."

"Fifty-two. They say weeks, months to live, maybe. It's pancreatic cancer. It's like the worst. It's fast."

"Weeks or months? No treatment? That can't be true."

"It's true. Mom's a wreck. The girls too. Mom's worried about the nursery. She can't run it by herself. Joanie and Kate are too young to be much help." Sam looked at the ceiling trying to hold back more tears. "And our dad's gonna die."

Claire held Sam's large, freckled hand and rubbed his thumb as she looked into his eyes.

"They'll be fine, Sam. You haven't had time to work out the possibilities." For Claire, the pain of the impending loss was very real. She grieved for the Wylders and herself and her own lost father.

"There aren't many options here." Sam bit his lip and shook his head.

"What are you saying?"

"I have to stay. I'll need to take over the business when I graduate."

"No Peace Corps?"

"No Peace Corps." There was no question in Sam's voice.

"Maybe later."

"There is no later. This is my life."

"We all have choices, Sam." Claire believed that, but it sounded hollow and cold saying it to Sam right now.

"Yes, Claire. We do have choices. And this is mine. I'm staying here to take care of my family. They need me."

I need you too, Claire almost said, but she stopped herself.

CLAIRE QUIT THE RESTAURANT—RELUCTANTLY, if she were totally honest—and began working at the nursery so Sam's mom could spend more time at the hospital. And while she liked working alongside Sam and looking up to see him across the nursery, she felt her world growing smaller, bit by bit. It consisted of school, the nursery, and Sam's family.

It broke her heart each time a customer asked about his father, but Sam continued to greet customers warmly. He smiled, nodded, and thanked them for their concern about his dad. "He's hanging in there," is all he'd say. "The nursery will stay open. We're not going anywhere."

It was clear that this was who Sam was and where he belonged. It was equally clear that Claire had no idea where she belonged.

TODAY, like many recent afternoons, Claire drove from the nursery to the Wylder house, stopping at Von's Market on the way for whatever she thought Sam's sisters might want for supper, mostly canned soup and sandwiches or Kraft Macaroni and Cheese. Claire still didn't have much of a repertoire in the kitchen.

She found Joanie sitting at the dining room table surrounded by a half-dozen cookbooks. Tears filled her blue eyes. Sam's eyes.

"What's up?" Claire set down the bag of groceries.

Joanie shook her head. Kate, the red-haired seventh-grader answered.

"She has to make a dish for her French class. Something besides French fries or French toast." Joanie handed Claire the mimeographed assignment sheet. Due next week. The teacher had reserved the home-ec kitchen.

"I can't ask Mom. Not now. Besides, she doesn't cook anything French."

"I guess there's nothing in the cookbooks?"

"Betty Crocker isn't exactly known for her fine French cuisine."

"No, probably not." Claire recalled a similar assignment in her own high school French class. "You're in luck. The French make great grilled cheese."

"Grilled cheese?"

"It's called Croque Monsieur. It's grilled cheese with ham, topped with béchamel sauce and broiled."

"Betcha-what?" Joanie's chin began to quiver again.

"Béchamel. White sauce. You know, butter, flour, milk..." Even Claire remembered that much from her junior high home-ec class. With Libby's help, she'd finally gotten rid of every lump. If she got stuck, she'd call Libby.

"That sounds pretty complicated." Joanie looked doubtful.

Claire opened the fridge and did a silent inventory. Butter. Bread. Ham. Swiss cheese. "Let's give it a try tonight. For fun." Joanie's face brightened.

"What do we do first?" Joanie asked.

"Stop crying. Start grating cheese."

Disaster averted. Or postponed anyway.

Later, after what turned out to be a pretty tasty dinner, she drove the girls the few miles to St. Jude Hospital in Fullerton. Sam and his mother sat in the dim room. His father seemed to be sleeping. Sam stood and kissed Claire's forehead.

"How was dinner?" Inez asked from her seat.

"Claire made fancy French grilled cheese sandwiches," Kate volunteered.

"Really?" Inez looked at Claire for confirmation.

Claire nodded. "Croque Monsieur. Or at least a reasonable facsimile. A trial run for Joanie's French assignment next week."

"It was good, but maybe too complicated for the assignment," Joanie added. "I wish there was something simpler."

"Sorry, I'm not more help right now, honey. What about a French apple pie?"

"Hmmm," Claire thought for a moment. "The French do a very simple, free-form pie called a galette." Her French teacher had made one.

"Free-form?"

"Yeah, you plunk the crust on a baking sheet, put the filling on top, fold the edges up and bake it. Voila!"

"That sounds a lot easier." Joanie looked relieved.

"Does it have to be apple? There is rhubarb in the backyard. Strawberries too." Inez offered. "That would make a nice pie."

Sam's father stirred. "Did someone mention strawberry rhubarb pie? My favorite." His voice was scratchy. Inez jumped up and held a straw to his lips.

"That's settled then. I'll make a sample tomorrow so Daddy can taste-test it." Joanie smiled now, proud she might please her father, make him happy one last time. Claire recognized that desire as one she had never outgrown.

That night, Claire went back to her apartment. Alone. And

that wasn't a bad thing. She had to study for finals, pack, and get ready to leave. It wasn't that she wanted Sam out of her life. No. She just needed some elbow room, a longer leash. His family, as much as she liked them—loved them—simply wore her down.

A WEEK OR SO LATER, an exhausted Sam stopped by her apartment after closing the nursery and seeing his dad at the hospital. It was late.

"Did you eat anything today?" The words, felt as if she were channeling Libby's mom whose philosophy was, "When in doubt, offer food."

"Not since breakfast. It got busy at the shop. There wasn't time…"

"Sit down. I'll make you a grilled cheese. American, not that fancy French one."

"I guess…" His voice trailed off as he looked around the apartment and then at Claire as she heated the griddle and got out bread, butter, and cheese. "You know I like this, coming home to you." Sam took a Coke from the fridge and opened it. "We could get married after graduation and…"

Claire knew if she married now, she'd never be alone—a prospect more troubling to her than always being alone. She was too selfish to be a wife. A mother. She'd be miserable and make her family miserable in return. How could she make Sam understand that?

"Or we could wait until I get back. It's only two years," Claire said as she plopped two sandwiches onto the griddle and listened to the satisfying sizzle. These arguments were always the same. He'd have done anything for her. Anything but leave his family. Anything but wait.

"If you loved me. . ." Sam stood behind her now, two hands at her waist. She leaned back.

"I do love you." Claire refused to use love as a weapon. Instead, she turned and kissed him, trying to reassure him. She stopped long enough to flip the sandwiches, then turned back as sorrow overwhelmed them both.

Their combined grief was present in every moment now, every act. Even lovemaking. Knowing that each time could be the last, she ached, missing him already. Tugging at the waistband of his 501s, and unbuttoning his fly, Claire dragged him down the hall toward her bedroom. He offered no resistance but surrendered as she pushed him to the bed. Frantic, they tore at each other's clothes, in a vain attempt to rip away the pain, the heartache, the hopelessness. They devoured the despair, transforming it, forgetting it, if only for a moment. Both finished breathless, in tears, and holding on for dear life.

The odor of forgotten and burning sandwiches reached them. Claire found her shirt and ran to the kitchen. The sight and smell of them nauseated her. She tossed them into the trash, turned on the exhaust fan and started over.

DAYS LATER, cardboard boxes and the contents of every closet and drawer were stacked haphazardly on her apartment floor. Surrounded by precarious piles of books and papers, she had just hung up from a phone call with her mother who had asked again about flying down for graduation. Claire hated to disappoint her but it seemed wrong to go through the whole cap and gown celebration with Sam's dad about to die. She heard only sympathy in her mother's voice as she agreed.

Hoping for a bit of diversion as she sorted through her belongings, Claire turned on the TV. The Tonight Show theme song had started when she heard a knock at the door. She answered the door to find Sam there, purple smudges of fatigue under his eyes. She kissed his cheek and noticed he hadn't shaved.

"Beer?" she asked.

Sam nodded, then turned down the TV as Ed McMahon intoned "He-e-e-e-e-re's Johnny!" He moved a stack of clean laundry off the couch and onto the floor while she opened two beers. Sam wrapped his arm around Claire's shoulders and she nestled into him and took a sip. It tasted bitter. Had it gone bad? She set it on the coffee table.

"How was he tonight?" Claire asked.

"Barely conscious," Sam said, giving his head a small shake.

"How...?" How can she ask that question delicately?

"Not much longer."

"Oh, Sam. I wish there was something more I could do to help."

"You're doing a lot now. Mom truly appreciates what you're doing at the shop and with the girls."

"I'm glad to do it. I wish there was more..."

"Marry me." Claire couldn't bear to refuse him again, to hurt him when he was so defenseless—even though her answer hadn't changed—so she said nothing. "I love you. I can make you happy."

"You do make me happy," Claire asserted. That was true.

"I want to spend the rest of my life with you. And I want that to start as soon as possible. You must see that life offers no guarantees. Will you marry me now?"

"I love you. More than anyone, ever. But I'm not sure I can make you happy and...."

"Don't be silly," he interrupted her. "Of course, you can make me happy. You already do."

"It's not silly. I simply don't know if I have what it takes to make anyone happy and be happy myself."

"Because of your dad," Sam said with a dismissive shake of his head.

"Yes," Claire said firmly, turning to face him. "Because of my dad. And my mom. They didn't exactly set a great example of 'until death do us part.' They tried to be married and couldn't do it. Love wasn't enough to make him stay. Maybe I'm not enough." Claire choked on that last bit. Looking at the ceiling, she fought back tears. She bit her lip before going on. "I can't marry you now. You're worried about your family. I am too. And I'm sorry. But that is no reason to rush into this."

"I wanted to marry you before Dad got sick," Sam protested.

Claire tried to remain composed, her voice measured. "I know. But his illness is putting an extra strain on you. On me. You aren't being exactly rational right now." She held up her hand. "Maybe I'm not either. I'm not sure what I want. But I know for certain what I don't want. I don't want to be married right now. I'm only twenty-one. There will be plenty of time. Later." She was crying now despite her efforts.

Sam sat forward with his elbows on his knees and looked straight ahead. "Damn it, Claire. My mom needs me. The girls need me."

And there it was. As much as Claire loved Sam, wanted Sam, she still wasn't certain she needed him. But his family did. She was suddenly serene as if the answer had simply been handed to her. She leaned forward, touched his bristled chin lightly and turned his face toward hers.

"Do what you need to do," she said plainly, without a hint of anger or doubt. "And Sam, be happy. But please, don't wait for me to change my mind."

Sam's blue eyes, that had always reminded her of sunlight sparkling on water, turned to cold, steely gray. He said nothing more but turned away from her, stood up, and walked out the door. He slammed it, rattling the windows. Heavy steps shook the building as he ran down the outside stairs. She raced to the window and watched him start his Jeep, turn on the lights, and disappear into the night. She reached out and touched the cool, damp window.

"I do love you. And I'm sorry."

———

CLAIRE DIDN'T TALK to Sam again, although she did attend his father's funeral. She greeted and hugged Sam's mother and sisters after the service. If she were going to be part of a family, this is the one she would choose. Sam wouldn't look at her, but she kissed his cheek, which felt strangely cool.

Alone, she walked out of the church and got into her car which was already packed for the drive back home to Nevada. There was no reason to stay even a moment longer. The fatigue and mild nausea that had plagued her throughout the spring's turmoil had finally subsided. She was ready to move on. She merged onto the freeway, blinked hard, squared her shoulders, and focused on the road ahead.

———

BACK IN CARSON CITY, Claire stepped out of the bathroom wearing the oversized yellow Wylder Nursery t-shirt she'd slept in. Sam's shirt. Claire followed the smell of coffee.

"Good morning, honey. I made a fresh pot of coffee," her mother offered. "Do you and Libby have plans today?"

"Hmmm. Maybe. I need to finish the last bit of paperwork and get it mailed. And I want to get in a run before it heats up." She'd grown used to the routine of a daily run, one that she'd tried to keep up in spite of the anxiety that had sapped her strength in the last few months. Her energy had returned. Along with her appetite.

Claire poured herself a mug of coffee and stood for a moment looking out the kitchen window at the lawn and tree-shaded patio before putting an English muffin into the toaster. She found butter and some of Fran McCormack's peach jam in the fridge.

"Are my shot records still in that box in the den?" One final piece of paper the Peace Corps needed.

"Along with everything else. You might have to dig a bit, I'm afraid. For some reason I can organize everything for my business, but not personal stuff." Claire believed the box held some link to her father that her mother found troubling to face, even after all this time. That knowledge made her feel more sympathetic toward her mother. Would she feel the same about Sam in the years to come? She looked down at the Wylder logo on his shirt—a line drawing of the front of the nursery. Her fingers touched the soft fabric.

The cardboard banker's box lay on the floor of the closet. She bent to pick it up and carried it back to the kitchen, setting it on a chair beside the table. The muffin popped out of the toaster, she buttered it, spooned on some jam, and sat down. As she nibbled at her breakfast, Claire glanced at envelopes, documents, and photographs one by one. Some items were familiar, triggering memories. She imagined them waiting for her to scratch at the surface.

She pulled out her green Girl Scout sash with badges she and Libby had worked on. Needlecraft. Camp cooking. Swimming. She was sure Libby had lots more. Of course, Libby had stayed in scouts through high school, while Claire had dropped out in junior high. Libby loved checking off the necessary tasks to accomplish the awards. Claire usually started off with a bang then lost interest. How many half-badges had she earned? And her dreary old report cards—mostly Bs and Cs— more evidence of her very pedestrian school career. The teachers' comments were consistent. Lots of promise. Does not apply herself. Seems unmotivated. She hoped she'd outgrown that. The report she'd written in fourth grade on JFK caught her eye, her first attempt at typing. She read the last lines.

...The new President wants to help people. He makes me want to help the world. When I am grown up I will help people too.

Maybe now, with the Peace Corps, Claire would fulfill her childhood wish. She took another bite of her muffin and smiled. And here was the shot record she needed. Setting it aside, she picked up a yellowed, official-looking document.

"Oh my god. . ." Her mouth hung open. The muffin dropped from her hand.

"What?" her mother answered from the front room.

"Mama, come here!"

"What?" she said again, this time from the doorway.

Claire shoved the document toward her mother. "Your marriage license, the date... You said you got married on New Year's Eve in 1948, but this says 1949. I was born in June of 1950."

Her mother said nothing, but bit her lip, scraping off a strip of coral lipstick and arching one eyebrow. Her shoulders slumped.

"You were pregnant?" An old lie, repeated so often it had replaced the truth. The earth shifted on its axis. Claire detected the slightest hint of relief in her mother.

"Yes, Claire. I was pregnant when we got married."

Her mother sat across the table from Claire, took the license from her, and studied it. Her hand shook.

"Oh, Mama. That's why Papa left? He'd been trapped into marrying you? Because of me? Because of a mistake?" For the first time, Claire saw before her, not the competent, respected businesswoman, but a frightened young woman in trouble. What would Claire have done in the same situation? Would she have married at twenty? No, she didn't think so. Baby or no baby.

"You had nothing to do with this and you weren't a mistake." Her mother sighed, touched Claire's hand, and held her gaze. In a voice that was nearly a whisper, she said, "You were a gift. However, my parents never approved of Claude."

"Because...?" Who wouldn't love her charming, handsome father?

Her mother patted her hand and gave a small laugh, shaking her head as if Claire were a little dim. "Because he knocked me up, honey. . ."

"And when Papa left?"

"I couldn't bear the 'I told you so' in their voices. We've pretty much ignored each other for twenty years." Her mother seemed to be trying to blink back the memory, or at least put it back in the box.

"You were really on your own." In that moment, Claire regretted every willful act and vowed to never again cause her mother hurt or disappointment. "Did you even have birth control back then?"

"Well, yes. Condoms. Diaphragms. Prayer." Her mother chuckled. "At least now you have the pill."

"Yeah, pretty fool-proof. No excuse but stupidity." Claire couldn't imagine being pressured into marriage. Or keeping a secret so huge.

CHAPTER SEVENTEEN

Now: This Old House

Claire and her mother didn't stay long at Libby's after the funeral. The accident, surgery, and two weeks at the rehab hospital had taken its toll. And despite yesterday's trip to the beauty parlor and her artful make-up, her mother simply looked worn out. More noticeable though, was that she'd lost confidence in her ability to make her body do what she wanted. Every step seemed slow and tentative.

Being responsible for another human being had slowed Claire too. Doctor appointments. Physical therapy. The pharmacy. Grocery shopping. Cooking. Laundry. Calls from her mother's office. Even as she checked items off her to-do list, Claire felt as if she were slogging through oatmeal. By evening, she found she had little energy for much more than watching the old Danny Kaye movies her mother was partial to. Claire had lost count of the times they'd watched "White Christmas." To top it off the owner of the antique shop on the ground floor had given notice. She'd be gone within a month. They would need to find a new tenant.

One private agenda item never made it onto the official list despite Libby's nagging. Grace. Claire had done nothing about her letter, hidden in the pocket of her duffle bag. Sharing the apartment meant that any communication with Grace would risk Sylvia's finding out. Even as an adult—perhaps especially as an adult—she couldn't bear to disappoint her mother. Was it shame? Not exactly. She was neither ashamed of having the baby nor allowing her to be adopted. No, her shame came from the lies she'd told to keep her secret. Not to mention depriving her mother of a grandchild.

Claire held their purses and unlocked the apartment door. Her mother started up the long flight of polished hardwood stairs. The slow, awkward rhythm of cane, right foot, left foot, pained Claire.

"Sorry. I hate how slow I am. These stairs. . ." her mother muttered with a groan.

"I know, Mom. Have you thought about moving?" Certainly, her independent mother wasn't ready for assisted living. Or was she?

"Every day. Besides, how much longer do you want to sleep in the den?"

"I'm fine." Sleeping on the sofa bed was not a permanent arrangement. Nonetheless, without a job, she had little money of her own. She'd sublet her tiny apartment in the Bronx to Enrique when she quit her job, but that merely covered the rent. She needed to find a job. One that was here in Carson City and flexible enough to allow her to take care of her mother.

"Well, I do own the whole damn building. When "Time After Time" leaves, maybe I won't rent it again." Her mother seemed to be thinking aloud as she scaled the stairs. "Once it's empty, I could remodel." She sighed heavily when she reached the top step. The room was dim except for the sunlight seeping in through the closed shutters on the tall, narrow windows.

"Remodel? Into what?"

"Another apartment. Perhaps an office."

"So, two renters to replace one? Is that even practical? What about parking? How does that solve...?"

"No renters." Her mother collapsed on the couch.

"What are you talking about?" Claire hung their purses on hooks by the stairs.

"I like where I live, but I can't climb those damn stairs anymore. At least I don't want to. What if I moved downstairs and gave you the upstairs? I don't need much space. The west half the ground floor would be enough and I could move my office into the east side."

"You'd close your office?"

"Let's call it, 'consolidating my interests.' Can you help me get my shoes off?"

"Sure." Claire bent and loosened the laces.

"God, I hate these oxfords. So ugly. The indignity of being an old lady is bad enough. But I do hate looking like one." She leaned back against the cushions and closed her eyes. "Sometimes I feel every one of my seventy years."

"Remodeling sounds like an awful lot of work."

"A remodeling project would give me something to focus on besides my recovery." Her mother looked up. "I'm sorry. I didn't even ask if you wanted to stay here. Maybe you have other plans."

Claire shook her head. "What skills do I have to make a living here in Carson City? Fifty is a little old to go back to cocktail waitressing."

BY THE MIDDLE OF JULY, Sylvia Jordan, still sporting a cast on her right arm, had met with a contractor and decided on a plan. She'd chosen colors and finishes, appliances, and floor coverings appropriate to the historic building. And while they were at it, she'd invest in a few accessibility features—wider doorways, a seat in the large shower, bars beside the toilet—just in case.

With the workers busy downstairs, Sylvia and Claire began sorting through her belongings upstairs. As organized as she believed she was, this enterprise still resembled an archaeological expedition. Clothing, jewelry, china, not to mention report cards, photographs, and art projects from Claire's childhood. Paring down seventy years of detritus to a small kitchen, a dresser, and a closet made Sylvia worry what the next step would be. A nursing home where her belongings would be reduced to a comb and toothbrush? She forced the thought from her mind as something pricked at her conscience. That box.

Sylvia knew what lay buried in the dusty bank box at her feet. And she knew it was time to confess another old sin to her daughter. The time had never seemed right. Maybe the time would never be right, but she needed to do it before Claire discovered the deceit on her own. That would be worse. Sylvia needed to disclose it now, so she could explain, somehow, what she'd done and why.

Could Claire forgive her? Could she forgive herself?

Claire sat on the office floor sorting old photos, wearing a faded baseball cap over her not-quite-grown-out shearing. Sylvia lost herself in a moment of admiration at her daughter's loyalty and courage in support of Libby. What an amazing woman she'd raised. In spite of everything, Claire had turned out fine. More than fine.

Sylvia's heart ached as she dug down into the box, rifling through layers until she found what she was looking for. There. A stack of envelopes, bound by a desiccated rubber band that crumbled to dust in her quivering left hand. She handed the small bundle to Claire.

"What's this?" Claire turned over one envelope and then another, her brows furrowed in confusion. "They're addressed to me. And they were never opened."

Sylvia's lips trembled. "They're from—from your father."

CHAPTER EIGHTEEN

Then: Help

*J*ack sweat as he helped Libby load her belongings into her dad's old wood-sided utility trailer, the one they'd taken to the dump and on camping trips for as long as she could remember. The ratty second-hand, faded brown couch had gone in first. She'd hated the scratchy, stained, and frayed upholstery almost from the beginning, but she'd only paid $15 for it at a garage sale. And she still had no money. Some of this stuff would have to do for a couple of paychecks. Her new job teaching first grade at Fritsch School would pay $7700 a year. Nearly $150 a week. More money than she'd ever earned in her life. She shoved in one last box marked "kitchen misc" and turned to Jack.

"I saw the sofa I want at Red Barn Furniture," Libby said. Jack busied himself tying down the load that now resembled something from the Dust Bowl. "I think I can manage a few hundred dollars by November."

"Why don't you wait?" Jack grunted as he pulled the rope taut, his long hair hooked behind his ear.

"Wait? No, I'm sick of that sofa. It's gross. I have to put an afghan over it to hide where the stuffing is coming out."

"I have fond memories of that sofa," he said with a little smile, complete with a gleam in his eye. That twinkle got her every time. If any child of theirs inherited that spark of devilishness... She shook the thought from her mind. Talk about counting chickens before they're hatched. While everyone assumed she and Jack would get married, the absence of a proposal—let alone a ring—left things decidedly undecided.

Jack threaded another rope across the load and through the slats. Finally satisfied, he finished off with a few expert Boy Scout knots. "Tell you what, you wait on buying the sofa and we'll buy something together. After we're married."

"No, I want a new sofa. I need a new sofa. I can't...," Libby stopped and looked at him. "Wait. What did you say? Who said we were getting married?" Lawyers. Can't trust them to make anything clear.

"I'm saying. I mean, we are getting married, aren't we? I just thought ...." His eyebrows crinkled into a peak as worry flashed across his face. Jack was usually so sure of himself. Libby chuckled at seeing this rare vulnerable side of him, however fleeting.

"You never actually asked."

"Do I need to? We talked. . . I mean, I love you. You love me, right? I thought. . . Listen, I'll be done with law school next June and take the Bar in August. I can clerk at my uncle's office until I pass." Jack still looked a little nervous. Sweat dripped down his temples.

He'd laid out a persuasive case as if Libby needed convincing. "Do you need to call any witnesses, counselor?"

Exasperated, Jack shook his head and sighed. He looked Libby in the eye and knelt on the sidewalk. Taking her left hand in both of his, he spoke in the fake Irish brogue he used to mock her. "Elizabeth Frances McCormack, I love you more than breath itself. Will you be marryin' me next summer or not?"

"Hmmm..." Libby made a big show of hesitating, looking at

the sky and tapping her index finger on her chin. Relief and giddiness overtook her, but she held the pose in spite of feeling Jack's grasp on her hand tighten. Finally, she said, "Sure and I'll be marryin' you. Anytime you want."

Jack rose and kissed her. His lips tasted of salt.

TWO WEEKS LATER, Libby sat sipping black coffee at the kitchen table, nibbling her breakfast of dry toast and grapefruit, and trying to ignore her mother's sticky buns on the counter. Not till she lost that freshman fifteen that'd been hanging around for four years. Or she fit into her mom's wedding dress, the one her grandmother had made. She scanned a bridal magazine, debating between turquoise and lavender for her wedding.

Claire had been gone a week and wouldn't be back for two years. Wouldn't even be home for the wedding. As much as Libby looked forward to marrying Jack, she had to admit she was a little envious of Claire's adventure. Maybe she should have pressed harder to apply when Claire did. Her mother had fought it, of course. The danger. Not only physical but the danger of losing Jack. Her mom worried he'd find someone else while she was off "globetrotting."

Now Libby would be teaching and getting married in the town where she grew up. Still the obedient daughter. Predictable. Conventional. She'd missed her chance and now she'd never go anywhere, do anything important. Worse yet, she was back at A&W until school started. She still loathed the brown and orange uniform—not to mention the work—and had to keep reminding herself it was only temporary.

She pressed her finger into a few remaining toast crumbs and licked them off. The phone rang.

"McCormacks."

"Thank God you answered."

"Claire, what's wrong?! I thought you were in Puerto Rico." Libby heard something desperate in Claire's voice.

"I *was* until..." Claire seemed unable to say anything for a few seconds. "I'm in Miami. I'll be in Reno by tonight. Can you pick me up at the airport? 6:45?"

"Airport? Sure. Claire, what's wrong? Are you sick? Did you flunk out of the Peace Corps already?" Libby was only half-joking. Had she been caught smoking pot at Peace Corps boot camp? Claire had cleaned up her act, but still.

"God, have I messed up! They sent me home."

"What is it, Claire? It can't be that bad. Whatever it is."

"I can't.... Oh God..." and the sobs started again.

"Take a breath. Tell me."

"I'm—I'm pregnant."

STORM CLOUDS BUILT all afternoon in preparation for a summer thunderstorm. The air crackled with anticipation as Libby drove to the airport, her fingers dancing on the steering wheel. She parked and walked through the small terminal, stopping to get a large fountain Coke. She stood at the window chewing the ice and checking her watch.

Claire stepped off the plane and down the stairs onto the tarmac. It wasn't until she entered the building and got closer that Libby saw the difference in her friend. Chunks of Claire's blonde hair had escaped its lopsided ponytail and hung in dull, greasy strands around her pale, puffy face. Libby stepped forward, hugged her friend, and felt a ragged sob rise in Claire's chest.

Libby cocked her head toward the exit. They said nothing as they maneuvered through the crowds and waited for Claire's bags. Libby sensed that any words now, no matter how benign, might send them both over the emotional cliff. They tiptoed along its rim in silence, eyeing the drop and the roiling torrent below. Had Claire made any plans? Would she want to go home?

"Where to?" Libby asked.

Claire shrugged. "Mapes?"

"Seriously?" An odd choice. Libby had never been inside the aging Art Deco hotel that sat in downtown Reno, on the edge of the Truckee River.

"Not likely to see anyone we know there."

A wall of stale cigarette smoke and the jingle of slot machines hit her as they walked in the door. Libby worried about the price, especially on a Friday night. There wasn't much in her checking account. She started to dig into her bag, but Claire stopped her and paid with one of a stack of travelers' checks. The clerk handed them a key and directed them to the elevator.

Once inside the room, they collapsed onto the one big bed and stared at the ceiling. As much as Libby wanted to jump in to solve this, she couldn't imagine how. She let Claire take the lead. More shuddering arose in Claire. Libby instinctively grabbed her hand.

When the wave of sobs passed, Libby started, "But how? You've been on the pill for, like, years. Right?"

"Yeah. Like clockwork."

"And you didn't even think you might be pregnant?" Libby rolled onto her side and faced Claire, propping her head on her hand. In profile, she noticed the slightest bulge of Claire's usually flat abdomen.

"Those last few months were horrible. Sam's dad dying. Finals. Sam pressing me to get married. Moving. It was all my brain could take in."

"But. . ." Libby couldn't imagine being so out of touch with her body that she would miss the telltale signs. Missed periods. Morning sickness. Something.

"It never even occurred to me. When I didn't feel well, I chalked it up to stress. I'd been running more. Sometimes runners stop having periods, right? Mine have never been regular. And I don't own a scale. Don't always wear a bra." Claire looked down at her swollen breasts. "Guess I'd better start."

Libby silently calculated when her last period was. Should she and Jack use condoms too, in addition to pills?

"It wasn't until that physical. You know, blood tests and stuff. The doctor must have thought I was an idiot." Claire chuckled and shook her head. "Me. Of all people to become a cliché. I tried so hard in the last couple of years. To be good. Not to be—you know—the town slut."

"You were never the town slut," Libby protested.

"No? Ask your brothers. They'll tell you." Libby didn't need to ask. But the past was past. With a baby, the only thing that mattered was the future.

"What are you going to do?" Libby knew what she'd do. Marry Jack. Tomorrow. But she wasn't Claire. And for once, she was glad.

"I'm not telling Sam," Claire asserted. Libby knew that tone. Once Claire got hold of any idea—no matter how ill-considered —she wouldn't let go. And Libby knew that the harder she argued, the harder Claire would dig in. But she had to say something.

"Sam loves you. He wanted to marry you, even without knowing about the baby."

"I know." Another sob made her stop. "He'd be—a great father. The best. But I— broke up with him because—because —I wasn't ready to be someone's wife. And I'm sure not ready to be someone's mother."

"But. . ."

"No." Claire shifted onto her side, mirroring Libby's head on hand pose. She struggled to speak. "If I'd found out—earlier,

I would have had an abortion. We wouldn't even be talking about it. Too far along now."

At the mention of abortion, Libby gulped. Catholic or not, in her heart it was simply not an option. "At least tell your mom."

"No. It would break her heart. Disappoint her one more time. I won't do that. You should have seen her face when I was accepted to the Peace Corps. Proud, you know?"

Sylvia Jordan was the most understanding mother Libby knew. Libby recalled the night when, at sixteen, she and Claire had gotten drunk on rum and Coke. When Sylvia came home she'd merely asked Libby to spend the night without telling her parents about the booze. Sylvia might be disappointed, sure, but she always stood by Claire. Always loved her.

"And finding out that Mom was pregnant when she married my dad. That they had to get married. I'm not repeating that little bit of history." Thunder rumbled in the distance.

"You—you'll give it up?"

"Uh-huh." Give up a baby? To be raised by strangers? Libby detected a slight shrug, a hint of hesitation, of uncertainty. Or maybe she imagined it.

"Where will you live till then? How will you live?"

"I don't know. That's why I called."

"My apartment won't do. Staying in Carson would be pretty risky." She stopped to think. Jack's place in Sacramento wouldn't work either. All his roommates are from Nevada. "I think there's some program for unwed mothers out at the old Stewart Indian School. Maybe Reno has something like that. Surely Sacramento does. We just need a phone number." Yeah, right. Just.

With a sigh, Claire stood, walked to the window, and pulled open the heavy drape. The blanket of dark clouds blocked any view of the sky. Libby joined her and reached for Claire's hand. Lightning flashed. She counted to herself. One... two... three. .

. Boom! Thunder shook the windows. Another flash. One...
two...Boom! "Storm's getting closer."

A few moments of awkward silence passed as Libby struggled to find a neutral topic. "I'm hungry. Let's see what they
have downstairs." At the hotel's all-night coffee shop, they
ordered patty melts, French fries, cherry pie, and large glasses
of milk. Claire merely nibbled at the crusty edges of her sandwich, while Libby devoured her meal. Those fifteen pounds
would still be there tomorrow.

Between bites, Libby said, "What we need most is
information."

"Yeah, but the Yellow Pages doesn't exactly have listings for
"girls in trouble."

"Hmm, a doctor or some agency maybe? Your therapist?"

Claire shook her head. "I called Lou, but her service said
she was on vacation."

An idea flickered in Libby's brain. "I might know someone
who could help." Why hadn't she thought of him before? Her
uncle Matt was a doctor in the tiny town of Bridgeport, a few
hours south.

They hatched a plan—or at least the seed of one. If it
worked.

Seemingly relieved, Claire finished her sandwich and pie. By
three AM they were back in their room, stuffed, and sleepy.
Libby prayed as she went to sleep, "Please. Please. Please."

IN THE MORNING Claire sat cross-legged on the bed, her hair
still wet from the shower. She listened as Libby telephoned her
Uncle Matt McCormack. Of all the people they knew, he was
the one most likely to have the information they needed. And
while Libby had assured her they could trust him—he was a
doctor, after all—Claire couldn't help but worry.

"It's my best friend, Claire. Uh-huh. Pregnant. No, not married." Libby sounded earnest and compelling. Claire chewed her thumbnail trying to fill in the blanks from the other side of the conversation.

"Probably adoption."

Libby shook her head. Her uncle must have offered some resistance. Claire regretted forcing Libby to argue a case she didn't truly believe in.

"She doesn't want to run the risk of seeing anyone she knows." A small smile of relief touched Libby's lips. "Thank you, Uncle Matt. Thank you so much." She looked at her watch. "We can be there about noon."

"He wants to see you. Give you a check-up before making any recommendations."

"I'm not sick, just pregnant."

"He's a doctor, Claire. It's his job."

AT NOON they pulled into the McCormack's driveway after a quiet ride down the highway. Well, quiet except for Claire's little sobs that erupted without warning. She kept repeating her silent I'm sorry mantra. She apologized to Libby, her mother, to Sam, to the baby.

A white picket fence bordered the shady yard of the McCormack's modest clapboard house a few blocks off the main drag. Claire remembered being here once, on the way home from a camping trip at Twin Lakes with Libby's family. Libby's Aunt Ellie, who looked a bit like June Allyson—petite with a blonde page-boy hairdo—greeted both girls with warm, sheltering hugs. The unexpected tenderness brought a lump to Claire's throat. She swallowed hard and wished people would stop being so nice.

Dr. Matthew McCormack was a taller, slightly older version of Libby's father. His hair—or what was left of it—was completely gray. He took Claire's hand and shook it slowly, looking deeply into her eyes. She bristled at being sized up. That was something she recognized.

Over a lunch of tuna sandwiches and potato chips, Libby's uncle started the conversation. "Claire," the doctor said, "Rethink keeping this from your mother. I've met Sylvia a few times at Mike and Fran's. I'm sure she'd be supportive. Please, give her a chance."

Claire listened respectfully as she chewed a bite of sandwich. It would break her mother's heart. More than that, her mother might press her to marry Sam and keep the baby, as she'd done. No. That would lead to more hurt down the road. Only this time she believed it would be her leaving a child, a marriage. No, she wouldn't risk hurting her child, Sam's child. She gave a small shake of her head.

"At least tell the father. This is his baby too. He has legal rights, not to mention responsibilities." He looked straight into Claire's eyes. Legal rights? Was that true? That hadn't occurred to her. Shit. She looked away.

After lunch, with Libby tagging along, the four of them walked over to Dr. McCormack's nearby office where his wife often filled in as his nurse. He unlocked the front door and held it until they were all inside the cool, dark room, then relocked it, and turned on the lights.

The waiting room was small and sparsely furnished, with a nubby, green sofa and three turquoise Naugahyde chairs. The blue-green shag carpet stopped at the receptionist's desk where dark marble-looking linoleum began. Slivers of sunlight bled through the Venetian blinds and onto copies of *Highlights* and *Readers' Digest* stacked on the coffee table. A *LIFE* magazine bore a photo and headline that proclaimed, "Liz Taylor is 40!" As the pair led her back to an exam room, Claire looked back over her shoulder at Libby who gave her a reassuring nod. Claire took a deep breath and willed herself to move forward.

The exam room looked and felt like the college health center. The same cold fluorescent lights. The same paper-covered exam table. Even the faded blue gown smelled the same. They left her alone to undress, but Claire heard whispering outside the door. She couldn't hear what they said, but there were definitely two fervent opinions. A murmured quarrel. Another apology needed.

She heard a knock.

"Ready, dear?" Mrs. McCormack asked.

"Yes." A hard, cold stone of dread sat in the pit of her stomach as the pair entered the room.

Dr. McCormack asked routine questions about her health history. Allergies? Previous surgeries? Childhood illnesses? Broken bones? His wife took notes. He checked her blood pressure. He listened to her heart, her chest.

"You say your periods have never been regular?"

"Um-hum. Been on the pill for years. Never missed one."

"You had no idea you were pregnant? No symptoms?"

"No." she shook her head, heaving a sigh. "Tired. A little queasy in the spring. But a lot was going on. I thought it was stress. Oh, and I had bronchitis."

"Were you on antibiotics?"

"Uh-huh."

"There is some new information coming out now that antibiotics may lessen the effectiveness of birth control pills."

"Seriously? Shouldn't that be on a warning label somewhere?"

"When was it?"

"Late February or early March?"

He took a strange device out of a drawer. It looked like a trumpet. Where was he going to put that? He must have seen the alarm on her face and smiled.

"This is a Pinard horn. Kind of a stethoscope for listening to the baby's heartbeat. Midwives use them. Hospitals and ob/gyns in bigger towns use electronics. Dopplers and such. This works fine, though."

"Heartbeat? Already?" She hadn't thought of it having a heartbeat, had barely begun to think of it at all. It wasn't a person yet, just a roadblock, an unexpected detour from her path. And another reminder that she wasn't in control.

"With this, I can usually hear it at about eighteen to twenty weeks."

He placed the wide part of the cold metal horn on her belly and listened. Shaking his head, he adjusted the instrument a few times before he was satisfied. "Bingo! Strong *swish-SWISH*. That's what we like to hear."

A heartbeat. A baby. Her heart filled with emotion—though exactly what she couldn't name. Tears filled her eyes.

"Now we'll confirm that by checking your uterus and cervix." She tensed. Once again, she was being invaded, violated.

"Deep, slow breaths in and out." Yeah, the breathing thing. Her muscles loosened. Mrs. McCormack held her hand as the doctor examined her, his gloved fingers up inside. Claire turned her head and shut her eyes against more tears. "Yep. Near as I can figure you're about four or four-and-a-half months along. You haven't felt any movement yet?" Claire shook her head as he snapped off his glove. "So, your due date should be mid-to-late November. But that's only a guess. You can dress now. We'll talk then."

He motioned his wife to follow him back into the hallway. More whispers sifted through the door. Definitely an argument, though she couldn't tell if either of them was on her side.

When Claire stepped out of the exam room, Libby was there. "Wow!" she said. "Four months already? Lucky you! I'd be sticking out a mile by now."

Claire managed a chuckle and a small smile. "Yeah, lucky me."

The doctor smiled and explained, "With Claire's height and long torso, that baby's had plenty of room to grow without being noticed. Come back to my office, girls."

Once they were seated in the small paneled office at the end of the hall, a look and a nod passed between Dr. and Mrs. McCormack. Some agreement had been reached. Claire's stomach tightened. What would they make her do?

Dr. McCormack spoke first. "There are some calls we need to make, but this is a weekend and that will have to wait, at least until Monday."

Claire's mind scrambled over the meantime scenarios. "I can get a hotel room until..."

Mrs. McCormack interrupted. "No, dear. We want you to stay with us until you make a plan. Until we find a place for you and the baby. Our kids are gone. We have room." Relief swept through her and she released a breath she didn't realize she'd been holding.

"But..." the doctor continued, looking at Claire over the top of his half-frame glasses. Here it comes. There's always a but. "This is only a temporary solution. It will give you a few days to figure out the next step. And while you are here, we're going to keep trying to convince you to inform both your mother and the baby's father."

"But..." Not that. Please.

"We're parents too, Claire. If our kids were in trouble, we'd want to know. No matter what." Mrs. McCormack's sweet and encouraging smile made Claire feel worse.

"Thank you." Claire nodded and gripped Libby's hand. These people weren't family. They barely knew her. Was anyone that good? And here she was deceiving them.

That afternoon, Claire walked Libby back to her car with repeated thanks and apologies. Libby whispered, "Why didn't you tell them about Sam?"

"I don't want any red-tape to screw things up. If they don't know who the father is adoption will be easier. Right?"

Libby stammered. "Maybe, but it also means I'll have to lie." Libby hated liars. And she was a horrible liar. It wasn't lost on Claire that Libby would need to keep this from Jack as well.

CHAPTER NINETEEN

Now: Today is Your Birthday

*A*n angry sob rose in Claire's chest as the earth quaked beneath her. This made no sense. Letters from her father? All this time, her mother had kept them from her? Kept him from her?

"I—I—I was afraid to show you."

"Afraid of what? My loving him?"

Her mother swiped at her cheek with the back of her hand. "Afraid of losing you."

"How could you! All this time. I searched for him—and you—you knew where he was?"

"He left us. He didn't deserve a daughter."

Claire couldn't speak but clenched and unclenched her fists. When she finally spoke, her voice caught.

"My whole life. I thought. . . I believed my father abandoned me. That he didn't think of me anymore—didn't love me. That I wasn't enough. And you—you let me believe that. Do you have any idea how cruel that was?"

"I—I'm sorry. That's all I can say. I was so angry when he left. So hurt and afraid. I only thought about punishing him." Her mother sobbed now. "I never meant to punish you."

Claire could no longer listen to or even look at her mother. Her whole life, everything she believed about herself had been a lie. Her beloved Papa had thought about her. Maybe even loved her. She held the small bundle of envelopes to her chest and stood, looking around for an escape, for privacy, for someplace she wouldn't have to share air with her mother.

"Claire…"

Claire put up her hand and turned away from the pleading in her mother's eyes. Clutching the envelopes, she ran down the stairs and out the front door. Turning left at the street, she continued to run. The rhythmic pounding of her feet on the pavement echoed the repetitive rhythm of her thoughts. How could you? How could you? How could you? Past houses. Past the church. Past the junior high. Up, up, up. Her chest heaved with sobs and ragged breaths.

She didn't stop until she'd reached the trailhead at the top of Kings Canyon Road. She sat on a boulder beside the trickle of a waterfall and let her heartbeat slow. Wiping her face with her t-shirt, she watched thunderheads build over the valley below.

Claire sorted the now crumpled stack of envelopes by the postmarks, all early Junes. She counted the letters. Fifteen, showing at least half a dozen different return addresses, up and down the west coast. San Diego to Seattle. He hadn't forgotten her!

She took a calming breath and unsealed the first one, sent in 1957. Her hands shook. On it, the three bears stood around a birthday cake. "Wishing a special someone a birthday that is just right," the card read. Her father had written "Happy Birthday to my Claire Bear. Love always, Your Papa Bear." Claire bit her lip, remembering their pet names for each other. She smiled at the seven crisp dollar bills he had included. Again and again, she opened, read, cried, and wiped her face with her now sweat-, tear- and snot-stained shirt. The final card sent for her twenty-first birthday contained a letter.

Dearest Claire,

It's hard to believe that so much time has passed. You are an adult now. You must still be angry at me. I can think of no other reason for you not writing. I will stop bothering you with cards. Nonetheless, know that I'm still your father and I love you.

I regret much. I hope you can forgive me one day.

I have enclosed a gift which will help start whatever life you choose. Not that money can buy happiness, but it can allow you a few choices.

Love,

Your Papa

Claire's hand trembled as she held a $10,000 savings bond in her hands, issued thirty years ago in 1971. What choices would it have given her? Would she have kept the baby? No. Her reasons for giving up Grace had nothing to do with money and everything to do with herself. That made her feel even worse.

A loud crack of thunder startled her and she looked up. The sky had turned dark. It would be raining soon. And she was nearly three miles from home. Shit. She wasn't ready to face her mother yet. Instead, she tucked the envelopes under her shirt and started to run down the hill toward her only refuge.

RAINWATER DRIPPED from the eaves on Libby's porch. Claire, drenched and shivering, rang the doorbell.

"What happened? Your mom called. Crying." The red bandana Libby had tied around her head made her look like Rosie the Riveter today.

Claire held out the bundle of letters.

"Birthday cards. From my dad. Fifteen of them."

"And she never showed them to you?"

"Not until today." Claire's anger rose again.

"Come in. Let's get you out of those wet clothes. Dry off in the bathroom, I'll find something." Libby's cancer seemed to be giving her a good day—a day without nausea, at least. She came back with a set of Carson High sweats and handed them to Claire.

"I can't go home yet. I can't look at her right now," Claire said as she stepped into the wash-faded navy pants and shirt.

"You can stay here, of course. But, first, tell me about the letters." Claire followed Libby to the kitchen. "You need something to drink? Wine? Tea? Whiskey?"

"Water first," Claire said as she took a glass from the cupboard and filled it with tap water. Wet or dry, running six miles—not to mention all those tears—dehydrated her. She stood at the sink and drank three full glasses before she spoke again. "How could she?"

Libby shrugged, shook her head, and retrieved an open bottle of Pinot Grigio from the fridge. Claire nodded. Libby poured one large glass and handed it to Claire, filling her own glass with seltzer. Wine and chemo didn't seem to be friends. Libby carried the bottle to the living room where they sat. The thunderstorm was roaring now. Lightning flashed and thunder rumbled close behind.

Libby sat in an overstuffed chair with her feet curled under her. "What did he say?"

Claire leaned forward, elbows on her knees. "That he loved me. Asked why I hadn't written back. He was sorry. He sent money."

"Money?"

"Yeah, he put dollar bills in each one. Seven on my seventh, ten on my tenth. He sent a savings bond too. For my twenty-first."

"You would have written, right?"

"Of course! If she'd ever shown me..." Claire yelled. Lightning flashed and almost immediately thunder boomed. The rain pounded on the roof.

"Your mom must have had some reason."

"She says she was afraid of losing me. And she wanted to punish him."

"By lying to you for nearly forty-five years?" Libby hated liars but loved Claire's mom. Claire imagined a scale trying to balance those two emotions.

If Claire put herself in her mother's place—young, alone, broken-hearted, angry—what would she have done? At twenty-six, she hadn't been much older than Libby's girls are now. Not much older than Claire had been when she found herself in trouble. Claire shook her head slowly and sipped her wine, reviewing her own decisions, and hearing echoes of her own life as thunder shook the house.

"But I kept a secret from her, too. A big one. And lied, again and again, to keep it from her."

"Not the same," Libby argued. "She withheld your father from you. She allowed you to believe he'd abandoned you. Not telling her about the baby didn't affect her at all."

"Except I deprived her of a grandchild. The only one she'll ever have. Mom's family pretty much disowned her when she got pregnant and had to marry. She was up the proverbial creek."

"Still. . . she's your mother." Libby's voice softened. "You never know. . ." Aaah. The scale tipped toward compassion in Libby's heart. As always.

Claire knew where this was heading. How would she feel if her mother died without some resolution, some reconciliation? Shit. Did that have something to do with why her mother had finally chosen to tell Claire? Was she worried about Claire finding them after she died? Without explanation?

"I guess I need to get over this." Claire sighed

"Well, not immediately. But, yes. Probably so."

The phone rang. Libby picked up.

"Yes, Sylvia. She's here. She's fine." Libby looked at Claire. "Let me ask."

Claire shook her head. No. Not yet.

When Jack called saying he'd be home late, Libby asked Claire to stay for what they always called "Perfect Dinner." Hors d'oeuvres and dessert. They nibbled and noshed their way through a box of Ritz crackers, cream cheese with pepper jelly, and half a tube of cookie dough.

Eventually, the rain stopped and the summer sun hung low over the Sierra in the freshly washed Nevada sky. Claire's fierce anger had dissipated along with the sudden storm and the wine. She and Libby had simply talked the heat out of the subject.

"Should I make up the guest room for you?" Libby offered with a yawn. She might be having a good day, but she was still sick.

"No. I think I need to go home and get this day behind me."

"You sure?"

"Not a bit." A part of Claire wanted to run away, to hide, and to punish her mother for robbing her of her father. But despite her grief and anger, Claire knew that running away was how they'd found themselves in this mess in the first place. She stood to find her shoes. "I need to do it anyway. No way through but through. Thanks for putting up with my rant."

"Anytime."

Claire strode the few blocks back to her mother's in the deepening twilight. She inhaled the fresh fragrance of damp sage that permeated the atmosphere. It cleared her head. Sobered her, soothed her. No small task. As she approached the building, she saw no lights in the windows. She opened the unlocked door and climbed the stairs. No music. No TV. The apartment was dark except for the dim remnants of light stealing in through the tall, narrow windows.

"Mom?" Panic gripped her belly. "Mom?"

"I'm here." Her mother's voice, coming from the direction of her chair, was little more than a whisper.

"You okay?"

"I'm sorry. I can't even say how sorry. . ." Her mother's voice broke. "I should never have allowed you to believe your father didn't love you."

Claire turned on the lamp. Her mother's eyes were red and swollen. Used tissues filled her lap. Had she been crying all day? As angry as Claire had been, here sat her mother, sad and devastated. Claire removed her cap and raked her fingers over the fluff covering her head.

Her mother pressed her thin lips together, revealing only traces of the lipstick she'd applied this morning, now spreading into the fine lines and creases around her mouth. "I'm so sorry."

Claire's concern for her mother's well-being overrode most of her residual anger. She felt empathy for the old woman before her and for the frightened young woman she must have been, faced with an uncertain future.

"I think I understand how you felt."

"I thought. . ." Sylvia tore at the tissue in her hands.

"You were angry. You were hurt."

"I loved him so much." She sniffed. "And he—he just left."

Claire sat on the ottoman, facing her mother.

"Did you ever talk to him? Did he ask to come back?"

"He called a few times, but I wouldn't see him." Her mother looked into the distance as though she were recalling a memory. "I was too stubborn. We both were. So foolish. So selfish."

Over the years, Claire had imagined a hundred sepia-toned scenarios in which her father came home. All of them ending with a blonde, pony-tailed girl running in slow motion into her father's waiting embrace and living happily ever after.

"Do. . . do you know where he is now?"

"No. I haven't heard from him in years. He could be anywhere. He could be dead." That last bit seemed to wilt her mother even further.

Claire refused to believe her father was dead. Impossible. She recalled her habit of searching for her father's name in phonebooks at the library, in every hotel, every payphone. Of course, that was in the days before the Internet. Surely, she could find him now. Claire shook that thought off and stood, shifting back into caretaker mode.

"Let's get you something to eat, shall we? How 'bout some cinnamon toast?"

Claire knew there was more to say but couldn't go into that yet. She loved her mother, yes, but wasn't quite ready to forgive her. This was too big. It would happen someday and it would end with her revealing her secret. But not yet.

CHAPTER TWENTY

Then: Can't You Hear My Heart Beat

*C*laire dragged the large suitcase she'd packed for the Peace Corps into the room that had belonged to the McCormack's daughter. She collapsed onto the narrow bed. She wouldn't let herself get too comfortable, though. That would be a mistake. As nice as the McCormacks were, they had only offered a few days of shelter while they put a plan in place. Whatever they suggested, she'd have no choice but to trust them and do as they asked.

The following afternoon, Claire came to a decision.

"May I use the phone, Mrs. McCormack? I'd like to call my mom."

"Of course. And please, call me Ellie. Or Aunt Ellie," she said looking up from measuring butter and sugar into a saucepan on the stove.

"Ok. Aunt Ellie it is." While it felt awkward, she appreciated the gesture.

Aunt Ellie smiled. "I'm glad you've reconsidered."

"I haven't changed my mind, but I need to tell her something. She'll be expecting postcards and letters from Puerto Rico. From Africa."

"So, what will you tell her?"

"Not exactly sure." Claire didn't want this kind woman to hear her lie.

"Use the phone in the den. It's more private."

Claire stepped down the hall to a room that doubled as a home office. She closed the door behind her. She looked at the bulletin board above the desk, layered with a clutter of birth and graduation announcements, wedding invitations, and photographs. Her breath caught at the sight of wrinkly red newborns in the photos. Tiny. Vulnerable. Photos of toothless baseball players and plump ballerinas reminded her that babies didn't remain babies. They were the most irreversible decisions people made. Jobs came and went. Even marriages could be undone. But if she had this baby—if she kept this baby—she'd be a mother for the rest of her life. Taking a deep, ragged breath, she dialed.

"Hello."

"Mama," was all she could manage.

"Wow! I didn't expect to hear from you. And all the way from Puerto Rico! How is it? All you expected?"

"Not exactly."

"What do you mean? Are you okay?"

"Not exactly." This was going to be harder than she thought.

"What happened?"

"I'm not in Puerto Rico. And I'm not in the Peace Corps."

"What do you mean?"

"Well, I've sort of been kicked out." That was true.

"Kicked out? Why? How?" Claire heard the disappointment in her mother's voice. The one thing she couldn't bear. With tears spilling over, her breath came between sobs.

"Got caught. Some pot. Holding. I'm so sorry." The pot was a lie. Sorry was the truth.

"Pot? You know better than that. What were you thinking?

And in a foreign country? My God. . ." Her mother's voice raised a few decibels. "And they only kicked you out?"

"I know." Claire gasped one big sobbing, sucking breath. "I'm so ashamed." She did know better. Only one little lie. So far.

"You're on your way home?"

"No, not right away. I'm in Florida. Ummm, Miami." And there was a second lie, although she had been in Miami two days ago. "I think I'll get a job here. Waitressing probably. I have enough money to get by for a while." She thought of the envelope of travelers' checks her mother had given her as a going-away gift.

"I wish you'd come home. No one will care."

That wasn't true. Carson City was a small town. There were no secrets. And her mother had bragged to everyone about the Peace Corps. She could practically her Mrs. Mac's tsk-ing.

"Or I'll come down there."

"No. I think I need to figure things out for myself."

"I hate the thought of you being alone. How can I reach you?"

"Nowhere right now. I'm calling from a diner. I'll call you as soon as I've settled in." She scrambled, making it up as she went along.

"There are a couple of letters here from Sam. You want me to forward them?"

"No." God, not that. "Not now. Gotta go. Someone needs to use the phone."

"But. . . if you aren't going away, maybe you and Sam could..."

"No, Mom. No."

"I'll hold them, though. In case you change your mind."

"I won't." She needed to close the door on the Sam-shaped corner of her heart. As much as she loved him, if she gave his baby away, she'd never be able to look into those blue eyes

179

again. He'd see the betrayal. The only way to move forward was never to see Sam again.

"If you need anything. . ." Claire was sure her mother meant it. She also knew what disappointment looked like on her mother's face. She'd seen it often enough: the lips pressed together, the sad and softened gaze as if she were watching her ideal of Claire fade before her eyes. Then, the ever-so-slight shake of her head as the real Claire came into focus.

"I need to go. Love you, Mama."

Claire put her head in her hands and wept. As saddened as her mother was with this news, it would have been so much worse if she knew the truth.

"Claire?" A few minutes later there was a timid knock at the den door. "Are you all right? I've made some cookies." Is that what mothers do? Offer something sweet to make you forget the bitter. Like the lollipop after a shot. Or the little mint that accompanies the restaurant bill.

Claire straightened and wiped her tears on her shirt. "I'll be right there."

Aunt Ellie stood at the kitchen sink, washing up from her cookie-making. Claire remembered these cookies from junior high home-ec class with Libby. Unbaked. Cooked on top of the stove and loaded with oatmeal, peanut butter, and chocolate. They lay cooling on waxed paper. She bit into one that was still a little warm. Fudgy, familiar, and comforting. Maybe moms were onto something. Aunt Ellie finished the dishes, dried her hands, and poured two glasses of iced tea.

"Let's take these out on the patio. There's a bit of a breeze this afternoon." Aunt Ellie led the way through the living room. Pictures of the McCormacks' two kids cluttered every horizontal surface and wall. Their daughter, Colleen, had married and moved to Florida. Their son, Doug, was in the Navy.

"They couldn't wait to get out of Dodge." Aunt Ellie settled into an aluminum folding chair. "Bridgeport was too small for them. Although I think Doug might come back when he finishes his tour. He says he misses the mountains."

The clouds changed shapes over the pasture land leading up to Twin Peak. Claire thought of the view out her apartment window in Fullerton—carports and the freeway. "I think I missed the mountains too." She couldn't imagine being stuck here though. Or stuck anywhere.

At that moment, something inside her moved. A gas bubble? A butterfly? She shifted slightly in her chair. No—there it was again. She flattened her hands against her belly.

"Oh my God!"

"The baby?" How did Aunt Ellie know?

"I think so. But it was so tiny. Just a flutter." Could she have missed it before?

"Quickening. It means you're about half-way through. The baby's as big as your two clasped hands."

Claire looked at her hands and felt an urgency she hadn't yet been aware of. November had seemed far away.

THAT NIGHT CLAIRE LAY AWAKE, staring at the ceiling. Moonlight filtered through the crisscross curtains on the window, reminding her of that night at the beach with Sam and the glowing waves. Bioluminescence. The baby moved again. A real baby now, no longer abstract. A baby with tiny fingers and toes and a heartbeat. A miniature version of Sam floated lazily in a dim amniotic sea. Dark red curly hair. A crooked smile. Freckles. Did newborns have freckles? A stream of tears trickled down her cheeks and soaked the pillow. Her heart ached. She missed Sam. Missed his strength, his calm, his protection. But marrying him wouldn't solve anything. Claire hoped that it wouldn't always hurt this much, that the hurt would fade with time. Without thinking, she began whispering to the baby.

Here's the deal, little Sam. I love your father. I really do. He is a good man. I'm the problem. Not him. Not you. I just keep screwing up. I won't take that chance with your life. You deserve better. You deserve two parents who won't let you down. Won't leave. But don't worry, I'll take care of you until you can breathe air. Until I'm sure you're okay. But then...

Claire sniffed and took one long, jerky breath. Then what? The profound weight of her responsibility sobered her. Like it or not, she was already someone's mother. She'd better start acting like one, even if it was only temporary.

Everything will be okay, little Sam. I promise. I won't let you down.

Claire got out of bed and tiptoed down the hall to the den. She turned on the light and found the Mono County phonebook. Her hands trembled. She opened to the yellow pages. There. A. Adoption.

MONDAY MORNING OVER BREAKFAST, Claire and Aunt Ellie compared lists. Claire's, the very short list of adoption agencies she'd found in the yellow pages last night. Ellie's, the half dozen charities she and Dr. Matt knew about. By noon Aunt Ellie had made phone calls to places up and down the sparsely populated Eastern Sierra. Some were run by churches. Some had long waiting lists to get in. Was unwed motherhood a seasonal phenomenon? Whatever the reason, it was limiting Claire's options. Only two sounded acceptable. And both were hours away in Ridgecrest and Victorville. They agreed to discuss it further when Dr. Matt came home at noon.

When Dr. Matt arrived, a little red-faced from his short walk home in the noon sun, Claire was setting the table and pouring glasses of lemonade. The three of them sat and began eating turkey sandwiches.

"Claire and I have been busy this morning." Aunt Ellie pushed the sheet of notes across the table toward her husband, which he perused while eating. He tapped one name and nodded.

"Sisters of the Sierra. Catholic, of course. Good people," he said. "That would be my first choice. And they'll help find a good family for your baby."

Aunt Ellie nodded. "That's my first choice too. One of the sisters spoke at my women's circle last year. Such a wonderful woman. Kind and compassionate and...."

"But I'm not Catholic."

"Makes no difference. They don't judge," Dr. Matt replied.

Claire doubted anyone could judge her more harshly than she judged herself. "That's probably why they have the longest waiting list. A month or more before they could take me."

"Hmmm." Dr. Matt shook his head slowly as he continued to stare at the list. "A month, you say?"

Claire nodded. Second best would have to do. Aunt Ellie tapped her husband's hand and he looked up at her. She tilted her head slightly and raised her eyebrows in an unvoiced question. Dr. Matt pursed his lips but didn't take his eyes from his wife's. They seemed to be having a wordless conversation. Finally, Dr. Matt sat back in his chair and spoke. "Maybe we can work out something if you're sure this is what you want."

What she wanted was no longer the issue. "I'm sure, but if it's going to be a month, I'll move to a hotel. I've got some money." Not a lot, but some. How long would it last if she had to pay for a room? And food? And bigger clothes? And how much would she have left to move on when this was all over? She'd need a job, but who would hire a pregnant girl?

"I think what Matt's saying—what we're saying, dear—is

that you can stay here, with us, until the Sisters have room for you."

"Are you sure?" Claire couldn't believe what she'd heard. The McCormacks nodded. "Thank you. I mean, I'll pay rent, of course, and get a job."

"We'll work out details, but yes, dear, you can stay." Relief and gratitude flooded through her. Little Sam even gave her a happy kick.

"And Claire?" the doctor said as he stood to go back to the office.

"Hmm?" She looked up.

"Please, tell your mother."

A DAY LATER, Claire made good on her promise to find a job. She dressed as neatly as she could, with the help of a few safety pins to hold where buttons and zippers would no longer close around her belly.

She asked at Busters—what passed for a supermarket in the tiny town—and at the Bridgeport Inn. But the job that came through first was at Jolly Kone, the local drive-in. Not waitressing, just counter work. Like the A&W. The manager was happy to hire someone already familiar with the tasks. And her condition wouldn't matter since they only needed extra help in the summer. She could start tomorrow.

That afternoon, she sorted through her clothes. Most wouldn't fit much longer. Aunt Ellie offered a few of Dr. Matt's old dress shirts and several of their son's left-behind XL t-shirts that might tide her over. Claire wished she could afford to buy a few things, but the Jolly-Kone wouldn't pay much. Aunt Ellie suggested a trip to Second Hand Rosie's, the thrift shop operated by the hospital auxiliary. And while Claire couldn't imagine ever being big enough to fill them out, she picked out several smocks and pairs of pre-stretched maternity pants. At least no one she knew would see her.

Over the next week, Claire tried to act as eager and helpful as Libby would. She did her own laundry and helped with meals and dishes. She even filled in answering the phone at Dr. Matt's office one morning. But as much as she tried to be like Libby, the role never quite fit. Libby's responses were too extreme, too immediate, and too visible. Claire knew that in her current situation, the risk of falling down the rabbit hole of emotion was too great. No, she needed a more serene role model, one whose exterior hid rather than revealed secrets. One whose image disguised rather than disclosed. But who?

The answer came as a surprise. Her mother. Of all people. Her mother projected calm, despite being the single mother of a troubled daughter. Had Sylvia Jordan always been that person or had she needed to learn the part? Empathy for her mother now bloomed alongside the guilt.

After a few phone conversations with Sister Ruth at Sisters of the Sierra, Claire received an inch-thick packet of mimeographed forms and information detailing the process. It all struck her as being cold and impersonal, like selling a car. The adoption would be closed. Neither she nor the parents would know the other.

"We've learned it's best for all concerned," was what the Sister said. Claire accepted those terms as a condition of the Sisters' help. She was in no position to argue. Still, it bothered her.

Reluctantly, Claire began completing the paperwork, understanding that she'd forever look into the faces of strangers searching for something of herself—of Sam—the way she already looked for her father. Her anxiety grew along with her belly. She trudged through endless weeks of summer, taking extra shifts at the Jolly Kone to pad her meager nest egg.

It didn't help that the exact date the Sisters would have room for her was in constant flux. One girl delivered early, another late, or changed her mind. The McCormack's calendar bore several erased dates but now stood a few weeks away in early August.

One Saturday afternoon in late July while Aunt Ellie was out, Claire and Dr. Matt sat at the kitchen table with tall glasses of lemonade. Claire had finished work for the day and propped her bare, swollen feet on a chair. Her toenails bore forlorn chips of pink polish and she scolded herself for not removing it while she could still reach her feet. No chance now. And what had happened to her ankles? They were no longer hers but had somehow become old Miss Mabel's. She heaved a giant sigh and took a long drink of lemonade.

Dr. Matt gave the sheaf of completed forms a final reading. She'd held onto them too long. Dr. Matt looked up from the papers, tapping a space she'd left empty.

"About the baby's father, Claire, is there no chance you'd reconcile? Unless you think he's dangerous, I mean…"

Claire shook her head. "No, not dangerous. The opposite of dangerous."

"Then help me understand." The doctor's gaze was earnest and kind, like Libby's father.

"He asked me to marry him right after graduation."

"So, you loved him?"

"Oh, yes." Her heart broke with how much.

"But…?"

"But I wasn't ready to get married, to be married. To anyone. I need to grow up first." She bit her lip and looked away. "But he refused to wait. We fought for weeks. We broke up. Then I found out my mom was pregnant when she and Dad got married. We all know how that turned out."

"Yes, but it doesn't always happen that way."

"What if I'm like my dad? What if I were the one to leave? I couldn't stand to be that person."

"I see," he replied in a neutral tone. "I still think it's a mistake not to tell him, not to give him a chance..."

His statement hung in the air. With a sigh, Dr. Matt slowly pushed the papers toward her. Claire held them a moment before sliding them into the large manila envelope and closing the metal clasp. Monday, she thought to herself.

The doctor spoke, more softly now. "You might be surprised to learn that even small-town doctors like me get letters—pleas, really—from childless couples wanting to adopt babies. I guess they figure there's always an off chance that some unfortunate young woman will drop one on my doorstep on her way through town."

"Has anyone ever dropped a baby at your door?" A vision of Moses in the bull-rushes came to her mind. Probably from watching "The Ten Commandments" on television.

"Not exactly, but I have helped place two children with wonderful families." Dr. Matt smiled.

"So, there are happy endings to sad stories?"

"Yes, there are. Babies are happy endings." He smiled again. "And beginnings."

They both looked up when they heard Aunt Ellie's car pull into the driveway. Claire dragged herself out of the chair and plodded to the sink with their glasses. Dr. Matt rose quickly to help bring in the groceries. Claire watched Ellie touch her husband lightly on the arm and say something Claire couldn't hear. Dr. Matt grinned broadly, kissed his wife on the cheek, grabbed two bags of groceries and practically danced into the house.

As the three of them put away groceries, Ellie retold the story.

"I ran into Gail Thorsen's mother at the market. Gail was our Colleen's friend from Girl Scouts and softball. Sweet kid. Took in every stray critter. No one was surprised when she became a vet. She even married a vet and took over his father's practice somewhere in Nebraska."

"She always had female troubles, even when she was young," Dr. Matt continued. "Horrible periods, fibroids... And she's been trying to get pregnant for a couple of years. A few months ago, they discovered a tumor the size of a tennis ball."

"Cancer?" Claire asked. So far, this story didn't seem to warrant their excited retelling.

"No, thank God, but they did a hysterectomy."

"How old is she?" Claire asked.

"Twenty-nine," both answered at once.

Claire didn't need to hear any more.

EARLY THE NEXT MORNING, Claire couldn't help but overhear one side of the phone conversation as Dr. Matt used the phone in the den. Claire tried to distract herself with an embroidery project she'd started, but the design swam before her eyes.

"Hi, Gail. Dr. McCormack here. How are you? ... Ellie talked with your mother. . . Told us about your surgery. . . Sorry to hear. . . You feeling okay now?.. Good. Good. . . Your mother said you're trying to adopt a baby? . . . We have someone here with a baby due in November. Unmarried...Fine healthy girl. . . Friend of the family. . ."

Did these people need convincing?

Dr. Matt went on. "Tall, blonde hair. Brown eyes. No, no. Not from town...Um-hum... No...Yes...Yes... Of course."

After he hung up, Dr. Matt stepped out of the office, smiling. "It looks like this might work. You may not need the Sisters after all. They'll talk to their lawyer, see what's involved. You ought to do the same."

"But I don't have a lawyer."

"You have Jack."

"Jack? Libby's Jack? He's not a lawyer yet. And he doesn't know about any of this."

"The adoptive parents' lawyer will do most of the work. You want someone looking out for your interests. Someone who'll protect you. You trust Jack, don't you?"

"Yes, but. . ." While she didn't want to involve anyone else, she knew she couldn't expect Libby to keep a secret this big from Jack for the rest of their lives. It wasn't a good way to start a marriage. Claire wouldn't risk hurting Jack and Libby's marriage before it began.

"Why don't you call Libby and see if she and Jack want to come down to talk it over? Soon." He handed her the phone.

"SHE'S WHAT?" Shock registered across Jack's face as he sat opposite Libby in the Ormsby House's coffee shop.

"Sssh." Libby looked around nervously and lowered her voice to a whisper. "You heard me. Due in November. Nobody knows."

"What about Sam? He'd stand by her, right?"

Libby explained Claire's decision as best she could. Jack shook his head in disbelief. She looked up at Jack.

"What if it were us? What would we do?"

"Get married and have the baby, of course," Jack asserted without hesitation. "It would change the schedule, but not the outcome. We'll be together no matter what."

That's why she loved this man. He stood firm while she flew off the handle. "She needs a lawyer. Uncle Matt suggested you."

"I still have to pass the Bar, remember?"

"Uncle Matt says that's not important, that you only need to look over what the other lawyer does. Answer questions, you know? How about Labor Day weekend?"

He sat back, crossed his arms, and frowned. "Did you forget we already had plans?" The little muscle in his jaw twitched.

They did have plans. She hadn't forgotten. Jack had planned a romantic weekend in San Francisco. "I'm sorry. But we can go another time."

"When exactly? You'll be working. I'll be in school."

Libby hadn't anticipated an argument. Didn't he understand how important this was? How could he put a vacation ahead of Claire?

"We could go Nevada Day. Or Christmas vacation," she offered.

"Maybe." Jack sighed then looked at her. His gaze softened a bit.

"I'm sorry. Really. But, what can I do? This is kind of a big deal."

"So are we, Lib. We're a couple now. We need to decide things together. You can't expect me to just get dragged along." He wore his thinking face now. His mouth twisted as he gazed up and off into the distance. "Tell you what. Have Uncle Matt send me the paperwork. Or better yet, have their attorney send it directly to me. I'll look it over and talk to Claire on the phone. We'll work out something."

"Thank you. I love you." Libby felt like they'd passed some critical milestone in their relationship. A negotiated settlement.

WITH THIS NEW plan for little Sam moving ahead, Claire's worries about where and how to live until November re-emerged. She'd begun scanning the classifieds, hoping to find a small, cheap apartment somewhere in town. All she'd found was a dingy single-wide mobile home, but when she mentioned it, Aunt Ellie had been surprised.

"Oh, no!" she'd said. "I thought you knew. The Thorsens are such good friends, we'll be happy to have you stay here."

This seemed too good to be true. "Until November?"

"Until November."

"But we'll need to renegotiate the room and board, at least."

"Not necessary. The Thorsens are taking care of that."

Nevertheless, Claire kept her job. She'd still need cash for after.

WHEN COPIES of the proposed adoption papers arrived a week later, Claire read through the labyrinth of legalese trying to understand. Lots of party of the first parts, whereas-es, and heretofores. During the first fraught phone conversation with Jack, she learned about something called "Termination of Parental Rights."

"It's a legal process that involves a court hearing." Her heart stopped for a moment. Breathe in. Breathe out.

"I have to go to court?"

"Yes. Or at least your representative. A judge must issue a decree that permanently ends your legal parental rights. It happens before the adoption is final.

"Can we do it now? I mean before...?"

"Unfortunately, you can't terminate your parental rights until you are a parent." He went on to explain something about legal risk and that the adoption of newborn infants is considered high risk. She couldn't take it all in. Claire hadn't considered this. She thought she'd sign papers with a promise, a contract of some sort, and be done.

"But as soon as she's born, right?"

"Well, the adoptive parents can take the baby, certainly. But the adoption can't be finalized for a while." Was he deliberately doling out information slowly, trying to lessen the impact?

"How long?"

"Six months."

OVER THE NEXT WEEK, Claire had more conversations with both Jack and Dr. Matt. More what-ifs plagued her. What if the baby wasn't healthy? What if little Sam were missing some fingers or...? Claire insisted that she be allowed to take care of the baby until the parents arrived, in case there was some problem. If there were—and if the parents changed their mind—she would keep her.

Dr. Matt worried that Claire would bond with the baby. She knew he was trying to prevent more heartache and disappointment for the new parents. Claire tried to convince him as well as herself, that it was her own protective instinct that was causing her to make this decision in the first place. Dr. Matt reluctantly agreed.

"I checked with my Family Law Professor. This is kind of unusual. You think you can do a better job than the nurses?" Jack probed in yet another phone call.

"That's not it. I don't want little Sam to know one moment of not being loved. Not one."

"I'll do what I can, Claire. Good thing the hospital is so tiny. Not much bureaucracy to deal with. If that's all..."

"One more thing. Put it in writing that I will never contact little Sam, but when she's grown, if she ever wants to contact me, I'm open to that."

THE LAST WEEK of summer finally arrived. Jack had put her conditions in writing but insisted that he speak with Claire face-to-face. He and Libby had driven down for the day and would get their San Francisco weekend after all.

After reviewing and signing the agreement at the McCormack's kitchen table, Claire addressed the big envelope to the Nebraska lawyer. The trio then walked to the post office to mail it and on to the Jolly Kone for celebratory root beer floats.

The late summer heat rose in waves from the blacktop that rolled through the center of Bridgeport. A bright blue, cloudless sky formed a perfect bowl overhead. American flags fluttered from every porch and flagpole around the small town. A crush of late summer travelers lined up at Jolly Kone's service window. Claire grew impatient waiting in line on her swollen feet and went around the back where she made two floats and poured herself a large vanilla Coke. After all those summers working at the A&W, she still couldn't drink root beer. It didn't seem to bother Libby, though.

They found a table in the shade. Jack and Libby sat opposite her. They talked and watched the tourists. Claire gasped. Her heart stopped. She grabbed her belly and bolted upright.

"Oh, shit!"

"What is it, Claire? The baby?"

"No! Sam!" she said in an emphatic whisper, before waddling to the rear of the drive-in, leaving Jack and Libby looking bewildered. She stepped into the kitchen's storeroom through the wooden screen door, which slapped behind her. From inside the dark storeroom, she could see out the long windows upfront. She ducked behind a rack of paper cups and watched as Sam and his lumpy roommate, Ron, walked up to the window to order. They waited for their food and looked around. Sam looked past Libby, then back at her, before walking over. Libby smiled and said something Claire couldn't hear. She tried to read their body language. Sam and Jack shook hands. An introduction to Ron. Libby shook her head, shrugged her shoulders. That's right, Libby, you haven't heard a thing. Jack nodded and motioned to the back of the building.

Sam and Ron disappeared and Claire went deeper into the dark and sat on a case of ketchup, behind a tower of hamburger buns. Her heart raced. Sweat trickled down her neck and between her breasts. What are they doing back here?

"So that girl knows Claire?" She recognized Ron's voice.

"Yeah, her best friend since they were kids."

"And she hasn't heard from her?"

Claire held her breath. No answer from Sam but she heard a door screech open and then close. The restroom door. Claire slumped and exhaled. Minutes later she heard running water and then the creak of the door again.

Sam spoke now. "You take the next shift behind the wheel. We can switch again at Adelanto."

They're heading south, back toward Fullerton. They won't be coming back through town.

Later that afternoon, Jack and Libby were getting ready to drive back to Carson City.

Claire offered her hand to Jack and said, "Thank you. I know you got dragged into this. And thanks especially for not saying anything to Sam."

Jack's kind eyes betrayed no judgment. "Not my story to tell." He pulled her into a warm hug. Libby was a lucky girl.

"Aunt Ellie will call me when you go into labor," Libby said. "I'll be here as soon as I can." Weather frequently closed the one road between Carson City and Bridgeport, even in the fall. "Hope that baby is considerate enough to arrive on a weekend. And during the day." Libby kissed Claire's cheek and patted her tummy.

"Well, if she's anything like her mother, she'll be late and cause the most possible trouble," Claire said as she closed the car door. Little Sam was a girl? No longer it? When had that happened?

CHAPTER TWENTY-ONE

Then: Will You Still Love Me Tomorrow?

*A*s time went on, Claire's restlessness increased. Despite her fatigue from long days on her feet at the Jolly Kone, sleep eluded her, no matter how many pillows she piled around her in bed. Out of desperation, she began spending nights in Dr. Matt's recliner. She read a bit, dozed a bit, but mostly rifled through possible scenarios of what life would be like once this chapter ended.

Carson City held absolutely no allure. She'd promised Libby to stick around for the wedding in June, but she knew that was only temporary. She wanted to put all this behind her. But aside from her degree and fluency in French, she had little to offer in the way of job skills. She was a waitress. Period. Maybe a fancy resort somewhere? A cruise ship? Airline stewardess? Sure, those would satisfy her wanderlust, they'd do nothing to quell her desire to atone for the mess she'd made of her life so far. Would the Peace Corps take her back? If not, were there other options?

A frustrated sigh heaved from her chest as she refocused her thoughts on what kind of life little Sam might have in Nebraska. No earthquakes, but tornadoes. What else? Claire flipped down the footrest of the recliner, rose with some effort, and lumbered to the bookshelf where the set of Encyclopedia Britannica stood. As she reached for the N volume, she felt pressure on her bladder and plodded down the hall to the bathroom for the zillionth time.

DURING ANOTHER SLEEPLESS night in September, Claire sat up at the kitchen table struggling to write letters to little Sam and her parents. She felt compelled to explain—to them and herself—why she couldn't keep a baby. How could she ever hope to justify not wanting her baby? Sam's baby. So far, her attempts had resulted only in a mass of crumpled, tear-dampened paper.

Sighing, she stood and set the kettle to boil. Maybe some chamomile tea with honey would help. She listened for the rattle of the boiling water, not wanting to disturb her hosts the whistle, and made her tea.

Once again, she began. In pencil. On scratch paper. If she ever got a draft she liked, she'd recopy it. And change all the pronouns, if necessary.

To the parents,

I am happy that you are going to raise my baby.

Claire stopped. "My baby" sounded too possessive of a baby who would no longer be hers. "This baby" seemed too impersonal.

I am happy that you are going to raise my̶ our baby. When I heard your story from Dr. and Mrs. McCormack, I knew you were the right choice. I feel as though I've been merely babysitting until her r̶e̶a̶l̶ parents arrived.

Although this baby was unplanned, she was never unloved. Her father and I loved each other very much.

Past tense. They had loved each other. She still loved him, but he couldn't possibly still love her. Not now. Not ever again.

I have taken good care of her for you, but raising a child is a lifelong commitment. I know I am not capable of providing the stability she needs and deserves. I trust that you will love her and give her what I cannot. I have given her life. It is up to you to give her a life.

She may have questions as she grows up, so I have enclosed a letter for her as well. As her parents, please do with it as you see fit.

I have faith that this is the way it was always meant to be and am at peace with my decision. She is and always has been your child.

~C.

Her letter to little Sam proved more difficult. New parents would be grateful to have the family they wanted—finally. A child's concerns might not be so clear-cut, especially as she grew up. What questions would an adopted child have? Who do I look like? Why didn't my birth mother want me? What's wrong with me? Didn't she love me?

Dear baby,

Wait, when would the parents share this? Probably not until junior high. Maybe later.

Dear ~~baby~~ one,

It is unlikely we will ever meet, but I wanted you to know a little about me. A person has a right to know where they come from.

Claire looked up from the page and sipped her tea. Would the new parents agree? Claire could only hope they would allow little Sam to see this letter, sometime. She started simply with the basics.

I am tall with blonde hair and brown eyes. I like running and the feeling of freedom it gives me. It might also be because I'm always late. I love to travel. Your father is also tall, with curly red hair and blue eyes. His skin freckles in the sun and he is extremely stubborn. Some people say I'm stubborn too. If stubbornness is an inherited trait, I'm guessing you got a double dose. Sorry.

Although I won't be there to watch you grow up, I know it isn't always easy.

What worldly advice could she give? Did she have any right to give advice?

My dad left when I was little, so it was only my mom and me. We didn't always get along. I guess I was kind of a handful, but she always stood by me. One thing she taught me was this: Life is living with our choices. Even when we don't make good ones, we can learn from them. I've made lots of mistakes and it took me a long time to learn the lessons. Like I said, I'm pretty stubborn.

You deserve the best possible life, dear one. I believe you deserve two good parents, who chose to make a family. I know I can't give you all you deserve. That is why I've entrusted you to Tom and Gail. I am grateful we found each other. Never forget, we did it for you.

Claire stood up and stretched, arms over her head. She bent to one side then the other looking out of the kitchen window. It was late now, after midnight. The house was quiet. Aunt Ellie and Dr. Matt had been in bed for hours. The full moon shone brightly on the mountains. Again, she thought of bioluminescence and Sam. Wherever he is, he might be looking at the moon too. Perhaps her father was as well. She smiled and sat down again.

My love for you is like the moon. It only appears to grow and shrink, but it never really changes. And even if you can't see it, it is strong enough to pull the tides. That's the love I have for you. Always.

~C.

LIBBY'S APARTMENT PHONE RANG. The bedside clock said 5:45.

"Sorry it's so early, but Claire's water broke. She's in labor," Aunt Ellie told her.

Instantly wide-awake, Libby thanked her aunt and quickly

called her principal, sounding as sick as she could. She'd planned ahead. For the last two weeks, she'd made sure her lesson plans were so explicit, so easy, that a well-trained Labrador retriever could handle them. Her suitcase was already packed.

Then she called her mother. A pre-emptive call with a prepared lie.

"I feel terrible. Sore throat, headache."

"Fever?"

"Maybe a little." Well, she was sweating.

"What do you need? I can bring it right over."

Crap. "No. I'll be fine. I have juice and soup. Aspirin. I'm going to crawl back in bed and unplug the phone. And I don't want to expose you to whatever crud those first graders have given me. You're just getting over bronchitis." Libby congratulated herself on that little touch.

"Well, all right. I hate to think of you all alone."

"Alone is exactly what I need, Mom. I'll call you if I need anything." With her parents living only five blocks away, alone was rare. It always felt like someone was watching, checking up on her. Claire was right. There was no privacy in a small town.

She called Jack, took a quick shower, and tossed her suitcase into the car along with snacks and tapes for the eight-track. Simon & Garfunkel, Judy Collins, Joni Mitchell. By seven she was headed south on US395. She prayed out loud, "Please, God. Please. . ." again, she wasn't sure what for. An easy delivery? A healthy baby? For Claire to change her mind?

CLAIRE'S MOOD brightened when she saw Libby at the door of the hospital room. Her contractions were still twenty minutes apart. Aunt Ellie showed Libby how to mirror Claire's efforts, breathing through each wave, trying to relax and not fight the pain.

Libby distracted and entertained Claire with stories of her more troublesome first-graders whose brains seemed to be coated in Teflon. Claire laughed as another contraction caused her to gasp.

Libby checked her watch and noted the time. When Claire relaxed again, Libby continued with how terrified she'd been at parent conferences. She laughed at how she was supposed to be the expert. Again, they laughed before another contraction gripped Claire.

"Well, at least I know why some of my kids are the way they are."

"Acorns and trees?"

"Exactly. Weird little kids have even weirder parents."

"They're lucky they have you."

"Maybe. But I may not be enough for some of them. Their holes are just too deep."

"But they're only in first grade. How far behind can they be?"

"About six years."

***

SOMETIME LATE FRIDAY AFTERNOON, everything simply stopped. No contractions. Nothing. Claire's cervix was simply stuck at six centimeters. The stout nurse named Verna, with purple varicose veins and a bit of a mustache encouraged Claire to walk. Libby and Claire walked up and down the hall until Uncle Matt stopped in after his dinner to check on her progress.

"Don't worry. It happens." He did, however, instruct Verna to attach a fetal monitor to the baby's head. "Just in case." In case of what was never stated. And then they strapped another device around Claire's belly to register her contractions.

A bit later, Jack arrived with a burger and milkshake from Jolly Kone for Libby but didn't stay long.

"I brought studying." He kissed Libby and left. Claire had to admit, he was one of the good ones.

With her labor at a standstill, Claire was more than tired. She was angry. This had gone on long enough. Evolution sure hadn't progressed very far if this was still how babies get born. And now, with the leads from the fetal monitor between her legs, the belt around her belly measuring her contractions, and the IV in her arm, she was trapped. Tied down. All she wanted to do was to run away.

"I think I know what's happening," Libby offered when they were alone again.

"My body is on strike?" Claire huffed.

"Somewhere deep inside, you understand that these are the last moments you'll spend with your baby." She squeezed Claire's hand. "I think you don't want to let go."

"Yeah, right!" Claire dismissed that idea as ridiculous. But she couldn't help imagining a conversation.

It's time, Mom.

So soon?

It's been nine months.

Not long enough.

I've got a life; you've got a life.

A life.

Yes, a life.

Don't leave.

I have to.

I love you.

I know.

LIBBY PULLED a deck of cards from her bag, sat on the bed, and dealt the cards onto the rolling tray-table. They were into their third or fourth game of War when pain once again gripped Claire's belly. Like the worst cramps ever, with maybe a stabbing thrown in for good measure.

"Oh, my god. It's starting again." Sure enough, the monitor showed a strong contraction. "Almost forgot why I was here." Almost.

The wave passed. Another one followed just minutes later. And another. Time was only measured in the minutes between contractions. Those intervals grew shorter and shorter. Libby kept track. Seven minutes. Five. Four. Claire's heart pounded. She was sweating and breathing hard. Like running a race. Not a sprint, but a marathon.

"Water."

"Sorry, ice chips only." Libby spooned ice into Claire's mouth.

"More."

Libby obeyed with a little chuckle.

"What's so funny?" Claire saw nothing funny in this.

"A little girl in class last week was crying at snack time. She'd packed it herself. A Popsicle. Or at least it was a Popsicle when she packed it."

"You mean? Oh…" and another contraction took hold of Claire.

Dr. Matt returned and lifted Claire's gown, placing his gloved hand between her legs to check her progress.

"How're you doing, Claire?"

"You mean aside from the fact I can't get this baby born?" Another contraction. Breathe in, breathe out.

"Yes, aside from that." He smiled. "You've made some progress. About eight now."

"I'm so tired though. How long has this been going on?"

Dr. Matt looked at his watch. "About eighteen hours."

"If I could catch my breath." She began to doubt her strength to finish this.

"That's what I think. We want you strong for the next stage. What do you say to a little pain medicine? That paracervical we talked about? Numb you right up. Then you can rest a little."

"Yes. Please." Another contraction, maybe the strongest yet, gripped her. Verna handed Dr. Matt a syringe. He waited for the contraction to pass. She felt the pinch when the needle went in, then nothing. Nothing. Minutes later, only the monitor indicated another contraction. Claire closed her eyes. No one would believe her, but she dozed. Nonetheless, each time she closed her eyes a nightmare hallway appeared. She couldn't open any doors. She tried door after door with no success. Until a new sensation gripped her. The urge to push.

"Libby!"

"Right here, Claire. Right here." Libby bolted out of the chair where she'd been nodding.

"Get the nurse. I have to push."

"Hang on."

"No way! If this baby is finally ready, I'm not hanging on! I'm pushing!"

Verna arrived at a trot. Another set of gloved fingers inside her. She nodded. "You're at ten, Claire. I'll get Dr. McCormack. We'll move you down to the delivery room."

"Libby?"

"Here. Don't worry. I'm coming with you. Let me get dressed for the big dance." Libby pulled on green scrubs then twirled as she tucked her hair into a surgical cap. More people arrived to wheel her down the hall.

"Well, Claire. Your baby will be here very soon." Dr. Matt patted her hand. Claire felt warmth from the bright flood lamp between her legs. A spotlight ready for the star of the show to appear.

She still couldn't visualize how an actual human being

would exit her body. Time and place disappeared. Existence was reduced to this table, Libby beside her, and the profound urge to push coming in ever-increasing waves. And Dr. Matt's voice. Calm. Patient.

"That's right, Claire. I can feel the head. Shallow breaths now. Don't bear down. Let me check how the shoulders are positioned. Good. Good. You're doing fine."

Repeatedly, Claire pushed, rested, and pushed again through the burning pain that threatened to tear her in two. She screamed. She swore. She called for Sam. And just when she thought she couldn't bear anymore, couldn't give anymore, she heard Dr. Matt say, "That's it. There are the shoulders. And... she's here! A beautiful baby girl."

Claire looked at Libby, whose face was wet with sweat and tears, then at the wet and wriggly child who had scarcely emerged from her body. She couldn't speak but choked back her tears. Well, little Sam, it's about time.

The baby didn't cry. She merely gave a good yell, as if to announce her arrival. Dr. Matt laid the infant on Claire's chest where she and Libby inspected her from the tufts of dark, damp hair on her head to the tips of ten tiny, curled toes. Dr. Matt said something about the placenta, then something about a few stitches. But Claire focused on her daughter. Sam's daughter. Love and pain exploded in her chest.

When Dr. Matt finished and left, Verna came to take the baby to the nursery.

Claire held tight. "No. Not yet. Let me have her. They promised. She's mine!"

Verna was firm. "Claire. She needs a bath. You need some rest."

"No! I'm not tired." Claire knew she was yelling but didn't care. Why wouldn't they let her keep her baby? She'd waited so long.

Dr. Matt reappeared and motioned to Verna to follow him into the hall.

Libby was beside her now, holding her hand.

"Take a breath, Claire. Nice and slow," she said softly. Claire obeyed with a ragged inhale. "Another." Again, she obeyed. "Another." Her anxiety began to ease, but as it did, it left in its wake a dark and unfathomable void. Libby used her first-grade teacher voice. Small words. Short sentences. "They need to take her down the hall. To the nursery."

"I can't."

"Yes, you can."

Claire gulped and held her daughter more tightly.

"Do you trust me, Claire?"

"Yes, but…" but what? There was no one she trusted more than Libby.

Libby smiled gently. "May I?"

Claire only nodded as Libby lifted the baby from her arms and handed her to Verna. Little Sam disappeared down the hall.

LIBBY CHECKED HER WATCH. A little after two in the morning. Verna had gone, but a new nurse, Lois, had given Claire some medication—a sedative maybe?—and something so her milk wouldn't come in. The baby was a few rooms away in the nursery.

"Tell me if she needs anything," Lois said to Libby. "The medication should make her sleepy." Libby nodded. Lois's soft-soled shoes squeaked a bit as she walked back to her station.

After the scene in the delivery room, Claire was unusually calm, zombie-like. Libby stood beside her in the dim room, but Claire looked beyond her, out the window, toward the dark night sky.

A faint smile appeared then faded from Claire's face.

"I named her." Her voice sounded thick. "I know it won't stick, but I did it anyway. Samantha Elizabeth Jordan. Little Sam." Libby handed her a glass of water and put the straw in her mouth. Claire sucked greedily then sighed. "Thank you. For everything."

"I guess I should be more careful what I promise from now on," Libby said.

"I wish. . . I wish you could be her godmother." Claire's eyelids drooped. She yawned.

"I'll be her fairy godmother."

Libby patted Claire's hand but she was already asleep. It was only then Libby realized how tired she was. She sat and closed her eyes.

"I called the new parents." Uncle Matt was tapping her shoulder. Libby must have slipped into a doze.

"Already?" The baby was only hours old. It was the middle of the night.

He looked at Claire's chart. "They're flying into Reno and driving down. They'll be here tomorrow afternoon."

"It's just…" What? What if that scene in the delivery room meant Claire was having second thoughts?

"The sooner the better, Libby. And they've been waiting for a long time. I'm headed home. Do you want to come and get some rest?" Libby shook her head. She'd stay with Claire.

Throughout Saturday, Lois brought Claire meals and checked her vitals, her bleeding and—after last night's episode—her mental state. Lois was maternal and sweet, a tiny, bird-like person compared to the sturdy, no-nonsense Verna. She seemed to have heard or surmised the reasons Claire would be going home without a baby and probably knew the adoptive family. Didn't Aunt Ellie say that the mother was raised here? Small towns were like that. No secrets.

By Sunday afternoon, Libby had slept a bit and taken a shower at Ellie and Matt's. She saw some improvement in Claire's coloring, her alertness. They'd brought the baby in a few times and let Claire give her a bottle of formula. There had been no repeat of that awful scene. Claire seemed to understand they wouldn't let her see the baby at all if she didn't behave.

When the adoptive parents arrived, Libby heard a commotion from Claire's room. She stood in the doorway and tried to look inconspicuous. The couple, who from this distance looked enough alike in size and coloring to be siblings, greeted Uncle Matt. Both had dark, curly hair. Both wore jeans, down jackets, and wire-framed glasses. They peered through the nursery window where Uncle Matt pointed out their daughter.

"How do they look?"

"Nice. They look nice," Libby said, choking back tears and telling herself they were happy tears. She realized her own emotions were a complex and potent cocktail of relief, sadness, gratitude, and anxiety.

Verna was back on duty. Along with pulse and temperature, she pressed on Claire's belly and inspected the bloody pad. She shook her head.

"I'm worried about her bleeding," she told Libby. "Should have slowed a bit by now. Let me check with Dr. McCormack when he's finished down there." She motioned in the direction of the nursery.

"Quite a scene," Libby whispered to Verna at the door.

"Yes, it is." Verna fought back tears as she took a tissue from her pocket and wiped her nose. "Gail grew up here. A darling girl. She'll be a wonderful mother. Your friend has blessed them with that baby. Truly blessed them."

As Verna spoke with Uncle Matt, Libby saw the look of concern on his face. He walked toward the room.

"We're going to keep you another night, Claire. The bleeding." He patted Claire's hand. "Being a little extra cautious. And we'll give you medicine to help you clot. That should do the trick."

Sunday night Libby called her principal and her mother, telling them she was still sick and adding two more lies to her weekly confession.

CLAIRE IS ALONE IN A DIM, empty hallway. She hears a baby crying from behind one of the many doors. Her baby. She tries one door. Locked. Why was it locked?! The crying continues, louder. Another door. Locked. She bangs her fist against another door.

"Help! Help me, please! My baby is crying! Don't you hear? Somebody help me. Do something!"

She runs, screaming, from door to door. Still, the baby cries. "I can't find my baby. I can't. . ." She collapses against a door, sobbing. The baby's cries are louder now, more desperate. "I'm sorry. I'm sorry. Sam, I'm so sorry. Someone, please, find my baby."

"Claire." Verna's voice. "Claire, wake up. You're having a nightmare."

"Help her. . ." Claire gasped, her heart thrashing against her ribs.

"The baby's sleeping, dear." Verna patted Claire's hand, then slipped her fingers around her wrist to check her racing pulse.

"I—I heard her— crying. I—I c-couldn't find her."

"It was a bad dream. Baby's fine. Sleeping like an angel." Verna said in a breathy whisper. She looked at Claire's chart. "It's time for some more meds. They'll help you sleep."

"I don't want to sleep." Not if sleep put her back in that hallway.

"Dr. McCormack left orders for a mild sedative if you woke up. Let's follow his instructions, shall we?"

Claire surrendered. "May I at least go to the bathroom first? I may need some help." She felt like a child asking permission. Powerless.

SUNLIGHT REFLECTED off the snow on Twin Peak and streamed into Claire's hospital room when she awoke Monday morning. While a fog of drugs and grief clouded her brain, she knew her time with Little Sam was running out. But when Jack told her there'd been a snafu regarding checkout her vision suddenly cleared, like he'd wiped the frost from a windshield.

"What?!"

"California law says that because this is a private adoption, you have to leave the hospital with the baby. Sorry." Jack shrugged.

How could she leave? Every time she'd tried to stand, her muscles and spine had turned to jelly, as though everything inside her had liquefied and was draining out. She wouldn't have been surprised if Dr. Matt wanted her to stay in the hospital another day.

The baby slept in her bassinet, with Libby hovering over her. Jack and Libby were to meet the new parents at Dr. Matt's office soon with little Sam.

"Easy girl." Jack reached out to steady Claire as she swung her legs over the side of the bed and tried to stand.

"I—I need to get dressed," Claire said. However, the mere act of reaching for her suitcase caused the room to swirl around her. She grabbed Jack's outstretched arm. After two more attempts at being upright, she gave up, fell back into bed, and collapsed inelegantly against the pillows. She closed her eyes and took several deep ragged breaths. Libby pulled up the sheet to cover her.

"I can leave the hospital in a robe, but Samantha needs to be dressed."

Jack looked at his watch and said, "I have a few things to take care of. Then I'll bring the car around. Twenty minutes, ladies?" They nodded. Claire sat up slowly.

"You have an ensemble for her coming out party?" The baby's eyes fluttered open as Libby picked her up from the bassinet.

"In the suitcase," Claire murmured.

Libby settled the baby on Claire's lap, her little head at Claire's knees.

"First things first, little girl," Claire whispered to Samantha. "You need a dry diaper. Always start a journey with clean underwear." Claire smiled that she—of all people—could give motherly advice. Gratitude that someone more capable and worthy filled her for a moment. That gratitude was quickly replaced by sadness that it wouldn't be her.

Libby tried to help, but Claire waved her off.

"Let me do this one last thing for her. Please." Her hands shook as she diapered and then wriggled little Sam's tiny pink body into a pale green nightgown adorned with embroidered daisies. "Remember this stitch? We learned it in Girl Scouts. We made hankies, right?"

"I remember. You sewed this?" Libby looked more closely at the flowers.

"Uh-huh."

"Nice. But what if Sam had been a boy?"

"Sailboats. I made both." Claire shrugged. "Didn't have much else to do. Aunt Ellie tried to teach me to knit, but I couldn't get the hang of it.

Claire held little Sam against her shoulder. She fit so perfectly under her chin, felt so right. Samantha yawned. Her sweet, milky breath caused a sob to rise in Claire's chest. She leaned back for a moment to gather strength for what was to come.

"This is stupid." Claire shook her head. "Someone who wanted a baby will have one. Little Sam will have a family. A real family. The kind she deserves. What's wrong with me?"

Libby handed her a tissue. "You just had a baby and your hormones are all mixed up." Libby looked Claire in the eye. "Second thoughts?"

The direct question snapped Claire to attention. Of course, she could change her mind. Nothing was final. For a moment, an imagined life with a baby reeled out before her toward— what? —a dead-end. While that may be the life she deserved, it wasn't the life little Sam deserved.

"No." She sniffed. "No second thoughts."

Lois was back on duty and appeared with a wheelchair. "It's time to go. Everyone ready?"

"Ready as I'm gonna get," Claire chirped too brightly, hearing the falseness in her voice. A hollow ache in her chest and belly told her she wasn't ready. Not ready to leave the hospital and not to leave little Sam. But she wouldn't give voice to those doubts now. No. She'd given her word. A promise was a promise.

―――――――

LIBBY WHEELED Claire out to the car where Jack waited with the motor running. The November sun shone without warmth as Libby held the baby. Jack helped Claire into the back seat. With awkward tenderness, Claire snuggled little Sam in the backseat, whispering to her throughout the short drive to the McCormack's house. *Be happy. I love you.* When they arrived, Claire kissed the baby's head and gave her one final affec-tionate squeeze before handing her to Libby. Jack practically had to carry Claire up the front steps where Aunt Ellie met them at the door. Libby followed.

"She doesn't look right, Aunt Ellie," Libby whispered. "Should she even be out of the hospital?"

"We'll keep an eye on her." Aunt Ellie led Claire back to the recliner and tucked an afghan around her. A silent Claire meekly followed directions. Something was wrong.

"At least you're here. Jack and I will be back in a while. Shouldn't take too long."

"I'll have lunch ready for you," Aunt Ellie said with a wave.

Sniffing and dabbing her eyes with the corner of the baby blanket, Libby got back into the car. Samantha's pink lips made little sucking motions. How could Claire give up her child? Did she think it as some sort of penance? Or maybe Claire believed the only way out was to move forward alone. Libby knew she'd never make the same decision.

Minutes later, Jack held the door to Uncle Matt's office open for Libby and the baby. The Bassetts sat in the waiting area with Uncle Matt. The woman flew out of her seat when Libby entered. Libby braced herself and prepared to hand off the baby. Instead, the woman stopped within inches of where Libby stood with the now wide-awake Samantha. The woman's chin trembled as she stood still, staring into little Sam's unfocused eyes.

"Oh, my God, Tom. Our baby." Tears had already streaked the woman's mascara behind her glasses. Her husband was at her side within seconds, his hand cupping her shoulder. His eyes soon filled too.

"Hello, sweetheart," he whispered while stroking the baby's cheek with his index finger. "I'm your dad."

Uncle Matt introduced them. Libby nodded and smiled as she handed off the precious cargo. She and Jack stepped back as a family was born.

The adoption wouldn't be final for six months. Libby would

have another six months of praying to do. What those prayers would be, she wasn't sure. She reached into her jacket pocket and withdrew the envelopes with Claire's letters and handed them to Gail.

"Claire, uh. . . the birth mother, wanted you to have these. She wrote to you and the baby. You don't ever have to read them or share them with the baby, but she wanted you to have them anyway."

A flash of recognition that another mother was involved here, passed across Gail's face. She nodded and pressed the letters to her heart. "Dr. Matt told us what you've done. We want to thank you for being such a good friend. Without you. . ." Gail sniffed. "And thank you, Dr. Matt, for bringing us together. Little Grace here is the answer to our prayers."

Grace. Libby felt a wistful smile cross her lips. Kindness. Mercy. Reprieve. She hoped Claire would find a bit of that too. That would be her prayer.

"AUNT ELLIE?" Claire whispered from the recliner late Monday night where she'd been watching Johnny Carson. Her voice sounded strange. "Aunt Ellie?!" She said it a bit louder.

"Here, Claire. What do you need?" Ellie entered the living room drying her hands.

"I think I need to use the bathroom. Maybe change that pad. I feel kinda wet down there. But I'm afraid to stand up."

"Okay. Take it slow." Ellie activated the recliner's lever for Claire. "That's right. Easy does it. Now try to stand. Slowly." Ellie's right arm was around Claire's waist. She grasped Claire's arm with her left hand for support.

"I feel a little woozy," Claire said as she stood up and then...

She must have fainted because she didn't remember

anything until she woke up lying in the backseat of a car, wrapped in a towel. Two towels. More? And they were sticky. Aunt Ellie was driving.

"What happened?" Underneath her on the seat was a plastic tablecloth.

"You fainted," Aunt Ellie said evenly. "You're hemorrhaging. Bleeding. Matt helped get you into the car. We're meeting him at the hospital." Claire felt the bump as they stopped at the emergency entrance. "Here we are. And here's Matt."

Claire raised her head once or twice to look down. So much blood. Cool night air struck her as two orderlies opened the car door and lifted her out and onto a gurney. Dr. Matt ran alongside as they wheeled her into the small emergency room.

Again, the room spun then disappeared.

This time she woke up in an operating room. Dr. Matt was talking to her.

"Claire, you're not clotting. We've cleaned you up, applied pressure. Given you more clotting factor. We've transfused you. But you keep bleeding." He was holding her hand.

"What...?" She could hardly form a thought, much less words.

"We're going to put you under and open you up. See if there is a tear somewhere. Something. But. . ."

"But?" She dreaded the end of the sentence.

"If we can't stop the bleeding, we'll remove your uterus."

"You mean...? But. . ." Her head was swimming.

"I don't like this either. But unless we can stop the bleeding, you'll die." Dr. Matt looked her in the eye. "I need your permission. And Claire, I need you to trust me."

A tear dripped into her ear. "What should I do?"

"Live, Claire. You choose to live."

Without another word, she nodded.

CHAPTER TWENTY-TWO

Then: Take Good Care of My Baby

*I*t was a little past 9 a.m. on the first Friday of December and Sylvia Jordan had been at her office for over an hour already, putting the final touches on the office Christmas tree. Jordan Properties now employed three full-time agents, a part-time receptionist, and Arlene, her office manager. Sylvia still handled most of the commercial properties herself, especially historical ones, leaving residential sales to others. The phone rang, and while Arlene answered, Sylvia lit a cigarette and stepped back to assess their progress. She hated it when it wasn't balanced. Or if it were overdone. There was a fine line between festive and tacky.

"Call for you, Sylvia. Fran McCormack. Line two."

Sylvia walked back to her desk, sat down, lifted the receiver, and pressed the blinking button.

"Hi, Fran. What's up?"

"I don't want to bother you, but Libby told me that Claire was coming back. Maybe next week. Have you heard from her?"

"No." She flicked an ash into the cut-glass ashtray on her desk and sat down. Sylvia wouldn't admit to Fran that she hadn't heard from her daughter in weeks. Fran and Libby must talk every day. She wasn't envious, exactly. But was there something lacking in her skills as a mother? Claire had a full, busy, grown-up life. So did Sylvia. They didn't need to be in each other's business all the time. She blew cigarette smoke out through her nose, releasing it into a blue haze above her head. "Maybe she just decided. She'll tell me." Won't she?

"Well, I guess she's going to share Libby's apartment, at least for the time being."

Sylvia wondered if she'd always be the last to learn anything about her daughter. Suddenly she didn't want to talk to Mrs. Frances McCormack, Mrs. Busybody Mother of the Year anymore. She stubbed out her cigarette and stood up.

"Well, thanks for calling, Fran. I'm sure we'll get the full story soon enough. Merry Christmas." Her daughter was coming home and Fran had to be the one to tell her about it? With Claire incommunicado, the least she could do was talk to Libby. She looked at her watch. Nine-thirty. Libby wouldn't be home 'til after school.

THE PHONE WAS RINGING as Libby unlocked her apartment door and ran to pick up. She glanced at the clock on the stove. Five-thirty. So much for teachers getting off work at three.

"Hello." She dropped her purse and book bag onto the kitchen counter.

"Hi, Libby. It's Sylvia Jordan."

"Oh, hi," Crap. Now, what lie would she have to tell?

"Your mom called this morning and said something about Claire coming home soon. She was sketchy on details. I thought maybe you had some more information." Couldn't her mother keep anything to herself?

"The truth is Claire hasn't told me exactly when she's

coming home." Actual truth. Uncle Matt said it could take a while to recover. Libby took a breath and shrugged out of her down coat, balancing the phone between her ear and shoulder. "Sometime in the next couple of weeks, I think." Truth.

"And she's going to live with you?"

"Um-hum. I've got that second bedroom. And she doesn't think she wants a place of her own since she'll be leaving again."

"Leaving again?"

"Yes. She'll stay until my wedding in June." Truth. "After that, she's not sure. She may go traveling again. You know Claire. Can't pin her down." More truth.

"Yes, I know Claire. I guess I was a little surprised that she hadn't let me in on her plans."

"I thought she had told you. I'm sorry." She sank into a kitchen chair, stretching the long, coiled phone cord from its base on the wall and kicking off her shoes.

"You've done nothing to be sorry for. You've been a good and loyal friend. But I worry about her, even though it may not seem like I do. And since the Peace Corps thing fell through, I've had this feeling that something was wrong. She may not want to talk to me. She may think I'm disappointed. Maybe I am, a little. But not disappointed in her. Disappointed for her."

"Me too."

"You'd tell me if she were in trouble, if anything were wrong, right?"

"Of course," Libby responded. That was a lie, a lie to keep a promise, but still a lie. Sylvia had become a friend too, so this deception sat in a dark corner of Libby's brain accusing her and making her doubt herself. She was still an honest person, wasn't she? The front door opened and she looked up to see Jack. "Jack's here. I'd better go. Goodnight, Sylvia."

Libby stood to hang up the phone as Jack carried the

fragrant pizza into the kitchen. She opened the fridge and retrieved two bottled beers.

"Trouble?" Jack asked as he reached into a drawer for the bottle opener. He popped the tops, which made that satisfying "ttsshh" they both loved. The sound of Friday. The sound of letting off steam, letting go.

"Claire's mom. My mom told her Claire was coming home before Claire told her."

"Her reaction?" Jack's mouth twisted into a grimace.

"Confused. Hurt. Left out." Jack settled himself at the table while she took plates from the cupboard. He opened the box and placed slices on their plates.

"What did you tell her?"

"What I knew. Not much. *Tried* not to lie." She took a bite and chewed. "I guess what bothers me most is that there isn't any privacy here. Everyone knows everyone's business. Their history. Their mistakes. There is simply no escaping any of it."

Jack seemed to be chewing on an idea. Finally, he said, "There's an answer to that."

"Witness protection?"

He smiled. "Not exactly. But close. I've been offered a job in Las Vegas. My uncle's opening an office there next year. He said he'd take me on as an associate if I wanted."

"I don't know." As much as she complained about her life here, she'd never seriously considered moving.

"It's a good opportunity. A chance to make a life of our own, if that's what you want."

"But what about my job?" She loved her job.

"You can teach anywhere, Lib. And the way Vegas and Clark County are growing, they'll need a ton of teachers to keep up."

Libby thought about what she wanted. The idea of moving, while intriguing, scared her. No. What scared her most was telling her mother. Would she let fear stand in her way? Uncertainty clouded her thoughts for the second time tonight. Who was she if she wasn't the loyal daughter who lived near her parents? The girl who never lied? Was she a good person or was she simply afraid?

A WEEK LATER, Claire slumped in the passenger seat of Libby's old blue Datsun. Low gray clouds and a mid-December drizzle shrouded the Eastern Sierra as they drove north home to Carson City. The one place she'd tried to escape for as long as she could remember. Even college hadn't been far enough. Now her mother and the rest of the town would know she'd screwed up. Again. And this time, worse than anyone suspected. She leaned her head against the cool window and squeezed her eyes shut against more tears. Sam's face appeared. And the baby's. And the blood. Her eyes shot open. Outside, the trees blurred through a rain-splattered window.

Libby glanced at her. Claire sighed. Libby hated liars and now Claire had forced her to become one.

"Why do I keep crying?"

"I think crying's a pretty normal response." Even after only a few months on the job, Libby's tone reflected the patient, soothing quality of a veteran first-grade teacher. She reached over and patted Claire's knee. "How can I help? Shall I call someone? Sam maybe?"

"What? God, no! You didn't see his face at the funeral. The way he avoided my eyes. No. Not Sam." She'd never be able to face him again after what she'd done, after what had happened.

"His heart was broken, Claire," Libby said, her tone matter-of-fact. They'd been through all this before. "You didn't see the worry on his face when he asked about you last summer. And that stack of his letters..."

His letters. Why wouldn't he just give up? "Toss them out.

Burn them. I don't care. Nothing he could say would change anything. I can't undo what I've done."

Libby kept her eyes on the road, her hands firmly at ten and two. The diamond solitaire on her ten o'clock hand glinted as she twirled her engagement ring. The sight of the ring made Claire's heart clench. Yes, she was grateful to Libby, who'd offered her a place to stay, but there was something else. A nugget of something bitter Claire didn't want to admit. Did she resent Libby because she had Jack? Was she jealous of Libby's happily ever after? Claire swiped at her face with her sleeve.

Libby opened the glove box and handed Claire a fresh tissue.

Claire dabbed at her cheeks and blew her nose. "This is the end of it. I need to move on. I'll stay for your wedding like I promised. But then…"

Then what? Claire couldn't imagine. But first, she'd need to stop crying.

A sleeping baby—her baby? —lay in a cardboard Bacardi box that someone—who?— set adrift on a wide river. The box floats away from her. In desperation, Claire strides into the water, trying to retrieve the child. Now there are more babies in boxes. More. Dozens of babies all drifting away from her. The water is now chest-deep and all the babies remain out of reach. Then Claire loses her footing and sinks below the surface. As she comes up for air, the current sweeps the boxes and babies around a bend and out of sight. "No! No! No!"

She awoke screaming, her chest heaving with wild sobs. Was her baby in need of saving? Or had she saved little Sam by her decision? She burrowed under the covers.

Now that she couldn't have a child, that's what she obsessed about. Who'd want her if she couldn't have children? The thought of disclosing her story to a potential partner felt impossible. And if marriage were out of the question, would she always be alone? Should she take back her baby in May?

Her mother's words echoed in her mind. Life was indeed living with your choices.

The phone rang, jolting Claire back to the present and Libby's quiet apartment. She arose and stumbled to the empty kitchen. Libby was already at work. After all, it was nearly ten.

"Hello?"

"Good morning, honey. Did I wake you?" her mother asked.

"No. I was awake."

"I have what looks like a Christmas card here from Lou. Can I drop it by on my way to work?" The name of her quirky therapist recalled the smell of incense. Claire took a deep breath and slowly let it out. No pleasant fragrance here, merely morning breath and her own unwashed body. When had she taken a shower? Yesterday? The day before?

No. Claire couldn't see her mother face-to-face. Not again. Sitting across the table, not looking her in the eye, during that one awkward, interminable dinner had been enough. She couldn't help the feeling that her mother saw the secrets that lay hidden below the surface.

"No, I'll—I'll be out later and stop by. Leave it on the table."

Claire forced herself into the shower where she stared down at her soft, white belly and the still angry purple scar running from hip to hip. She let the hot water run long after she was rinsed. Only when it ran cold did she step out. In her search for something clean to wear, she found only her running clothes. After all, she hadn't run since...when, exactly? Before little Sam was born, certainly. A walk to her mother's house would be a good place to start. Dr. Matt had cautioned her not to run for a few more weeks.

Cold air struck her as she opened the door. She rushed back inside for a heavier jacket, hat, and mittens. Her first few steps were tentative, as though she'd forgotten how to move forward, but after a few minutes she picked up her pace. By the time she reached her mother's house six blocks away, her breath came in gasps. She retrieved the key from under the mat and stepped inside.

Her mother's house—tastefully decorated for the holidays—smelled of lemon oil. The cleaning lady must have been here yesterday. The remains of her mother's breakfast—a clean coffee cup, one small plate, and a table knife—sat in the dish drainer. The order stood in sharp contrast to her room at Libby's. Claire found the envelope from Lou and ripped it open to find a UNICEF Christmas card with a handwritten note tucked inside. A trip to Napa Valley. A new grandchild. A bumper crop of avocados on her backyard tree. Reading the newsy letter brought Lou's warm and vivid presence into her mother's dining room. Claire felt herself lighten for the first time in weeks. She stuffed the letter into her pocket and quickened her step back home.

Back at the apartment she dug through the box of odds and ends she'd brought with her. Where was it? Of course, it was at the very bottom. She grasped the address book and flipped to the well-worn page as she walked to the phone in the kitchen. She dialed and waited as her heart pounded.

"Dr. Kozel."

"Hi, Lou. It's Claire. I—I got your card. And I'm sorry to disturb you. I can call back if this is a bad time. You can send me a bill for a phone session."

Lou laughed. "I think you're entitled to a freebie. I care about you. What's up? The baby? Is the baby okay?" Claire heard the concern in Lou's voice and was glad she'd at least told Lou about the pregnancy.

"Baby's fine. A little girl. With a nice family, I think." Her words stalled. "It's—it's me."

"Tell me."

"I—I—I can't."

"Claire," Lou said. "Of course, you can tell me."

"No. I can't—have—more—b-b-babies."

"I don't understand."

"There was a problem. I almost died. They took my…"

"A hysterectomy?"

"Yes." She sniffed and dragged her sleeve across her face. Where was that box of Kleenex? She spun off a length of paper towels and rubbed at her nose.

"I'm so sorry."

"That's why I called. I can barely get out of bed. Or stop crying."

Lou didn't answer right away. Finally, she said, "You've racked up some pretty big losses lately. Sam. The Peace Corps. This baby. More babies. I think you're grieving."

"Grieving? How could that be the right word? No one died. I just don't know what to do."

"But you do know what to do." Lou's voice was gentle, but her words caused a silent argument to erupt in Claire's mind. Why did Lou do this? Always assume she was stronger, wiser than she felt? "You practice breathing and walking and eating and living until those things begin to feel normal again."

"You mean fake it 'til I make it?" That didn't seem like very sound advice.

A soft chuckle burst from Lou. "The answer will come in time. You don't need to solve your entire life today. Right now, you can't see farther than the headlights on a foggy night. But keep driving. Slowly. In time the fog will lift. You'll see the path ahead."

"What if I don't? In six months, I have to surrender her all over again. Permanently. You know, sign more papers. I'm not sure I can do that."

"Give yourself time to heal. Use that time."

"It's—it's so hard."

"I know. But, Claire, did your uterus define you before?"

"Well, no."

"Then the loss of it shouldn't define you now."

Claire was skeptical. "I'll try to believe that," she said, shaking her head. Yes, she'd called for advice, but what she got sounded more like platitudes. Anger bubbled up from somewhere. "Merry Christmas, Lou."

She slammed the phone into the cradle.

Immediately she regretted her action. Lou was right. Perhaps the same process that got her past the rape would help. Where to start? She looked around to see the sink full of dirty dishes and sighed. Lou once suggested that almost anything could become a meditation if she were present in the moment. Well, this was something.

Claire breathed in the clean fragrance of dish soap as she plunged her hands repeatedly into the sink, establishing a soothing little cadence of wash, rinse, and set to drain. She even scrubbed the sink, wiped down the counters, and started a load of laundry.

Satisfied with her accomplishment, she lit the burner under the teakettle and searched the cupboard for some chamomile tea. As the tea steeped in her cup, she opened yesterday's *Nevada Appeal* to the classified section.

Jobs. Female.

CHRISTMAS PASSED QUIETLY and Claire tried to move ahead. Now, in the deep dark heart of an Eastern Sierra winter's night, she unlocked the apartment door and pulled off her boots. She shook the January snow from her coat and hair as quietly as she could. Libby was already asleep. Eight hours on her feet in high heels was killing her, but the tips were good. Nothing else paid as much as cocktailing in a casino. At least not with her skills and in Carson City. She still couldn't believe she was back here. How many years had she dreamed of escaping the role she had played here? The bad girl. The wild girl. The one with so much wasted potential. Such a disappointment to her mother. No matter how diligently she focused on her goal, seeing people she knew—and who knew her—while dressed in this skimpy dancehall girl get-up at the Ormsby House Hotel-Casino—well, it was mortifying.

It didn't help that her body had changed. While thin, her formerly perky little breasts simply weren't. She'd lost muscle tone. She felt soft and squishy. The results of increased exercise were slow to materialize. Furthermore, it was still a struggle to get through a shift without a clench in her heart or the start of tears. There was no predicting what would set her off.

Tonight had been a perfect example. Her high school French teacher, Mr. Barton, sat in a cozy corner booth of the bar with an attractive woman Claire assumed was his wife. It was a special occasion. He wore a jacket and tie, while she wore a cobalt blue cocktail dress. Here was someone she respected and from whom she had always wanted respect in return. When he looked up and recognized her, standing there in her push-up bra and black fishnet stockings, she saw the look in his eyes. It wasn't esteem. She had feathers and sequins in her hair, for God's sake.

"Home for good now, Claire?"

"No, Monsieur Barton. Only 'til summer. Libby's getting married in June."

"I heard. Did you finish school?"

"*Oui. J'ai reçu un diplôme avec un dégrée en français.*" She smiled and hoped he'd be proud of her accent and her degree in French.

"*Grand! Que ferez-vous avec lui ?*" That was always the next question. What will you do with a degree in French?

"Travel." She shrugged one shoulder.

Mr. Barton nodded. "Didn't I hear something about the Peace Corps?"

God. Couldn't anyone keep their mouth shut?

"Yes, sir, but I changed my mind." She doubted he bought it. He'd probably heard the marijuana story. Once again, she had lived up—or down—to everyone's expectations. She had failed to redeem herself in her own eyes, in her mother's. If she got far enough away, Claire still believed that there was a chance that she could become a better person. Carson City was simply too small. No room to breathe here, to grow beyond expectations, to outrun her reputation.

At the moment, Paris seemed far enough. If she saved like crazy and sold her car, she might be able to stay away for a few months. Then maybe she'd be ready to find a real grown-up job. Or maybe she'd stay in Europe and work. That's why she wore this cocktail uniform, why she smiled at her customers. They were her ticket out. She straightened her shoulders, inhaled, and smiled.

"What are we celebrating tonight?"

"Tenth anniversary."

"*Félicitations! Ce que je peux obtenir pour vous?*" Claire had turned away then. They hadn't seen her tears.

Now, standing in front of the bathroom mirror, removing the overdone eye makeup that was part of her cocktail regalia, Claire wept again.

LITTLE BY LITTLE, by fits and starts, winter surrendered its grip on Carson City in the same manner and at about the same pace as Claire's gloom lifted. Lou had been right. Again. Claire had written to thank her and apologize.

Today, on a bright May morning, the cottonwoods were greening as Claire ran back down the hill from her routine run up Kings Canyon. The fresh air in her lungs energized her entire body. Some days she even felt the tiniest bit hopeful. Libby and Jack's wedding was a month away and then she'd start her own adventure. With the help of a travel agent, Claire had already purchased a Eurail pass and made her initial airline and hotel reservations in Paris. Her passport had arrived three days ago. Next month, she'd be running along the Seine.

The mailman was at her apartment door when she ran up. "Hi, George." He'd been the mailman in this neighborhood since she was a child. He delivered to her mother's office, Libby's parents' house. Everyone she knew.

"Glad I caught you, Claire. You need to sign for this." He raised a large, thick manila envelope in her direction. "Looks important."

Claire nodded as she signed. Probably tickets or something. "Thanks. Have a good day." She gasped when she saw the return address. Omaha. Her hands shook so badly her key couldn't find the lock. Would George have noticed the return address? And if so, who would he tell?

Jack had already walked her through what the next steps would likely be—a few witnessed and notarized signatures since she was out of state. She'd worried about who she could turn to for that, without anyone in town knowing or asking too many questions. Jack had kindly alerted his uncle's law office in Reno to expect her call.

───────

CLAIRE DELAYED OPENING the envelope all day, avoiding what she knew she had to do. Instead, she spent the day cleaning the apartment to within an inch of its life.

"Are we shooting a Clorox commercial? Are we expecting company? The health department?" Libby asked as she entered the apartment after school.

"No. But look at what arrived today." Claire, wearing rubber gloves and a bandana, cocked her head toward the kitchen table where the unopened envelope sat.

"You want me to open it?" Libby offered that afternoon

"No." Claire's heart was in her throat, remembering another envelope and Sam's eyes on her when she got the acceptance letter from the Peace Corps. This was worse, although she knew what it contained. She took off the gloves, her hands shaking as she picked up the envelope and flipped it over revealing the seal. She pried it up gently and removed the sheaf of papers. Watery words whirled before her eyes.

Termination of Parental Rights. Adoption Order.

A WEEK LATER, Claire climbed the stone steps of the historic building that housed Earl Cooper's law office. She'd declined Libby's repeated offers to accompany her. This was something she had to do by herself. For herself. For little Sam. Besides, she didn't want Libby to have to witness something she didn't entirely support. With Libby there, Claire worried she might not follow through on her plan.

"I'm Claire Jordan to see Mr. Cooper," she announced to the gray-haired woman wearing a gray twin-set and pearls seated at the first desk. Her mother called such women "wrens." They tried not to draw attention to themselves. Fran was one. Her mother was not.

"We're expecting you, Miss Jordan. I'm Marge and will act as your notary and witness."

Jack's uncle was a portly man with a flushed face and a walrus mustache. He stepped out of his office and introduced himself, shaking her hand. He invited her into the conference room signaling Marge to join them. Marge stood, stuck a pen in the tidy bun at the back of her head and followed them with what Claire guessed were her notary stamp and a large note-book. Marge closed the door behind them.

"Jack explained your situation and sent us copies of the documents. Do you have any questions, Miss Jordan?"

"I tried to read all this, but the words got in the way."

The lawyer smiled and nodded. "It's pretty straightforward. You are giving up the right to raise this child. She will no longer be yours."

Giving up? No! Claire protested silently. She hadn't given up anything. Like a good mother, she'd made a plan for the care of her child.

"I—I understand. But somewhere in there does it say that if she wants to contact me someday, I'm okay with that?"

Mr. Cooper paged through the document to find the right section. He nodded. "Yes. It appears so." Jack had indeed left a trail of breadcrumbs that her clever and curious daughter might follow one day. And little Sam's new parents had agreed.

CHAPTER TWENTY-THREE

Now: Somebody's Baby

*I*t was Claire's turn to accompany Libby on what could be her final chemo infusion. For weeks this summer, teacher friends and neighbors—dubbed "Libby's Rack Pack" —had happily chauffeured Libby to and from appointments and brought meals several times a week. Today, wearing a "Bald is the new black" t-shirt and a colorful knit cap with brown fringe, Libby settled into a recliner under a blanket as the nurse hooked up the IV.

"New hat? Claire asked.

"Uh-huh. Aunt Ellie made it." Libby ruffled her fingers through the brown yarn framing her face. "Looks almost like hair, right?"

Indeed, it did. Clever of Aunt Ellie to think of that. Once again, Claire marveled at Libby's ability to find some humor, some happiness even in this experience. Libby closed her eyes as the cocktail of lifesaving poison dripped into her veins.

"How are you and your mom doing?" Libby asked without opening her eyes.

"Ok, I guess." Claire shrugged. This morning she and her mother had avoided talking about the birthday cards, careful not to touch the still-tender bruise. Claire's fiery anger had burned itself out leaving only a few embers amid some cold ashes. It still hurt, but she'd begun to acknowledge the risk her mother had taken in opening that old wound. That courage may have taken a lifetime to reveal itself, but Claire had to admit, her mother was one gutsy broad. She knew she'd need some of that courage.

"When are you going to tell her about Grace?" Libby's earnest blue eyes opened.

That was always the question from Libby. As urgent as Claire's need to establish contact with Grace was, she wouldn't risk that until she'd told her mother the story. The whole story.

"Soon. Maybe today."

"How...?"

Where and how should Claire begin the conversation? With Sam? The Peace Corps? The photo? And how would her mother respond? Anger? Sadness? Disappointment? Hurt? All of them at once? For the remaining time at the infusion center, Claire and Libby tried to imagine and respond to all the possible scenarios. Claire hoped she could find a happy ending to the telling of this story.

After Claire dropped an exhausted Libby back at home and tucked her in bed, she began to wonder when she had become this person, this caretaker. Had she finally at this late date, developed some capacity for putting other's needs before her own? For mothering? Nonetheless, Claire's thoughts reverted to dread and self-doubt as she drove home.

LATE THAT AFTERNOON, Claire removed a manila envelope from her duffle and placed it on the dining room table in the patch of light streaming through the window. She poured two glasses of tea.

"How about taking a little break, Mom? I need to talk to you about something."

"That sounds ominous." Her mother tightened the closure on one more bag of surplus clothing to donate. She dragged the bag to lie with the others at the top of the stairs. Her mother wasn't using the cane this morning. More progress.

They sat opposite one another at the table, but Claire avoided her mother's eyes. The spoon and ice clinked against the glass as her mother stirred Splenda into her tea. Claire stalled, despite her many mental rehearsals, fiddling with the envelope's clasp until it broke.

"You were brave to show me those birthday cards." Claire's voice was little more than a choked whisper.

"I'm sorry it took me so long. I was wrong, but..."

Claire held up her hand and interrupted, "I think it's time I share my secret. To be honest with you."

"Have you been dishonest?" Puzzled lines appeared on her mother's forehead.

"Yes, Mom. A long time ago. A lifetime ago. I kept something from you."

"Oh, honey, I know you were a pretty wild kid. What does any of that matter now?"

"It matters because it changed my life. Forever."

Claire pulled the photograph of Grace from the envelope and slid it across the table to her mother, who now looked confused.

"Who is this?"

"My daughter. The daughter I had in 1972. The daughter I gave away."

"A daughter?" Her mother's eyes were transfixed by the young woman in the photograph.

The words, locked deep in Claire's heart for nearly thirty years, all needed to come out. Each part of the story vied for space to tell itself. Claire took another sip of her tea to settle her nerves and find the thread of the story.

"You remember Sam, don't you?"

"That nice boy with the garden shop? Of course. Oh, Claire...does he know?" She asked, her eyes riveted to the photo.

Claire shook her head, then looked at the ceiling in a thin attempt to keep from crying. The words tumbled out, in no particular order. A jumble of memory and pain and regret, punctuated by sobs and gulps of air. Sam's proposal. Her refusal. His father dying. The Peace Corps. Libby. Dr. Matt. The adoption. The blood.

When the torrent of Claire's words finally stopped, she saw tears in her mother's eyes. Her mother said, "I'm so sorry" as she reached across the table and clasped Claire's hand in both of hers.

"Sorry?" Neither she nor Libby had prepared for that reaction.

"Sorry, you went through all that alone. That you didn't feel you could tell me." Her mother dabbed at her eyes with a tissue. "I told myself years ago that I wouldn't do what my parents had done. You know, shut me out, abandon me. And yet I did it anyway."

"I didn't want to disappoint you." Claire gulped down a sob. "And I thought you'd make me marry Sam."

Her mother's hand now covered hers. "You didn't want to start out the way your dad and I started out."

"Or end up the way you ended up."

"Again, I'm sorry. For everything."

"Me too." Claire's breath and pulse slowed again.

"What's her name?"

"Grace."

"Oh, my. That was my grandmother's name, you know."

"I—I didn't know that. Her parents named her."

"She has your eyes. You see that, right?" Her mother shook her head slowly in wonder.

Claire felt the slightest bit of hope. Maybe their bond could knit itself back together. She removed Grace's letter from the envelope.

"She wants to meet me."

A WEEK LATER, Claire stood at the doorway of what would be her mother's "great room." An ironic name for the combination living/dining/kitchen in the small downstairs apartment. The windows were wide open to the summer heat as two masked workers sanded the hardwood floors. Her mom was directing the staff at her large and soon-to-be-vacated real estate office this morning, getting things ready for the move into the small office which would fill the eastern half of the ground floor.

If Claire needed office space, this would be big enough for— what exactly? What skills did she have after a lifetime spent on the road? Or would that be too much togetherness for her and her mother? The phone rang and she ran up the flight of steps to catch it before the machine picked up.

"Hello," she panted.

"Claire Jordan?"

"Yes," she said, beginning to think it was a telemarketer and she'd raced up the stairs for nothing.

"This is Grace Bassett. In Omaha."

"Oh. . . Grace," Claire croaked before her heart rose into her throat and she lost the ability to form words.

"I received your letter."

"I—I apologize for taking so long. My—my mom and my best friend were both ill. I was sort of overwhelmed. They're better now." Claire wouldn't admit the real reason to Grace nor her uncertainty about what to write. She'd finally decided to match what Grace had shared—a couple of paragraphs with her contact information and her willingness to be in touch. Claire looked at the smiling photo of Grace now posted on the refrigerator door. She shouldered the phone and opened a bottle of water.

"I'm glad you wrote. I have great parents, by the way. But when you're adopted, there are always questions. Or at least there were for me."

"For birth-mothers, too. I wondered what your life was like. Every day." Claire reminded herself to breathe. She gulped water, trying to dislodge whatever was stuck in her throat. She removed the photo from the door and sank onto a barstool. She cleared her throat. "So, what is your life like?"

"My life is good. Very good." Grace's sweet chuckle made Claire smile into the phone.

"You can't imagine how glad I am to hear that. You finished school?" Silly. Of course, she's finished with school. She's almost thirty.

"Yeah, nursing. A BSRN from South Dakota State."

"A good career. They'll always need good nurses."

"That's what my parents say. But I felt I couldn't stay in the Midwest without experiencing something more exotic. Someplace not quite so—I don't know—white bread and mayonnaise? At least once."

"I can understand that." Was there a genetic predisposition for adventure-seeking? What else had Grace unwittingly inherited. Recklessness? Stubbornness?

"My folks hated the idea." Of course, they did. "I spent two years in Africa with the Peace Corps. Child and maternal health."

"I was on my way to the Peace Corps when I found out I was pregnant with you." Claire heard a sharp intake of breath.

"I just got goosebumps."

"Me too."

"So, you didn't go?" Grace's voice had an empathetic quality now. Do they teach that in nursing school?

"No, but I've been to Africa since then with several other relief organizations. Child and maternal health." Claire stopped a moment, remembering. The work with babies had proven too painful for her. "Eventually I moved into funding education and economic development, mostly in Haiti. Where are you working now?"

"I'm working at a hospital in Omaha. Labor and delivery. And I'm getting married next summer."

"Someone from home?"

"Yes. We grew up together."

"So, you were friends before you fell in love?"

"Yeah. My mom says that's a good way to start."

"I agree." Claire nodded into the receiver. "Such an exciting and happy time in your life."

"Part of that happiness is finding you. Are you married? Did you have more children?"

"No, never married. No more babies." Claire felt the ancient hollowness deep in her belly, but she did not want Grace to feel sorry for her. "We can never tell what turns our lives will take. I have good friends. I've had a good life." This was getting pretty deep for a first conversation. The dialog stalled for a moment. Grace spoke up.

"Umm, my mom's here. She wants to say something." The reference to another woman as Grace's mom, stung for a second, even though Claire knew she'd done nothing to warrant the title.

"This is Gail. I wanted to say thank you. You blessed us. Tom and I feel so fortunate to be Grace's parents." Gail's voice caught. "We thank God for you and Grace every day."

The words, the emotion caught Claire by surprise. She pressed her lips together as her chin trembled. Several long moments passed before she could respond. "No. Thank you."

Grace came back on the phone. "Mom's crying."

"Me too," Claire managed between sniffs.

"Well, since neither of you can talk through all the bawling, let me tell you that Mom and I are going to my grandmother's in Bishop over Labor Day weekend. We fly into Reno on Thursday morning and drive through Carson City on the way. Could we meet somewhere for lunch?"

"Of course!" Anytime. Anywhere.

"I'm glad you turned out to be so nice, so normal." Claire laughed to herself at being called normal. But then, Grace hadn't met her yet.

A BABY'S cries echo through that large house with long dark hallways and countless locked doors. Claire can never find the baby. This time, however, she discovers a previously unknown set of French doors at the end of a hallway. She opens them cautiously and steps through. She stands on a sunny balcony overlooking an expansive, formal garden filled with flowers planted in colorful patterns. As she gazes out across the peaceful scene, she realizes the crying has stopped.

Claire rolled over and looked at the clock. Six-thirty. A.M. Grace and Gail would arrive around twelve-thirty. While the few emails they'd exchanged assuaged much of her uneasiness, Claire's nerves fizzed as she repeated the mothers' refrain of, "I only did what I thought was best." How much could that excuse?

Rising from the sofa bed, she ran her fingers through the still short bristles of her hair and performed an abbreviated sun salutation in the tiny space between the bed and the desk. As she finished, she heard her mother in the kitchen. Only a few more days of sharing the apartment, which had seemed to grow smaller lately. Her mother's new place downstairs was nearly ready. The speed and efficiency with which the job had been completed was a testament to not only her mother's skills and connections but also her reputation for not tolerating delays.

Claire stepped into the kitchen.

"' Morning, Mama."

"Good morning. I didn't wake you, did I?" Her mother filled the coffee maker with fresh water.

"No. I was awake." Claire measured coffee into the basket, lost count, dumped it back into the can, and started over. She pushed the brew button and ran downstairs to get the paper from the stoop. Buster, who'd been waiting under a parked car, greeted her with an impatient yowl.

"Good morning, Buster." He bore the scars of a rough, adventurous life, but seemed to have settled into old age with some calm. She stepped back inside and scooped kibble into his bowl. He rubbed against her leg and permitted a brief scratch behind his ears before turning his attention to his breakfast. Claire breathed in the fresh morning air and climbed the stairs.

Her mother opened the paper. "This is a pretty exciting day, becoming a grandmother and all."

"A little belatedly, but yes." Claire couldn't say she was becoming a mother though. Maybe it was too late for anything meaningful. Perhaps meeting Grace would be enough.

"Are you sure you want me here? I don't want to intrude."

"I'm sure. No more secrets." Besides, her mother possessed social skills Claire didn't. Sylvia Jordan, the consummate hostess, could put strangers at ease.

Claire poured two cups of coffee and sat at the counter. Her mother, perched on a barstool, kept the Business section of the *Nevada Appeal* and handed Claire the front page. Claire liked to read the Opinion page first, then the comics and horoscopes. Only afterward did she scan the rest of the paper for news that interested her.

Claire stood to pour more coffee. She wasn't hungry but thought she'd better eat something. "English muffin?"

Her mother nodded. "There's some of Fran's peach jam in the fridge. I think it's the last jar I have." Fran McCormack's peach jam was legendary and even more prized now that there wouldn't be anymore.

"I'll ask Libby."

"No, her family should have whatever is left. We'll make do with Smuckers." Her mother looked briefly at the half-full jar of jam with the handwritten label before turning her gaze out the window. The loss of Fran was oddly painful for her mother. The two had frequently been at odds. The toaster dinged, bringing her mother's attention back to the room.

"What's for lunch today?"

"That chicken salad of Libby's. The one with grapes and cashews."

"Mmmm. Need any help?" While she appreciated her mother's offer, this morning, it put Claire on edge. Perhaps they had been living in close quarters for too long. Each of them had lived alone for so many years, they were unaccustomed to all this togetherness. Claire scolded herself for her adolescent reaction and quickly replaced it with gratitude. After all, her mother had been the one who stayed. She took a breath before responding.

"I only need to cut up the chicken and assemble the salad. Not much. How about setting the table?" Claire used paper towels as napkins and had trouble remembering on which side to place the fork. "Maybe you could do something with those flowers I bought yesterday? And arrange the brownies on a plate?" She'd opted for store-bought brownies but didn't want them to look store-bought.

"Of course. How about getting the good dishes down?"

Claire put down the half-eaten muffin and stood barefoot on a chair to retrieve dishes from the top shelf of the built-in china closet. Her mother's daintily patterned Bavarian china and pink Depression glass stemware would stay in Claire's apartment after the move. There was no room downstairs. While her mother seemed perfectly willing to sell or donate them, for some reason she could not name, Claire was not. She recalled drinking ginger ale from the goblets on New Year's Eve, and orange juice for her birthday breakfast. Even after her father left, her mother had made an effort to make holidays special by using the good china.

A goblet slipped from Claire's hands and shattered on the hardwood floor.

"Oh no!"

"No matter." Her mother set down her coffee cup.

"But. . . I'm so sorry. . ." Claire nearly cried as she looked at the shards of pink glass. She felt childish and clumsy.

"It doesn't matter. Honestly. I'll get the broom. You stay up on that chair."

"Yes, Mama." Even now, someone else was cleaning up her mess.

AFTER SHOWERING AND DRESSING, Claire looked at herself in the bathroom mirror. She couldn't do much about her still-too-short hair but put on a little eyeliner and some rosy lip-gloss. She shrugged at her reflection and turned her attention to the lavish application of Windex and Lemon Pledge.

Wine, sodas, and iced tea were chilling along with the assembled salad. Her mother had not only arranged the flowers and set the table, but she'd also dusted the brownies with powdered sugar and placed them on a pedestal cake-plate with a paper doily.

Now, a little afternoon, Claire sat near the tall windows that faced King Street, alternately gazing from the street to the apartment with more than a tinge of anxiety. Grace and Gail would undoubtedly be judging her. Was she good enough? She realized she would be judging Gail as well. Was she good enough?

"Everything looks lovely, dear. It will be fine." Her mother tried to reassure her from where she sat thumbing through a magazine. Claire suspected she was only feigning indifference.

Claire's hands squeezed themselves into tight fists. She'd spent a good portion of her life concealing and then running away from this one incident. In a few minutes, she'd confront the consequences of that choice in the flesh. "What if. . . what if she doesn't like me?"

"She already likes you. And she's half you, remember? Besides, how could she not like you?"

"Let me count the ways." Claire turned toward her mother. "Mothers and daughters don't always get along. You and I didn't."

"That's different. We had proximity working against us. Mothers are always in their daughters' faces."

"You mean she'll like me because she doesn't know me?"

"No dear. But you two missed those awful adolescent years. You're both adults now. You're meeting on even ground."

Claire glanced out the window for the hundredth time and gasped, "Oooh! They're here!"

Grace and Gail got out of their little rental car. Grace stood nearly a head taller than Gail. Sparks of copper in Grace's curly auburn hair escaping a messy bun stirred something deep in her memory. The square shoulders, the way she squinted as she looked up at the building. Oh, my God. This was Sam's child. Her heart leaped into her mouth and stopped her breath.

Unable to contain herself, Claire flew down the stairs.

"I saw you drive up. I couldn't wait," Claire said breathlessly. The three laughed nervously, hesitated, and then fell into a warm embrace. They climbed the stairs. Claire introduced her mother when they reached the top.

"Nice to meet you, Mrs. Jordan. You have a lovely home," Gail said, offering her hand.

"Please, call me Sylvia," her mother said with a slight catch in her voice, the only sign of the emotion bubbling below the surface. Was that a tear about to spill down her cheek? Claire hugged her mother's shoulder then and offered cool drinks.

"I'll be moving downstairs next week. I had a fall on the stairs a while back. I think I need to live somewhere flat."

"Claire told me about your fall. You seem to get around okay now," Grace observed. There was only a hint of a limp now, after six weeks of physical therapy.

"Oh, yes. I'm fine—it's only the stairs . . ."

They sat down for lunch. Claire passed the salad and rolls and worried about what to say. Gail spoke first, clearing her throat.

"Part of my wanting to meet you was pure parental pride. I wanted to show Grace off to you. What a truly beautiful gift she was." Gail beamed as she spoke, her blue eyes crinkling behind her glasses. Gail must be close to sixty and yet she didn't appear to be wearing make-up. Not even lipstick. Her glow came from somewhere inside.

"I don't blame you." Claire felt some pride too, although she knew hers was unearned.

"When we flew out to pick her up, I was so focused on finally being a mom, I didn't think much about you. I'm sorry. I was so grateful to be getting a baby, this baby." Gail patted her daughter's hand.

"You weren't supposed to worry about me."

Gail took a bite of salad. Sadness briefly flashed across her face while she chewed. "We'd wanted a baby for so long. And then I had that hysterectomy. Those were dark times."

"I understand." Claire wouldn't say how deeply she understood. Dark times indeed.

"And when Grace was accepted into the Peace Corps and I

knew I wouldn't see her for two years, my heart nearly broke."
Now Gail grasped Claire's hand, looking into her eyes. "But
you said good-bye for—forever."

"Not the same at all. I didn't have a lifetime of shared expe-
riences and memories. I knew what Grace needed and what I
had to do. What I'd promised to do. I wouldn't go back on
that."

"Still. . ." Gail shook her head.

"May I ask a few questions?" Grace said.

Claire looked at her and swallowed hard. Here it comes.
"Sure."

"Who is my father?" Despite being part of a loving family,
Grace wanted more. A biological connection? Claire could iden-
tify with that. She longed to know more about her own father.
So far, her internet searches had led to dead ends. Phone
numbers that were no longer in service. Letters returned. How
does a person simply disappear? Was he some sort of
vagabond? In witness protection? A spy? Was he dead? She
refused to believe that.

"Sam." The knot in her stomach tightened as she intention-
ally withheld Sam's last name. Yes, a few secrets remained.
They had to—unless and until she told Sam everything. And
she couldn't see that happening. Ever. "He was a good man. I
loved him very much. That's where you got your red hair. But
he doesn't know about you. I don't know what his life is like
now. It doesn't seem right to spring this on him. I'm sorry."

"You didn't tell him you were pregnant?" It was hard not to
hear an accusation in her question, although there was only
kindness in her dark eyes.

"Let's not pry," Gail warned.

"It's all right. You see, we had already broken up when I
learned I was pregnant." Claire recounted more of her story,
starting with her father leaving.

Her mother spoke up then. "Claire had just learned that her

244

father and I had rushed into marriage when I learned I was pregnant. That didn't work out. I'm sure that contributed to her decision."

Claire smiled, grateful for her mother's defense.

"I knew if I told Sam, told anyone, they'd try to talk me into getting married."

Grace nodded. "But Mom said you named me Samantha. You must have still had feelings for him.

"I did. As I said, he was a good man. But I wasn't good enough to be your mother. I was stubborn and selfish. I wasn't willing to give up my plans." Claire admitted. Now, Grace knew the truth.

"Not selfish," asserted Gail, looking into Claire's eyes. "You gave us Grace. That's the most generous thing you could have done. You weren't selfish. Not one bit."

Claire considered what Gail was saying, thinking that she might indeed have done the right thing, but for the wrong reasons. Did that still count, Karma-wise?

CHAPTER TWENTY-FOUR

Now: Leaving on a Jet Plane

$\mathcal{L}$ibby counted the slices left of the three pizzas she'd ordered tonight. Norah and Annie were both home for a change and she knew Claire would show up—eventually. For nearly a year now, Claire had been part of the Cooper family's Friday night tradition.

"Sorry I'm late," Claire announced as she stomped the mid-January snow from her boots on the doormat in Libby's entry. She then unpacked a six-pack of micro-brew and two pints of Ben & Jerry's. Maggie jumped up to greet her.

"Maggie, down!" Libby scolded the aging border collie.

"I have news," Claire said as she opened a beer and then scratched behind Maggie's ears.

"You're leaving?" Libby knew this day would come. After taking the first quarter of school off to fully recover, her energy was back to normal. Her most recent bloodwork revealed no cancer. Even her hair had grown back.

"No. I'm staying! I want to be close to Mom." She took a slice of vegetarian from the box, sprinkled it with red pepper flakes, and sat down. "I'm opening a travel agency. A little one, anyway. A desk in mom's office." She took a bite and chewed slowly before continuing. "The internet travel business is growing, so I want to offer something different. Customized tours. Literary or spiritual, maybe? Or eco-touring? What do you think?" Claire sat back and took a long drink of her beer.

"I love it!" Libby felt relieved and happy.

Norah asked, "What about service vacations? Like the Peace Corps only short-term. You know, building a house, digging a well, or cleaning up after a hurricane?" Libby was grateful and proud of her daughter's contribution. This child had been a rebellious and selfish brat for most of her teens.

"Ooooh, I like that idea. I still have lots of contacts. You're so smart!" Claire said.

Norah beamed at the compliment. Norah and Claire had developed a special relationship. They often ran together, taking Maggie along. Lately, Norah had expressed an interest in Claire's relief work.

"Now I need your help. What should I call it? Escape Plan. Or Runaway, maybe?"

"So, autobiographical?" Libby laughed and reached for a notepad and pencil. "Annie, what do you think?"

"Well, if you're going to do stuff like a Jane Austen Tour or one based on the DaVinci Code, how 'bout Book Tour?" Of course, Annie was her reader.

"Yes, but that's not all. I'd like to offer spiritual ones too. Not only the Holy Land but Buddhism, Islam, Santeria...you know, ashrams in India. Retreats."

"Hmmm. . ." Everyone turned to look at Norah. "Spirit Quest?"

Claire chewed and swallowed. "Not bad. But wouldn't that put off people asking for help booking airline tickets to Minneapolis? I don't want to be too specific."

"Ticket to Ride?" offered Jack, who had been finishing off the last of the deep-dish pepperoni.

"And the teacher suggests, "Choose Your Own Adventure," Libby added.

Norah rolled her eyes. "I loved those books, Mom. When I was eight."

Jack, swallowed the last of his beer. "Maybe we're trying to be too clever. Claire isn't well-known here, but Sylvia is. Jordan Properties is an established entity. Use that familiarity to your advantage, especially since you're sharing an office. Maybe something simple like "Jordan's Journeys?"

Heads nodded all around.

"Need an assistant?" Norah asked eagerly.

"Maybe, but first I need some customers."

Libby was proud of Claire. She'd remade her life and was settled—happy even—and connected to those whom she loved and who loved her. Even Grace was part of her life. Maybe she didn't need a man, but didn't she want one?

In March, the ad appeared in the *Nevada Appeal*.

Jordan's Journeys

Customized tours. Specializing in travels off the beaten path.

Literary. Spiritual. Historical. Epicurean. Eco-touring. Adventure. Service.

A FEW MONTHS later in mid-May, Libby looked at her watch and stood in the crowded Disneyland Hotel conference room. The four-day literacy conference was winding down. One more session tomorrow morning and then a quick flight home in the afternoon. But this afternoon she was on a mission unrelated to teaching. She donned her sunglasses, shouldered the swag-filled Scholastic tote, and hurried toward the exit.

Last night in her hotel room, she'd opened the Orange County phone book and looked for Claude Jordan. He wasn't listed. Then, on a whim, she'd flipped pages until she reached the Ws—Wylder. She scanned down until her eyes stopped at Sam. Sam and Christine. Stone Hedge Court. Yorba Linda. Sam and Christine. Crap. Then she'd turned to the yellow pages. Nurseries. Wylder Nursery. See ad on page 582. A half-page ad. Expensive. They must be doing well. "Growing to meet your needs. Visit our newest branch!" and "Thistle Dew Nicely~Flowers and Gifts" next to a photograph of a petite, smiling blonde in a butcher apron that read, "Christy" in big, bold letters.

All night Libby debated with herself. The evidence pointed to an intact marriage. But certainly, people got divorced and remained business partners, right? She wasn't stalking Sam. No, she was merely gathering information. Still, she wouldn't tell Claire. Or Jack. They'd only discourage her. No, this is something she had to do. Libby wasn't sure what her goal was other than satisfying her curiosity. She needed to see for herself who Sam had become.

A map with a highlighted route lay on the passenger seat of the rental car. A neon pink sticky note held a scribbled address. The concierge at the hotel had assured her that the route he chose was the fastest and easiest despite her trepidation about Southern California freeways. He estimated half an hour. Libby's pulse quickened as she started the engine. She turned on the air conditioner and pulled out into traffic. She breathed a little easier once she merged onto the freeway.

Libby exited the freeway and turned onto Yorba Linda Boulevard where she found the Wylder Nursery parking lot crowded on a sunny Saturday afternoon. At least she wouldn't be the only person in the place. She parked and willed her heart to slow the ka-thump, ka-thump, ka-thump that she was sure was audible to anyone within a one-mile radius. She scanned the layout. Her mother would have loved this. Clear signage designated areas for sun and shade plants, perennials, vegetables, trees. . . and the most adorable Victorian-style green-house, Thistle Dew Nicely.

The little blonde—whom Libby recognized from the ad as Christy—carried a large arrangement to a waiting delivery van. Several helpers followed her with successive armloads of flowers. Must be a wedding. Christy ran back to the shop and returned with a clipboard which she proceeded to hand off to a red-haired twenty-something man who was presumably the delivery driver. Their son? Ka-thump, ka-thump, ka-thump.

The van drove off. Then she saw Sam. He approached Christy and said something Libby couldn't hear. Christy responded with a laugh. Sam bent to kiss the top of her head and loped back to someplace inside the nursery.

Well, there you have it, Libby. Nothing for Claire here. Move along.

CHAPTER TWENTY-FIVE

Then: We've Only Just Begun

*L*ibby and her mother had reached a momentary truce. Planning her wedding had not brought out the best in either of them. Every item from the guest list to the length of Jack's hair caused a row. No detail was too small to escape Fran McCormack's notice and critique. But today, their reflections in the full-length mirror of the small dressing room at the church belied the tension frothing beneath their smiling exteriors.

"Elizabeth Frances McCormack, you look beautiful! Just beautiful," her mother said. Wow. Her mom never complimented her without some equivocation. There was always some caveat, some minor correction. Here, let me fix this. Don't slouch. At the very least, there was an exasperated head shake accompanied by tsk-ing.

"Thanks, Mom."

Libby did feel beautiful. She'd lost that fifteen pounds and done a few repairs and alterations—mainly letting out the bust —on her mother's vintage 1945 ecru gown, the one sewn by her grandmother. It fit perfectly. The cap sleeves. The princess seams. The covered buttons. The wide scoop neckline, extending to the tips of her shoulders, covered in something her mother called "illusion." Libby chuckled to herself that a long-line strapless bra was responsible for another illusion.

The fact that Claire would be her only attendant had been the focus of another clash with her mother, who'd urged Libby to choose someone "more appropriate." Teacher friends, sorority sisters, cousins—anyone without Claire's shady reputation that her mother still tried to keep separate from Libby. Libby had stood firm. Only one. Only Claire.

Another argument stood out now as she was about to become Jack's wife. Her name. When she'd mentioned not changing it, her mother had been shocked.

"I'd think you'd be proud to take Jack's name!"

"I'm proud to be a McCormack." And she was.

"Marriage means sacrifices, Elizabeth. Each person gives up something. Perhaps you aren't mature enough to marry if that's your attitude."

"Is it immature to want to retain some piece of my own identity? Besides, the man isn't expected to change his name."

"What does Jack say? Doesn't he want you to take his name?"

"He says it's up to me. After all, it's my name." When she'd complained to Jack about her mother's response, he'd encouraged her not to give in to her mother's intimidation.

"But what will my friends think?" her mother had snorted. "That you're some bra-burning women's libber? Think about that!"

Libby had felt her face flush. Why did her anger always show like this? "Your friends are not my concern. Frankly, it's none of their business. And from now on, it's none of yours. It's between Jack and me. Period."

Libby smiled now, remembering the stunned look on her mother's face. The subject hadn't come up again. Nor had Libby revealed the offer of a job at Jack's uncle's new office in

Las Vegas. Vegas was booming and Jack's family lived there, so the offer was tempting. Nevertheless, to keep the peace in the weeks before the wedding, Libby kept her mouth shut. Once they'd made a decision, she and Jack would announce it. Together.

"Flower delivery!" Claire called as she entered with two bouquets and handed one to Libby. Following Sylvia's advice—which only served to aggravate her mother further—Libby had chosen a profusion of bright pink and yellow roses, blue delphinium, and daisies. The colors of wildflowers. Libby had even let Claire select her own dress, a long halter sundress in pale periwinkle blue. Claire's long blond hair was braided and pinned up off her neck, with sprigs of baby's breath tucked in here and there. Libby's hair was pulled up under a fall of heavily lacquered false curls. No chance of ruining this do, come heat, humidity, or hurricane.

Her mother looked at her watch. "I'll send Dad back." She kissed Libby on the cheek and clucked under her breath, "At least she could have worn a bra."

Moments later, Libby's dad poked his head in the door.

"Ready, Little Bit?" he asked. Libby smiled.

"You bet, Daddy." For all the tension with her mother, her dad always calmed her. Made her feel safe and secure. Jack did the same thing. She heard organ music now. Her pulse quickened with pleasure as she took her father's arm.

Claire walked down the aisle in cadence with the music. When she was in place, the organ chords announced Libby's arrival. One hundred pairs of eyes were on her now, but the only ones she saw were Jack's. He looked—well—he looked awed. Libby beamed back at him, her heart nearly burst. After today she would be proud to call herself Elizabeth McCormack-Cooper.

FEELING SOMEWHAT TIPSY, Claire teetered on her platform sandals as she stood in the shade next to Libby and the keg of beer. The ceremony in the dark, cool, ancient sanctuary at St. Teresa of Avila Church contrasted with the brightness of the reception in the McCormacks' backyard, where everything was in bloom. Mason jars holding bouquets of cut blossoms lined up along the centers of the long tables Libby had borrowed from school. The buffet of cold ham, rolls, baked beans, and assorted salads crowded tables on the patio. Claire sipped her beer.

Earlier, Dr. Matt and Aunt Ellie had taken Claire aside to inquire about her health and her plans. Now, they chatted with her mother, causing her belly to twitch with anxiety. Earl Cooper had discreetly nodded his greeting earlier. Claire had fretfully chewed the nail polish off her thumb and now hid it inside her clenched fist.

Libby's mother talked with Jack's parents and Uncle Earl over their glasses of beer. The beer was doing its job. Everyone seemed to be enjoying themselves. Even Libby's older brothers, John and Patrick, in town with their wives and children were laughing over something. John's puffed up carriage and crew-cut never let anyone forget his status as a naval officer. Nevertheless, he avoided making eye-contact with Claire. No doubt he was as embarrassed as she was about a long-ago one-night stand. He'd been so full of himself after graduating from Annapolis and before heading off for sea-duty. He was kinda dull and a bit of a bully, but for some reason, they'd had sex. Quick and unsatisfying sex. Claire hoped Libby never found out. While she had no personal history with Patrick, she was pretty sure he was in on the secret. Libby's brother Keith—who was still her favorite—was the kindest and gentlest, the most like Mr. Mac, and was headed to grad school to become a family counselor. She and Libby had laughed at the McCormack clan's need for an in-house therapist.

Speaking of which, Mitch's attempts at sobriety seemed to be taking the day off. He'd started drinking well before the reception. When he passed by Claire on his way to the keg, he'd called her the Maid of Dis-honor. And so taken by his cleverness, he'd repeated it loudly to John, who'd snickered. One more reason she was happy to be leaving Carson City behind her.

Libby swept a stray curl behind Claire's ear.

"When do you leave for Paris?" Libby asked. "You told me, but I've forgotten again. . ."

"Wednesday. Early." Claire drained her cup and reached to refill it.

"I won't see you after today." Libby's chin wrinkled like she might cry.

At that moment, a shriek erupted and Claire caught a sudden movement in her peripheral vision. Mrs. Mac aimed her all-too-familiar pointer finger at Libby as she practically flew across the yard toward them.

"Jack's got a job in Vegas? You're leaving?!" Mr. Mac stood and followed his wife. Jack rushed to Libby's side. All eyes followed as Mrs. Mac screamed at Libby.

"I—I—we..." was all the stunned and red-faced Libby could utter.

"When were you going to tell us?"

Claire felt some sympathy for Mrs. Mac, who seemed to be a little worse for the beer. Her lipstick smeared, her corsage askew. Still, Claire wouldn't stand by and watch her embarrass Libby. And certainly not at her wedding. Like a traffic cop, Claire stepped between Libby and her mother and put up her hand.

"Stop," she said with enough force that Mrs. Mac froze, eyes wide, face flushed, mascara streaming. Claire stood still despite the fierce shaking going on inside her. What had she done?

"Let's take this inside, Franny," Mr. Mac said, his hand

cupping her shoulder. In a small, silent parade, the five of them walked past the gawking guests and into the house. They sidled past friends who were manning the kitchen and down the dim hall into Libby's old bedroom. Jack closed the door behind them.

Sobs choked Mrs. Mac's words as she turned on Libby. "How c-c-could you m-make plans like this without t-telling us? We're your p-p-parents. Your f-family."

Claire squared her shoulders and stepped between mother and daughter again. It took considerable energy to turn down her volume.

"Yes, you are her parents, but she's married now. Remember?" Claire said, gesturing toward Libby and Jack, who stood together, dumbfounded.

"But leaving town? I thought..."

Claire took another deep breath and in the calmest voice she could muster, said what must have been lurking beneath the surface for years.

"You thought what? That Libby would remain your obedient daughter forever? That things would always be the same?" Claire took another breath. "You've often said you wanted Libby to think for herself and not be so easily influenced by others. Especially me. But what you meant was that you didn't want her influenced by anyone but you."

"But..." Mrs. Mac spluttered. "But, her family is here..."

"No," Claire continued, her voice practically a whisper. "Your family is here. From now on, Libby's family is wherever Jack is."

Mrs. Mac's face crumpled in shock.

His arm still around his wife, Mr. Mac spoke to his daughter. "You do what you and Jack think is right, Libby. Your mother was—surprised. That's all." He led his wife upstairs to collect herself.

Claire's heart galloped. Had she overstepped? Could Libby forgive her?

"Wow." Jack was beside Claire now and planting a kiss on her cheek. "Maybe you should be the lawyer instead of me."

Claire laughed a nervous laugh. "I'm sorry. I don't know what happened there. So, you're moving to Vegas?"

Libby shook her head and smiled. "We may have to now."

By mid-July Libby and Jack were home from their honeymoon in Yosemite. Jack studied for the bar and commuted to his uncle's office in Reno. Together they'd started a list of the pros and cons about moving to Vegas. That chart had remained on the kitchen table for days. Each of them added advantages or disadvantages as they thought of them.

For Libby, using reason—and not emotion—to come to a decision was new. When written down in black and white, the choice was easy. The job in Vegas would focus on gaming law, an area Jack cared little for. Working in Northern Nevada and near the capital could mean the potential for work at Nevada's Supreme Court or the AG's office. Those were appealing. Libby loved her job and her school and hated the idea of starting over. And they both loved the proximity to Lake Tahoe, the trees, the mountains, and the changing seasons. Vegas was simply bare and hot by comparison. As it turned out, the only compelling reason to move was to get away from her mother. Like cutting off one's nose to spite one's face. That knowledge gave Libby a sense of her own power that she was determined to hold onto.

This morning she reread Claire's most recent postcard. Libby couldn't help comparing their honeymoon camping trip with that trip to Paris. She scratched at the souvenir mosquito bites on her legs. She and Jack would take a trip like that someday. She stuck the postcard onto the refrigerator and looked over her to-do list.

Thank-you notes. This Photo by Unknown Author is licensed under CC BY-SA

This Photo by Unknown Author is licensed under CC BY-SA

Gifts put away. This Photo by Unknown Author is licensed under CC BY-SA

This Photo by Unknown Author is licensed under CC BY-SA

Exchange 4 crockpots and 3 fondue sets (an ice bucket and some good wine glasses?)

Deal with all the boxes (Jack)

Deposit wedding checks. This Photo by Unknown Author is licensed under CC BY-SA

This Photo by Unknown Author is licensed under CC BY-SA

Buy photo album (large) and extra pages. This Photo by Unknown Author is licensed under CC BY-SA

This Photo by Unknown Author is licensed under CC BY-SA

Assemble wedding album

She poured another cup of coffee and settled happily into the task of sorting photographs and mementos into piles, arranging them in sequence, writing on the back of each photo —who, when, where. While that scene with her mother had somehow not been caught on film, a few photos did show her becoming increasingly disheveled. Her dad had quietly apologized to Libby, explaining that her mother had been so anxious about the wedding, she'd taken a tranquilizer before the ceremony with a shot of whiskey. And they all thought Mitch would be the one to make a scene. Ha!

JACK WALKED in after work carrying the mail as Libby placed the last photo in the album.

"It's all done," Libby said proudly, closing the book. "Our entire married life in one album."

"All six weeks, eh? You gonna keep this up?"

"Probably not, but it feels good to have this done. I hate loose ends."

Jack scanned the envelopes and handed one to Libby. "Speaking of loose ends."

It was addressed to Libby McCormack in clear, bold script. The return address read, "Sam Wylder, Yorba Linda, California."

CHAPTER TWENTY-SIX

Now: I Will

Claire dozed on the mid-September flight to Omaha and awoke sweating. Shit. Another hot flash. Even without a uterus, she hadn't escaped menopause. Sitting up, she took an ice cube from the cup on the tray table and let it melt on the back of her neck. A chill dripped down her back as she opened the air conditioning vent and ran her fingers through her damp hair.

The invitation to Grace's wedding—a mostly family affair—had surprised Claire. She'd considered not attending, to avoid awkward introductions and small talk, but Grace had stubbornly insisted. She learned how hard it was to say no to one's child.

The view out of the window revealed a flat, nearly featureless landscape aside from the patchwork of fields. No mountains. No river-carved canyons. No wonder Grace wanted to see more of the world. When the pilot announced they were arriving, Claire took several long deep breaths to cool and calm herself.

Gail waved as Claire stepped out of the gate. They greeted each other with warm hugs as a quiet man wearing aviator sunglasses and a buzz-cut disguising a deeply receding hairline looked on. Tom. Grace's dad.

Gail had invited Claire to come to town early to attend the rehearsal dinner on Friday night and to stay through Monday. At their house. Gail wouldn't hear of her getting a hotel room. Both mother and daughter had been so persistent, Claire had finally relented. Now though, she felt a definite chill coming from Tom. Uneasy didn't begin to describe her feelings. Nevertheless, she was determined to break the ice somehow. If she couldn't, she'd change her plane reservation and leave right after the wedding, using her elderly mother as an excuse.

"You must be Grace's dad." She put out her hand.

Tom's smile was closed-mouth and tentative, his manner cool but polite as he shook her hand. The exact opposite of the warm, bubbly Gail.

"Let's get your luggage," Tom offered.

"This carry-on is all I have. I never check a bag. After traveling for a living, I got pretty good at packing light. Lost bags can be a nightmare in third-world countries." She felt compelled to keep talking, filling the space between them.

"Makes sense," Gail replied. "We don't travel much."

"I'm sure a veterinary practice makes it hard to get away."

"It does, but we have a new partner now," Gail added. "One of Grace's cousins, Laura, finished her training last year. We should be able to get away more often now, won't we Tom?"

"Uh-huh," he replied.

"And with Grace living out of state, we'll have to travel if we want to see her." Claire knew that Grace's fiancé had been offered a job at the University of Oregon.

"Grace got a job?"

"Not yet, but she's not worried. Plenty of jobs for good labor and delivery nurses. She's also applied for jobs in public health and at the campus clinic." Remembering campus health, Claire nodded.

Tom led them toward the exit past the Omaha Steaks kiosk. Their oversized SUV bore a Bush-Cheney bumper sticker and a Jesus fish.

"An outdoor wedding sounds lovely."

"Humpf...that sure wasn't our idea. That was all Grace," Tom said. "A wedding should be in a church. But our girl is pretty stubborn. Even threatened to elope." Unwittingly Claire had touched a sore spot.

"What are parents supposed to do?" Gail shrugged. "Every young woman deserves the wedding she wants. At least our old pastor—the one who baptized her—is performing the ceremony." Gail patted her husband's arm.

Claire scrambled to find a safe topic. She remembered her mother's advice. Let people talk about themselves. Look for common ground. Nevertheless, the drive to the Bassett's house was short and mostly silent. Their tree-lined neighborhood featured older homes, many sheathed in white asphalt shingles. Tom parked in the driveway beside the house. Three medium-sized dogs of indeterminate breed greeted them at the back door and yipped in greeting but didn't jump. Gail excused herself to make lunch.

"Good dog. Good dog. Yes, you're a good dog!" Tom rewarded each with a scratching of ears. "Meet Belle, Booger, and Blue."

"Well, hello kids," Claire bent and offered her hand for a sniff. "They're great. Somehow, I thought you'd have, um. . ." Belle rolled over for a belly rub.

"Bassets?" Tom chuckled. "We had one years ago. Stretch. But these guys needed us."

"It's hard to imagine anyone not wanting these guys. They're wonderful."

"People are strange. They don't realize that when you adopt an animal, it takes time to train and care for them, to help them become a pet you can live with." Okay, finally a topic he wants to talk about.

"People give up?"

"Every day. You have no idea how many are dropped off at our office in the middle of the night. Sometimes in a crate. Sometimes tied up. Some are sick or injured. But all of 'em are scared." Tom looked away for a moment, obviously remembering something sad.

"But you can't take them all in. You'd be overrun."

"No. The local Humane Society is great. And there are specific breed rescues. Beagles, Dalmatians. . ."

"But, older dogs? Mutts?" Now Booger and Blue were rolling over, insisting on their belly rubs. Claire squatted on the linoleum floor, surrendering to their demands.

"Yeah, they're harder to place. If we don't have a quorum, and they get along with the rest of the pack, we'll consider adding one. In the past, five was our limit. Beyond that, they don't get enough attention, in my opinion. But with Grace gone, I think three may be all we can handle."

"At home, I sometimes run with my friends' border collie. I've never had a dog. Always gone too much. I do have a part-time cat though. Big ol' marmalade guy."

"Part-time?"

"Sort of came with the house. He lives outside. Comes around to say hello every day. We feed him. And once when he was hurt, he allowed me to get close enough to get him into a crate and to the vet."

"And?"

"Needed to have a wound cleaned up. Gave him shots while we were there. Since then we seem to have an understanding."

"Cats are funny. You don't choose them. They choose you."

Just then, Grace burst in followed by a tall, broad-shouldered young man in basketball shorts. They'd been running.

"You're here! Adam, this is Claire Jordan." Tom backed away then and disappeared down the hall with Claire's bag.

"Pleased to meet you, Ms. Jordan." Claire looked up into kind blue-gray eyes. He must be at least six-four.

"It's Claire." She offered her hand, which was swallowed whole in Adam's. "I'm happy to meet you, too. Grace has told me so much about you. Congratulations on the Oregon job. You must be excited."

"Yes, ma'am. But a little sad, too. Our families are here," Adam sighed.

"New beginnings are always a mix of emotions. Excited, scared, hopeful, anxious..." Claire imagined Tom and Gail's heartbreak at having their only child live halfway across the country. She felt a little guilty for her happiness that Grace and Adam would be closer to her.

After lunch, Claire excused herself and settled into a sweet room with flowered wallpaper, a patchwork quilt, and a white Bible on the nightstand. She kicked off her shoes and stretched out on the bed, hoping she could settle her mind, calm her unease at being here in a strange place surrounded by near-strangers.

Claire's standard technique to calm herself—slow and rhythmic breathing—must have worked. When she opened her eyes, the sun's lower angle made the light golden. Through the window, she watched Tom play with the dogs in the large shaded backyard. He tossed balls, which the dogs joyfully retrieved and dropped expectantly at his feet. Anyone who loves animals the way he does isn't a cold or unfeeling person. And anyone who raised Grace. . . No. He's a loving, protective father. He perceives Claire as a threat. And like one of those awful people who abandon dogs at his office. Claire felt a stab of recognition. That's it.

She changed into running clothes and shoes and went out to the yard.

"Mind if I take someone for a run before supper?"

"Really?"

"Yes. I like running with a four-legged friend. And after the plane ride, I need to move." Belle dropped the ball at her feet, sat, and looked up eagerly. "Who needs a little exercise?" Claire tossed the ball.

"They all do. We didn't get our run in earlier, that's why I'm out here now. I should go too. Let me change. It won't take me but a minute."

"Sure." This was better than she'd hoped.

Tom returned in a t-shirt and shorts. They headed down the flat, tree-lined street, but soon came to a trail with a few walkers, joggers, and other dogs. Tom had Booger and Blue on long leashes. Claire ran alongside Belle, her new best friend. The dogs knew the drill. They stayed close and didn't bark or stop to sniff and pee.

"The circuit is about two miles. Okay?"

"Piece o' cake. I'm used to running at 4700 feet. And uphill." No brag, just fact. The humidity here gave the air weight though, reminding her of the years spent in the tropics.

Tom ran ahead in silence for several minutes. Claire took the initiative and caught up to him. "Thank you for allowing me to stay in your home."

"Grace insisted. And like you heard, she's pretty stubborn." He shrugged.

"I'm sorry to have been the cause of any trouble. I offered to stay at a hotel. But Gail..." Claire was grateful they were running. It made conversation easier.

"It isn't any trouble. But they'd met you. I hadn't. I guess I'm a little hesitant about who I invite into my home."

"I don't blame you."

"Sorry. It wasn't my intent to make you feel unwelcome." Intent or not, that was certainly the effect.

"You haven't." Politeness won out over the truth.

"Grace and Gail are the world to me. When I think about potential threats to my family, I see red flags. Even though Grace is a grown woman, I'm still her dad." He stopped to catch his breath and wipe the sweat from his face with his shirt. "Not sure what your motives are, I guess."

"My motives?" Claire stopped to look at him. The dogs took the opportunity to sniff and pee.

"What do you want from Grace?" He slid his sunglasses down his nose and looked straight into Claire's eyes.

She returned his gaze. "I'm not sure I want anything. Of course, I've wondered about her. Worried about her. Was she healthy, happy? But I made a decision when she was born and I stuck to my promise."

"Until...?"

"Until I received Grace's letter. I can't deny that I feel a huge sense of relief and pride and even love."

"But you gave her up." They stepped aside to let a young woman pushing a three-wheeled jogging stroller pass. Tom smiled and nodded.

"Yes, but I didn't abandon her. I made a plan. I chose you and Gail to parent a baby I knew I couldn't raise. And from the woman Grace has turned out to be, I am more certain than ever I made the right choice."

Tom kept his eyes fixed on her. "So, you don't want. . ."

Claire tried to convey assurance. "Grace already has two parents."

"When I heard you weren't married, didn't have other children, that perhaps. . ."

"I wanted yours?"

"Something like that." Tom turned and resumed running. Claire followed.

"As for not marrying, I never found anyone worth the trouble."

"But no more children? That would cause most women considerable grief. I remember what Gail and I went through."

Claire weighed what to say next. "For me, it wasn't a choice. There were complications after Grace was born. She would be my only child."

"I'm sorry." Tom stopped again and looked at her over his sunglasses. "Yet you say you are at peace with your decision. I suppose I find it hard to believe that some part of you doesn't regret giving her up."

"And I wouldn't be honest if I told you I never ask myself, 'what if...? '"

"I hope there's a but coming. . ."

"Yes." Claire took a deep breath. "The but is I didn't think I'd be a very good mother. I made a lot of mistakes when I was young. Hurt people I loved. It wasn't until my thirties that I figured out how to do better. How to be better."

The house was visible now. They let the dogs off-leash and watched as they bounded forward. Claire and Tom walked the rest of the way, catching their breath and slowing their pulses.

"So, all your relief work. . ." Tom stopped to look at her again.

"If we ever were to meet, I didn't want Grace to be ashamed of me. In some way, I think I became who I am because of Grace."

Two days later, Claire arrived at the University of Nebraska Alumni Center with Gail, Tom, and Grace. After helping to carry the dress and veil upstairs to the bride's room, she slipped back down to the shaded, tree-lined outdoor chapel space. Folding chairs were arranged for guests. A few of Grace's friends worked to put the final touches on an arbor. They sprinkled sunset-colored rose petals on the spot where Grace and

Adam would stand in an hour. A soft breeze rustled the leaves and began to cool the air.

Tom spoke to one of the tuxedoed young men who would stand up with Adam. He motioned to Claire.

"Zac Powell, this is our friend, Claire Jordan. This is Adam's twin brother, Zac."

"Hello." Claire held out her hand. He was even taller than Adam. "Adam and Zac? A to Z?"

"Yes, ma'am." He smiled. "Mom's little joke. She says we were all the kids she'd ever need."

Tom then gave instructions. "When guests start to arrive, I'd like you to seat Ms. Jordan in the second row, right behind Gail and I."

Uncertain, Claire said, "I don't want to be any trouble. Somewhere at the back is fine…"

Tom shook his head. "No. This is what Gail wants. What we want."

Zac nodded. "Anything you say, Dr. Bassett. Let me know when you're ready, Ms. Jordan."

Claire went back upstairs, hoping to catch a glimpse of the preparations going on in the bride's room. She heard the giggling and squealing that were hallmarks of any female gathering. It didn't matter what the culture or language. All young, happy women sound the same. Then it was silent. Claire peeked in and saw all heads bowed, all hands folded as the pastor prayerfully asked God's blessing on the proceedings. She bowed her head until she heard the Amen.

"Claire, where did you go? We've been looking for you." Gail smiled and waved her into the room.

"I was trying to stay out of your way. This is your day, not mine."

"Don't be ridiculous. The photographer is here. I want a picture of you and me with Grace."

The sight of Grace in her wedding dress took Claire's breath away and caused a lump to rise in her throat. Auburn curls tumbled down her back and a tiara so perfectly placed that it looked as if she wore it every day. The simple, strapless gown of champagne lace and satin suited her long, elegant body. Claire recognized her own dark eyes shining back at her and couldn't speak as she and Gail stood on either side of Grace while the photographer snapped away.

"So, mother of the bride and...?" he asked.

"The other mother of the bride," Grace answered.

Claire smiled, wishing Grace's other father could be here too.

CLAIRE SAT in the second row as Zac escorted Gail down the aisle, smiling at each of the hundred or so family and friends gathered in the twilight. When the music changed, all eyes turned to watch the procession of bridesmaids and groomsmen.

Once the wedding party was in place, Gail stood, giving the silent signal to everyone else. Claire stood and watched Tom and Grace begin their walk down the aisle to the hymn, "Blessed be the Ties that Bind." At that moment, Gail turned and took Claire's hand, holding it tightly. Together they watched their daughter step toward her future.

The pastor led the touching ceremony, getting a little misty during his brief remarks as he reminded them to care for each other and be each other's priority.

"Who gives this woman to be married to this man?"

"Her mothers and I." Claire heard a catch in Tom's voice. He stepped back and handed Grace off to Adam then reached for a handkerchief. Tom, the gruff old bear, had a heart of marshmallow cream when it came to his daughter.

The reception, a sit-down dinner inside the alumni center,

was followed by toasts. Friends told stories and offered their best wishes to Grace and Adam. Then it was Tom's turn.

"Thank you all for being here to share in this happiest of celebrations. Each of you is here because you have been a blessing to Grace or Adam. Each of you shares some of the credit for the wonderful people they have become. Gail and I thank you for that. And we thank God for you." He stopped, looking from Grace to Gail and back again.

"But there is one person I want to single out this evening. One person without whom none of us would be here tonight." He looked directly at Claire and smiled. "Gail and I would like to publicly and profoundly thank Claire Jordan for choosing us, for allowing us. . ." Tom swallowed hard to compose himself. ". . . for giving us Grace."

Audible sniffs and sighs filled the room as Claire felt all eyes fixed on her. Tom continued, "We rarely get to see the effects of our decisions or God's will made manifest. Claire, I ask you to look around this room and see how many people's lives you changed for the better. We thank God and thank you for this most precious gift."

Glasses were raised and clinked as Gail took her hand. With chins trembling, hearts overflowing, Claire and Gail gazed, teary-eye to teary-eye, mother to mother.

CHAPTER TWENTY-SEVEN

Now: I Say a Little Prayer

*T*o Libby—cancer-free for over two years—every morning was a gift, especially bright spring mornings like today. Running a bit behind schedule, she mentally checked off the items she needed for an early meeting while looking for her shoes. There. Kicked off last night beside her chair.

A loud thud from upstairs startled her.

Jack called to her. She ran up the stairs where she found him curled up on the bathroom floor, his face contorted in pain.

"Jack! What happened? What hurts?" Dear God. Please...

"Can't—breathe. Chest—heart?" he gasped, his face glistening with sweat. Libby saw fear in his eyes and raced to the bedside phone to dial 911. Back at his side, she covered him with his thick robe and pulled a few towels off the rack to cushion his head as she gave their address and described Jack's condition. The dispatcher instructed her to give Jack a baby aspirin, unlock the front door, and control any pets.

"Of course, but please hurry." Please, God. Don't let him die.

Libby found the aspirin bottle and slipped a tablet into his mouth. She sprinted to unlock the front door, put Maggie in the backyard, and ran back upstairs. Winded, she sat on the floor beside him stroking Jack's forehead and holding his hand. His eyes never left hers.

Within minutes, the sirens screamed outside, identical to the screams inside her head.

"Up here! Upstairs!" Libby called out when she heard them enter. She nodded at the young uniformed emergency crew—a male EMT, a female paramedic—and stepped out of their way. They asked questions. She answered as best as she could. No, no drug allergies. Yes, he takes medicine for high blood pressure, handing over the prescription bottle. No. No cardiac events before. A few minutes ago.

They clearly knew what they were doing, but the frenzy of activity looked and sounded like chaos to her. The words and numbers she heard might as well have been in a foreign language. The heart monitors blipped, the two-way radio crackled in a blur of noise and commotion until they had him loaded onto a stretcher and into the ambulance. Libby started to climb in too, but the female paramedic gently stopped her with a light touch on her hand.

"You can follow us, Mrs. Cooper."

"But…"

"You'll want your car at the hospital," she explained. Well, yes. She supposed so, but…

With the rear doors shut, the ambulance pulled away. A yellow school bus drove past, reminding her it was still a school day. She ran back through the house and into the garage. She pulled out her cell phone and dialed Sub Services as she started her car.

"Hello. This is Libby Cooper," she said, shouldering her phone and backing out of the garage.

"Yes, Mrs. Cooper. How are you today? Need a sub for that training next month? Lots of calls coming in today."

"No. I need one today. This morning. Now."

She stopped at the corner. Barely.

"It's a little late, Mrs. Cooper. A substitute might not get there in time for school to start at 8:30. You don't have before school duty, do you?" Libby couldn't believe this conversation. Jack might be dying and she was being scolded about calling so late?

"My husband had a heart attack. The ambulance just took him away. You're saying I should come in because it makes your job hard?!"

She rolled through the next stop sign.

"Well, no. I guess not. But when you don't give us enough notice. . ."

"Next time my husband has a heart attack, I'll ask him to have it on the weekend," Libby yelled into the receiver. She pressed the end button hard and immediately dialed her principal.

"Not to worry, Libby. We'll take care of your class. You take care of Jack. Let us know what we can do."

"Thank you," she whispered as she parked at the hospital. Libby felt a sob rise in her chest as she ran into the ER, still wearing her slippers. Breathless, she stepped up to the intake desk. "My husband, Jack Cooper was brought in. Where...?"

"Yes, Mrs. Cooper. He's already with the ER doctor. But we need some information from you."

Libby stood answering more questions, digging out insurance cards, and signing authorizations. All this nonsense when all she wanted was to be near Jack. To tell him she loved him. To pray.

By the time she finished the paperwork, the young ER doctor found her and told her they'd done another EKG and were taking Jack to the cardiac cath lab. They'd alerted the cardiologist who would meet them there. He'd find the blockage and clear the artery.

"May I—may I see him?"

"Of course. But only for a moment. He's been sedated. You may follow him as far as the lab's waiting room."

So many wires and tubes were connected to Jack that Libby immediately thought of Jean Luc Picard and the Borg from Star Trek.

"Resistance is futile," she whispered to Jack as she squeezed his hand. A faint smile flashed across his lips, then quickly faded. "I love you." She kissed his cheek and watched as he was wheeled through the double doors. Libby sank into a plastic chair in the empty waiting room wondering what to do next. After a quick call to Jack's office, she called Claire.

"What's up? Playing hooky?"

"It's Jack. Heart attack. We're at the hospital."

"Oh, no. What do you need?"

"Shoes." Libby laughed when she said it, although the laugh became a sob. "What happens if…"

"If you don't have shoes?"

"No, silly." And she laughed again. "If Jack dies."

"He won't," Claire interrupted. "He wouldn't dare, not with Annie's wedding coming up. Besides, I'd kill him. You tell him that." Libby smiled, grateful for her friend.

CLAIRE ARRIVED with shoes and a latte and sat with her in Jack's room through the afternoon. The cardiologist had put in a stent and assured Libby that this was a survivable event. He wouldn't miss Annie's wedding.

"Do you want me to go home with you tonight? I can stay over if you want." Claire asked before she left. "We could get a little drunk."

"No. I'll be fine. I'm probably going to take a hot bath and crawl into bed."

"Okay, but if you change your mind—even late—call me." Claire hugged Libby and left. Moments later, Libby saw that Jack was sleeping peacefully. Tonight, she could face neither the wreckage of their bedroom nor the emptiness of their unmade bed. She spent the night at Jack's bedside.

THAT SPRING AND SUMMER, Jack had become a model patient. He ate better, exercised more, and had lost almost thirty pounds. Libby too had lost something—her need for control and her need to please. She'd stopped saying yes to every request. Cookies for the PTA. Chairing a committee. Organizing Reading Week. She'd learned to say, "Let me get back to you. I need to check with Jack first." She felt infinitely lighter. She lived in the moment—or tried to. And this moment was all about Annie.

Libby heard her cue, the *plinka-plinka-plinka-plinka-plink* of Kermit's banjo and stood. The intro to "Rainbow Connection" produced audible sighs from those gathered for Annie's wedding to Josh Martin in his parents' backyard. Libby stood and watched Jack escort their daughter down the aisle. Jack beamed, his twinkly eyes shining. Libby breathed a little prayer of gratitude for her daughter's happiness and Jack's full recovery.

Norah, Annie's only attendant, continued to work for UNICEF—the job Claire had helped her get right after 9-11. Claire had been right about Enrique, her former co-worker. He and Norah had been together for a year and had recently announced their engagement.

Jack squeezed Annie's shoulder and kissed her before handing her off to the practically giddy groom. He stepped to his spot beside Libby, took her hand, and kissed her on the lips.

"You look like a bride yourself," he whispered. "Will you marry me?"

"In a heartbeat."

HOURS LATER, Libby wilted into a chair beside Claire and Sylvia who were sharing a slice of wedding cake. Tiny lights twinkled in the trees and shrubs surrounding the Martins' yard. Candles glowed in lanterns suspended by wires from the lower tree branches. Libby slipped out of her shoes, letting the cool, damp grass beneath the table tickle her bare feet.

"Libby, the cake was beautiful. Which bakery?" Sylvia asked.

The cake was lovely and simple. Annie had wanted chocolate cake with chocolate icing, decorated with fresh flowers. Period.

"No bakery. It was Karen, a friend from school. Everything you see is the result of Annie's fairy godmothers and their husbands." Besides doing the cake and flowers, they'd barbequed chili-lime chicken and kept bowls filled with spinach salad and wild rice pilaf. Thank God for good friends.

The only family who had helped with the wedding were her brother Keith and his partner, Daniel, who had been manning the bar all evening. The others hadn't even offered. While Mitch—sober for a year—was there, he seemed focused on his latest girlfriend, whom he'd met at an AA meeting. John, now retired from the Navy and divorced, lived in Atlanta and worked for a hi-tech firm. He'd flown in yesterday and would leave tomorrow. Patrick had called and apologized. A dozen cattle were sick with something. None of the far-flung cousins, while invited, could make it either. Libby hadn't seen most of her nieces and nephews in years. So much for the close family her parents had raised.

Their mother had been gone for two years and their father had failed quickly in the nursing home. He was confined to bed, in what Libby secretly prayed were the last stages of his Alzheimer's-induced decline. Her twice-weekly visits to Carson Pines, if noticed at all, seemed only to upset and confuse him.

"Your friends did everything?" Sylvia seemed to take in each detail.

Libby nodded. "Annie and Josh asked that the money we'd set aside for a wedding be a down payment on a little house. Annie is the practical sort. She even wore mom's wedding dress."

"I remember that dress from your wedding. Fran made it, right?"

"My grandmother did."

"They both would have been so proud." Sylvia sipped her wine and smiled at her daughter. "Did you help too, Claire?"

"I contributed beer and wine."

"And the honeymoon," Libby added. "Claire gave them a week at one of those all-inclusive resorts in Cancun. They fly out tomorrow afternoon. That'll give Annie a week before school starts."

"Professional discounts." Claire shrugged. She'd made all the travel arrangements for the wedding too. Claire's travel business was doing well.

Sylvia emptied her glass and yawned. "I think I'm ready to go home now, Claire. This is way past my bedtime."

"Sure, Mom. I'll drop you home and come back to help clean up."

"Don't bother," Libby said. "I think we've got clean-up covered, but don't forget brunch tomorrow. You too, Sylvia. About ten?"

Watching Sylvia and Claire disappear into the mild, starry August night, Libby missed her mother.

AFTER MIDNIGHT, a still shoeless Libby said goodnight to the last of the guests. The happy couple had taken off an hour ago for a B & B in nearby Genoa. The fairy godmothers were finishing the dishes, stacking the rented chairs, and piling an Everest of trash bags beside the Martins' garage.

Libby breathed a happy sigh. In two days, she and Jack would be taking off for their own honeymoon. A week in Paris. She couldn't believe they were finally going. In the past, something had always interfered and made them cancel their plans. Nothing would stop them now. Nothing. Everyone was happy and healthy. Settled. Even Mitch, bless his heart, drank iced tea all evening.

Still a little tipsy and dreaming of a moonlight stroll down the Champs-Elysees, Libby gathered her purse from its hiding place in the pantry. It vibrated. Her phone. Probably Annie saying goodnight. Or she'd forgotten something. Libby looked at the display. Carson Pines. Seven missed calls. Three messages. Daddy.

AFTER LISTENING TO THE MESSAGES, Libby looked up from her phone. The first person she saw was her brother John, who hadn't yet left for his hotel. He insisted on coming along to Carson Pines, although there wasn't anything anyone could do now. Their father had been dead for two hours.

They were still in their wedding clothes, although Jack had removed his tie and coat. Libby reluctantly pressed her swollen feet back into her shoes as Jack drove. John phoned Pat from the backseat.

"I don't know what happened, but you can be sure I'll find out," John declared. Libby heard no grief in his voice, only anger.

Libby's own emotions were a bittersweet pudding of grief and relief. Michael McCormack had stopped being the father she adored. That man had been gone for years. Gone were his ubiquitous, clip-on bow ties, and his Irish temper rising at the evening news. Gone were his boisterous songs and animated recitations of "The Cremation of Sam McGee" and "The Wreck of the Hesperus" on long car rides. A lump rose in her throat thinking of that Dad, the one she missed. Her father had been reduced to a set of bodily functions requiring maintenance. It felt cruel, but she thanked God for taking her father. Finally.

Barb, a middle-aged nurse with spiky copper-colored hair and rhinestone-studded half glasses buzzed them through the front door. Libby knew this woman from previous emergencies with her father and appreciated her kind but frank, no-nonsense demeanor.

"I'm so sorry, Libby. We called and left messages, but…" she began to explain, and then noticed how the trio was dressed.

"My daughter's wedding."

"What happened?" John asked, getting right to the point.

"This is my brother, John McCormack. He's visiting from Atlanta." That's why you've never seen him.

Barb nodded before continuing. "About 7:30, the CNA checked on him and noticed your father was having some trouble breathing. She alerted the RN on duty."

"And?" John injected.

Barb looked at him oh-so-briefly before returning her attention to Libby. "And we administered some medicine to make him more comfortable. We gave him oxygen…"

"And then what? You let him die? Didn't you call 911 or get him to the hospital? What kind of place is this?" John, used to being in charge, tried to bully the nurse. Libby knew Barb was not easily intimidated.

"We had a signed DNR. No extraordinary measures were to be taken to prolong your father's life."

John then turned on Libby. Literally.

"Who signed that? A man who didn't even know his own name? I can't believe..."

"I did." Libby interrupted.

"You? You got to decide? What gave you the right? You let our father die?" A purple stain spread over his neck and face. Even his scalp, visible beneath the military-style haircut, flushed with rage.

Jack stepped in then and opened his mouth in defense, but Libby put up her hand. She squared her shoulders and pulled herself up to her entire five-foot-two height. She stared up at her big brother.

"Since I was the one who stayed, the one who took care of them, Mom and Dad gave me the power, John."

"When did that happen?" His tone was just short of mocking.

Jack now spoke up; after all, he'd drawn up the papers. "Five years ago. We all sat down and talked about this. Your parents were very clear."

"I wasn't there." Was he ever?

"You were invited," Jack continued. "Everyone was. But decisions are made by those who show up."

"So, you used that power to end our father's life?"

Libby felt years of frustration rise inside her, but she refused to cry or yell. She banked the coals of those feelings and lowered her voice. She gritted her teeth and spoke slowly as she would to a six-year-old who had gotten on her last nerve.

"What life was that exactly, John? The life in which Dad didn't remember who or where he was? Or who we were? The life in which our father had to be diapered and fed like a baby? The life so important to you that you haven't seen Daddy in over a year? Is that the life you wanted to continue?"

"I don't...I have...I can't..." John spluttered, unused to anyone's defiance, much less his little sister's.

"If you'd been here—or even visited now and then—you would have seen what little life Dad had left."

"But still, it wasn't up to you to decide."

"No, John, it wasn't up to me. It was up to God. Are you second-guessing God now, Commander McCormack?" John stood with his mouth agape. Adrenalin coursed through Libby's veins, but she felt totally in control. Not to mention a little taller.

Barb took advantage of the pause in hostilities. "Would you like to see your father? We've called the funeral home, but they're waiting for your okay to remove his body."

The three followed the nurse down the hall. Jack held Libby's hand and despite her grief, she smiled.

BRUNCH the next day was a tense affair with John still pouting from last night's exchange. He was the only one who exhibited any emotion at all. Yes, her father had died, but he'd been gone for years.

Libby spent most of an hour that Sunday morning on the phone and out of earshot. When she finally emerged from the den, Jack cocked his head and raised his brows in a wordless query. Libby gave him a small conspiratorial nod and announced that the priest at St. Teresa's had agreed to meet with them at two that afternoon to discuss funeral arrangements. Libby hoped the presence of a priest would put them all on their best behavior—or rather, put one sibling on his best behavior—as they settled the details.

"Some people have plane reservations," John said.

Libby shrugged and said, "If you can't come, we all understand."

Keith handed her a mimosa.

"To Dad." She raised the goblet and gratefully downed the contents. Keith refilled her glass.

FOUR MCCORMACK CHILDREN, Libby, John, Keith, and Mitch, accompanied by Jack, waited in the office of the new priest. Sunday was the busiest day of the week, but Libby had insisted and the kind Father had acquiesced.

At 2:10, John checked his watch and looked around the room anxiously. Libby saw him roll his eyes when the young Puerto Rican priest rushed in, apologizing.

"I am Father Tomás," he said as he shook hands and introduced himself to Libby's brothers. To Libby and Jack, he offered, *"Lo siento.* I am sorry for your loss. It is good to have so many family members together at such a sad time, no?"

Libby nodded.

"I have heard that your father was well-known and well-loved in this community. A much-beloved teacher for many years. Many will wish to pay their respects. To remember him, yes?"

John started before Libby could open her mouth. "Most of our family lives elsewhere, Father. It will take several days to make travel arrangements. So maybe next weekend? I have to fly out today but I can be back by next Friday or Saturday." He looked at his Blackberry, then at Libby. Of course, the family should accommodate his schedule, after all he's done.

Libby knew what she was going to say. She began in the same first-grade teacher tone she had used the previous night. Slowly.

"We agree there is a logistics issue. Our daughter was married last night. She's leaving on her honeymoon today and won't return for a week. As a teacher, she doesn't have much flexibility for vacations. We've already told her to go ahead with her plans."

"Good," said Keith. "I was worried she'd feel obligated to stay." Mitch nodded his assent as well. Only John shook his head.

Libby continued. "And Jack and I are leaving the day after tomorrow for Paris. We won't return until a week from Wednesday."

John pounded his fists into the arms of the chair. "Well, that's great, Libby. Dad is dead and you're going to Paris. I would think the least you could do is stick around to bury our father."

"Let's not talk about the least one can do, John." Libby only gave her brother a fleeting glance before returning her gaze to the priest, who now showed little creases between his thick, black eyebrows. His dark eyes darted between the two siblings. A bead of sweat dripped from one of his side-burns.

Libby began again. "What we'd like is a small private mass for the immediate family in the little chapel tomorrow after-noon. Whoever can make it, that is." She looked at John. "And then burial next to our mother at Lone Mountain Cemetery immediately following. I spoke with both the funeral home and the cemetery this morning. They assured me they could have our father's body prepared." It was a rush, for which she would pay extra, but Libby had been firm. There would be no delays.

"Why the hurry? I'm flying out today. Is this some sort of test? And what about a public funeral? Our father deserves some acknowledgment of his contributions to this town." John's voice rose sharply, his face once again flushed. "And what about the rest of the family? You're being pretty selfish, Libby."

"Now just a damn minute, John!" Jack cut in. "You have the nerve to call Libby selfish? After all she's done for your parents?"

Libby touched Jack's hand. God, she loved this man. She offered her proposal. "We'll have a public memorial service later when everyone can return. Your kids too, John. And Pat's family."

Keith and Mitch both nodded. John started to argue but stopped when Mitch said, "Three against one, John. Unlike the Navy, this family is a democracy." Not exactly, Libby thought, but it's nice to have some support.

"What about Pat? Doesn't he get a vote?"

"I called him this morning. He agrees with me. With us." The Navy had been outmaneuvered.

Father Tomás swiftly accepted the plan and looked at Libby.

"Would one o'clock tomorrow work for you, Senora Cooper?"

"That will be fine," Libby stated. She watched him write it on his calendar.

"And when would you like to plan the memorial service, Senora Cooper? September? October?"

Again, Libby was ready with her answer.

"Friday afternoon of Thanksgiving weekend, Father. It's our dad's birthday." While she wasn't asking approval, she saw out of the corner of her eye that both Keith and Mitch were grinning at her. John stood and stormed out. He gunned the engine of his rental, kicking up gravel as he sped out of the church parking lot.

As they rose to leave, Jack squeezed her hand and whispered in the French they'd been practicing, *"Très bien, mon chéri. Formidable!"*

CHAPTER TWENTY-EIGHT

Now: Tea for Two

*T*en A.M. was too early to check into her hotel. Besides, Claire worried that if she stopped anywhere, she'd lose her courage.

It had been at least thirty years since she'd driven this stretch of Southern California freeway. In that time, Orange County had grown into a vast and carefully landscaped mosaic of concrete, greenery, and billboards. Her rental car nearly drove off the road when she read one proclaiming, "Wylder Nurseries: Celebrating 50 years in Yorba Linda. Grow with us! Newest branch opening soon!"

The reunion with her father would be a surprise, just as his leaving had been. She told herself she held no expectations. Still, she could not quell her fears as she stepped out of the car in front of Bradford Square Assisted Living. The familiar scent of jasmine triggered poignant memories. Automatic doors opened into what looked like a hotel lobby, decorated in soothing peaches and blues. She smelled coffee and freshly baked cinnamon rolls. Nicely-dressed residents watched a nature documentary on the large television or chatted in comfortable-looking chairs.

After signing her name at the reception desk, she was directed to the elevator. She bobbed her head to the piped-in sounds of Herb Alpert and the Tijuana Brass. Claire straightened her shoulders as the doors opened and nervously smoothed her navy-blue linen shirt, regretting her choice. After six hours of travel, the shirt resembled a used paper napkin.

Knocking on the numbered door, her hammering heart raced the approaching footsteps. The latch clicked. The door opened and she looked into the eyes of the tall, silver-haired man in a coral polo shirt. Long ago she'd forgotten what her father looked like, had given up even trying to recall his face, his smile. Nonetheless there he was, beneath the soft, wrinkled skin of his cheeks, behind the thick glasses. Papa.

"Claude Jordan?"

"Yes. Do I know you?" He struggled to recall her face as though he were flipping through a mental Rolodex.

"You. . . you used to. I'm Claire. I'm your daughter." The words barely escaped her throat.

His expression changed almost instantly from confusion to elation. "My, dau…. Oh, my land! I never thought…How did you…?"

"Hello, Papa."

"What a happy surprise." He stood back, shaking his head slowly, never letting his eyes leave hers. His tears began to pool and she felt her own. "You were—you were just a little girl. It's been so long."

Claire couldn't find her voice. "Almost fifty years," squeezed out.

"Time does have a habit of slipping through our fingers. Come in. Come in." Claire stepped through the door and her father closed it behind her. "How did you find me?"

"The Internet. But it wasn't easy. You've moved quite a bit." The death of Libby's father —and those birthday cards—had finally compelled Claire to find her father before it was too late. After weeks of cyber-sleuthing—she'd even set up a Google Alert—Claire had finally found what appeared to be a current address and phone number. She'd debated spying on him from a distance. But merely seeing him wouldn't be enough. Not nearly enough. She had to meet him, to look into his eyes. She had, however, called. Once. A lump had risen in her throat as she'd listened to his message, "This is Claude Jordan. Sorry to have missed your call..." She'd hung up without saying anything.

Her father nodded and shrugged. "How are you?"

"I'm good."

"May I offer you something? A cup of tea, perhaps? I have Earl Gray. Or are you one of those herbal gals? I think I have some chamomile."

"Tea would be perfect. I love Earl Gray."

Her father stepped into the little kitchenette of his tidy studio apartment while Claire looked around. No photos of grandchildren. No evidence of a wife. A package of McVities Digestives lay on the kitchen table next to *The Los Angeles Times*, open to the stock report. The walls displayed world art, mostly small watercolors or line drawings of places she recognized. Paris. The Greek Isles. The pyramids of Mexico. Had he visited all those places too?

She leaned against the kitchen counter and watched her father fill a kettle and set it to boil on the two-burner stove. While still taken aback by her visit, her father's charm kicked in.

"Tell me about your life."

"I went to college, Cal-State in fact." She tipped her head toward the nearby campus. "Traveled. Worked for relief organizations. You know, nonprofits. Now I have a little travel business."

"I love to travel."

"I remember," Claire said softly, recalling the map tacked up on her bedroom wall.

"I'm sure you do." He shook his head. "I'm sorry about that. It was my job. Your mother hated it, of course. She got tired of being alone. We fought whenever I came home."

"So, you stopped coming home?" She tried not to sound accusatory, not angry, not hurt. But she felt fifty years of pent-up sadness, resentment, curiosity, and something else she couldn't name.

"This is difficult to tell you, after all this time." He placed two white cups with saucers on the counter with a teabag in each. "I loved your mother. Loved you. But Sylvie was a stubborn woman. She gave me an ultimatum."

"An ultimatum?"

"Yes. She told me she couldn't go on being only half married. Having me home less than half the time. We argued about it for a year before I left. Your mother wanted me to give up traveling and live in that little Podunk town. She made me choose. I was selfish. A few years later, I guess they would have called me a male chauvinist, expecting the little woman to sit at home and wait for my return. Frankly, I'm ashamed of myself now."

This last exchange seemed to take something out of her father as if he'd been saving it up to tell someone.

The kettle whistled. He poured boiling water into the cups and offered a plastic beehive of honey. Claire accepted it and squeezed a bit into her cup. They carried their tea to the sitting area and sat down, he in an armchair, she on the loveseat. She stirred her tea. The perfumey fragrance of bergamot reached her nose and she knew it would forever be imprinted on her memory of this moment.

Where had she figured in this story? Had he ever thought about her, loved her, missed her? Claire wanted to say all of this but didn't. Couldn't. He was an old man now, and alone.

"Did you ever want to come back?" That sounded too needy even as it came out of her mouth and seemed to hang there between them. She sipped the sweet tea, trying to remove the bitter taste of her words. Her father dipped his teabag in and out of the steaming cup, as though strengthening the tea would fortify him for what was to come, what he needed to say.

"I did. But again, your mother thought it would be hurtful, damaging for you to have such an unstable home, with me coming and going."

"And so, you stayed away." Claire sighed and shook her head.

"And so, I stayed away." His gaze dropped from hers.

"Didn't you want to visit me? Something?" She didn't care if she sounded needy now. Her breath came in short gasps.

"Oh, honey. I wanted to visit you. But that was part of our agreement. I would leave and not see you again." He reached out and patted her hand. "I hid out a few times to watch you on the school playground. I saw you graduate from high school. And I sent you birthday cards. Every year. Didn't you...?" His look was pained, beseeching.

"Mom didn't show me the cards until a few years ago."

"Sylvie kept those from you?"

"Uh-huh." Claire bit her lip. "I grew up believing you didn't love me. That you'd abandoned me." Her throat constricted with the sensation that always preceded tears.

Perhaps the parent who stayed needed to maintain the upper hand, the high ground. Did she blame either of them more than the other now? They were both perpetrators. Certainly, they were all victims. Claire was crying now. She felt six years old again, as though she'd done a belly flop at the pool and had the air knocked out of her.

"I'm so sorry." He reached out and patted her knee and handed her his handkerchief. "I regretted the decision almost as soon as it was made. I wrote to your mother repeatedly to ask her to reconsider. But fifty years ago, I made a choice and…"

"…life is living with your choices," Claire finished, sniffing.

He nodded, smiling. "Funny. You know where your mother got that saying?"

Claire shook her head.

"It's what her father said when he forced us to get married. I'm a little surprised that Sylvie would use it on you."

Claire sat stunned with yet another revelation about her mother.

"And after you were grown—and I hadn't heard from you—I tried to let it go." Her father paused to let that sink in. The earth was shifting for him as it was for her. He took another sip of tea. His hand trembled slightly.

Claire blew her nose as her sobs subsided.

"How is your mother?" he asked.

"She's well. Still has the real estate office. We live in the Sweeney building. The first one she bought."

"You must be married with children now, right?"

"I never married. But I do have a daughter. Grace." She reached for her purse and removed an envelope of photos.

"You raised a daughter on your own?"

"No." Claire smiled, shook her head, and recounted the story. No more secrets. "And now Grace is pregnant, due any day. I'm about to become a grandma."

"And that would make me a great-granddad. Hmmm. Sounds like you've made a good life."

"I guess. You?"

"I guess."

He described working his way up the medical supply company's corporate ladder. He'd done very well but had moved many times. By the time Claire was in college, he was no longer in Orange County. He moved to Sacramento, the Bay Area and finally to the headquarters in Seattle. When he retired, he came back to Orange County, a place with more sunshine and where he still had friends. At 80, he played bridge, bingo, and nine holes of golf every week.

As he finished telling his story, there was a knock at the door. He stood to answer and Claire collected the now empty teacups, taking them to the sink.

"Are you ready for bingo?" Claire heard a female voice.

"Sorry, it slipped my mind. But come in. There's someone I want you to meet."

Claire was drying her hands as she turned to the door.

"Claire, I'd like you to meet my friend, Inez Wylder. Inez, this is my daughter, Claire."

Inez Wylder. Sam's mother. Shit.

"Claire, what a surprise!" Inez reached for her hand and shook it. Although her hair was white, it was still styled in a no-nonsense pixie cut. She seemed as cheerful as ever.

"You know each other?" her father looked baffled.

"Yes—um—we knew each other a long time ago when I went to school here. I dated her son Sam." Claire had just spilled every last bean to her father. He was sure to catch on that this was the Sam, her Sam. Her chest constricted.

"Claude, if you want to skip bingo, I'll go without you. I don't want to intrude. You never mentioned a child, although I do see a resemblance."

Her father replied, "Well, we've been out of touch for some time. Claire was catching me up on her life. It sounds like you might have some catching up to do as well. Please stay. Would you like some tea?"

Inez declined the tea and decided to skip bingo. She sat down next to Claire, who hoped Inez couldn't hear the thundering of her heart.

"It's been such a long time. You look well. As beautiful as I remember. Tell me about yourself, Claire."

Claire repeated the highlights of what she had told her

father, minus any reference to Grace or Sam. Would her father catch on? Claire listened for any information about Sam in Inez's stories. The Wylder children and grandchildren all took part in some aspect of the business.

"And Sam's wife, Christy, opened a floral and gift shop in the nursery. Quite unique." There it was. He's married. Good for him. "She came to work at the nursery soon after you left."

"I'm glad he married. And he's happy."

"Yes, he was happy."

"Was?"

"Oh, you wouldn't know. Christy died in a car accident while she was out on a delivery. Almost three years ago."

"Oh, no. I'm so sorry." Poor Sam. Claire's heart ached. "And their children?"

"Three boys, all grown, of course. The two older ones—Ben and Marcus—have coped pretty well. I'm still a little worried about Jacob though. And Sam took it very hard. We all did. She and Sam were a good team. He's just now beginning to act like the Sam we know. He's a slow healer."

"I'm sorry. It must take you back to...."

"Yes, but after Lee died, focusing on my children and the business helped. That's what I encouraged Sam to do. It's good to get back into normal life as soon as you can. Even if you don't feel normal. Pretty soon life becomes a habit again."

"Good advice," her father said.

"I agree," Claire added, remembering Lou's similar advice.

"You didn't have any brothers or sisters, did you? I thought I remembered you being an 'only. '"

"Yes, it's just me. And my mother."

"But you have your father."

"Now I do. I just found him."

"Claude, were you lost?" Inez teased.

He smiled. "Yes. Lost to Claire anyway. When her mother

and I divorced, I—I—left. I haven't spoken to Claire since she was six."

Inez's face bore no judgment. Then she tilted her head and smiled. "With all this reconnecting, Claire, perhaps you'd like to see Sam."

Claire wasn't at all sure about that. This would be a lot to spring on Sam. Poor Sam. After all these years.

"Not sure we'd have much to say..." except that we have a daughter and a grandchild on the way. She caught her father's almost indiscernible nod of encouragement, silently urging her, willing her to say yes. He didn't understand. She'd spent a lifetime avoiding Sam.

"Nonsense. I know my son. He'd love to see you again. And Kate and Joanie remember you so fondly. Joanie passed French that awful year because of your help. And Kate still makes that breakfast thing you taught her. Some sort of babies? And those fancy French grilled cheese sandwiches?"

"Dutch babies and Croque-Monsieur." They remembered that? Funny. Her kitchen repertoire hadn't grown much since that time.

"You're in luck. It's Kate's birthday barbeque tonight. And I'm inviting you both. I'll tell Sam I'm bringing a couple of friends."

"Well, I..." Claire did not want to see Sam. Not now. Maybe not ever.

"We accept," her father interrupted. "Thank you, Inez."

Inez stood to leave.

"This has been a lovely surprise." Claire hoped that sounded sincere. "Can we take you with us? I have a car."

"One of the boys usually picks me up. He can take all three of us."

"You're sure?" Claire was anything but sure.

"Yes. See you downstairs at five. It's casual. Just the family."

Claire and her father sat back in silence for a few minutes, processing all that had occurred in the last two hours.

"So, Sam is the..." her father asked gently.

"Uh-huh," Claire clenched her lower lip between her teeth.

"I won't say a word if that's the way you want it."

Claire nodded. Anxiety tightened its grip.

"Lunch is in a few minutes. You can be my guest. I'd like to introduce you to a few of my friends. Show you off."

"Of course." All she'd eaten today was coffee, peanuts, and some Bloody Mary mix on the plane.

Her father escorted her down the hall, into the elevator, across the lobby, and into the dining room, his hand at her elbow. Inez was already seated, smiling and gesturing to two seats she appeared to have saved at her table.

CHAPTER TWENTY-NINE

Now: Time in a Bottle

*C*laire needed to sort out the morning's events and work through her trepidations about tonight. She'd called Libby, but it had gone to voicemail. So, she pulled on running clothes, filled her water bottle, and headed for the hotel fitness center's treadmill. Running's steady rhythm—right, left, right, left—steadied her.

Claire never meant to find Sam. No, she had locked that door years ago. Is that why she ran? To outrun her past, her regrets? And yet, as hard as she ran, those feelings threatened to overtake her. She bumped up the machine's incline to its max. What would Sam be like now? People change. And thirty years was a long time. She pictured her relief clients, women of forty who looked eighty—aged by tragedy, poverty, hunger, illness, abuse, and neglect. Perhaps life had hardened Sam. He might be someone she wouldn't even recognize.

Nonetheless, the only Sam she could conjure was her old Sam.

Thirty minutes later, with sweat dripping from every pore and endorphins flooding her brain, she gulped the last of her water. Her anxiety had lessened. At least a little. Seriously, what could go wrong?

Back in her room, Claire pulled the one, wrinkled, just-in-case dress from her duffle. Hanging it in the bathroom while she showered should do the trick. She stripped and turned on the shower and hoped the pelting of the water would wash away the residual uneasiness about tonight's impending encounter. Guilt niggled at her every time her thoughts meandered to what she had concealed. And from Sam, the most blameless of all people.

Finally, wrapped in a towel, she opened the mini-fridge and considered the array of maxi-priced mini-options. Four-dollar candy bars, bags of almonds, Diet Cokes and tiny six-dollar bottles of wine. She chose a bag of nuts and a White Zinfandel, just to take the edge off.

Claire pulled the sleeveless, paisley maxi dress over her head, then applied a little blush, eyeliner, and mascara. She stood back to evaluate. Not bad for a middle-aged spinster. Except for that crease between her brows. She tugged unsuccessfully at her short bangs trying to hide the Grand Canyon on her forehead. Could there be a drive-thru Botox place nearby? This is Southern California after all. Shrugging, she drank the last of the wine, put on earrings, and found her platform sandals—the shoes she'd bought on her last trip to Paris. With their ankle ties, Libby had laughingly called them her hooker shoes.

For once, Claire thought she'd arrive at her destination a few minutes early, but then she remembered she'd neglected to put on deodorant. Then she couldn't find her room key. She was nearly to the car when she remembered a wrap. Shit. Back to the room. She looped the turquoise pashmina around her shoulders without glancing back at the traitorous mirror. By the time she started the car she knew she'd be late. She took several more breaths and willed her anxious heart to slow. It did not obey.

Minutes later, Claire parked next to Bradford Square's entry, gathered her purse and wrap. The car beeped as she locked it. Starting for the entrance, something stopped her. She spun and noticed her shawl caught in the car door. Beep, unlock, open, remove, close, beep, walk.

"Shit," she muttered.

"Pardon me. Is this yours?" She turned to see a tall man with a neatly trimmed beard and sunglasses dangling an earring between his thumb and index finger.

Claire reached up and felt her ears. Sure enough. She extended her hand.

"Thank you," she uttered, looking up into the stranger's face. Her heart gave a few syncopated beats. A tremor ran down her spine and settled somewhere just south of her belly button. She nearly toppled off her shoes. "Sam?"

Confusion crossed his face as he lowered his chin and looked over his sunglasses. Sam's clear, lake-blue eyes searched her face. He still had a full head of curly hair with only a little gray. Not salt and pepper. More like cinnamon and sugar. While no one would describe him as overweight, he was substantial enough that Claire felt his gravitational pull. Is that why she'd been so root-less since she'd left, so unanchored? The realization stunned her.

"Claire?"

"Uh-huh," she breathed. Her heart thudded in her chest as she caught a whiff of his clean, just-out-of-the-shower-smell. God, she loved that smell.

"What are you doing here?" She heard only surprise in his voice, although her guilt couldn't help but add some small indictment.

"My...my dad lives here."

"So does my mom."

301

Bradford Square's shuttle bus pulled up to the entrance. They stepped aside as a half dozen people exited carrying shopping bags from Target and Walgreens. Sam removed his sunglasses revealing the skin of a man who spends his days outside. Freckles crowded his face and forearms. He nodded in greeting as the residents passed.

"I saw her today. She invited us to dinner." Claire watched Sam for some reaction, some indication to ease the awkwardness of the moment. Nothing.

"When Mom said to expect two more for dinner, I thought it would be a couple of her bingo buddies."

"I think my dad's a bingo buddy. Claude Jordan." Inez hadn't told Sam who she'd invited? "I'm sorry if..."

"I've met Claude. I didn't know his last name. I thought..."

"Yeah. I just found him—then today, uh—your mom..." Claire couldn't form complete sentences. She looked at her watch. "I said I'd be here at 4:45."

"Looks like you're a little late." Sam smiled. Even his beard couldn't hide those deep dimples. The knot in her belly loosened but failed to untie completely. They walked together to the elevator. The doors opened and their parents stepped out.

"Oh, good. You've already met." Inez's smile seemed conspiratorial as she nudged Claire's father with her elbow. Inez kissed her son's cheek. "Wasn't this a nice surprise, Sam?"

"Yes, Mom. A very nice surprise." Claire warmed under his gaze. Or was it another hot flash?

Sam drove them to his house in Yorba Linda's Country Club Estates—the same house his parents had owned back in the sixties. Inez explained that Sam and Christy had purchased it and raised their three boys there when she'd moved to a nearby condo. They'd added a pool and done other remodeling. Claire thought of her tiny apartments. The last one in New York would easily have fit inside Sam's three-car garage.

Sam's sisters met them at the door. They couldn't look more

different and still be sisters—like Audrey Hepburn and Stevie Nicks. Joanie was delicate, dark, gamine in a striped top, black capris, and ballet flats. Kate was taller, with mounds of long strawberry blonde curls, wearing layers of gauzy fabrics. They didn't seem at all surprised to see Claire. Inez must have told them. Several grown children with spouses or dates arrived. No grandchildren that Claire could see. Kate kissed her big brother and grabbed an open bottle of wine and three glasses. Joanie took Claire by the arm and practically dragged her to a patio table on the far side of the pool.

"Hey! Where...?" Sam protested mildly, but Joanie shushed him with a look. Claire pleaded wordlessly as she looked back at Sam. Kate poured while Joanie started the questions, as Claire chose a seat that afforded her a view of the entire yard.

"What happened to you? Where did you go?" Joanie asked before tasting her wine.

Claire chose her words carefully. "Home, at first." She wouldn't lie, but she wouldn't reveal any more than necessary.

"Weren't you joining the Peace Corps? I thought that's why you left." Kate's tone was softer than her sister's.

"Peace Corps didn't work out. But I lived in Paris for a while. Worked in the travel business. Then various relief organizations."

"We never heard a thing from you. Not even a postcard." Kate seemed hurt, as though Claire had broken up with her.

"I'm sorry."

"It must have been a terrible fight. We thought you and Sam would get married," Joanie added, her tone serious. "It took him a long time to get over you." Her words stung.

"Me too. I'm not sure I ever met anyone like Sam. He's kind of the gold standard." His sisters nodded. Claire clenched nervously at the dress fabric pooled in her lap. She looked across the pool at Sam, who was laughing with several of the men. Of course, Claire had had crushes, affairs. That on-again, off-again thing with Dave. But, like a jacket that never fit right despite how perfect it looked on the hanger—or on someone else—she'd never found "the one." After a while—when was that, exactly? —she simply gave up trying. She couldn't stand the disappointment when each Tim, Nick, or Barry turned out not to be Sam. The heartbreak went both ways, of course. She hated herself for being this way—for punishing men simply for not being Sam.

"Then I really don't understand," Joanie's tone was earnest. "If you loved him so much, why did you leave?"

Claire stiffened at the directness. Maybe Joanie had had a head start on the wine, too.

"Timing." She gave a slight one-shoulder shrug, belying the strength of that argument. "I wasn't ready to settle down and Sam wasn't willing to wait. I had to prove I could stand on my own two feet."

"How'd that work out for you?" Joanie lowered her chin and looked at Claire through a fringe of dark lashes and mistrust.

"Mostly I tripped over them."

"But you could have come back. Why didn't you come back?" Kate asked.

"I thought he might hate me" ...for leaving and not telling him about his child.

"So, you never got married?" Kate seemed to be hoping for some happily-ever-after for this story. Claire was sorry to disappoint.

"Nope. That's one mistake I never made. Maybe the only one." Please don't ask about children. Her dress was crumpled again. She tried to smooth it with her sweating palms.

"But you've had a good life? A happy life?" Kate asked, again trying to lighten the mood.

"Yes, in spite of everything," Claire stated confidently and took another drink.

"So, what do you think, Joanie?" Kate cocked her head.

For a moment, Claire had forgotten these women weren't her girlfriends. They were Sam's sisters. His self-appointed guardians. This had been an interrogation.

"We don't want to see Sam hurt," Joanie said, direct as always.

"I didn't come here to see him. My father lives here." That was the truth, but now that she'd seen Sam, she couldn't deny there was still something. Questions roiled in the now wine-clouded sea of her mind and threatened to pull her under. She hoped answers would float to the surface.

"Yes, but here we all are anyway. Maybe Joanie and I are a little overprotective. He's had a difficult time since Christy died. Please consider that before you start anything," Kate warned.

"I'm only here for a few days."

"But he's been watching you since we sat down," Kate said under her breath. Claire looked across the yard and saw Sam staring at her. She felt an illusory bubble of hope rise unexpectedly. Could she keep it from bursting on the thorny truth? Claire emptied her glass and looked for an exit. Instead, she saw Sam smiling and sauntering around the pool toward her. The sky blue of his shirt stood out against the dense green of the landscape in the deepening twilight. It nearly matched the blue of the pool. The low angle of the setting sun caught a few coppery glints in his hair. His comfort in his own skin, his compassion, had always put her at ease. It did so now. Somehow, he'd found his way into that dark, Sam-shaped space in her heart and lit a candle.

"Mind if I have a word with my date?" His sisters gave Claire warning glances as they made lame excuses about being needed in the kitchen and scurried off.

"Date?" Claire asked.

"I'm sure that's what Mom had in mind." It was hard to read what was on his face.

"How do you feel about that?"

"Better than I have in a long time." She felt his hand at her back. "Let me show you Christy's garden." Claire wobbled unsteadily along the gravel path to the back of the large lot. The combination of wine and platform sandals was not working in her favor. She warned herself not to drink anything more until she'd eaten. Sam picked at a few dead blossoms.

"Our son Jacob usually takes care of this. It looks a little neglected, I'm afraid. He's been busy with opening our new branch."

Claire knew nothing of gardening, but if this was unkempt, she couldn't see it. Of course, compared to most Nevada gardens, this place was Eden, even with a few dead flowers.

"Christy was an artist. This was her studio. I know the names and growing habits of everything you see, but she—she made it beautiful." Sam dropped the dry blooms on the path to join the fallen leaves.

"I've never seen such a lovely garden. I'm happy you found her," Claire admitted.

"Actually, she found me." Sam chuckled. "Chased me around the nursery for over a year after you left, before I even noticed her. I'd guess you'd call her 'tenacious.'"

"Well, she caught you and made you happy. I'm glad." Claire remembered Sam's stubbornness. Christy must have been a worthy opponent and partner.

Sam looked away. "Not sure I'll ever really be over losing her. It was so sudden. Not like with Dad, when we knew the end was coming. Christy left on a delivery and just never came back." His Adam's apple bobbed as he swallowed hard.

Claire squeezed his hand and attempted to finish a conversation she had alternately dreamt of and dreaded. She hoped putting it out there would give her some closure.

"You know, I'm sorry I couldn't marry you back then. I wasn't ready. I was scared."

Sam smiled a small, tight smile and nodded. "I know. After

raising three boys, twenty-one seems so young now. Too young. You were right." He took her hand and they stood face to face. "But I did love you."

"I never doubted that. And I'm still sorry. Although each of us found the life we were meant to have."

Sam looked away and nodded. When he turned back to her, he said, "Tell me about yourself."

Once again, Claire summarized her life.

"You never wanted to settle down?"

"No."

"How long have you been back home in Nevada?"

"Three years." Sam's eyes narrowed as he gave her a wry, lopsided smile. Was he teasing her about finally settling down?

"Dad! Dinner's ready. Grandma said to come and find you."

Claire looked up to see Sam's thirty-years-younger doppelganger rounding a corner of the house and striding down a gravel path. Instinctively, she dropped Sam's hand.

"Claire Jordan, this is my youngest son, Jacob."

"Nice to meet you, Ms. Jordan."

"It's a pleasure, Jacob. And it's Claire. Please." Jacob gave his father a wary look, trying to figure out who this strange woman was.

"Claire is an old friend from college. Her father lives at Bradford Square. You remember Claude, don't you?"

"Oh, yeah, okay. Well, like I said, dinner's ready. You'd better come before the ribs are gone."

Jacob left, seeming relieved to have completed his task.

Claire turned and started toward the house. Sam took her elbow and stopped her gently. "I'm glad you came tonight," he said. She leaned toward him but caught herself. Sam might be glad now because he doesn't know anything. He doesn't know he has a grown daughter and a grandbaby on the way. Would there ever be a right moment to tell him?

They walked back to the patio where a long buffet table was

set up. Everyone served themselves and settled into comfortable chairs and around tables, finding their own groupings. Inez waved them over to sit with her and Claire's father. Sam brought another bottle of wine.

Inez led them through dinner conversation centered on the many places Claire and her father had traveled and Claire's work, easing the four of them through what could have been an awkward evening. Of course, the wine helped.

After birthday cake and a few yawns from the old folks, Joanie and her husband volunteered to take them back to Bradford Square on their way home. Of course, it was Joanie. Her intentions had been clear all night. Stay away from my brother!

"Claire, how about I take you back to your car after a while," Sam said. "It'll give us a chance to—um—catch up." His smile melted Joanie's objections, but she flashed Claire a cautionary glance.

Claire kissed her father's cheek and whispered, "How about brunch tomorrow? Can I pick you up at 10?" Perhaps time constraints would rein in her other impulses. While her father hadn't exactly been "Father Knows Best," she needed some advice. He quickly agreed.

Others left, one by one until the house was empty.

Claire removed her troublesome shoes and stood at the sink doing the few dishes that hadn't fit in the already humming dishwasher. Sam finished placing leftovers in the refrigerator. Her nerves settled as she stacked one large platter after another onto the granite counter.

"You don't have to do those. I remember how you hate washing dishes."

"I hate doing my own. I don't mind doing someone else's."

Claire looked up to see Sam behind her, reflected in the window. He placed his hands on her waist and she leaned back into him. A luscious tingle shot through her body. She tried to be rational about what she was feeling. She'd had a lot of wine.

She knew what sexual attraction felt like and it had been a while. But standing in the kitchen with Sam was different, something she had only ever felt long ago—and only with Sam. An intoxicating brew of excitement and comfort, of the new and the familiar. Pleasure and protection. Is this what Libby and Jack felt after all these years? Is this what she'd been missing?

"Come with me. I'll put another log in the fireplace outside."

Claire dried her hands and followed Sam back out to the patio. Only in Southern California would someone have a fire in an outdoor fireplace on a warm autumn evening. They sat comfortably on the padded rattan loveseat, their bare feet up on the matching coffee table. Sam placed his arm around Claire and she settled back against him. The air was fragrant. Soft jazz was coming from somewhere. Maybe now she could tell him.

But then, Sam turned her head and kissed her tenderly. As the kiss deepened, she hurtled headlong down a rabbit hole into a timeless, past-present space where she and Sam were and always had been in love. Every cell of her body vibrated. Blood roared in her ears, as she careened and spun out of control—until—until she caught a glimpse of what lay ahead. A rocky cliff with raging rapids far below, complete with flashing barricades that read: Beware! Keep away from the edge!

Claire panicked and pulled away. Inhaling sharply, she sat up straight.

"What's wrong?" Sam's forehead crumpled with questions.

"It's just—I—I don't—think this should go—any further tonight. We haven't seen each other in a long time. And all the wine..." She licked her lips and tasted Sam.

"We're not exactly strangers."

"But we are." A small resigned nod accompanied his heavy sigh. "Maybe you'd better take me back to my car."

"If that's what you want."

"Not what I want." Claire smiled sadly, hoping to soften her words. "But tonight, it's what I need." She stood to find her shoes.

They agreed to spend Sunday together. Later that night, alone in her hotel bed, Claire ran through potential scenarios. None of them ended well.

CHAPTER THIRTY

Now: Tell Him

The next morning, conflicting urges of profound thirst and the need to pee roused Claire from a restless, dream-filled sleep. The one-two punch of the previous day's events and too much wine played hell with her subconscious as well as her body, leaving her with disturbing after-images of a thundering, slow-motion avalanche.

Claire reached for a bottle of water from the fridge to make a single cup of coffee and used the remainder to take three aspirin. No way through but through. While the coffee brewed, she checked her phone. Libby might have called. It was dead. Where was the charger? Why hadn't she plugged it in last night? By the time she found it, the coffee was ready. She gulped down two scalding swallows hoping to clear her head.

It was time to come clean with Sam. She drank the rest of the coffee as she dressed for a run. Once outside, the sunny morning and a light breeze lured her away from the hotel's treadmill and toward the Cal-State campus. She estimated it was about two miles away and checked her watch. Plenty of time.

She stuck to main roads and soon crossed under the 57

Freeway. She ran toward the deserted campus. Few familiar landmarks remained. The older buildings still bore the hexagonal, beehive motif that had been ubiquitous in the seventies. More substantial structures dwarfed them now. Life had gone on. Things had changed. She'd changed too. Could she convince Sam of that? Would he ever trust her again?

Claire turned and ran back to the hotel. With each step, she repeated a mantra. Tell Sam about Grace. Tell Sam. Tell Sam....

CLAIRE'S FATHER was already in Bradford Square's lobby when she arrived. His face brightened as she approached and he kissed her cheek.

"I noticed Marie Callender's around the corner. How does that sound, Papa?"

"They have a nice Sunday brunch. Champagne too, if I recall. Might have to wait for a table though."

"Do you mind?"

"Not a bit, if I'm waiting with you." Claire's heart melted a little as she recalled dates with her father at the Pine Cone Café. When she was little, love meant cherry cokes and shoestring fries. What did it mean now? Mimosas and Eggs Benedict?

"Walk or drive?" she asked.

"It's a beautiful day. Let's walk." Father and daughter stepped out into a golden morning.

Her now fully-charged phone vibrated in her jacket pocket. Gail's photo smiled from the screen and she answered.

"Today's the day! Grace's in labor. We're all at the hospital." Claire could hear the grin in Gail's voice.

"How far along?" Claire's heart rose to her throat.

"Already at five centimeters. Halfway there. She's smiling, giving you a thumbs-up."

"Keep me posted when you can. But focus on your girl." Claire remembered her plans to spend the afternoon with Sam. As much as she wanted to be in on every detail, she shouldn't be a priority for Gail or Grace. And she didn't want to have to take an awkward phone call. She wasn't that good a liar. "Not sure where I'll be today, so maybe you'd better text me with updates."

"Will do. Keep her in your prayers."

"Always." Claire looked at her father, who'd heard most of the conversation as they walked.

"A big day, huh?"

"Uh-huh," was all she could manage. A low rumble began in her chest, an echo of last night's troubling dream.

"It seemed you and Sam got along well. I guess you had a lot of catching up to do."

"We did. But I couldn't tell him everything. At least I didn't. I didn't tell him about Grace."

"That would put a fly in the ointment, all right." Her father held the door as they entered the restaurant's noisy waiting area filled with families. Claire gave her name to the hostess who estimated a short wait since there were only two of them. They stood by the window.

"I never tried to find him. Never meant to tell him anything."

"But, now? Now that you've seen him?"

"Maybe I should leave." Her father couldn't mask his disappointment. Claire was disappointed in herself. "I know it makes me sound like a coward. But if I tell him, he'll be hurt and he'll hate me. If I just leave, he'll be…"

"He'll still be hurt. Think of what your mother withheld from you and how much that hurt when you found out." Her mother's actions had erased any chance at a connection with her father. Until now, anyway. Claire didn't want to be that person. No. She would tell Sam. Today.

THREE HOURS LATER, Sam turned onto Pacific Coast Highway. Claire lowered the window hoping the ocean breeze would dispel the dark storm churning in her head. She closed her eyes and breathed in the salt air. An Isak Dinesen quote came to mind, something about saltwater being a cure for anything. Claire wasn't so sure it could cure this.

Her phone vibrated for the first time in over an hour. "Stalled at 7," the text read.

"Something important?" Sam asked.

"Just—um—an update." Not a lie. Not exactly.

"Going well?"

"A hiccup." Her daughter—their daughter—was giving birth to their grandchild hundreds of miles away. Claire recalled that her labor had stalled and experienced the same hopeless, helpless feeling she felt now. Biting her lip, she tucked the phone back into her pocket and felt a distant avalanche rumbling toward her in slow-motion.

Sam signaled and pulled into a turnout. She remembered this place, where Sam had shown her the glowing waves that night. "Bioluminescence," he'd told her then. That word was forever linked to this place and that first kiss. She'd never forgotten it. It had become an incantation, a mantra she used to conjure that feeling of protection. Standing at the overlook, she glanced up at him as he turned. He kissed her, tentatively, like that first time. For a moment, that kiss erased all other thoughts and feelings.

"Let's go down to the water," she whispered in his ear. He led the way down the steep path to the beach. They removed their shoes and played tag with the small waves that reached the shore, before settling down side-by-side on the sand, looking out to sea.

Claire despaired at her weakness, her deception. But she

could neither bring herself to break the spell of this moment nor to stop thinking about Grace. She took the phone from her pocket and looked at the small screen. Nothing. She buried the phone back in her pocket and looked at the horizon. They talked about other things. Sam's boys. The nurseries. Her travel business and the job she was most proud of, her relief work.

"What did you do?"

"Mostly sweat. Drank bottled water. Slept under mosquito netting."

"But what did you accomplish?"

"We gave women opportunities to start small businesses, taught them how to keep chickens and goats. We bought sewing machines. We vaccinated babies and taught girls to read."

"Sounds rewarding." It had been, but she didn't want him thinking of her as Mother Teresa. Better put the kibosh on that right now.

"I haven't been completely honest with you."

"What do you mean?" His hand left hers. He turned toward her, but she couldn't face him.

"You know that I never married."

"Yes, but I'm sure…"

"No, let me finish. Please. I had a child. A daughter." She swallowed hard and turned to look into his sun-crinkled eyes. She saw grief there, his still-broken heart. Her story would add to that grief. "And I…"

Sam shook his head and put a finger to her lips. "Let's not dwell on the past today."

"But I…"

"There will be time for stories later." Sam's tone was firm. He wrapped his arm around her shoulder. Claire leaned into him as they watched the waves wash away her resolve. Claire felt her heart lie with every beat.

The rest of that afternoon, Sam's body rarely left hers,

seldom broke the connection they both seemed intent on making. He held her hand. He wrapped his arm around her waist or shoulder as if trying to convince himself she was real. Each touch was as painful as it was pleasurable.

"How 'bout we go back to the house? Swim, maybe?" he said as the sun began to sink toward the horizon. "There are plenty of leftovers from last night. Wouldn't take much to turn them into dinner."

"Sure." Leftovers. She knew what happened when you left them too long. "Can we stop at the hotel first to pick up my swimsuit?" Something rumbled inside Claire. She would tell him before the baby arrived. She had to.

Sam followed Claire into the hotel room. She pulled her phone from her pocket and set it on the nightstand so she could see the flash of an incoming message as she dug into her duffle. Sam took her hand then, turning her and kissing her deeply. Claire closed the gap between them, ignoring her fears. Her body responded in all the ancient ways, arching and aching. Her hands sought the nape of Sam's neck, his ears. Sam's found her back, her buttocks and she found herself in a time and place in which their lives—their shared lives—held infinite possibilities and promise.

She only pulled away when she heard her phone vibrating and saw the flashing light. Sam looked over her shoulder as she picked it up.

"Congrats Grandma!" the text read. She gasped.

"Your daughter?" Sam asked.

"Grace."

"Grandma? Your daughter had a baby and you weren't there? Where is she?"

"Oregon."

"What? Wild horses couldn't have kept me away." Of course not. Sam is a real parent.

"Her mother's there. She—she's fine."

"What do you mean? You're her mother."

"Only biologically. I surrendered her for adoption." Claire was never sure what words to use—surrendered, abandoned, gave away? And how many more words for what she felt now—regret, guilt, sorrow?

"I see." Sam frowned and stepped away from her. "Maybe you were right. We are strangers. Maybe you'd better tell me the whole story." He sounded like a dad now, trying to get to the bottom of his child's misdeed. And she was that child, caught in a lie.

Her shoulders slumped and she sat on the bed. Where to begin? No words came.

"How old is she?" Sam finally asked.

"Nearly thirty-one."

Sam's coppery brows met.

"So, she was born in like, what—1972?"

Claire opened the attached photo. The image of the chubby cherub and her beaming red-haired mother brought her heart to her throat.

"You mean she could be—my—our—?"

"Not could be. Is." Claire handed the phone to Sam who stared at the screen. The avalanche buried her. She couldn't breathe.

Sam's eyes remained glued to the phone. He listened in stony silence while Claire sobbed and stumbled through the panic she'd felt when she learned she was pregnant, her doubts about being a good enough mother. The painful decision to give up their daughter, a child who would be her only baby ever. And the happy reunion with Grace.

Claire held her breath, paralyzed, waiting. He said nothing but stood and shoved the phone back at her. Tears scorched her cheeks as he turned and stepped toward the door. This was it, wasn't it? She'd hurt him. Again.

"This is a lot to take in," he said without looking at her.

"You tell me I have another child—a daughter—and now, a granddaughter."

"I'm so sorry. You must feel…"

"I don't know what I'm feeling right now." Claire started the mental list. Anger. Hurt. Betrayal.

"This must be a shock, but…"

"You have no idea." He put up his hand to halt any more words. "What hurts most is you didn't trust me. I thought we at least had that." His voice rose. At last, he faced her. "I loved you, Claire. I would have taken care of you. You didn't have to go through that alone."

"But, I couldn't…"

"No, you wouldn't," he hurled back at her. "That's the key. You had a choice. You chose to run away. From a life with me, and our daughter." Sam reached the door and opened it. He stopped. His chest heaved. He shook his head once and was gone, slamming the door and pounding down the corridor.

LIBBY WAS PACKING up after yet another Sunday afternoon at school preparing for Monday. How many weekends had she spent like this? Every one of them, for thirty years. Her cell phone rang.

"Hey. Claire! How'd it go with your dad?"

"Good and then not good."

Libby heard the breathy sadness in Claire's voice. "Oh, no. What happened?" She dreaded the answer.

"Everything." Claire's ragged voice pierced Libby's hope for her happiness.

"What do you mean?"

"I met my dad. That was all good. Then guess who dropped by?

"His girlfriend?"

"No, Sam's mom. She lives there too and invited us to dinner at Sam's."

"With his wife? Oh my God. Did you go?" Libby dropped her book bag and sat in a small chair at the reading table. This could take a while.

"Yes, but his wife died. Three years ago. Car accident." Three years? That would have been about the time of Libby's little spy mission. "Then we spent today together." Claire continued with the telling. Sam. The baby. Sam's anger.

Libby heard Claire crying. She waited for the sobs to subside. They always did, but you had to shed the tears before you could move on. After several long moments, she asked, "What will you do now?"

Claire sniffed. "Call the airline and change my reservation."

"Coming home?"

"Not yet. I've got to meet my granddaughter."

CHAPTER THIRTY-ONE

Now: The Stuff That Dreams Are Made Of

*O*ctober had whizzed past as Libby immersed herself in plans for Thanksgiving and her father's memorial service. After some initial resistance to holiday travel, everyone eventually accepted her invitation. All her brothers and their families—even the married children—would be in Carson City for the entire weekend. Close to thirty for dinner. Claire had handled all the airline reservations and rental cars for the group in addition to securing a block of hotel rooms for the out-of-towners.

Today, Veterans Day, Libby had set aside to organize Norah's room. It had become the designated drop-off for anything Libby hadn't known what to do with. Now it was uninhabitable—filled with not only Norah's leavings but also several boxes from her parents' home. Libby would give other family members one last chance to take what they wanted. Annie had taken Fran's recipe box and compiled the favorites into a scrapbook. She'd even made copies for everyone.

For motivation, Libby watched several episodes of "Hoarders." She then armed herself with trash bags, a Sharpie, and a stack of large sticky-notes. With a third cup of coffee in hand, she began by labeling four corners of the room. TOSS. SAVE. DONATE. And one pile with a large question mark.

As she sorted, Libby considered what she was ready to live without. How much did she and Jack need? Was it time for a smaller house? A smaller yard? Maybe no yard, now that Maggie had died. Certainly, a house that was easier to maintain. And what did she want to do with the rest of her life— their life? Both she and Jack had had health scares. Their priorities had shifted. If they wanted to make a change, now was the time.

Jack felt it too. He was back in a busy private practice but volunteered more time at the legal clinic and with the ACLU. Friends suggested he run for District Judge but his heart wasn't in it. The work intrigued him; a campaign did not. He wasn't ready to quit lawyering altogether but was ready for a change. Just what, he hadn't figured out.

Throughout the morning, Libby opened one memory-filled box after another. In one she found her pink plastic-bound diary with a now-broken lock. She opened it and read several passages written in careful cursive.

August 21, 1959

Dear Diary,

Today Hawaii became a state. Now there are 50 states. Alaska was number 49 in January. I wonder what they do with all the old flags?

She placed the diary in the growing SAVE pile. But just 'til she'd shown Claire.

Now on to Norah's things. Her older daughter had given Libby carte blanche to toss anything she'd left behind. If she hadn't needed it in ten years, Norah figured she wouldn't need it again. Libby took her at her word. Abandoned shoes, clothes, especially coats and boots went into the donate pile.

Libby pulled two boxes of vintage *National Geographic* from under the bed. As a child, Norah had devoured each new issue, just as Libby and Claire had. Those magazines had been windows to a world they longed to explore. Maybe now she and Jack could be more than armchair travelers.

The last box was labeled "Norah—Desk, etc." She opened it to discover Norah's entire childhood preserved. Unlike an archeological dig, with of strata defined by time, it looked as though her daughter had merely dumped all her drawers and sealed the box. Plastic barrettes. Happy Meal toys. Long-dry markers. Notes origamied into secret packages. College recruitment brochures. That girl had saved everything. Toss. Toss. Toss.

A large envelope jammed in the bottom of the box caught Libby's eye. Peace Corps. No doubt part of Norah's exploration before accepting the job with UNICEF. She'd been inspired by Claire's work. Hmmm. Libby removed the contents. A letter thanking Norah for her interest. A booklet displaying full-color photographs of projects and people around the world. Libby turned page after page. Something inside her clicked and opened. A window let in a shaft of light. An old dream poked its head in, crooked its finger and...

"Jack! Come here! I've got an idea!"

CHAPTER THIRTY-TWO

Now: Stormy Weather

*I*nez Wylder looked at the kitchen clock. Sam would be here at any moment to pick her up. The Wylders would enjoy their Thanksgiving feast in Joanie's yard. A tent and outdoor space heaters would keep everyone comfortable on what was turning out to be a rather gray Southern California day. The half-hour drive would give her a chance to talk with Sam. That surprise reunion with Claire two months ago had briefly brought Sam back to life, but her abrupt disappearance had pulled him down again. Some misunderstanding? A quarrel? Surely her son wasn't to blame.

Since Sam had been silent on the subject, she'd asked Claude if he knew what had happened. He'd only said, "It's between them. They'll have to work it out." Inez suspected he knew more than he would say. As frustrating as it was, she admired his loyalty to his daughter, especially after such a long separation. Did he feel this was some sort of test? Still, the questions would not leave her alone.

Two knocks interrupted her thoughts.

"Happy Thanksgiving, Mom." Sam entered, wearing a familiar wool plaid shirt that seemed a bit too large. "Something smells good." As requested, Inez had made her spicy butternut squash and apple casserole. Its enticing aroma filled her apartment. She removed it from the oven and placed it in a towel-lined cardboard box.

"I used fresh ginger this time. And more black pepper. Always fiddling with the recipe." She pulled on a festive burnt orange cardigan with a sheaf of wheat embroidered on the back. "I'm most thankful that I only had to make one dish."

Sam picked up the boxed casserole. As they walked to the elevator, Inez's mind scrambled to start a conversation that would get her son talking about Claire.

"I thought of inviting Claude to dinner, but he said he was flying up to spend the holiday with Claire and her mother." Inez watched her son for some reaction.

Sam looked away and asked, "Are you up to training the new hires on wreaths and garlands this year?" Drat. He'd changed the subject. She pressed the elevator button. The door opened and they stepped in.

"Of course. Next week?"

"Monday at nine. Just five newbies. The returnees have already started on the preorders. Joanie has everything ready at the Yorba Linda store." The elevator door opened and they stepped out.

Once on the freeway, Inez tried again. "When I thought about inviting Claude, I thought you and Claire might still be seeing each other. You seemed to get along so well."

"Mom." He shook his head and glanced at her. "I don't want to talk about it."

"What happened?" Claire was only here for two days, for goodness sake. How could things go so wrong so fast? And what could be troubling him months later? Staring straight ahead and gripping the steering wheel, his shoulders crept toward his ears.

"I don't think I can trust her." He shook his head slowly.

"Trust her? What? Why?"

"She lied. For over thirty years. She lied." The dense Thanksgiving Day traffic slowed to a crawl. He looked over at her now, his eyes betraying a hurt she'd hoped never to see again. And a spark of something else. Anger?

"You haven't seen her in that long. Are you saying that she lied thirty years ago and you can't trust her now?" Inez kept her eyes on her son as he struggled to control his temper, his words. Honesty was number one of Sam's core values. But what difference could a lie make now, after all these years?

"She had a baby, Mom. My baby. She gave it away. And she never said a word."

Reaching out and touching her son's shoulder, she bit her lip against speaking too soon, too rashly. Another grandchild.

"A child?"

Sam nodded. "A daughter. And now a granddaughter, born in September." A great-grandchild? Oh, my. No wonder...

"And she told you when she was here?"

"Yes, but I don't think she intended to. I found out by accident. If you hadn't invited her to dinner that night, I still wouldn't know."

A pregnancy, a child. That was troubling. Sam and Claire had both been young. And stubborn, God knows. But was that act so unforgivable that he would cut Inez off from her great-grandchild? She had to find a way to fix this. Minutes passed before she said, "Maybe if you step back. You know, look at the big picture."

"Big picture?"

"What was going on when you and she broke up?"

"I didn't break up with her, Mom. She left."

"Because...?

"Because she didn't want to get married. She said she wasn't ready to settle down. She was joining the Peace Corps, remember?" His voice was sharp with barely controlled rage.

"I remember. And…?"

"And I got angry."

"Did you know she was pregnant?"

"No. Of course not. I don't think she even knew."

"So, what would you have done, I mean, if you'd known?"

"Married her…"

"But she didn't want to get married." Inez waited, hoping Sam would see his part in this.

"But…"

"But nothing, son. She wasn't ready for a family. She told you that. You pressured her. She bolted."

"But a baby…"

"Yes. A baby. Would you have raised a child on your own?"

"I wasn't given the option, Mom. Don't you see? She just gave her away." Inez remembered Claire's relief work and her efforts to help other women in desperate situations and understood.

"I doubt it was an easy choice. And she didn't just leave the baby on a doorstep, did she? Did she make a plan? Is that baby happy and healthy now?"

"I guess…" he shrugged.

"Well, it sounds like Claire did a good thing. Maybe the best thing she could have done at the time."

"I don't know…"

"And if things hadn't happened exactly the way they did, you never would have married Christy. You wouldn't have had your wonderful boys. Honey, you found someone who didn't need convincing. Someone who wanted a family. With you."

Sam seemed to be considering that last bit.

"But how can I trust her?"

"She might not feel that she can trust you." That was hard for a mother to say, but it was true.

"What do you mean? I'm not the one who…"

"Not the one who blew up when he learned about the baby?"

"I didn't blow up!" he yelled.

Yeah, not much. Sam stared at the road now, white-knuckling the wheel and panting like a bull.

Inez lowered her voice and went on. "Life is short. Sometimes unexpectedly short. You and I understand that better than most." Inez knew forgiveness and trust were two-way streets but allowed herself to hope that Sam and Claire could find a way. "Don't close the door on a chance at happiness. Promise me you'll at least think about it."

They drove the rest of the way in silence with Sam flexing his taut fingers on the steering wheel.

THROUGHOUT THE DAY, Inez watched her son. His usual pleasure in the company of family was noticeably absent. Sam's appetite for holiday foods was legendary, but today his fork seemed to merely move mechanically to and from his plate or push food around. His mind was elsewhere.

"So, Sam, how many Christmas trees did you order this year?" Kate had to ask twice as Sam pulled himself back from somewhere far away.

"Hmmm?"

"How many trees did you order?"

He shrugged. "That's Ben's department." He nodded to his eldest son.

Ben answered with numbers for each of the three stores, broken down by type of tree. Noble fir. Silvertip. Douglas fir. Cut vs. living trees. Inez paid no attention. She focused on Sam. His plate was still half-filled with tepid mashed potatoes and congealing gravy.

As Joanie's husband began clearing the table, the teenaged

cousins dispersed to avoid being called into service. Sam rose and took his traditional station at the sink. He shooed the others toward the television and football, isolating himself in the kitchen. Twenty minutes later, Inez joined him.

"Here, let me help," she offered. She began to wipe a large platter. "You didn't eat much. You feel okay?" Standing this close to him she noticed what she hadn't before—hollows in his cheeks and darkness shadowing his eyes. This not eating business had been going on for a while. Probably weeks, probably since...

"I'm fine, Mom. Just not hungry." She didn't believe him. But she knew better than to push him beyond what she already had.

The sun was setting by the time the last of the pots, pans, and platters were washed and put away. Coffee was brewing and soon someone would want pie. Sam turned to his mother.

"Thanks," he said as he pushed the start button on the dishwasher.

"It's just dishes, kiddo."

"Not just the dishes. Everything. Do you think one of the others could take you home? There's something I need to take care of."

"Now?" He couldn't mean to go now.

"Yes, now. Like you said, 'Life is short.'" He wrapped two dinner rolls up in a napkin, kissed her cheek, and left.

CHAPTER THIRTY-THREE

Now: Tears in Heaven

*D*uring yesterday's larger-than-usual Thanksgiving gathering, Libby asked everyone to look once more at the last of their father's belongings which she'd arranged on Jack's workbench in the garage. A music box that played "When Irish Eyes are Smiling." Three books of poetry. Two old Timex watches. A tackle box and fishing creel. A tiny set of nesting screwdrivers. A shoebox filled with her dad's clip-on bow-ties.

First Mitch, then Keith, and finally Pat, John, and their children slipped out to the garage. She didn't see what they took, but each emerged smiling as if they shared an inside joke. As the only girl in the family, she was accustomed to being left out of the boys' club.

Dinner had proceeded without incident. Even John had made an effort to be pleasant and helpful, if not exactly warm. He seemed honestly chagrinned and embarrassed by his earlier behavior. His transition to civilian life had not been smooth, but he was trying.

Libby sat in the front pew of the former St. Teresa sanctuary. A new larger church had recently been built across town. This familiar and historic building had been turned into a performance hall but was a fitting venue for her father's memorial service. Occasionally she turned around to see who was there. Friends from school, former students of her father, neighbors. Claire arrived with both her parents. Libby smiled and nodded in their direction, happy to see that little reunion.

The video slideshow Annie had created detailing Mike McCormack's life played while guests arrived and took their seats. Keith had built a soundtrack of traditional Irish tunes to accompany it. Murmurs and chuckles arose from the crowd as the photos dissolved one into another. Libby checked her watch. It was after one now. Jack and the rest of the family still hadn't taken their seats. Where were they?

A final smiling and bow-tied photograph of her father held on the screen as the strains of "Too-Ra-Loo-Ra-Loo-Ral" floated across the sanctuary. Voices sang along to the familiar lullaby. Loud voices, including several slightly off-key baritones. Who in the world—? Libby turned to see. A lump rose in her throat and her eyes clouded with tears as she saw the entire McCormack clan, parading down the aisle, singing. Each one—male and female alike—sporting one of her father's clip-on bow-ties.

CHAPTER THIRTY-FOUR

Now: Even Now

*C*laire stood at her living room window. It was only five o'clock, but the weak November sun had already dropped behind the mountains. For much of the day, the wind had roared, driving snow across highways and down necks. It seemed to have stopped now, although a thick blanket of clouds blocked any stars.

Thanksgiving weekend wasn't too early for a snowstorm, but Claire wasn't sure she was ready for the cocooning of winter yet. Then again, perhaps that was exactly what she needed. If only she could somehow hit fast-forward and speed up the metamorphosis. Into what she couldn't say. Her wild early years had not brought her any real contentment. Nor had the years of doing good. Something was missing. She wriggled her toes inside heavy socks and pushed her hands deep into the pockets of her fleece hoodie. Buster looked up at her from a pool of streetlamp light. Maybe this would be the winter she'd bring the stubborn old grump in at night. Maybe this would be the year he'd let her. The habit of being alone was a familiar one and hard to break.

In the two months since her trip to California, Claire had

sought distraction in activity during the day and too much wine at night. She poured herself into her travel business, connecting with more guides and service projects in foreign cities. She created a website. She ran more and added two Pilates classes to her weekly routine.

Yesterday's Thanksgiving dinner with her parents at Glen Eagle's Restaurant had gone surprisingly well. Of course, pre-dinner martinis and a bottle of excellent Pinot Noir relieved much of the awkwardness. This afternoon, they'd all attended the memorial service and reception for Libby's father. So, this is what it's like to have a family, to be a family.

Her parents were downstairs now. What could they be talking about after all this time? Could they forgive one another? Certainly, some ties couldn't be mended. Or shouldn't be. Thoughts of ties brought her back to Sam. No chance of mending there. While they couldn't deny the attraction, neither could they deny their natures, nor their painful past. A past that should remain buried.

An ache filled her chest and caused her to shudder. That past had led to Grace and her baby. There were no regrets there. Okay, maybe a few about what she'd missed, and the lies. But holding her granddaughter for the first time and feeling that wave of unconditional love wash over her had erased any doubt that she'd made the right choice. No matter what Sam thought. With Gail and Tom as her parents, Grace had grown into an intelligent, strong, and caring young woman.

Claire took comfort in that and clicked the TV remote. No signal. The satellite dish must have filled with snow. Disappointed, she selected CDs and pressed the buttons, settling in for an evening in which The Beatles, Simon and Garfunkel, and even James Taylor and Carly Simon were together again and on endless repeat. She added a log to the fire, poured herself a glass of wine and settled herself on the couch, allowing herself just one last solitary wallow. Tomorrow she'd pull herself together and get back into real life. Her real, satisfying—if solitary—life.

She swallowed the last of the wine and reminded herself that Grace, Adam, and the baby would stop by for lunch on Sunday, on their way back to the Reno airport. They'd spent Thanksgiving with Grace's grandmother—her real grandmother—in Bishop. Claire had resigned herself to the few hours here and there she might get to spend with them. She'd send birthday cards and spoil her with good books and a small college fund she'd established with that savings bond from her father.

And she would be grateful.

At least she could get Sunday's soup started. Libby said it's better if it sits a day or two anyway. Removing Jack's Pozole recipe from its place on the refrigerator, Claire found the big knife, the cutting board and began assembling the ingredients from the pantry and fridge. First step: chop bell peppers and onion. Her nose and eyes grew red and watery. Halfway through the second onion, she surrendered to the tears. The phone rang. Caller ID showed her mother's name.

"Hey, Mom. Does Papa need a ride back to his room yet?" She wiped her hands on a towel and sniffed.

"No, I'll call him a cab. Are you okay?"

"Yeah, I'm chopping onions and having a good cry while I'm at it."

"Oh, I'm sorry. But, well—there's someone here who came to the wrong door. He meant to see you. I was only calling to see if you were decent."

"Yeah, I'm decent." She looked down at her sweatpants and hoody. Decent, but not exactly company-ready. Wait a minute. He? "Who would be out on a night like this?" But her mother had hung up. Who would go to the wrong door? Everyone knows she lives upstairs. A delivery? She wiped her face with a kitchen towel, checked her reflection in the microwave, and shrugged.

Moments later, she heard the doorbell. She turned on the porch light from the top of the long flight of stairs and began a wary descent. Her pulse quickened as an odd trick of the light through the door's etched glass obscured her vision. A tall, silhouetted figure caused her to stop a few steps from the bottom hoping the image would clear. Nope. Two more steps. She gingerly bolted the chain. Too late for an actual threat. Her mother wouldn't have sent him if he were dangerous, right?

Claire opened the door a cautious crack and gasped. She saw Sam's tired and whiskery face, his eyes looking directly into hers.

CHAPTER THIRTY-FIVE

Now: Shower the People

"*S*am? What the…"

"I'm sorry." His voice was soft but sure. Claire unhooked the chain and opened the door.

"What do you have to be sorry for?"

"So much."

"Me too."

They kissed then and held each other in the glow of the porch light, mumbling more apologies between more kisses and ignoring the old marmalade cat who wound around their legs.

At the top of the stairs, Claire helped Sam off with his jacket.

"What do you need first? Food or drink? Sleep or shower?"

"First, I need to pee."

They laughed and she pointed to the bathroom.

"About that drink…" he said when he returned.

"Beer? Scotch?" she asked.

"Beer." He slumped onto a stool at the kitchen counter as she opened a bottle of winter ale and handed it to him. She refilled her glass with wine and stood opposite him.

"I can't believe you drove in this weather."

"It wasn't snowing at my house," he shrugged and took several long swallows of his beer. "I guess I wasn't thinking. And airports were all tied up with holiday traffic and weather delays."

"When did you leave?"

He looked at his watch. "Last night. After ten, I guess. The drive took a little longer than expected."

"Jesus, what is that? Like eighteen hours?" The drive usually took only half that.

Sam cocked his head toward the window. "Chain controls. Road closures. Whiteouts. I got just beyond Bishop and finally had to stop and go back."

"I hope you got a room somewhere to wait it out."

"No room at the inn. I slept in the car for a few hours in Denny's parking lot. That was this morning, I guess. When I woke up a CHP cruiser was parked next to me. I figured they'd know what was going on."

"And?"

"They advised me to wait it out. So, I sat inside Denny's."

"Like in college."

He nodded and smiled. "Not exactly. I didn't try to stretch one cup of coffee for over five hours. I'll have you know I ordered real food and tipped very generously. I read several newspapers then tried to take a little nap this afternoon, but after all that coffee, I wasn't very successful." It was only then that he looked around and registered the state of the kitchen. "Expecting company?"

"Not 'til Sunday, but I thought I'd get a head start."

"Am I in the way?"

"Not at all. It's just family."

"Family?" Confusion showed on his face. "I saw your parents downstairs."

Claire smiled. "Grace."

His eyes widened in what looked like wonder. "And her... and the..."

Claire pressed her lips together and nodded. "Uh-huh. Husband and baby. They've been seeing family. In Bishop."

His jaw dropped. "Small world."

"Yes. Yes, it is."

Claire wanted nothing more than to get this man to her bed but knew he must be exhausted. She needed—they needed—to take it slow. Besides, she selfishly wanted him fully functional.

"You brought a bag?" she asked. He nodded. "Why don't you get it and take a shower while I clean up this mess?"

Twenty minutes later, Claire had bagged up the chopped veggies, tidied the kitchen, and turned down the bed. Sam exited the bathroom wearing only his boxers. Claire gestured to the bed.

"I'll let you sleep here. It's a better bed and I'm sure you're a wreck. I'll take the fold-out in the den."

A look of disappointment passed over his face. "It's a big bed, Claire. I think there's room for both of us."

"I thought that you needed sleep," Claire teased.

"I do. But I came here to be with you." He pulled her closer and touched his lips to hers in a kiss that held promise. "I think we've been apart long enough."

By the time Claire had brushed her teeth and put on her pajamas, Sam's eyelids were drooping. She curled up into the curve of him, relishing the sensation of his chest on her back and the luscious clean scent of him. Sam's breath on her neck became warm and regular as they nestled together under the down comforter. Soon he was asleep. A sense of comfort and safety replaced Claire's initial excitement and she too succumbed to sleep. The deepest she'd had in months.

Morning dawned bright and clear and found them still spooned. Claire rose and looked out at the impossibly blue sky overhead, at a world frosted, glistening, and new. What a difference twenty-four hours can make. Shivering, she turned up the thermostat before crawling back into bed and resuming her position tucked up against Sam's warm torso and legs. He stirred and wrapped his arm around her belly. He kissed her neck, sending a pleasurable shudder down her spine. His big hand moved now, caressing her breasts, her belly. Then it moved lower, lower, until he found the sweet spot he was searching for. She moaned and turned to face him.

"Good morning," she said.

"The best…"

"You know, I'm not young anymore," Claire apologized, looking into Sam's eyes.

"Me neither. And I'm a little out of practice."

"Like riding a bike," she mumbled. They explored each other's bodies with both tenderness and hunger. They slowly and softly awakened themselves to what Claire hoped was a second chance at happily ever after.

THE AROMA of coffee greeted Claire as she stepped from the shower. She dressed quickly and joined Sam in the kitchen where he was scrambling eggs in a bowl. He stopped to pour her a cup of coffee.

"Mmmm, thank you. Sorry, there's not more to work with." She pulled a frying pan from the cupboard and butter from the fridge. "There is some good sourdough for toast. And jam. I'll get that started."

"No problem. It was a risk to show up like this." Sam was attending to the eggs in the pan now, not looking at her. "And it could have been awkward if…"

"If I'd had another guy here you mean?" She loaded bread into the toaster.

"Yeah." She couldn't remember the last time she'd had a man in her kitchen or bed.

"What made you come here?"

"My mom. She made me see my part in this. That I drove you away." Claire had always liked Inez but was surprised that she'd confronted her own son.

Claire buttered the toast. Sam served the eggs. They sat side by side on bar-stools.

"I was so afraid of hurting you. Again," Claire confessed.

"Or me getting angry, again?"

She shrugged one shoulder. "When I told my dad I might just leave town without telling you, the disappointment on his face about killed me. He reminded me of the damage secrets can do, the walls they build."

"Are there more secrets I need to know about?"

"Nope. I think I'm secret-free at this point." Almost. She felt a smile form on her lips.

They spent Saturday morning sheltered in the apartment. Their rhythms and movements adapting as they bumped companionably into each other in and out of the bedroom. They worked together preparing the pozole and setting it to cook in the crockpot. He washed. She dried. Claire shared pictures of Grace and her family.

That afternoon, they walked the snowy streets to Libby and Jack's hand-in-hand. Libby stood open-mouthed at the door. Tears filled her friend's eyes as she embraced them both before inviting them in. Jack offered them hot, rum-laced cider as they sat before a blazing fire in the living room. Claire related the saga of Sam's journey.

"We have news of our own to share," Jack announced with a grin.

"We're both retiring in June." Libby seemed hardly able to contain her excitement.

"Retiring?! But you're so young!" Claire objected.

"Not that young. I've been teaching for thirty years."

"But both of you? What will you do?"

Jack answered. "We've filed applications with several humanitarian organizations. Ones that focus on human rights and education. We hope for the Caribbean or Latin America. Or maybe Eastern Europe." His eyes danced.

"What? When did this happen? You never said anything…"

"It happened while I was going through all our stuff, all my parents' stuff. I'm ready to be rid of it. Besides, I was always jealous that you got to go off and do what you did."

"Jealous? But you had everything. A happy marriage. Children. A career." Wasn't that enough?

"And all the constraints that go with them." Had she and Libby switched places now? She squelched the pang in her heart that Libby would no longer be nearby, but was happy that her friend was finally able to follow her own path. Everyone deserves that.

―――――

SUNDAY MORNING WAS ONCE AGAIN bright, although the streets now bore muddy streaks of slush. Claire's mother and father invited them downstairs for breakfast. Her old favorite, Dutch Babies, served with berries, whipped cream, maple syrup, bacon, and hot coffee. And today there was champagne with which Sam toasted new beginnings. Her parents seemed almost giddy, hinting at something Claire couldn't quite put her finger on. Her phone vibrated.

"Hi, Grace. How's everything?"

"We're on the road. The flight's on schedule. It looks like we'll be at your house around eleven. We need to leave by two. Sorry for the short visit."

"No worries. We're—uh, I mean—I'm grateful to see you at all." She withheld any mention of Sam. "See you soon."

"So, I'm going to be a surprise?" Sam asked, his eyebrows raised.

ONCE AGAIN UPSTAIRS, Sam busied himself bringing in a stack of wood and building a fire in the fireplace. Claire set the table, shredded cabbage, and sliced limes to garnish the soup. They paced the apartment, giggling when one would catch the other peeking at the street. She'd just put a pan of cornbread into the oven, when Sam called out, "That's them. They're here!" She stood next to him at the window overlooking the street with his arm around her waist. Adam lifted the baby from her car seat and wrapped her in a puffy pink blanket. Grace looked up and waved at Claire in the window. A question registered in her eyes.

Together, she and Sam ran down the stairs to open the door and welcome their guests.

"Grace, this is Sam."

"Oh, my God. Sam? You mean...?" Claire nodded. Grace immediately held out her hand. "I'm so glad to meet you."

"Me too." Sam's voice sounded small and tight as he pulled Grace into a warm embrace, then held her at arms' length and looked into her eyes. He was fighting back tears, a fight that Claire and Grace had already given up.

"Okay, everybody. Upstairs," Claire said. "I don't want my granddaughter out here any longer than necessary. Although with all those layers of quilting and fleece, I'm sure she could survive anything short of a return of the Ice Age."

Upstairs, Adam handed the baby off to Claire and offered his hand to Sam.

"Adam Powell."

"Sam Wylder. You can't know how happy I am to meet you and your little family."

"And Sam," Claire said after unwrapping the pink and ginger bundle in her arms, "I'd like you to meet your granddaughter, Miss Samantha Bassett Powell."

"Samantha?" Sam looked up at Claire, then at Grace. A chubby fist wrapped around his finger.

Grace explained. "That's what Claire named me when I was born. She said she called me 'little Sam' the whole time she was pregnant. We wanted to honor her sacrifice, her gift, and give her back the Samantha she gave up."

Claire placed little Sam in her grandfather's waiting arms. The pair appeared fixed on one another for several long moments. Sam was speechless. Then he kissed Samantha's head and whispered something in her ear. When his gaze shifted to Claire, he mouthed a silent "Thank you."

"Yoo-hoo! Claire! Is there room for us?" Claire's parents stood at the bottom of the steps.

"Sure. The more the merrier. Come up and meet your great-granddaughter."

Claire made the introductions and invited everyone to sit. There was small talk and laughter. Sam handed his phone to Adam for a photo with Claire, Samantha, and Grace. "My mom needs to see this. My boys too. Maybe it'll inspire them to get started on the next generation of Wylders."

The timer dinged and lunch was served.

Half an hour later, Sam was snuggling little Sam in a quiet corner the living room, swaying and singing to her softly. She'd gotten fussy during lunch and he'd volunteered, causing a lump to rise in Claire's throat. Both Sams seemed smitten.

The doorbell rang again. The entire Cooper clan—Libby, Jack, Norah, Enrique, Annie, and Josh stood outside.

"We had to stop by. Just for a minute. To see the baby."

"Of course."

For once, a room filled with friends and family did not send Claire looking for the nearest exit. She had no desire to escape the crush and cherished the warmth, the closeness, the ties that bound her to every person gathered here in her home. Why had she run away from this?

Throughout the next few hours, Claire caught Sam simply staring at Grace. Her red hair and freckles, the long and lean body made it hard to deny the resemblance. She was Sam's. Hers. Theirs.

WHEN EVERYONE HAD LEFT and it was once again just the two of them, Sam added another log to the fire. Claire collapsed onto the sofa with Sam's arm around her, curling her feet under her and leaning into his shoulder.

"This has been the best day I've had in a long time. I have no reason to be proud, and yet, I am," Sam said.

"Me too. Isn't little Sam just the prettiest baby ever?" Even as she said it, she knew pretty wasn't enough. It never had been.

He kissed the top of her head. "Pretty, like her Grammy."

Claire chuckled. "I hope little Sam never doubts she's enough. That she's loved just because." It had taken Claire a lifetime to learn that she was enough, that the best people love you not for how you look or what you do, but just because.

"Yes, a lucky little girl." He pulled Claire closer.

"Isn't it odd though, starting our life together as grandparents? Usually, that's where people end up." Sam kissed her then and for once she let the kiss carry her forward, not back. Finally, she had to ask, "But what's next? For us, I mean. We haven't been very good at staying together."

"You mean, how does our story end?" He lowered his head and looked her in the eye. "That depends on what you want. What do you want, Claire?"

Claire swallowed hard. Grace or the universe or whatever

had insisted that she and Sam be together at last. She knew what she wanted. There was no longer any doubt, only love and hope, and the knowledge that was enough. Maybe more than enough.

"All of it. Always. With you. I want us."

"It's about time."

– THE END –

ACKNOWLEDGMENTS

Because the gestation period for this novel has been over ten years, there is a cast of thousands who've had a hand in its birth. So many midwives!

Going back to nearly the very beginning, my fifth-grade teacher, Miss Lucille Webb at Bradford Elementary School praised my story "Forty-Niner Come to Visit" in such a way that made me believe I could—and perhaps should—be a writer. However, while I loved writing, I was never fast, always taking too much time puzzling and worrying over every word, every line. For years I stuck to writing silly little poems, light-hearted fare reminiscent of the humorous ditties my grandfather penned, celebrating birthdays, weddings, and other life events. So, Grandpa Joe gets a nod of thanks as well.

I was lucky enough to begin my teaching career with a wonderful writing role model, Janet B. Sheridan. She encouraged me to take an intensive summer writing course offered by the Northern Nevada Writing Project, whose philosophy was "We practice what we teach. We write." I became a Teacher Consultant and facilitated workshops for teachers and parents throughout Northern Nevada. Through the NNWP, I also joined a writers' group. We met to eat, drink, and critique each other's work for over ten years. With their help, I gained both skill and confidence.

At about the same time, I began paying attention to "Fresh Ideas," a women's column in Carson City's newspaper, *The Nevada Appeal*. My friend, Abby Johnson contributed to the column and when I asked her about it, she responded, "You want to join us?' The paper's editor at the time, Barry Smith, had seen a few of my fervent letters to the editor. Barry seemed to think I fit into what he called the column's cadre of "tree-hugging-granola-eating-vegetarian-feminist" point of view, which countered the paper's more conservative male columnists. Thus, I began fifteen years of meeting deadlines and wordcounts while trying to say something meaningful about the personal side of politics—kids, education, women, and families. Thanks, Abby and Barry.

In 2008, my writers' group buddy, Joan Atkinson told me about NaNoWriMo—National Novel Writing Month—in which writers challenge themselves to create a novel in one month. She dared me to give it a try. I agreed. After all, I'd recently retired from teaching and had a few brain cells and a little time to spare on a story that had been rolling around in my head for decades. The story would feature themes of lifelong friendship, lost love, found love, family, and second chances. Because of Joan, I had something to edit. And edit. And edit. Thanks for being my cheerleader, critique partner, and midwife-in-chief.

Now I had 70K words inspired by true events and held together with a litter of sticky-notes and Dove chocolate wrappers. Sure, it was a little rough in spots and probably had a few gaps in the plot. Nevertheless, I believed I could get it into shape during the following year.

Cue the deep, resonant voice of an omniscient narrator: "Little did she know…"

Enter another friend, local legend, Marilee Swirczek,

founder of Lone Mountain Writers at Western Nevada College. When I ran into her and told her that my story involved a little mid-life romance, she said, "Oooh, we need that!" and invited me to join LMW. From the wise, honest, and kind members of the group, I heard that I had produced some great writing without any discernible story. Fortunately, the group included several English professors who offered both criticism and encouragement in equal measure. Thus began ten years of trying to find the thread of my story. I owe a deep debt of gratitude for the patience and perspective of the countless members who have streamed through the group in that time. While Marilee passed away in 2016, she still sits at my shoulder while I'm writing and rewriting. Thank you, Marilee.

To my dear friend and sister-in-spirit, Gail Crane Sweeney whose giant heart and commitment to family in all its forms provided the seed of this story, thank you. This is not your story, but you certainly inspired it. You showed me that happy endings are possible when we choose to love and to hope.

To my beta readers—Joan Atkinson, Robyn Laguzza, Anne LeFevre, and Wilma Counts— You are the best, even when you told me that my writing was not. I learned something with every pass, every note in every margin. Thank you.

And to all my friends and family who keep asking when this thing will finally be published, thanks for asking. Here it is. I hope it's worth the wait.

To my daughters, Joanna and Katie, for being the happy, healthy, independent women you are. Thank you too for only giving me small, everyday worries, and not big ones. You make me proud and I love you too much.

Finally, to my sweet, kind, reliable, and good-looking husband who's been keeping our little ship afloat for nearly fifty years. I don't say thank you often enough. Even when you recently shook your head and said, "You know, someday you'll just have to let it go and publish." Thanks, I needed that.

THANK YOU

Thank you for reading *Us, Now and Then*. I sincerely hope you enjoyed this novel. In today's online marketplace, reader reviews are vital for any author hoping to stand out in out in a field of millions of eBooks available. Your review doesn't need to be long—just a few words, expressing how you felt about the story— whether you liked it or not. It would be much appreciated.

Thanks again,

– Lorie

www.lorieschaefer.com

ABOUT THE AUTHOR

Lorie Smith Schaefer has lived and worked in Northern Nevada for over forty years.

Her career in elementary education included many years as a Teacher for the Carson City School District and Teacher Consultant for the Northern Nevada Writing Project. For fifteen years she contributed tree-hugging-granola-eating-vegetarian-feminist columns to Carson City's *Nevada Appeal*.

Retired now, she lives in Reno with her husband where she spends her time avoiding housework by reading, writing, and watching her granddaughter grow up way too fast.

Made in the USA
Monee, IL
21 February 2020